THE GIPSY SCHOOLBOY

or the Mystery of a Dark Night.

Edwin J. Brett
"Boys of England" Office, 173 Fleet St.
and all Booksellers.

"RALPH PENDARVEN FELL TO THE FLOOR WITH A DULL THUD."

THE

GIPSY SCHOOLBOY;

OR,

The Mystery of a Dark Night.

COMPLETE.

BEAUTIFULLY ILLUSTRATED.

LONDON
"BOYS OF ENGLAND" OFFICE, 173 FLEET STREET, E.C.
AND ALL BOOKSELLERS.

"'ROGER MALTBY, I BELIEVE YOU ARE A VILLAIN!' CRIED REUBEN."

THE GIPSY SCHOOLBOY;

OR,

THE MYSTERY OF A DARK NIGHT.

━━━━━━━►•◦•◦•◄━━━━━━━

CHAPTER I.

IT was a night of storm and darkness, some sixty years ago, as two men were hurrying as if for their lives' sake along the white, chalky road leading from Tregeis to Pendarven, on the coast of Cornwall.

On one side lay the black and solemn-looking country, over which the wind and rain were driving, while on the other, not many yards from the road, was the restless sea, whose hoarse murmurings could be heard above the roaring of the blast, as the billows tumbled in from the wide expanse, and broke in tumultuous masses against the jagged rocks.

Both men were attired in much the same fashion—knee breeches, gaiters, rough coats, fur caps—but it was easy to see that one was much younger than the other, and from his walk and build generally it seemed that he belonged to a different class from his companion.

"This is a strange welcome home, Reuben Pendarven," said the elder man, with a chuckling laugh. "Seems as if the very elements are up in arms to drive you back again."

"Don't talk nonsense, Caleb," said his companion, testily. "I ought to thank heaven for sending the wind and the rain so that no man can see and recognise the face of the one who has been made an outcast—almost an outlaw."

"Nay then, be not offended, Reuben," said Caleb Lee, whose dark and swarthy features, and black, restless eyes proclaimed his gipsy birth. "I did but jest. Outcast, outlaw, or whatever you may be, I shall never forget that you saved the life of my only child at the peril of your own. Strange it is, though, that

we should have to pass Pendarven Castle to-night. But hark! what is that?"

Both men paused to listen.

At first nothing came to them, except the wash of the waves below the cliffs, the pattering of the rain against the leaves of the trees, and the howling of the angry wind.

But after a moment the strange sound was heard once more.

The solemn tolling of a bell.

They looked from one to the other in wonder.

What could this mean?

It was not the tolling of the church bell at Pendarven at this time of night; that was most certain.

Ding, ding, ding!

Monotonous and at intervals the sound rolled out over the dark landscape.

"The sound comes from the castle," cried Reuben, suddenly. "It is the alarm bell. No one tolls that except in cases of dire necessity and danger. Great heavens! my uncle, perhaps, is dying with my forgiveness unsaid. Let us hasten on."

The gipsy caught him by the arm.

"Have a care," he said. "Do not plunge into unnecessary danger. Take heed that you do not go to find a curse instead of a blessing."

"I will risk that," cried Reuben Pendarven, as he quickly shook himself free from the gipsy's grasp. "There is danger threatening the house of Pendarven, and that is enough for me,

"Hark! there it is again."

Ding, ding! went the monotonous bell once more, and away Reuben dashed through the storm of rain and wind, followed by the gipsy.

"Ever headstrong," muttered Caleb; "ever putting himself into danger for others, and yet an outcast from his home."

As they went on, they could see the high, dark, gloomy towers of Pendarven Castle rising up before them on the cliffs, gloomy and threatening, behind masses of black pine trees—not a light to be seen anywhere save in one of the topmost turrets.

Yet still the bell kept tolling dismally —more indistinctly now as they approached—and jerkily, as if the one who held the rope was struggling with some person who was trying to prevent the ringing.

Reuben Pendarven dashed forward more hurriedly still at this.

His mind was in a whirl of contending emotions.

Four years before our story opens he had been compelled to leave the country.

Always a spendthrift, he had been set down by his friends as a ne'er-do-well, and when tidings had come to them that he had disgraced the family name in order to obtain money, he was not only forbidden his uncle's house, but warned to quit England or be prepared to suffer for his crime.

That he was innocent they would not believe.

Circumstances were certainly against him, and he was too proud at last to take any steps to clear himself.

Since his departure his uncle had married, and his wife had died, leaving one child—a son—who on this eventful night had just completed its second year.

Richard Pendarven, stern man as he was, had loved his wife dearly, and loved his son still more, with a passionate worship.

He seemed to live only for his child, which was his heir, which was to perpetuate the family name, which would keep the castle and its belongings free from the grasping hands of his younger brother.

And so since the death of his young wife he had lived at the castle almost alone, with two servants, in fact, as his only companions.

There was danger threatening the young heir of Pendarven from those who in the event of his death would benefit to the extent of thousands.

It was to this strange and desolate home that Reuben and his gipsy companion were now hurrying.

He had good reason to trust Caleb Lee, king of the gipsies.

Five years before, when Reuben was a lad of eighteen, he had saved Miriam, the daughter of Caleb, from certain death in the deep mill-stream, and during his illness afterwards he had been tended carefully by gipsy hands.

During that illness, too, the secret came out that Reuben had gipsy blood in his veins—that his father, Robert Pendarven, had stooped to marry a maiden of Romany birth, and so the tie was made doubly strong, and the house-dweller was reckoned as one of the king's tribe.

This proved of great service to Reuben in the time of his trouble.

There was no necessity for him to leave England when he was cast out and persecuted by his family.

Disguised as one of the tribe he remained securely in their tents, as far from the malevolence of those who knew him as the probable heir of Pendarven as he would have been in the jungles of India.

It was a strange chance which now brought him to the wild coast above which the old castle reared its sombre head, and feeling as if fate was leading him by the hand to the scene of former joys and sorrows, he ran rather than walked to the great eagle-mounted gates, and across the grounds to the building.

To his astonishment he found the door wide open.

The lamp was burning in the hall.

Everything was apparently in its usual place, but all was solemnly still.

The bell had ceased tolling.

Not a sound was there to show that anything was living in the place.

"This means some deadly crime— murder perhaps," cried Reuben; "at all hazards, I shall enter!"

Then, seeing Caleb hesitate, he added—

"Nay, fear not; you must come with me. Where I go so also can you, my friend."

Drawing from beneath his rough coat a sword artfully concealed, he was about to enter and rush up the silent staircase, when four men, completely masked, rushed through a side door into the hall.

They stood aghast as they saw Reuben and the gipsy at the door.

Then, with a quick command to those with him, the leader dashed with uplifted sword towards the newcomers.

Both Reuben and Lee, the latter of whom had only a heavy bludgeon, were somewhat taken aback by this sudden assault, and the men had made a rush upon them before they had really time to prepare themselves.

Nevertheless, they quickly recovered their presence of mind, and Reuben, making a furious advance upon the leader, endeavoured to prevent his escape.

But in vain.

The four men made a feint of attacking the two at once, and then suddenly turned and fled.

This was no time for hesitation.

A feeble toll came from the bell in the tower again, a toll which made the four figures pause in their flight an instant, though they immediately resumed it.

"Follow me!" cried Reuben to the gipsy.

And without waiting even to see if Caleb Lee followed him, he rushed up the wide, polished oaken staircase of the castle, with every nook and cranny of which he was familiar.

As he went up he searched on both sides of the mansion, but all the rooms were empty.

In one, the study, which was Richard Pendarven's favourite haunt, there were signs of a deadly struggle; papers and books were strewn about the floor, while chairs were overthrown, drawers dragged out from their places, and the heavy curtains before the windows were torn as if someone had clutched them madly for support.

Leaving this chamber, convinced now that some terrible deed had been enacted within the precints of the old castle, Reuben, still holding his drawn sword in his hand, rushed upwards towards the turret chamber.

He knew that the alarm bell, unless rung by ghostly hands, must have been set in motion by someone whose interest it was to alarm the neighbourhood, and so he paid no heed to other open doors, but made his way straight to what may not inaptly be termed the belfry.

Reaching this, just as a feeble thrill of sound trembled once more upon the night air, they saw an awful sight.

Richard Pendarven lay upon his left side, blood streaming from his chest, and stagnating in little pools round him, his right hand still holding in a weak clutch the rope of the great bell.

"Great heaven! there is murder here!" cried Reuben. "Give me your flask of brandy, Caleb. Quick, man, quick!"

He knelt down and lifted the sufferer's head upon his knee, the head of a man some forty years of age, with hair streaked prematurely with grey.

A handsome face, with regular features, and a look of calm resignation, even in the face of death.

A few drops of the strong liquid seemed to revive him, and opening his eyes, he gazed fixedly at Reuben.

"Heaven! it is Reuben!" he said, and fainted.

"Let us not stop here!" cried Caleb Lee, who had no wish to be seen by any one of the neighbours that night in the company of Reuben Pendarven. "Let us carry him down to one of the other rooms—one of the bed-rooms. It will be better for him, and more easy for us to escape if anyone approaches. If we were found here—alone—in this house of blood, we should be accused of murder."

Reuben made no reply to this.

He was too much excited and overcome by this strange home-coming.

He raised the form of the evidently dying man in his arms, and with Caleb's aid gently bore him down the wide stairs.

No one was about.

No sign was there of anyone approaching from without.

The house nearest the castle was far distant, and no doubt the tolling of the alarm-bell had been unheard in the driving storm.

Reuben bore the senseless master of the castle to the stately bedchamber, which he knew was his, and then administered more brandy, chafing his hands, too, placing his head in a comfortable position, and holding to his nostrils some strong salts, which were ready on his dressing-table.

Presently Richard Pendarven opened his eyes once more, and glanced round him.

He was sufficiently revived to know where he was.

He cast one anxious look at the familiar objects in the chamber, and then his eyes fell on Reuben.

He put out a white, trembling hand, and took that of his nephew.

"Ah, Reuben!" he said, with a deep sigh, "so you have come to me at last. Give me some more brandy. Let me have strength ere I die to tell you all—to crave your forgiveness, to leave to you a legacy of vengeance. Ah, Reuben, to think we should meet thus!"

He paused, and Reuben, who had waited anxious to catch every syllable that fell from his uncle's lips, gave him some more of the invigorating spirit, saying—

"Talk not of the past. At such a time as this, it is I who should talk of vengeance, not you. Tell me all quickly, while there is time."

"I will, Reuben," said Richard. "Let your friend stand near the door to listen for footsteps. I have a sacred charge to give to you to-night, and but little time in which to do it. If you had not arrived, another death—the terrible death of a poor innocent, would have happened in the castle to-night."

Caleb Lee at once did as he was directed, taking up his position near the door, where he could hear what the master had to say, and also notice if any one approached from without.

"Reuben," said Richard Pendarven, speaking quickly and firmly, though in a low voice, "about a year after your disappearance through what I now know to be a most unmerited accusation, I married a young and lovely girl, who made me during our few months of marriage a true and devoted wife. The only thing which any one could allege against her was that she was of gipsy origin."

Both Reuben and Caleb started.

"Like my mother," said the former.

"Yes, like your mother," returned Richard Pendarven. "But listen. Your uncle Hubert was furious. He had hoped that, as you were gone, an outcast —no one knew where—on the face of the earth, his son, Ralph, your cousin, would inherit all. Judge then his hate when two years ago my wife presented me with a son, yielding up her life at the same time, but making the trust all the more sacred in my eyes because she died in giving it to me. Hark! what was that?"

A strange scratching sound was heard upon the old staircase.

All listened.

But it was not repeated.

"It is only the rats," cried Caleb Lee, "but I will be upon the watch."

"Well," resumed Richard, with a shudder, "since the day of her death I have renounced the world. I have lived here with two servants (who went by my permission to the town to-night), and my life has been occupied in one incessant attempt to guard him from his uncle. To-night he came here (I knew him even under his mask), and demanded to see him. I told him that the child—my darling Rupert—was away at nurse; miles, miles away, out of his reach. But he swore it was false, and ransacked the house from top to bottom.

"Not finding him, the cowardly murderers demanded money, and failing in their efforts to intimidate me, attacked me, and left me for dead. I managed to crawl from the study up to the turret chamber, while they were ransacking the lower part of the house and the cellars in search of treasure, and I rang the alarm bell again and again. But I suppose in the storm no one heard me, save you. And now, Reuben," said the master of the castle, dropping his voice to a whisper, and pressing his hand warmly, "now comes the secret. Do you see yonder picture?"

He pointed as he spoke to a large oil-painting low down on the wall, the figure of an old cavalier, a Richard Pendarven, of the time of the Commonwealth.

"Touch the hand of that figure, Reuben, the right hand. Then press it hard, that is my secret."

As he was speaking, the picture had moved from its place, and disclosed a small door.

"Enter, lose no time, there is no danger, Reuben," cried Pendarven, speaking firmly, almost authoritatively, though he was dying fast. "Bring the child and a large casket that lies near it."

Reuben, thus adjured, at once entered the little ante-chamber.

It was a tiny room, but fitted up with

every comfort, its little window overlooking the prettiest part of the grounds, its hangings light and graceful, pretty pictures and flowers scattered about.

And in a cot, peacefully sleeping, dreaming of anything save the perils that surrounded him, lay Rupert Pendarven, heir to the castle and its fortunes.

The casket was near to him, on a table, a heavily filled one and richly inlaid, too.

Reuben, however, managed to raise the boy without awaking him, and holding him on his left arm, he seized the casket with his right hand, and hurried back to the room.

He had been absent but a few moments from his uncle's side, but the change that had taken place in that short time was remarkable.

Richard Pendarven's face was bloodless, his eyes wild and staring.

Before he had been kept up by the excitement of narrating his wrongs, and by the sudden and strange re-appearance of Reuben, just in time, as he hoped, to save the child from its cowardly enemies.

Now the stream of excitement had ceased to flow, and he collapsed, as it were, losing heart and strength altogether.

When he saw the child he beckoned feebly for it to be brought to him, and kissed it fondly, passionately.

Then he relinquished it to Reuben.

"Reuben," he murmured, "the sands of my life have nearly run out. I have wronged you in the past, but I have bitterly repented it. Forgive me, and swear to me to save my child, to keep him from his enemies until he is old enough to do battle for himself; swear to avenge me and the wife, who I solemnly believe died through fear of Hubert. Swear it, Reuben."

And so, more to please the dying man than because he knew what to do, or understood what he was saying, he said—

"I swear!"

"That is well," pursued Richard Pendarven, feebly. "In that casket you will find papers and every proof necessary to show that this child is lawful heir to my fortune. Save one. That one I leave to you to discover. In the box, too, is a large sum of money, and four blank cheques signed by me. Fill them

in and get them cashed instantly, Reuben. I—I am losing sense and sight. Take care of him, Reuben. May heaven so deal with you as you deal with that fatherless and motherless babe."

He grasped Reuben tightly by the hand, he tried to swallow a little brandy held to his lips by Caleb, but in vain.

The end had come.

Presently he whispered—

"You have sworn, Reuben."

"Yes; and though I may truly say that a price is set on my head, I repeat my oath to protect him and to assert his rights."

"Then heaven's blessing and the last blessing of a dying man rest upon you."

These were the last words Richard Pendarven ever uttered.

In another moment his spirit had fled.

There was nothing more to do there.

Hastily, though reverently, Reuben drew the sheet over the face of the dead man, and with the baby in his arms, crept down the staircase preceded by Caleb, carrying the casket.

All was very still now save the storm without, which was uninterruptedly raging as before.

Not a sign of any human being was to be seen either in the house or grounds, and so, quickly though cautiously, the two men hastened across the velvety lawn in the direction of the road.

They had their burdens concealed as well as they could beneath their coats, and with their weapons clutched in their right hands they pressed on in the storm.

As they reached the road the four masked men sprang upon them.

"Who are you, and what have you got there?" shouted the leader of the party.

"Our business can have nothing to do with you, Hubert, Pendarven," said Reuben. "Let us pass."

"Ha, you know me!" cried his uncle. "Then there is more reason to be rid of you."

And he attacked Reuben fiercely, aided by another of his companions, while the other two assaulted Caleb Lee.

Burdened as they were, there could have been but one end of the conflict if at this moment there had not been heard a sound of ill-omen for the assassins.

The rapid rush of horses' feet.

They knew at once that the double patrol was approaching.

To Reuben and Caleb this meant safety and protection; to the others it meant arrest, disgrace, death.

The assassins, therefore, knew that they had no time to lose.

They attacked the two companions more fiercely than ever.

But at this moment Caleb contrived to draw his pistol, and firing, brought one of his assailants to the ground.

This precipitated matters greatly.

The sound of the pistol would, of course, arouse the patrol—would cause them to hasten to the spot, and the arrest of the murderers of Richard Pendarven would be certain.

"We must be off and away," cried the leader of the gang, "but your life first I'll have," and with the words he made a sudden lunge at Caleb, running him through the chest.

The gipsy staggered and nearly fell.

But though the wound was a desperate one, it did not for the moment deprive him of consciousness.

He managed to draw his other pistol and to fire just as the others thought themselves sure of victory.

He winged his man, who staggered back, and at that moment the thunder of the patrols' horses on the hard, chalky road was heard rapidly approaching.

It was perilous to remain longer.

The three assassins accordingly, with curses hurled at their opponents, dashed off along the road, and left Reuben and the wounded Caleb to themselves.

It was no part of their design to be found by the patrol.

The events of the evening were very difficult of explanation, and Reuben had not hinted wrongly when he said a price was set upon his head.

Years might have to roll by before he could clear his name from the false accusation against him.

And so, though he would be true to his trust, though he would honourably carry out the promise he had made to his uncle, he must remain for a time concealed—must in fact hide away like a criminal.

The dead body in the road, too, was something they would find it difficult to account for.

So, in spite of the desperate nature of Caleb's wound, they hurried as best they could across the road, and succeeded in making their way into Pentland Woods before the patrol came up.

"How much farther have we to go?" said Reuben, presently, as they pressed on, Caleb ever and anon having to pull up, overcome by the excruciating pain he was suffering. "I thought you had arranged with the boys to pitch their tents on the edge of the wood here."

"No; on the further margin," said Caleb; "on the hills which overlook the sea. They are not far, however. I shall be glad indeed to reach them, for I feel my life is sped. I have, I know, but a few hours to live."

He took from his pocket as he spoke a flask containing brandy, and drank a goodly draught.

This revived him a little, and he was able to hurry on more quickly still, until presently they came within sight of some lights, which showed that they were near the encampment.

Caleb's strength was rapidly giving way.

The casket was by no means a trifling weight, but still he struggled on manfully, speaking as little as possible, and, in fact, only speaking when it was necessary to give Reuben a direction.

Presently they reached the encampment, where, beneath the shade of some immense trees, which kept off the worst of the storm, the fires were burning and supper was being prepared.

The appearance of Reuben and Caleb were greeted with acclamation, but the joy of the gipsies was soon turned to horror and grief, when Caleb, staggering forward, fell in a heap at the opening of his tent and fainted.

The wounded king of the gipsies was quickly carried into his tent, and one of the lads, mounting a rough pony, set off at once towards the village to seek a doctor.

But Caleb's hours were numbered.

Revived by some cordial administered to him by Nona, the gipsy queen—his wife—he raised himself presently on his elbow and beckoned Reuben to him.

"Reuben Pendarven," he said, in a hoarse voice of agony, "as I told you in the woods, my life is spent. I wish to leave to you the care of my tribe. You are of gipsy blood; the true blood of the Romany runs in your veins, and I know that no worthier successor than you can be chosen by my people. I appoint you, therefore, king in my place. No one will think of disputing the right of the man who saved my Miriam's life. Nona, where are you?"

His voice was very feeble as he said these last words.

"Here I am, husband," said the gipsy queen, as she knelt down by his side. "Can you not see me?"

"All seems very dark—the thrust from that villain's sword has done for me," he said. "Is Miriam here?"

"Yes, I am here, father," said the young girl, a black-eyed, robust, lovely specimen of the gipsy race.

"I bless you both," he said, "with my last breath. May the curse of the Romany light on those who injure you! To you I leave a sacred trust—the little child whom Reuben brought to the tents to-night. He will be followed—pursued —everywhere. His enemies will be ever on his track. I wish you to aid him, to cherish this child, too, whose mother was a Romany, who will some day be rich and powerful and able to reward you."

"We want no reward," said Nona, "to aid one whom you leave in our care."

The gipsy queen was weeping silently, though her voice was firm and her accents decided.

"And now," said Caleb, "bring Seth Allen, Joshua Lee, and Hugh Blacklock here, that they may hear what we have to tell. Reuben will tell them the secret, and they must swear to keep it."

Nona gave him a draught of the cordial to rouse up what feeble ray of life was left within him, and then Miriam, issuing from the tent with the two-year-old boy closely pressed to her breast, went out to summon the three gipsies—heads of the tribe—to the beside of the dying man.

The men—not very bright specimens of humanity, especially Hugh Blacklock —listened in silence to the story which Reuben told.

He had been with them now for some time, and was a favourite with most of the tribe; but when the gipsy king told them of the fact that he had appointed Reuben his successor, significant glances were exchanged between them, and it was evident to all present that their hearts were full of jealousy.

Reuben, in fact, doubted the propriety of telling them at all the secret of Pendarven Castle, but in that spot Caleb's word was law.

By an oath—the most terribly binding —they were forced to swear to guard the infant, to obey Reuben, and aid him in all things.

This solemn scene was just over when the doctor, who had been fetched by the gipsy boy, arrived.

It was a task by no means pleasant to him.

The ride from the village was a long and lonely one, and he shared the very common prejudice against gipsies.

But he was a man of humane mind, and having been assured that it was a case of life and death, he had ridden over with the lad from sheer kindness, not expecting to receive any benefit or reward.

He was too late for any useful purpose.

Internal hemorrhage was going on; but he had brought with him a soothing draught, which eased the sufferer's pains and enabled him to talk with less effort.

The doctor gazed earnestly at Reuben when he saw him standing by the rugs and skins which formed the bed of the gipsy king.

He had known Reuben Pendarven years before, when the breath of suspicion had never passed over his name.

Was this dark-bearded, bronzed man the youth whom he had been acquainted with in those far-back times?

"What do you think of him, doctor?" said Reuben, as they drew apart from the rest for a moment. "Is he as bad as he supposes?"

"He will die before morning," said the doctor; "nothing can save him. But may I ask your name?"

"Reuben Lee. I am king of the gipsies when he dies."

He looked straight into the doctor's face as he said this, with a calm and resolute look which the other seemed to understand at once as a warning not to ask further questions.

"Ah, to be sure! A passing resemblance to an old friend of mine," he said. "A person more sinned against than sinning, I fancy. Well, well, this is a very sad affair. I must go now. If I remained I could do no good. Come to me in the morning or send."

And so the doctor, refusing the gold

which Reuben tried to press upon him, went off.

Ere dawn, the spirit of the gipsy king had passed away.

In three days more he was buried, being supposed to have been the victim of some brawl on the highway.

The body of the dead man found by the patrol was evidence of a deadly conflict of some kind.

But no one else was known to have taken part in it.

The other assassins did not come forward to claim the man who had been shot by Caleb in self-defence, and the mystery of the murder at the castle was supposed not to be in any way connected with the midnight affray in the road.

Within a few days Hubert Pendarven appeared on the scene, and took possession of the estate of the murdered Richard Pendarven.

The existence of a young heir was known to many, and the two old servants swore that they had left him alive and well in the castle when they had quitted the place that night.

But no trace of him could be discovered, and consequently, until it could be, Hubert was by law acknowledged as the rightful heir.

During all this time, even when the body of the murdered master of Pendarven was committed to the grave, and his brother shed false tears of sorrow before a large gathering of tenantry and friends, Reuben made no sign.

Miriam had taken charge of the forlorn little waif, the cousin of the man who had saved her life; and in spite of her youth (she was only seventeen) fondled and tended it as if it had been her own.

This task might naturally be supposed to have devolved on her mother, Nona.

But, since the death of her husband, the gipsy queen had been strangely wild and distraught, and seemed scarcely to notice the existence of the helpless babe.

Miriam's eyes often filled with tears as she fondled the little nursling and pressed it to her breast, and Reuben often wondered why she had conceived so great a love for it.

But others were not blind if he was.

Hugh Blacklock had noticed, with bitter anger at his heart, the tender glances which the gipsy maiden cast upon Reuben—her willingness to do his slightest behest—her gentleness to him in all things.

Blacklock loved Miriam passionately, as strongly as it was in his wild and desperate nature to do, and when he heard one night, about two weeks after the death of the master of Pendarven, that Reuben had given the word to strike tents next day and move to another county, he made up his evil mind for action.

Reuben had good reasons for removal.

He had thoroughly examined the papers in the casket, and found all the proofs complete save one, and that one the most important.

The marriage certificate of Richard Pendarven and Mona Lehman was wanting, and to obtain this he must quit Cornwall, and make his way to Dorsetshire.

On hearing this bit of intelligence, Hugh Blacklock sought out Seth Allen and Joshua Lee, and drew them apart from the rest.

"Friends," he said, "I have made up my mind to one thing, and I want you to help me. Reuben is a house-dweller — his blood is only half Romany—he is a usurper—one of us should have been king when Caleb died. I shall go to Hubert Pendarven and tell him of this child, and obtain a grand reward, which you shall share if you help me."

The men shook their heads.

"No," was their answer. "No," they had sworn and they would keep their oath.

Hugh, however, was not so squeamish.

Besides he had another incentive to action.

He desired to get Reuben out of the way, to place the child in such peril that he would fly with it to some other quarters, and so leave the coast clear for Hugh's wooing Miriam.

So that night he slunk off towards the castle.

The domestic who answered his summons stared in surprise at the rough-looking form as it stood in the dim light of the old porch.

"My master will not see you, I know," he said. "You had better send some message."

"Oh, yes, he will see me," said the man with a sneer. "Tell him I come to speak of a child who——"

"Hold!" cried a stern voice, and the master of the castle strode out of the dark hall—tall, dark, sinister, evil-browed—and stood before him with an angry light in his eyes. "Prate not your business here, enter and tell your story to me."

With a sidelong glance of triumph at the servant, whose imperturbable face expressed no signs of surprise, Hugh Blacklock entered, and followed Hubert Pendarven to his study.

The master of the castle closed the door, and flung himself angrily into his easy chair.

"Now then, what have you to say, and what folly was it that you were about to pour into the ears of my servant?"

"It was no folly, Mr. Pendarven," replied Blacklock. "He refused to bear my first message to you, and I was about to send one which would certainly have obtained me admission, though it would have told nothing. Listen. If it is of any use to you to have the child of Richard Pendarven in your power, you can have it ere dawn of day."

"And the reward?" asked Hubert, eagerly.

"A thousand pounds and the situation of gamekeeper on your estate," replied Blacklock.

"Good," said Hubert; "that is not unreasonable. Tell me all you know."

Never before was danger so near the innocent head, which was pillowed then on Miriam's breast, as at that moment when these two men drew their chairs close to the fire, and spoke in whispers of their cruel schemes of villainy and murder.

CHAPTER II.

A SNAKE IN THE GRASS.

IT was just before dawn, and darkness was heavy over everything.

In Pentland Woods all was very quiet.

The gipsies were resting peacefully before their departure for another county; the horses standing tied to the vans ready for a start.

Miriam had on this night yielded up her charge of Rupert to Reuben, excusing herself on the ground that Nona was wild with grief at the idea of leaving the spot near which her husband was resting in his last sleep, and that she was not fit to be alone or unwatched.

The girl's love for her mother was well known, but even this, had not Reuben's mind been preoccupied, could scarcely have accounted for the wild eagerness with which she pressed her charge on the new king of the gipsies.

And so now the little heir of Pendarven lay close to the strong man's heart, as he rested on a couch of rugs and skins, fully dressed, just where he had thrown himself after seeing to all the preparations for the morrow.

But all were not asleep in the tents, though Nona had worn herself out at last with her sorrow, and was slumbering calmly.

Miriam, when Hugh Blacklock had crept away from the encampment after his futile interview with Seth and Joshua Lee, had followed in his wake, and seen him take the high road to the castle.

She had not troubled herself to go farther.

Her object was to save Rupert and Reuben from danger, and so, having ascertained enough for her purpose, she returned to the tents and waited in concealment.

Meanwhile, just before dawn, a dark form came cautiously out of the denser parts of the woods into the comparatively open space where the gipsy encampment was situated.

It was Hugh Blacklock.

He glanced everywhere around him, peered into the tent which he shared with Seth Allen, to see if he were sleeping or had noticed his absence, and was on the look out, and made, in fact, a tour of the encampment.

Then, having satisfied himself apparently that all was well, he began stealthily to approach the tent where Miriam was accustomed to lie with her mother and little Rupert since the death of Caleb Lee.

Then he cautiously raised the covering.

In one hand he held a dark lantern, and in the other a knife.

He was determined to succeed at all hazards.

If Nona or Miriam made an outcry he would silence their voices for ever.

Turning the light partially on, he dropped on his hands and knees, and peered in.

Nona lay fast asleep.

But she was alone.

Blacklock withdrew with a curse.

"What does this mean?" he muttered; "what trick has been played upon me?"

Rising to his feet again, he paused to think.

"Ah, I have it," he cried, after a moment; "the child's with Reuben."

Without further hesitation he cautiously crossed over.

One glance into the tent was enough.

There was the babe calmly sleeping in the strong man's arms.

A sinister smile overspread the face of Blacklock.

Then he was about to go down on his hands and knees, still grasping the knife more firmly than before, when a form—that of a woman with her head closely enveloped in a hood—stood before him.

It was Miriam, though in the darkness he knew her not.

"Stay, Hugh Blacklock," she said; "one word with you."

He muttered a fearful curse.

"What want you with me?" he cried.

"I am Miriam Lee, and I have followed you this night," she answered.

"And whither?" he cried insolently.

"To the castle," she said confidently.

"Well, and what then?"

"You mean harm to Rupert Pendarven, and I am here to prevent it," she cried. "I know what you would do. You would steal the innocent babe, and give it into the charge of Hubert Pendarven. Go! Leave the tents, and I will not arouse the tribe. If you remain, I will tell all I have seen—all I know, and you will be driven forth an outcast, whom no other tribe will receive amongst their number."

The man advanced nearer to her.

She saw the glitter of his long knife, even in the darkness, and kept prepared.

She knew that this man was the most desperate of all the tribe.

"Keep your distance, Blacklock," she cried. "I can hear you well where you are. You have heard what I had to say."

"Yes. What if I refuse?"

"I will arouse your comrades."

"Listen then," said Hugh, in a hoarse voice; "there are more reasons than one why I hate Reuben. I love you wildly—madly. It is the one hope of my life to be able to win you. Long ago before you saw this man you used to be kind to me—to listen to my words, and I had every hope of winning you. But since the house-dweller came to our tents all has been changed. You love him, though he knows it not—love him when he would scorn you, could he but see it. Ha, ha! Miriam, the daughter of the gipsy king, trying to win a man against his will."

"Stand back! approach no nearer or I will cry for help," she cried.

He was still gliding closer to her.

"Listen," pursued Blacklock, "I have loved you—worshipped you like a slave. I have nourished hopes of being king, with you for my queen, until this white-skinned, fair-talking fellow, who has been driven from among his people, came to our tents. But I have sworn you shall be mine, and that oath I will keep."

"You do not always keep oaths," said the young girl. "You swore to protect this babe."

"Bah! we waste time," said the gipsy. "I have sworn you shall be mine, and as that is the dearest wish of my heart, I will keep my vow. Fly with me to-night, Miriam, bring the babe with you, and——"

"No more," cried Miriam, "I will listen no longer. I warn you in time. This child, whose helplessness makes cowards of all his enemies, has three protectors—myself, my mother, and Reuben Pendarven, whom no bribes and no threats will move. So waste no further words. Go while you are safe, and trouble us no longer."

With an oath he made a sudden spring at her.

His object was not murder.

He hoped to wound her—to cause her to swoon, so that he could carry her off swiftly to some part where he could conceal her from her friends.

But he had met his match.

Miriam knew too well the character of Hugh Blacklock to trust herself in his presence unarmed.

As he sprang forward something glistened in the night air; there was a sudden report, and with a bitter curse Blacklock staggered back, shot in the shoulder.

In an instant the tribe was up and stirring.

The gipsies were like soldiers, used to be aroused at the first alarm, and consequently, ere Hugh Blacklock had fairly recovered from his surprise, and the sudden attack which had been made upon him, the Romany were thronging to the spot, grasping glittering knives in their hands.

Hugh, however, had no idea of being taken in such a scene.

He knew well that no charge he could bring against Miriam would be listened to, and so with a curse—loudly vented—he dashed away, and fled through the woods.

The men had lit torches, and had listened in a wondering group to the story which Miriam had to tell, but at the request of Reuben, no one thought of going after the fugitive.

"He is cast out," said Reuben; "let him find friends elsewhere. Henceforward whoever helps or shelters him is an outcast from the tribe."

It was now so near the hour of dawn that it was deemed useless to retire again, and accordingly, as the first grey tints were breaking over the sea, the women began to light the fires for breakfast, and the men to get the horses ready for a start.

Indeed, now Reuben was anxious to be off as soon as possible.

Now that Blacklock had turned traitor it was difficult to know what other attempts might be made by Hubert Pendarven to recover possession of the child.

Reuben had been left in a state of comparative wealth by his uncle Richard, and had every means of paying for any search that could be made.

But he knew that until he could obtain some certain knowledge as to the proofs he required, it was best to remain among the people whom he could depend upon.

Early morning saw the caravan, therefore, slowly passing from the woods.

The sun, a frosty sun in the first days of spring, was brightening the dark old towers of Pendarven Castle as the vans went slowly by.

This was the first time that Reuben had been near the spot since that fatal night when Richard, his uncle, and Lee, the gipsy king, had yielded up their lives to the hands of assassins.

Everything was calm and still.

And, up at one of the windows, Reuben, walking on in his gipsy dress at the head of the horses, saw a man, tall and dark-bearded, gazing down at the line of waggons.

He knew him at once as Hubert, his uncle.

He guessed, too, the evil thoughts in that man's heart.

Blacklock's revelation had told him where the child was; but there was no legitimate reason for claiming it, and getting it into his own possession.

To do so would be to acknowledge the identity of the young heir of Pendarven, and once openly in the care of his uncle, he would be watched in such a way as to render it impossible to harm him.

No!

He must get him into his power secretly or not at all.

He must let the child go off with his strange protectors, and Hugh Blacklock must follow them.

CHAPTER III.

A GIPSY MARRIAGE—TIME FLIES—RUPERT THE GIPSY BOY.

REUBEN'S caravan made its way safely to Dorsetshire.

It was a county he knew well, and on the road, which he was able to pick out readily, having passed over it many times, he did not make any special haste

Before the terrible death of his uncle, he had lived on the bounty of the gipsies.

Now he was a rich man.

He had thousands in the bank in his own name as guardian of young Rupert Pendarven, and there also had been deposited the proofs of the boy's identity.

No one knew of his wealth save Caleb Lee, and he had carried the secret with him to his grave.

Miriam knew that Reuben had a little gold.

But she never dreamed that there was a small fortune lying in the Cornish Bank to the name of Reuben Pendarven.

On the road to Dorsetshire he had abundant chances of studying the character of the gipsy girl.

One evening, just as they had partaken of the last meal, he drew her apart from the rest.

"Miriam," he said, taking her hand, "it depends upon you whether I remain with the tribe or not."

"With me?" said the girl, trembling.

"Yes. I love you, Miriam," continued Reuben, passing his arm around her waist. "In the days gone by I loved you well, but I would not dream of telling you of it, because I was poor, friendless, and under a cloud. Now I am no longer poor. The same cloud hangs over me, but that will soon be dissipated. Tell me, Miriam, will you be my wife? Will you share with me really the burden of this secret? I so fear to lose you when I am compelled to be away, or I would not ask you until all was settled."

He drew her towards him.

She nestled in his bosom.

And so the betrothal was settled.

A week after a wedding took place, and Miriam was hailed Queen of the Gipsies. But there was also a marriage at the little country church, with only a pew-opener and the clerk for witnesses.

Somehow Reuben felt safer now that Miriam was his wife.

He told her of his wealth after they were married, and was scolded accordingly.

But she was indignant when she heard the story of his wrongs.

He had been, as he acknowledged, a spendthrift.

He had spent money recklessly, until his friends would supply him with no more.

Then he was accused of forging his uncle Hubert's name.

This had been done by a bosom friend of his who fled the country when he had done the deed, succeeding, however, in fixing the guilt on Reuben ere he went.

Until this man was found and forced to confess, a price was upon Reuben's head, for in those days forgery was punished by death.

He thought himself on the track, however.

A week after the humble wedding, which brought such joy to both their hearts, Reuben quitted the tents, leaving them and the infant Rupert in the care of Miriam and her mother and Seth Allen.

He was disguised in such a manner that no one could have recognised him either as Reuben the gipsy or Reuben Pendarven the outcast.

He was dressed like a gentleman who had just returned from abroad, in a suit of expensive and well-fitting travelling clothes, his bronzed face, with its black, well-trimmed hair being shaded by a wide felt hat.

No one could possibly have imagined what he had gone through, or what secret he held within his bosom.

His destination was Merton-on-the-Arrow, in the pleasant county of Dorsetshire; for at a church somewhere in the neighbourhood of this place Richard Pendarven had married sweet Mona Lehman the gipsy, one of the great family of the nomads who are spread over England.

Our hero's position was one of great danger.

A large fortune, and retribution, too, hung on the caution and wisdom of Reuben, for who was to tell who had visited Merton first—who knew what emissaries from Hubert Pendarven had tampered with those in charge of the registers?

Hubert no doubt knew the exact place where his brother was married, and the date also; and if so there was no doubt in the mind of Reuben that he had on some occasion, prior to the murder, stolen the certificate.

So, naturally, Reuben resolved to be very cautious.

There were three churches in and about Merton-on-the-Arrow.

But he believed that the church in

the wood must be the place he was searching for.

To this accordingly he went.

Roger Maltby, whose son was sexton of Merton-on-the-Arrow, was a man of about fifty years of age, though looking seventy.

He was sitting in the porch of his little cottage when Reuben approached.

"Good morning, sir," said Reuben. "Can you direct me to the house of Roger Maltby, clerk to the church in the woods?"

"I am Roger Maltby, at your service," said the old man, bowing, and rubbing his hands together servilely.

"Indeed! then may be we can transact business here without the necessity of going up to the church," said Reuben. "Do you know the names of Pendarton and Clara Absalom?"

The clerk eyed him closely.

"No," he said, after a moment, still keeping his eyes on Reuben, "I do not. Is it a burial, or a birth, or a marriage?"

Reuben laughed.

"Well," he said, "there have been all three, but not here. But it is a marriage I am looking for at the present moment. Can you spare the time to consult the register with me?"

"Certainly, sir," said Maltby. "That is my business—I will at once go with you."

The clerk opened the church door, and in a few minutes they stood in the vestry.

"Hold the lamp, sir, if you don't mind. The book can't be far off."

Somehow or another a deadly faintness crept into Reuben's heart.

With many an exclamation of regret and surprise, the little man sought everywhere around for the book, but in vain.

"This is very strange," he said presently. "I do not know where else to look. I must ask the vicar, and my son, and the verger, and so on, and perhaps they may be able to throw some light on the subject."

Reuben could hold his peace no more.

"Mr. Maltby," he said, eyeing him fiercely, "I have not only wished to see the marriage register of Pendarton and Absalom, but of Richard Pendarven and Mona Lehman. Ha! you know that name."

The clerk had given a slight start.

But it was very slight, and he soon recovered himself.

"No, the name is not familiar," he said. "I was at that moment thinking whether Pendarton had stolen the volume. He was here, and he remained here a few moments while I went to another part of the church."

"What Pendarton?" asked Reuben severely.

"The Pendarton that married Clara Absalom."

This was enough.

He caught the clerk by the arm.

"Roger Maltby," he cried hoarsely, "you are lying to me. Pendarton and Absalom are two names which I thought of accidentally on the road. It is the marriage certificate of Richard Pendarven I want, and that I demand of you."

"You are a madman!" cried the clerk, wrenching his arm free. "I didn't much like the look of you when I first saw you."

"You will like the look of me less when you see me again, no doubt," said Reuben. "I charge you with destroying or making away with the marriage certificate, or the book containing the marriage certificate, of Richard Pendarven and Mona Lehman. But, perhaps, we can come to terms."

"I don't know what you mean," said the clerk, shrinking away from him.

"I will make myself plainer, then," returned Reuben. "Tell me what you will take to bring me that book, no matter where it may be, or tell me the name of the man into whose possession you gave it?"

"I don't know what you mean," said Roger, making his way towards the door. "I wish you would speak to the vicar about this matter and not to me."

"Roger Maltby," said Reuben sternly, "you do understand me, and I believe you are a great villain. I shall go to the vicar and explain everything. If he can, or will, do nothing to help me, or force you to discover where you have placed the book, or how it was destroyed, or to whom it was given, be assured you will not escape me. I will hunt you down surely and remorselessly, even to your death!"

He turned to go as he spoke, and the old man did not detain him.

But he was evidently suffering from deadly fear.

Reuben tried him again. On reaching the vestry he said—

"Once more I give you a chance. If you will restore to me or enable me to procure the volume I want, or only the certificate, I will give you two thousand pounds."

The old man turned pale and trembling.

"I can't do it," he said. "I don't know what you mean."

And so Reuben left him.

His heart was full of anguish now.

By any open attempt at forcing Roger Maltby to divulge his secret, he would be delivering himself over to the law and to death. And yet how could he rest in peace in the face of this terrible injustice?

At the vicar's house no greater good attended him.

The worthy man was shocked at even the suggestion of his clerk's iniquity, and made every inquiry in the neighbourhood.

But in vain.

Nothing could be elicited from Roger, or his son, or his friends, and vowing vengeance against those who had participated in the deed of villainy, Reuben Pendarven once more turned his back upon the place.

"I regret," he would say to Miriam, "that I ever had the charge of young Rupert thrust upon me. But I had not the chance of refusal when my uncle was in the very throes of death."

So time went on.

Twelve years passed, and the babe, which had been rescued on that night of storm and murder, had grown to be a lad of fourteen, tall, well-made, and handsome.

He was a great favourite with the gipsies, was recognised, in fact, as one of themselves, and was admired and envied by many of the youths for his cleverness in riding, shooting, leaping, setting traps, in fact, everything which is taught in a rustic, wandering life.

During all these years no one had appeared in the shape of an enemy.

Reuben had heard secret news from the castle.

Hubert Pendarven had married again; his son by his first union had been placed at a school in the vicinity to receive an education befitting the heir of the family, and everything appeared to be going on smoothly and well for the assassin who had robbed Richard of life amid the tempest of that winter's night long ago.

Reuben had made no sign.

He dared do nothing yet, and, in fact, he had almost begun to despair.

He had taught Rupert the rudiments of an excellent education, and had resolved to send him to school.

An incident, however, occurred at this time, which forms the real beginning of our story.

Rupert was out on the margin of some woods, not far from the borders of Cornwall, engaged in his favourite pastime of fishing, when he was accosted by a somewhat rough voice.

"I say, youngster, can you tell me the way to Brackenbury?"

The voice was quite unfamiliar to Rupert, and when he glanced up the face and the form of the speaker were as unknown as his tones.

What he saw was a man of about eight and thirty years of age, dressed in a velvet coat, hunting breeches and boots, and a dark hunting cap, mounted on a beautiful bay horse.

He eyed Rupert curiously as the boy looked up, but the latter did not seem to notice his intent gaze.

"Brackenbury is a good distance from this place," he said. "You've got to go across the wood, and across Mellon's plantations, and then along the high road to the turnpike."

The horseman seemed struck by a sudden idea as he gazed upon the lad.

His face flushed with some pleasurable emotion, and an evil triumph came into his eyes.

"I'm certain I'm not mistaken," he muttered to himself, "those are the Pendarven eyes—the features altogether. At any rate it won't do any harm to put myself on the scent."

"Well, my lad," he said aloud, "as you say Brackenbury is a long way off, and as I see you have your pony tied to the tree yonder, what say you to showing me the way and earning a piece of silver?"

The boy's cheeks flushed with wounded pride.

"GILES CAME SLILY UP BEHIND HIM."

"I'll show you the way, but I don't want your money," he said.

And putting up his fishing tackle he prepared to mount his shaggy little friend.

"I'm certain I'm on the right track," said the stranger exultingly to himself.

But he exulted too soon.

As Rupert was about to mount his little pony, a loud voice was heard crying—

"Stop, one moment, Rupert!"

And Reuben strode upon the scene.

"Where were you going?" he cried, to the startled boy.

"To show this gentleman the way, cousin," he said gently.

Reuben, while our hero spoke was eyeing the horseman intently.

"Nay, then you must not do so, my boy," said Reuben. "That man is one of your deadliest foes. Ay, frown as you will, I know you again, Hugh Blacklock, in spite of the years that have gone by—in spite of the gentleman's clothes you wear. Go your way in peace. I'll harm you not, though you did try to injure my Miriam—my beloved wife. But I warn you not to come in this boy's way. I am ever on the spot to defend him, ever on the watch for you and others. Nay, say nothing—I will not listen to you. Come, Rupert, let us go."

He took the boy's arm as he spoke, and drew him into the cover of the woods.

Hugh Blacklock gazed after them with irresolute malignity for a moment, and then, with a fearful oath, he rode away.

"Never mind, Reuben Pendarven," he said, between his clenched teeth. "I shall be even with you yet. That's the boy, and if he isn't up at the castle within a week or so, then my name isn't Hugh Blacklock."

Meanwhile, Reuben, with his face agitated as Rupert had never seen it before, had led the way into the wood, and sitting down upon a fallen tree, motioned the boy to sit beside him.

"Rupert," he said, "the time has come at last when I must tell you your whole story, for your enemies have at length crossed your path. You must know all in order to be able to guard against them, and then for a time we must part."

"Part?" repeated the lad, in surprised and sorrowful accents.

"Yes, for a short time," said Reuben; "you must go to school some day to prepare yourself for a great and happy future, and it may as well be now when there is great need for concealment. But listen while I tell you your story, and learn a lesson of vengeance to be cherished in your heart for ever."

And so, out in that forest stillness, our young hero listened to the story of his strange birth, of the wrongs of his mother and the cruel death of his father until his blood surged with anger.

Springing to his feet, with one hand he grasped that of his cousin, and raising the other above his head, he cried—

"Fear not, cousin, I will be true to my trust. And here I swear that my father's foul murder shall be fully and fearfully avenged!"

CHAPTER IV.

BLAKESLEY HALL SCHOOL.

ABOUT a fortnight after the events narrated in our last chapter, a new boy arrived at Blakesley Hall School, near Tregeis, in Cornwall.

Blakesley Hall School was a grand old red brick house, standing not far from the seashore.

It was provided with large recreation grounds, orchards, kitchen and vegetable gardens, and fields beyond.

The master was Dr. Walton.

This school shared the honour of education with Huntly Hall Academy, which was one of the eccentricities as also the notabilities of the neighbourhood.

It was called "Hungry Hall" by the boys at Blakesley Hall, and well it deserved the title.

The boys were all of the same type, lanky, starved-looking creatures, who had often been seen to pick up a crust or any other morsel that had been flung away in the streets of Tregeis.

The two ushers, Messrs. Meekly and Small, looked as if they never saw a piece of meat from one year's end to the other.

But the master, Dr. Carver (whom the boys of both establishments had christened Dr. Starvem), was a being of a different mould.

He was somewhat below the middle height, but egregiously fat.

Strange rumours floated about in regard to this establishment.

It stood on an island in the middle of an arm of the sea, and not one of the scholars could make their way to the mainland without permission of the masters, the boats being kept securely padlocked.

Circumstances combined to cause the house to enjoy a very evil reputation, and it was openly asserted by some people that boys were placed there to be got rid of.

However this might have been, they were a curious lot; and the crowd of lads assembled on this half-holiday in the recreation grounds of Blakesley Hall School were indeed a contrast to them.

On this occasion they were discussing the arrival of a new boy.

He had arrived about an hour before, brought by a dark gentleman, in a brougham.

"What's he like ?" asked a stout, fair-haired lad, whose name was Tom Warner, and wore his hat far back off his forehead.

"Tall for his age—fifteen or thereabouts—dark, straight features, rather haughty," was the reply given by a merry-eyed fellow named Bob Lander (known in the school as "the Gossip").

At these words another boy strolled near the group.

"Haughty is he ?" he cried ; then I will soon teach him his manners. I'll have him for my fag. Lewis," he added, turning to a meek little fellow near him, "I release you from service. What is this new chap's name ?"

"Rupert Clifford," said the Gossip; "and he doesn't seem to me the sort of fellow to be a fag to anyone. I wouldn't try it if I were you, Pendarven; it's no use making a row directly a new boy comes into the school."

"It's your fault," replied Ralph Pendarven (son of Hubert, and consequently Rupert's cousin), "you shouldn't have talked about his haughtiness. You know how that annoys me."

"All right; do as you like," said the Gossip, "only mind—we're all witnesses that you've given up the services of Tony Lewis, and so if you don't make the new fellow obey you you've no fag at all."

"I'll chance that," said Ralph. "Ah! here comes your paragon I suppose."

Descending the steps which led from the school-house into the play-ground, was Mr. Tobias Littleton, who, from his height and his slender proportions, was known as Long Toby.

By his side was a boy whom we need not describe, as he was none other than Rupert Pendarven, who, by Reuben's wish, had assumed the name of Clifford.

Ralph turned colour slightly as he saw him approaching.

The Gossip observed this, and down went the circumstance in his mental note-book.

But of course nothing could be said now.

Long Toby, who was really a favourite with the boys, was soon among them introducing the new scholar.

The usher told them that he was the son of a gentleman in a high position, and he hoped that they would show him that he was among gentlemen.

And then, with a few cheery remarks, he left them.

The instant Rupert and Ralph looked into each other's faces, they took a mutual dislike to one another.

Ralph, because he saw before him a frank, handsome boy, who seemed bold and brave and true.

Rupert, because he recognised in the other an ignorant and over-bearing temper.

"Well, let's go into the fields and have a game of cricket," said Hal Armstrong, a jolly lad about Rupert's own age. "Do you like cricket, Clifford ?" he added, putting his hand in a genial way on Rupert's shoulder.

"Yes, I do very much, although I'm not a good player," replied Rupert, "but I'm persevering, and shall soon learn, I hope, so I'll join you if you'll allow me."

"Allow you ?" cried the Gossip; "why, we shall be glad to have you."

"Stop a moment," cried Ralph. "This is all very well, but we are going along anyhow. The new boy hasn't been put through his facings yet."

"What do you mean by that?" cried Rupert, turning fiercely upon the speaker.

Ralph did not like the looks and bearing of Rupert, so he moderated his tones and said—

"Oh, it's usual to ask a few questions when a new boy comes. "What's your name?"

Rupert smiled.

"The tutor told you that," he said; "but in case your hearing is defective, or you may not have been listening, I repeat it—Rupert Clifford, son of Gerald Clifford of the Larches, Besborough-on-Sea, age, nearly fifteen, weight, I don't know how much, temper good, warranted to work as well as play—that's all I need tell you, I think."

A loud chorus of laughter followed this sally, which was wonderfully discomfiting to Ralph Pendarven.

He changed colour, and cast an angry glance round the eager circle of his schoolmates.

What he saw depicted on their faces was by no means encouraging.

A spirit of insubordination seemed to be abroad.

However, he was not to be driven from his purpose.

"Very good," he said; "I am glad you are able to work, and are of a lively disposition. It is a rule that every new boy on entering becomes the 'fag' of the eldest scholar who wants one, and as I have just discharged mine, you will take his place."

"Much obliged, I'm sure," said Rupert, with a merry laugh. "Will you kindly tell me the duties of the peculiar being called a 'fag?' I have not been at a large school like this before, and I am always anxious for information."

"Oh," cried Ralph, who was angry indeed at the merriment the new boy was exciting against him, "you'll soon find that out. You'll have, among other things, to see that my washing things are ready in the morning, clean my boots, look out words for me in the dictionaries, prepare——"

"Stop—pray stop!" cried Rupert, in assumed horror. "I'm not up to any of it. I should only make a muddle of half the things, so if there's any honour attached to the office, pray give it back to the poor boy you've discharged, for I must decline it. And now let's be off to the cricket-field."

The lads round tittered loudly, and indulged in a variety of antics.

It was too much for Ralph, and, white with anger, he advanced towards Rupert.

"You're mocking me," he said. "That's a thing I won't stand."

"I can't help that," said the gipsy schoolboy. "I never asked you to stand anything. I'm used to do what I please, and say what I please, and I'm sure I'm not going to be brow-beaten by you."

"I'm not brow-beating you or attempting to do so," said Ralph, trying to appear calm; "but I tell you plainly what it is. I've been used to have my way as much as you have been, and in this school I allow no one to master me."

"Pray do not think that I wish to do so," said Rupert, who felt his anger rising. "You'll never find me interfere with anyone who does not interfere with me. But I warn anyone who tries to play any ungentlemanly tricks on me that I can and will take my own part."

"Don't let's have a quarrel, Ralph," said the Gossip. "Wait till he refuses to 'fag' for you, that'll be the time to punish him."

Ralph thought a moment.

An instant's reflection told him that he might get into serious trouble by forcing a quarrel on a boy who had only been a few minutes as it were in the school.

And besides, he somehow or another wanted to have a serious consultation with himself before he went further in the matter.

He made no objection therefore to the proposed delay.

"Yours is good advice, Gossip," he said. "Look you, Clifford, you're my fag, and no matter whether you like it or not, you'll have to begin your duties to-night. If you don't, then you'll see that unpleasantness will happen. I don't intend to stand any of your bounce."

Rupert bowed mockingly.

"Until then, your royal highness," he said, "we will defer the conversation."

And he turned to Hal Armstrong.

"My friend, what is your name?"

The lad told him, and hoped that they would be chums.

"Well, Hal, I hope so," returned Rupert. "And now let us adjourn to the cricket-field. The presence of royalty in the person of the mighty Pendarven is oppressive."

With these words he turned away, and Hal, anxious to avoid further quarelling, hurried with him towards the cricket-field.

Ralph Pendarven walked moodily away amid the unrestrained titterings of the boys around him.

"He's hard hit," said the Gossip to Tom Warner. "I don't remember his ever having such a reception before."

"No; and I don't suppose any boy ever before had such a tanning as Rupert Clifford will get if he refuses to fag for bully Ralph."

"He will refuse."

"Then Ralph will have his revenge," said the Gossip; "and you know it is the rule of the school not to interfere if a fight takes place."

"I'm not so sure about his getting a hiding," returned Tom Warner. "It strikes me there's plenty of bone and muscle about that youngster. He's as straight as a lathe, and tall for his age."

"But Ralph is the strongest boy and best boxer in the school," suggested the Gossip.

"I don't know that," said Tom. "He's never had a try at Ship Ahoy yet."

"Ship Ahoy," it must be explained here, was the name given to a lad, of about Rupert's age, whose father was a sea-captain, and who affected to be nautical in his ways.

His dress was as nautical as it could be in a young gentleman's school; wide trousers, short jacket—colour, navy blue—navy shirt, very low in the neck, tied by a loose handkerchief with ends waving about.

It was not all affectation, however.

He really liked the sea, was ultimately going to a naval college, and was about as good-hearted and jolly a fellow as any in the whole school.

His real name was Jack Amberley, but he had obtained, in consequence of the habit he had got of singing out to his comrades in the playground, the nick-name of "Ship Ahoy!"

"No," replied the Gossip, "he hasn't tried Ship Ahoy yet, and I don't know how that would be; but we must have patience until to-night. If the new fellow's in our dormitory there'll be a row, I know."

And with these words they dismissed the probable scene of the evening from their minds, and started off to the cricket-field.

Meanwhile Ralph Pendarven walked slowly towards the same spot, his mind full of hate and anger. He had made up his mind to thrash Rupert.

He was the acknowledged head of the school in the playground, by dint of being bully over the others.

He was a strong fellow, had thrashed most of the fellows into obedience, and was left alone by the rest for fear of punishment.

But in school he was by no means a shining light, principally because he hated the very notion of work.

He recognised in Rupert a lad who not only defied him, but one who had a clearer head, and a more genial manner.

"I hate his name, too," he muttered to himself as he went. "It puts me in mind of that gipsy brat who is wandering about in the world somewhere, claiming to be my cousin. Only let him refuse to-night to do what I tell him, and then let him see what he'll get. I'll nearly kill him."

"Who is this boy who is so bumptious, and talks about making me his fag?" asked Rupert of Hal Armstrong, as they went on towards the cricket-field.

"Don't you know?" said Hal. "He is the head of the school out in the playground, at cricket, boating, and so on. His name is Ralph Pendarven."

Rupert could not avoid a start.

Fate was certainly working things in strange ways.

He had learned from his cousin Reuben the true history of his life.

He knew consequently that this boy was the son of the man who had murdered his father; he was in fact his cousin.

No wonder then was there that there should be antipathy between them.

Hal Armstrong noticed the start, for they had been advancing arm-in-arm.

"Do you know Ralph then by name?" he asked.

"Why?" replied Rupert.

"You started when I mentioned it."

"Did I? Oh, that's nothing. I have heard the name often mentioned by my father," said Rupert; "but I have never seen one of the Pendarven's before."

The conversation flagged now.

Rupert, in fact, had fallen into a deep train of thought, and was wondering what could be the end of all this strange mystery.

"My poor mother!" he said inwardly, "if only she had kept a copy of her certificate, this would never have happened. The witnesses at least would have been forthcoming, and I should not have had to masquerade under a false name."

His cogitations, however, were quickly cut short, for they arrived in the cricket-field and sides were made, the Gossip being captain of one eleven, and Ralph Pendarven captain of the other.

As the Gossip had promised, he chose Rupert Clifford on his side, and very well indeed did our hero acquit himself.

His gipsy experiences had taught him to be a good runner, and to have a quick and ready eye.

These qualities made up for his want of absolute knowledge of the game, and when it was over, and he was found to have made twenty runs, and to have been a splendid fielder as well, he received congratulations all round.

There was time for some races after cricket, and in spite of the exertions they had gone through, the boys quickly came to the scratch after a short period of rest.

Rupert eagerly joined in these, and came off the winner, far ahead of Ralph Pendarven, who had run his best.

Things began to look ominous for him.

"Ralph has got his match," said Tom Warner.

"Yes, and so have I," said Ship Ahoy, hitching up his belt with a laugh. "But I mustn't grumble. Sailors can't be expected to be good runners."

On the road home Ship Ahoy spoke to Ralph of the day's proceedings.

"I think it'll be bad form for you to pick a quarrel with the new boy, Ralph," he said. "I think he bids fair to be a jolly fellow. It would be a pity to give him a bad opinion of the school directly he comes into it."

Ralph laughed—a very harsh and unreal laugh.

"Oh! he won't have a bad opinion of the school," he said. "You fellows have pretty well shown him how ready you are to fall down at his feet and worship him. It is only myself that he will dislike, and that is very immaterial to me."

"Well, he seems a jolly chap," said Ship Ahoy, "and see what a splendid fellow he is in all our sports."

"No doubt he will be a great acquisition to the lower forms," said Ralph jeeringly, and he walked swiftly on a-head.

Of course it was the very success on the part of Rupert Clifford of which Ship Ahoy had spoken that was so bitter to Ralph Pendarven.

It made him all the more resolute in his determination to vent his spite upon our hero, and he almost longed for the moment to come when he would have the chance of fighting with him and humiliating him.

CHAPTER V.

TRYING A "FAG"—AN UNEXPECTED DENOUEMENT.

THE dormitories at Blakesley Hall School were eight in number, and that in which Ralph Pendarven was head boy only contained eight scholars.

These had been Ralph, the Gossip, Tom Warner, Ship Ahoy, Hal Armstrong, Peter Bannerman, an American lad, and two smaller boys, Oswald Peacock, nick-named the Bird, and Lewis Allenby, the comic boy.

The American was removed to another room to make way for Rupert.

Had Dr. Walton only known the events which had happened in the playground, he would not most likely have dreamed of placing him in that bed-chamber at all.

At eight o'clock the room was full, and Rupert had been shown his bed.

"I say, Rupert," said Hal Armstrong,

as they sat on the side of the bed, pulling off their boots, "have you brought a big box?"

"A what?"

"A big box—you know, full of nice things for us. Cakes, and tarts, and wines, and—and all manner."

Rupert laughed.

"Yes," he said, "I have brought a big box of niceties. My father told me that every young gentleman was expected to give a school treat, and he saw to the box himself. I don't know a bit what is in it."

"Oh! that's jolly," said Hal. "It's a long time now since we've had a new boy, and so we're eager for a good spread I can tell you."

"Here, you Clifford!" cried a voice at this moment, "come and take my boots off."

It was Ralph's voice.

Rupert took no notice; he was close to him, but he affected not to hear.

"I'm as anxious as you to overhaul the box," continued our hero, "but I thought——"

"Do you hear, Clifford?" cried Ralph again. "I told you you were to be my fag. Come and take off my boots."

"What a noise that fellow keeps making," said Rupert, as he took off his jacket and waistcoat. "I was going to say that I thought it would be better to make a picnic of it out in the fields or woods where all the school could enjoy it. Ha! what's that?"

A boot, hurled by Ralph Pendarven, had caught him a heavy blow on the side of the head.

On such occasions as these the boys expected a little amusement, and got it.

But this seemed to be no case of amusement in any way.

It promised to be too serious an affair for merriment.

When Rupert turned in the direction from which the boot had been thrown, his form was drawn up erect to his full height, his eyes were glistening with a desperate light, his bronzed cheeks were pale, his lip white and quivering, and his hands clenched.

All the proud sensitiveness of his nature was aroused, and those who gazed upon him held their breath almost in awe.

"Who threw that thing at me?" he asked.

Then, as his eyes alighted on the insolent face of Ralph Pendarven, he strode towards him.

"I need not ask," he cried, hoarsely. "I know who did it now. I can read it in your sneering face. Take that, coward."

His clenched fist was raised with the rapidity of lightning, and as it shot out Ralph Pendarven fell to the floor with a dull thud.

"All the fat's in the fire! We're going to have a blaze up!" cried Lewis Allenby, the comic boy, as with one somersault he turned head over heels from one bed to another, nearly knocking the breath out of the Bird.

Ralph rose up astounded—furious, with the very devil in his eyes.

"You cad!" he cried, "how dare you strike me? I'll give you such a thrashing for this as you never received in your life."

"I've never had one yet," said Rupert, calmly, holding himself prepared for any attack.

All his coolness had returned.

His gipsy blood had been roused, and had run riot in his veins when the missile had been hurled at him.

But he had returned the blow, and his generous nature saw in that sufficient expiation of the affront.

"Then have one now," said Ralph.

And he aimed a blow at our hero, which, had it taken effect, would have doubtless interfered greatly with his power of sight on the following day.

But it was skilfully warded off, as Rupert cried—

"Not this time!"

And the next moment Ralph was sitting in a most undignified position on the floor of the dormitory.

This was enough for those around.

Not that anyone was very sorry that Ralph had found his master.

But they knew well that if the quarrel was allowed to progress much further, the masters would be up, and great unpleasantness would arise.

It was Ship Ahoy who rushed between them.

"One word, shipmates," he said, in his usual merry way; "I know this quarrel has got to be fought out, but don't do it on the quarter-deck. Wait till you can get down in the steerage—

in other words, my friends, stop this for to-night, and have it out in the five-acre field to-morrow after school hours. What say you, lads?"

And he glanced round inquiringly at his companions.

A murmur of approval arose from all of them.

They too were anxious not to arouse the masters.

They had had on previous occasions abundant proofs of how the principal and his colleagues looked upon scenes like this in the schoolhouse itself.

"I agree with Ship Ahoy," said Hal Armstrong. "I don't believe in fights in the dormitory. If there must be a set-to, let it be out in the open, where no one will interfere."

"Yes, that's the way," put in Tom Warner. "We don't want the master up. Don't you remember when Oswald and Bertie Roberts had a fight, how the doctor came up, and when he found what was going on, he punished the lot of us?"

"Yes, I do remember it well," said Ship Ahoy. with a grimace; "and that's just why I don't want it to occur again. It's all very well to be mast-headed— I mean punished—for another messmate now and then, but I don't like to be a martyr more than now and then. Well, Clifford, what do you say?"

Rupert was about to speak, when Hal Armstrong, who was nearest to the door, said—

"Hush, boys! I hear someone on the stairs."

In an instant some of the lads had rushed to bed, while the others went on coolly undressing as if nothing out of the way was happening.

Ralph looked very savage.

He had an uncomfortable feeling that his comrades were taking part against him.

Nothing is so exasperating as a sudden fall from popularity.

"I hope you're not having one of your larks at our expense, Hal Armstrong," he said. "I can't hear any noise at all, and I'd just as soon have it out here as not."

"Listen, and judge for yourself, then," said Hal.

All were silent.

In a moment they heard a heavy tread, and presently, the door opening, revealed the face and form of "Long Toby," *alias* Tobias Littleton, the usher.

He glanced anxiously round the room.

But from the faces of the boys he could discover nothing, except that Ralph Pendarven looked very much annoyed at something.

Long Toby had not lived for such a time at the academy without knowing something of the ways of the boys, and he guessed at once that the acknowledged captain of the school had been attempting to browbeat the new-comer.

But he made no allusion to his own thoughts.

"Young gentlemen," he said, "Dr. Walton wishes to know what is the cause of all this unusual disturbance?"

"What disturbance, sir?" asked Ralph, in a kind of angry, yet respectful way.

"You must know what I mean. Master Pendarven," said Long Toby. "We were in the room underneath, and it seemed to us as if boots were being thrown about. Voices were loudly raised also. At any rate, the doctor says that if you can't keep better order in this room, he must put someone else in it as monitor."

This was gall and wormwood to Ralph.

To be reprimanded before Rupert was humiliation indeed.

Everything, in fact, seemed combining to rouse up a deadly feud between the cousins.

However he knew that nothing would be gained by being insolent to a tutor, so he said respectfully—

"Perhaps there was a little more noise than usual, sir, as we were talking to the new boy; but I will see the room is more quiet now and in future."

"I hope you will," said Long Toby, who never liked any unpleasantness. "Good night, young gentlemen."

"Well, Clifford," said Ship Ahoy, as soon as Mr. Littleton had gone, "is all arranged as we suggest? That you go to bed quietly now, and fight in the five-acre field to-morrow?"

"I will do just as I am forced to do," said Rupert. "I did not commence this fight. I was insulted and struck. Whenever I receive a blow, I give one back. For my part, I am quite satisfied, and want no fight."

"I expect not," said Ralph, sneeringly.

"I suppose you know that out in the open field I should give you too good a thrashing."

"As for that," returned Rupert, whose gipsy blood could stand no sneers, "if I had you out in the fields now, I would wring your nose for you, and throw you into the first horse-pond near to cool. But by to-morrow, perhaps, my temper may have calmed down, and I will leave it entirely to my schoolmates to arrange everything. I'll fight or not, just as they like. Now, boys, for bed."

"A Daniel come to judgment!" cried the comic boy, diving into the wrong bed, and being expelled at once by a vigorous kick, unnoticed in the exuberance of his joy.

"Oh, I am quite satisfied," said Ralph. "I will leave it entirely to my comrades."

Ship Ahoy and the others soon settled all preliminaries.

The fight was to take place in the five-acre field the next day at five o'clock.

The dormitory after this was quiet enough.

The boys, tired out after their cricket and their races, were thoroughly ready for sleep, and all save two were soon locked in the arms of slumber.

The two exceptions were Ralph and Rupert Pendarven.

The former was a prey to the most intense rage and mortification.

He had never, since his entrance into the school, been made such an exhibition of.

And in his own heart he was doubtful of the morrow.

Not that he feared the contest as a contest.

Bully and arrogant as he was, he was no coward, and the proud blood of the Pendarvens ran in his veins.

He dreaded only disgrace.

Rupert, on the other hand, calmly regarded the coming affray.

He was a hater of fights of all kinds, but his cousin Reuben (now his supposed father) had instilled into his mind the notion that he must always hold his own against all comers, and he consequently was resolved to do his best in the forthcoming fight with Ralph.

That was not what he was thinking of now.

His thoughts were busy with the tents he had left, the people who had been kind and gentle to him ever since the hour when he had been brought a helpless babe into their midst.

The house which Reuben had taken at Bessborough-on-Sea under the name of Gerald Clifford had held him only a few weeks, and there he had had, at any rate, the companionship of his cousin.

But here, among strangers, he felt a yearning for the green fields and woods.

But he remembered his family motto, "Brave, but patient"—and burying his aching head and burning eyes in his pillow, he sought sleep at last, and found it.

CHAPTER VI.

THE FIGHT IN THE FIVE-ACRE FIELD—A TERRIBLE ENDING.

NEXT morning was his first taste of real school routine.

When dressing, Ralph refrained from making any attempt at the tag business, and so Rupert's real *début* as a scholar was unmarred by any untoward incident.

He had been so well instructed by Reuben, so thoroughly initiated in school discipline, so ably "coached up" in general subjects by his well-educated and intellectual cousin, that he made a most excellent "first appearance," and took at once a high position in the classes.

Little did the masters, who smiled upon him for his acute answers, imagine that the rudiments of learning had been instilled into him in the leafy coverts of the woods.

The day passed rapidly, and at length the "fateful" hour arrived when the meeting was to take place in the five-acre field.

It had been so arranged that only the elder boys knew that anything was on the *tapis*.

The younger ones were induced to go off on an expedition of their own, and only eight lads were present at the combat.

It was a lovely evening.

The sun was shining brightly over meadows and cornfields, and its rays were dancing brightly on the surface of the river close at hand.

The open spot where the fight was to take place was shaded by lofty and thickly-foliaged trees, and a cool breeze was blowing.

Preliminaries were soon arranged, and the two boys—placed face to face with their waistcoats and jackets off—were left to themselves.

"This isn't the sort of fight I like to see," said Ship Ahoy to the Gossip. "They look too angry. Whoever wins, there'll be bad blood between them always."

"Yes; Ralph was foolish to go on with it," said the Gossip. "He must have seen that the new one wouldn't stand his nonsense."

"Ah! there they go at it."

Ralph struck the first blow, a heavy one; but Rupert, who was calm and collected, warded it off with apparent ease, and returned it with interest.

He did not give a knock-down blow, but one nevertheless that made his adversary stagger.

And so the fight went on.

Rupert was not exempt from punishment.

Once the spectators fancied he was going to be grassed.

But he quickly recovered himself, and rushing in, he struck Ralph a blow that sent him heavily to the ground.

The Gossip, who was Ralph's second, quickly had him on his knee in true orthodox fashion.

Ralph was badly shaken, and the Gossip hoped that the fight was over.

"I think I would give up now, Ralph," he said. "This new chap is too much for you."

"Give up—never! I'll fight to the death! Oh, how I hate him!" cried Ralph. "Only let me get a few chances of landing my blows."

So the fight began again.

Rupert, during the short interval of Ralph Pendarven's collapse, had recovered entirely his breath and his self-possession, and his opponent found his blows warded off with a masterly hand.

Again and again Ralph was either sent staggering back or cast on the ground, until derisive cries greeted his frantic attempts to strike Rupert in the face.

Exasperated beyond endurance by this, Ralph lost all command over himself, and as he came up for the last time, he aimed a ferocious kick at Rupert's leg.

The cowardly attempt succeeded to a certain extent, but Ralph in doing it fell to the ground.

In an instant all the gipsy blood rose up once more in the veins of Rupert.

His face grew deadly pale as before, and suddenly stooping he caught Ralph up by the belt, and lifted him in the air.

"I'll teach you," he cried, in a stern, hoarse voice, "to try your dastardly tricks on me."

Then before anyone could divine his intention, he had begun rushing headlong towards the banks of the river.

He seemed for the moment as if endowed with superhuman strength, and carried his burden as lightly as he could have done a child.

Anything cowardly or underhanded roused up the passionate part of his temper, and made him for the moment uncontrollable.

As soon as they saw what he was going to do the boys followed.

"He's going to give Ralph a ducking for that kick," said Ship Ahoy. "Shiver my timbers! if I don't think he deserves it too. The cowardly sneak! to kick when he was beaten fairly."

Not one of them thought of the danger any more than the gipsy schoolboy did.

Arrived at the bank of the stream Rupert poised Ralph in the air, and cast him in.

"Take that, you coward," he said, "for kicking me."

At the point where Ralph was thrown into the water the river Dart made a long bend, and the rush of water to that part of the bank was very great.

The Dart was a tidal river, though a small one, and the tide happened at this moment to be running down towards the sea.

The water consequently came up with a dash and a swirl, and as Ralph Pendarven fell into it, he was at once seized by the rushing waters and borne away.

A cry of dismay broke from the lips of the boys on the bank.

Rupert stood as if transfixed with surprise and horror.

He had never bargained for such a result as this.

He knew nothing of the river or its dangers, nor had he paused to think whether his adversary could swim or not, or, whether, even if he could, the stream at this point would not be too powerful for him to resist.

He had simply intended to give Ralph a ducking, and drag him out at once; but seeing what had happened so suddenly he was for the moment bereft of all power of action.

Meanwhile Ralph, who was making but ineffectual efforts to right himself in the water, was being borne rapidly away.

"What is to be done?" cried the lads. "No one can swim at this point well enough to save him."

"Can he swim?" asked our hero, as he quietly began getting off his boots.

"Yes, pretty well," said the Gossip.

"All right then. I'll save him," said Rupert, who had divested himself in an instant of all but his shirt.

"No, no; you'll both be drowned," was the cry.

But Rupert smiled.

"I say yes," he answered, preparing for his dive. "I threw him in, and so, if I can't save him, I must share his fate."

Generous heart!

He did not think of the kick or the coward blow which had been the immediate cause of all.

In another moment he had dived, and for a few instants was lost to view.

Then he came up with his head well above water, looked round to see where Ralph was, and swam away at a spanking pace, with the rapid tide, in the direction of the enemy he was trying to save.

"They can never get ashore again," said Ship Ahoy. "The tide's far too strong. They'll be carried out to sea and drowned."

"It'll be a fine story to take back to Dr. Walton," said the Gossip.

And so the eager boys, talking anxiously the while, ran along the margin of the river, not thinking whether they were in bounds or not, until presently, just as Rupert had nearly reached him, Ralph Pendarven threw up his hands and sank.

CHAPTER VII.

AFTER THE BATTLE.

A SIMULTANEOUS cry of horror broke from the lips of the schoolboys, as they saw the head of Ralph Pendarven disappear beneath the waves of the fastly-flowing river, just at a point too where the tide was strongest.

But the next instant their attention was attracted more forcibly by Rupert himself, who dived down recklessly in search of the foe who had insulted him, but whose life he was now resolved to save at the peril of his own.

He reappeared after a few moments, and a loud cheer resounded from the side of the river as the boys saw that he had hold of Ralph by the hair.

The other boys were swimmers to a certain extent.

But, with the exception of Ship Ahoy, not one of them seemed to care to run the risk of aiding Rupert in his struggle with the swiftly-flowing river.

He, however, had been quietly divesting himself himself of his clothes, while our hero had been swimming swiftly along with the rapid tide, and now just as Rupert was trying to make for shore, holding the head of Ralph by his hair, he sprang in.

He was a beautiful swimmer.

"Hold up, Clifford, lad," he said; I'm coming to the rescue!"

With a steady stroke he made his way in the direction of the two lads, and presently reaching them, he found that Ralph had fainted, and that our hero was nearly exhausted.

"I'll help you," he said.

And with his left arm he contrived to hold up the drowning boy—partially keeping his head above water and swimming with his right arm.

At length, by efforts which, considering the ages of the lads, were truly superhuman, they succeeded in bringing Ralph ashore.

They found that he was still breathing, and two of the strongest boys at once began to carry him towards the schoolhouse.

Reckless of the anger of the schoolmaster, one of them had run on with the news, and so when they neared the academy they were met by Long Toby and Donald McDonald the drill master.

"Bless the bhoys, what have they been doing?" cried the latter, "it's drowned the lad is, entoirely."

"No, I think not, sir," said Lewis Allenby, "his heart is beating."

"Let's hope it is," said Long Toby, severely, "the boys are so strictly forbidden to swim or row on the Dart, that I wonder how this could have occurred at all."

The insensible lad was quickly put to bed, the doctor, whom one of the scholars had fetched on his own responsibility, arrived shortly and Ralph regained consciousness, though he was too weak and confused to tell anything about his accident.

Under these circumstances, Dr. Walton sent for Rupert.

Our hero had not arrived at the school for some little while after the other boys.

He too was very exhausted.

His struggle to save Ralph had been a desperate one.

And he knew that he would have a by no means pleasant interview with Dr. Walton.

However he did not shirk it.

The schoolmaster eyed him very severely as he entered the room.

"I am very sorry to think such a disgraceful affair should have happened so soon after your entrance into the school. It seems to me that you were the ringleader of the whole affair."

"Will you allow me to explain, sir," said Rupert.

"Certainly; that is what you are here for."

"I should be very sorry indeed," said Rupert, "if I thought I had behaved in a manner seemingly disrespectful to you. But I think when you know all, sir, you will say that I am not so very greatly to blame as you think."

"Very well, my boy," said the doctor, kindly. "I am here to hear everything you have to say. I shall only be too glad if you can exonerate yourself."

Rupert made no hesitation.

He told his story freely from beginning to end.

Dr. Walton listened patiently.

"Well," he said, "this is a very sad affair. You see it comes of giving way to ungovernable temper."

"But I hope, sir, you do not think I meant to drown my schoolfellow."

"No, no! but your recklessness might have resulted in your doing so," said Dr. Walton. "I should be acting wrongly if I did not punish you severely. I must think what can be done. Go now to your room."

When Ralph recovered, which he did after a day's rest, he received a severe lecture.

"I don't allow fagging," said the master, "and never will if I can help it. You have brought your misfortunes upon yourself. I shall certainly punish Rupert Clifford, but still he is not so very much to blame, after the way in which he was treated directly he came to the school."

A severe imposition, a half holiday spent in school, sufficed to show the displeasure of Dr. Walton.

And then, except that Ralph was a trifle ill and pale, and less of a bully, the school went on as before.

It might naturally be thought that the reckless bravery of Rupert would have won for him the friendship of Ralph Pendarven.

But it was not so.

His courage and coolness in the face of danger had only succeeded in intensifying the hatred which his cousin felt towards him.

Such heroism as he had shown was more than his cousin could comprehend.

Rupert made the first advance.

But in vain.

His kind words were treated with disdain and contempt.

"I wish to have nothing to do with you," said Ralph. "You can avoid my company as I shall avoid yours. I hate you, and will yet have my revenge."

On the very night when the catastrophe occurred, Rupert dispatched a letter to his cousin Reuben, acquainting him with the presence of Ralph at the school.

On the third day he received a letter which surprised him.

He had expected that Reuben would at once suggest his withdrawal from the academy.

But he did not.

"Things are working well," he said. "I fancy that it is all for the best that you should have Ralph Pendarven under your eye."

Three weeks after, however, he received another note.

It had apparently been written in a great hurry.

It merely said—

"Meet me in Pentland Woods, near the Three Oaks, at seven to-morrow evening. Something has occurred to render it unpleasant, and even unsafe, for me to show myself near the academy. You know the spot well; you must make your own excuses to the master. I may send a messenger instead of coming alone."

The receipt of this note caused great anxiety to Rupert.

He was very ill, unable in fact to show up in the playground, except with the help of a schoolmate.

The cold which he had caught by his action in saving Ralph Pendarven, had settled in his limbs, and to meet Reuben, as desired, he would have to walk some distance.

What then was to be done?

He could not confide in Dr. Walton without betraying the trust given him by Reuben.

In these circumstances he looked round him for a confidant.

There were in the school at this time two brothers named John and Alfred Aylmer, the former about fourteen, the latter a little over fifteen.

Both of them were pleasant companions and trustworthy friends, and to Afred Rupert appealed for advice.

"Well, Clifford," said the lad, "if you are prevented from telling the master, what is to be done? You can't go in the state you are in."

"Certainly not," said Rupert.

But, just as he was about to add something, Alfred said—

"If you do not mind, I'll go for you; I should like the adventure."

Rupert considered a moment.

"Well," he said, "as my cousin said he may send a strange messenger, there might be danger, and why should you incur that for me?"

Alfred Aylmer laughed.

"Oh, as for that," he said, "I call it romantic nonsense. There won't be any danger, I hope. If there is, why not incur it as well as you. I look forward to it as a piece of fun."

"Very well," said Rupert, after some further hesitation, "I think I will agree. But there is one thing—you must remember, romantic or not, this matter must be kept a profound secret. My cousin, if he comes himself, will not tell you his business, nor will his messenger, I expect, do so. You will be given a letter for me; this you must defend, if needs be, with your life."

"All right," said Alfred, "and now you must explain to me all the details. I shall make an excuse to go out, and you may depend upon my doing my best, and keeping secret."

His eyes were full of pleasurable excitement as he spoke.

He was a lad of a most adventurous turn of mind, and he regarded this little episode with perfect delight, besides he was really fond of Rupert.

Everything was quickly settled, and when Rupert went up to bed, long before the others, in consequence of his illness, he felt confident of his friend's success.

By his own wish, he had Rupert's clothes and hat on.

"If the messengers are strangers," he said, "they will be likely, perhaps, to refuse any information if they think I am not the one they seek, and so I shall let them fancy that I am Rupert Clifford."

The brave little lad was off punctually at the appointed hour.

It was a very fine evening, and the lad felt his spirits rise at the prospect of his adventure.

Little did he know to what he was going.

Little did he dream what the end of his evening's walk would be.

Little did he imagine that he was walking to his death.

He had received such minute descriptions from Rupert, that he had no difficulty whatever in finding his way.

He reached the Three Oaks in Pentland Woods about a quarter-past seven.

It was then rapidly getting dusk.

All was very silent and gloomy in the forest.

The wind had been lulled long ago, and scarcely a breath moved the branches of the trees.

But brave Alfred Aylmer went on unhesitatingly.

Though the meeting, and, indeed, the whole affair was something very incomprehensible to him, he enjoyed its mystery thoroughly.

No notion of fear entered his head.

There seemed no reason why any harm could come to him.

He passed on through the silent woods, therefore, until, by some narrow and somewhat intricate paths, he reached the spot known as the Three Oaks.

This was a point in the forest where three massive trees, three real giants of the forest, stood by themselves in the centre of a high ground, which was made nearly into an island by a stream which flowed almost completely round it.

It was a pleasant place in the day time.

All around—in the summer days—poured down the golden sunlight, bright, steady, burning, while underneath the shade of the giant oaks it was cool and refreshing always, not a ray of light being able to penetrate the leafy covert.

There was but little left of sunshine on this evening.

A few rose-flecked clouds hovered about in the air, but in the recesses of the wood all was cool, shady, and solemn.

No sign of human life was visible.

Alfred threw himself down on the cool velvet sward and waited.

And being a boy, a boyish bit of devilment entered his mind.

If Rupert's cousin Reuben made his appearance presently, he would, of course, only represent himself in his real character as Alfred Aylmer; but if the newcomer was a stranger, he would pretend to be Rupert.

He was dark, he was dressed in our hero's jacket and cap, and he would have every chance of passing himself off.

Some time elapsed ere any footsteps were heard.

Then they could be made out crawling furtively through the brushwood.

What could this mean?

Why was there necessity for secrecy?

For the first time a sense of danger, perhaps murder, entered the boy's mind.

A sense of insecurity took possession of him.

He did not indulge in it long.

Why, in fact, should there be any peril for him.

Presently he saw a man cautiously emerge from the brushwood and glance curiously and eagerly about him.

The newcomer caught sight of him after a moment, and giving a whistle to some companion who was invisible for the time being, he advanced towards Rupert.

He was a dark and sinister man, and evidently of the gipsy type.

But he was not Hugh Blacklock.

If he had been, he would at once have known that the boy, whom after an instant he confronted, was not our hero.

"You are Rupert Clifford, I believe?" said the man approaching.

"Yes," said the thoughtless boy.

"Ah, you are punctual," said the man. "I and my friend yonder didn't hurry, for we thought there'd be some bother about getting away from the school."

As he spoke another man appeared.

A fellow of the same dark type of the first speaker.

Alfred Aylmer began to feel uncomfortable.

There was something sneering in the smile, and in the manner of the men, that made him fear an unpleasant end to his adventure.

Should he confess that he was not Rupert?

However, he answered calmly—

"No, I had very little trouble in getting away. The trouble will be in getting back."

The men exchanged glances.

"I don't think there'll be much trouble on that score for you."

"Why not?"

"Because I don't think you'll be going back just yet. And perhaps not at all."

"Oh, I must," said Alfred, "and if you don't mind, I would be obliged if you would let me know at once the message."

"That's just what we can't do," said the first speaker; "we was to 'ave given ye a message from Mr. Reuben, but now he's a-coming to see you hisself. Giles, go and tell him the young gentleman's here."

With these words he flung himself on the velvet sward.

"All right," said the other man, and began at once to crawl away through the dense woodland at the rear of the place where Alfred Aylmer was sitting with his back against one of the famous oaks.

"Don't be long, Giles," said the other.

"No, I'll be as quick as lightning, Bob," he answered.

And with a sneering chuckle he was gone.

Somehow things didn't seem at all safe to the lad after this.

The sun had set now.

The wind blew cold and with more strength, rustling the leaves of the great trees with a dismal sound.

Alfred began to be more nervous.

Had he by his own imprudence brought himself into peril?

Whatever he had done, it was too late now to alter it.

He must put up with the consequences.

The man chatted about one thing and another, about school, about Reuben's delay, about the lonely woods and murders done there.

All this was done to distract the boy's attention from what was happening.

And that was something terrible.

Like one of the Thugs (those pestilent murderers of India) a man was creeping up behind the boy.

This was the villainous Giles.

Evidently murder was his object.

The murder of the boy whom he took for Rupert.

But why this caution?

Why did they not at once seize upon the unfortunate lad and slay him?

The reason was that they were acting on orders.

He was to be killed.

But no blood was to be shed.

Something far more cowardly was to be attempted.

The man came cautiously on.

The other fellow preserved a wonderfully calm demeanour.

He was in fact fully prepared to act his part.

"Well, I hope you will not keep me long here," said Alfred, after a moment, feeling as he spoke a kind of superstitious awe over him.

The man did not reply.

Everything around was very still now.

"I shan't be sorry when I'm back at the school," he thought.

But that was not to be, poor boy!

The man Giles came slily up behind him, his long, skinny, but nervous hands were stretched forward, and then the neck of the unfortunate lad was grasped in a deadly grip.

The act was terribly sudden and effective.

There was only one struggle from that poor brave boy, one awful and smothered cry for mercy, and then all was still in the woods once more.

Death—a cruel death—had silenced the once happy and innocent voice which had resounded within its shades that day.

CHAPTER VIII.

WAITING FOR ALF'S RETURN—THE SEARCH IN THE WOODS—A HORRIBLE SCENE.

IT was with a great feeling of consternation that Rupert saw the time go by, and no sign of the return of Alfred Aylmer.

The latter was a good chum and a cheerful friend, and he earnestly hoped that no evil would befall him.

But he dismissed the idea again and again as the time went on.

Why should there be any danger in meeting Reuben?

Despite the fact that he knew that his path was surrounded by enemies, he was innocent of such ideas of wrong as would have suggested to him that he would be led out for a deliberate murder.

However, a dozen things might happen.

And so, as darkness settled down over the school, and no sign of the return of Alfred Aylmer was to be seen, he began to feel very nervous.

"DR. CARVER SAT DOWN IN A BOILING HOT POOL OF GREASY LIQUID."

But what could he say or do without betraying the whole affair?

He certainly began to blame himself greatly for allowing Alfred to put on his clothes, but he thought it was only a boy's whim.

But he felt as if he had been guilty of something criminal.

Still the hours went on.

The absence of Alfred was not observed by the elders of the school, and so the place was closed up, and before ten o'clock all was silent.

For a long time Rupert was unable to court sleep.

He seemed to see before him all manner of terrible visions.

He did not know what might detain his cousin Reuben, or what in fact might be the special business upon which he wished to see him.

So there were two reasons why there might be delay.

In the first place, Reuben might not have been to time.

In the second place, the business on which he came might necessitate Alfred Aylmer's going with him for a time.

These reflections caused Rupert's mind to be soothed a little, and towards morning he fell into a deep slumber.

At dawn he was awake again, and his mind in a whirlwind of contending emotions when he knew that his school-mate had not returned.

He scarcely knew what to do.

The secret of the intended adventure in the wood had not been confided to anyone.

Not even the brother of Alfred knew anything of the mission which he had taken upon himself.

In these circumstances, Rupert re-solved to wait until midday, and then, if he heard nothing about the friend who had aided him in his trouble, he would be compelled to volunteer a statement to Dr. Walton.

He had not to wait for midday.

The absence of Alfred Aylmer was observed long before that hour.

He had not been noticed as leaving the school in any way stealthily, and consequently it was at once set down by the masters that the boy had run away.

It was decided at once that a letter should be dispatched to his parents.

But Rupert stopped this in time.

He plucked up courage, and asking for a private interview with the principal of the academy, told his story.

At least as much of it as he was able to tell without compromising himself and Reuben.

It will be remembered, of course, that the latter was imagined by the doctor to be the father of our hero.

"Dear me," said Dr. Walton, "this is a very strange affair. It is a most mysterious thing that your father should ask you to act in a manner which tends really to subvert all discipline."

Rupert felt that the remark was not unmerited.

But he knew that Reuben was not to blame.

He knew indeed that his self-sacrificing heart was working in all things for his good.

And yet it was difficult indeed to account for the strangeness of the pro-ceedings.

"I have no doubt my father would be sorry to think he had done anything to annoy, or injure the discipline of the school," said Rupert, "and no doubt in the future he will be able to explain everything to your satisfaction. But I am really anxious about poor Alfred."

The doctor's brows contracted in anger.

"Anxious!" he cried; "no doubt you are. I fear you will find more cause for anxiety than you imagine. I fear also that you have been allowed too much of your own way, and that you have no idea of the strict manners which should guide a gentleman. You should have asked me to send someone, as you were not well enough to go, and depend upon it I would have respected your secret."

"I am very sorry indeed, sir," said Rupert, with bowed head.

"I trust you are," said Dr. Walton. "But no regrets will be of any use now. We must act at once, for the lad may be in danger. He may have met with an accident in the recesses of the wood, where he would, of course, be unable to make anyone hear, no matter how loudly he called. Do you know the spot well that he went to?"

"Yes, indeed."

"Well then, do you think you are well enough to show anyone the way?"

"Yes," said Rupert, "I am much better than I was. Perhaps the fright has driven away my pains for a time. I am ready to go at once."

"Very well," said Dr. Walton. "I will order the pony-chaise, and you and I, and Mr. Lyttleton, and John Aylmer, will go in the wood, and make inquiries in the neighbourhood if we find nothing there."

They were not long in starting.

Rupert had indeed spoken truly.

The alarm excited in his breast by the disappearance of Alfred Aylmer seemed for the moment to have driven away his illness and to have given him fresh strength.

It was Jack Aylmer who was the most upset and silent of the whole party.

On reaching the wood, they dismounted at the point shewn them by Rupert, and leaving Bobbins, the groom and page boy, in charge of the pony, hurried in the direction of the Three Oaks.

We have said how solemn and gloomy the recesses of this wood looked at night.

Even now, in the middle of the day, it was still and suggestive of dark deeds.

Rupert trembled as he advanced.

Something seemed to tell him that he would make a terrible discovery.

Evidently something was wrong.

They were not long kept in suspense.

As they reached the point called the Three Oaks, they saw an awful sight.

The body of poor murdered Alfred Aylmer suspended by his neck to the branch of a tree.

For an instant no one spoke.

Exclamations of horror shuddered from their lips.

"What can be the meaning of this dreadful deed?" cried Dr. Walton at length, as he glanced round him and saw not the slightest sign of a struggle.

"He must have committed suicide," said Mr. Lyttleton, the usher.

"And yet, how can he have done that?" asked Dr. Walton, incredulously.

"You see, sir," said Mr. Lyttleton, "he could easily have done it in this way. He could have climbed the tree, and then affixed the cord to his neck, and afterwards to this branch, which is a very strong one, and thrown himself off."

"Truly, he could have done so," said Dr. Walton. "But why should he commit such a determined suicide?"

"Ah, that is a thing which seems strange," said the usher; "but still one never knows. Such strange things do happen."

"Rupert," asked Dr. Walton, suddenly, "have you any enemies who could have done this?"

Our hero was deadly pale now.

He knew—at least he felt certain that this unfortunate lad had fallen a sacrifice for him.

He must have been taken for him, or proclaimed himself as Rupert, and so been murdered.

The idea of suicide never took root in his mind at all.

He told his suspicions at once.

"That letter must have been a forgery," said the master, who was overcome by great emotion, "written on purpose to draw you to this spot. It is a most terrible thing. Mr. Lyttleton, pray drive over to the town and fetch Dr. Watson. I don't wish to cut the lad down till he arrives. Poor little fellow, he has been dead many hours."

The usher went off at once as directed, leaving Dr. Walton walking up and down, deep in thought, while Rupert knelt by the side of John Aylmer, who was weeping violently.

When the doctor came, accompanied by two police-constables, the body of the unfortunate young adventurer was cut down and examined.

"This is no suicide," said Dr. Watson, as he glanced at the marks on the neck.

"What then?" asked the schoolmaster, eagerly.

"I believe that the lad has been strangled by some strong man's hand," replied the surgeon, "and then hanged after. This has been done to cover a murder. But we must have a proper investigation."

And so they had.

But nothing was discovered.

By Reuben's desire, Rupert kept back as much as he could.

Reuben, it need scarcely be said, knew nothing of the letter which had been sent.

But both he and our hero could guess readily whence it derived its origin.

Either Hubert Pendarven had discovered Rupert's whereabouts, and openly declared war, or Hugh Blacklock was the author of the letter and the murder too; working it for his own interests, to get the large reward promised by the assassin master of the abbey.

However this was, Colonel Gerald Clifford, as Reuben was now called, gave no sign.

He dared not yet declare himself.

The ban was still on his name, and in those days of sanguinary punishments, he knew well that he would stand no chance.

And with his safety was bound up that of Rupert, and keeping the solemn vow he had taken to Richard Pendarven in his dying moments.

And so this mystery passed away for the time.

The most strenuous efforts were made everywhere to discover the assassins, but in vain.

But both Rupert and John Aylmer had sworn to discover them.

The murder had created between the boys a firm link of friendship, and our hero, as he gripped the hand of the now brotherless lad, said—

"John Aylmer, I swear, if I am spared, I will avenge your brother's death. Those who killed him did so because they mistook him for me. They are my enemies."

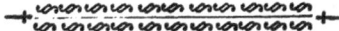

CHAPTER IX.

THE PICNIC.

THE light-hearted boys, who were at first so inexpressibly shocked by the tragic end of Alfred Aylmer, soon regained their elasticity, and things continued to progress much as ever at Blakesley Hall Academy.

Rupert had of course been greatly upset and horrified.

But, like others of his age, he could not mope for long, and in a couple of months poor Aylmer's death was a thing of the past, to be remembered only when the chance came of avenging it.

One day a whole holiday was given the school in honour of the birthday of one of the ushers.

It was a warm and lovely day, and consequently no one dreamed of suggesting that they should remain in the house.

"Let's have a picnic in the woods," cried Rupert. "Let us go into the town, buy some provisions, and cook them, like the gipsies, in the open air."

His idea was received with acclamation.

But to Rupert it was a joy unspeakable.

Since the time when he had been brought, a two-year-old babe, to the tents, he had only spent a few months in the abodes of the house-dwellers, and his heart yearned for one of the old woodland feasts, if it were but a few hours.

The proposition was laid before the headmaster, and was at once acceded to.

So the spot destined for their day's amusement having been settled upon— a spot, be it said, in a direction opposite to the Three Oaks—a party of youngsters were left to gather sticks, and the teachers remained there to "superintend arrangements."

The elder boys, including Ralph and Rupert, went up to the town to get food and utensils.

The two latter had patched up a hollow truce.

It was by Reuben's wish that this was done.

He had heard with the deepest horror of the awful catastrophe which had happened to poor Alfred Aylmer by ruffians who mistook him for Rupert.

It, of course, explained the fact that the identity of our hero was known.

But this did not greatly disconcert Reuben Pendarven.

He gave our hero injunctions to be more careful, and wrote a long private and explanatory letter to Dr. Walton.

But beyond that he did nothing.

Reuben himself was supposed by Hubert to be once more abroad, and "Colonel Gerald Clifford" was supposed to be a person who had taken a fancy to Rupert, and resolved to educate him.

Ralph had received a severe letter from

his father, warning him against open quarrels with Rupert.

This may appear surprising.

But it is not on reflection.

Ralph knew nothing of that terrible night of storm and crime when Rupert was saved by Reuben.

And certainly Hubert had no desire that his son should know that he was an assassin.

As the dozen boys trotted off along the sunlit road from the woods to the town, no one seeing them would have imagined for a moment that there existed a deadly feud between Ralph and Rupert.

"This is a jolly holiday," cried "Ship Ahoy," as they hurried on; "we should never have thought of a picnic if it hadn't been for you, Rupert."

"Certainly not gipsying," said Ralph, with a covert sneer.

"Perhaps not," said Rupert, with a slight flash of the eye. "I've been with the gipsies, and know their ways. I can show you how to make up the fires, and sling a soup cauldron, or broil a fowl, or anything."

"That's jolly," said Lewis. "We shall fancy ourselves hundreds of miles away from schoolrooms."

"And wish ourselves there too," laughed Rupert, "but we must contrive to borrow a large pot of some kind. We shall be lost without that."

They were not long in reaching the town, and having decided what they were to purchase, they went in different directions, appointing a general rendezvous in half-an-hour.

Many things were bought and stowed away for future use.

But we must follow Rupert and Ship Ahoy.

These two went in search of the more substantial part of the feast, and first and foremost a search was made for the stew-pot.

They had almost despaired of finding this, and Rupert already began to feel glum, when Ship Ahoy cried out—

"Avast there—shiver my timbers!"

"Well, and after all that?" laughed Rupert.

"Why, let's steer down this lane here," said the boy. "I've just remembered old Mother Grigson."

"Who's she?"

"The 'tuckout-shop' woman,"

"Well, and what of her?"

"Why, if we buy some things of her, and leave a deposit, she will lend us what we want."

"I hope so," said Rupert. "I was beginning to give up in despair."

The lane was a narrow little winding one, with green hedges and white cottages.

They found the old woman sitting at the cottage door by the side of a table under an awning, displaying temptingly cakes, sweets, ginger-beer, and lemonade.

Ship Ahoy was well known to her.

But Rupert was a new customer, and her smirks and curtseys were a sight to see.

"What a lovely day, sir," she said, "but very hot. I can recommend that lemonade; it's fresh and beautiful."

Both the thirsty lads indulged in a refreshing draught.

Then they made sundry purchases of cakes and so forth, and after this the grand question was mooted.

The old woman laughed and put up her hands.

"Law! you boys, you know how to enjoy yourselves. Going a-gipsying, eh? Lawks-a-daisy! When I was young I liked nothing better, but that's a many years ago, I can tell ye."

This talk was all very well.

But the boys wanted to be off.

"Well, Mrs. Grigson," said our hero, "can you lend us the big saucepan? We'll leave you the price of it, and pay for the use of it."

"Bless yer souls! Yes, I'll lend it you. But it's a very big one, and you'll have all your work to carry it, it's so okkard. Wait just a moment."

And so the garrulous old woman went in.

All this time they had unconsciously been the object of careful scrutiny.

Two men of the tramp type had been leaning over a fence near at hand—two brutal-looking ruffians.

If the voice of Alfred Aylmer had not long since been dead, had not the secret of his awful fate been hidden in his early grave, he could have told them that these two men were none other than the two assassins.

The cowards, Robert and Giles.

But, of course, to Rupert and Ship Ahoy their faces were quite unfamiliar.

They had stopped smoking when they saw the boys.

They wanted to have a good look at them, and were afraid that the aroma of their coarse tobacco might attract attention.

"Blow me, if I don't think that's the youngster we ought to have settled," whispered Bob.

"The dark one?" asked his companion.

"Yes. Ye see the face is almost the same, and he's darker. His eyes are real gipsy, and no mistake."

"What's to be done?"

"Nothing," growled Robert. "We can't kill the whole lot. We must find out whether we're right. We'll have a nearer squint at 'em."

"Hey, youngsters!" he cried, in a loud voice, as the old woman disappeared inside the cottage.

The boys turned round startled.

They had seen no one near save Mrs. Grigson.

Rupert flushed as he caught sight of the two men.

Their faces were to him a revelation.

They were true Romany, but of the worst kind.

"What do you want of me?" he said, going up closer.

"Only a bit of 'bacca," said Bob, in a whine, which sounded queerly coming from his hoarse throat. "We're stone-broke."

"All right," said Rupert, as he handed the man twopence. "Is that all?"

"That youngster suspects me," was Bob's inward thought.

But he answered—

"That's all, and good luck to ye."

"Good day, and *cushgar bok*" (Romany for good luck), cried Rupert laughing.

And he went back to the cottage.

"What do you think of that, Giles?" said Bob, in an undertone. "The insolent young whelp boasts of his Romany."

"Yes, and knows we don't mean him any good," said Giles. "Howsomever, if we get the order to do for him again, we can't make a mistake a second time. I should know him anywhere."

Meanwhile, old Mrs. Grigson had reappeared, bringing with her a large iron pot with a swinging handle.

Rupert's eyes twinkled at this.

"Oh, that's the very thing!" he cried, as he seized it. "Come on, Ship Ahoy. Put on all sail, as you say, and let's sail ahead."

With a wave of the hand to the old woman, the two boys then hastened off in the direction of the rendezvous.

This was a little green in front of a tavern at the outskirts of the town, just before the entrance of the road leading to the woodlands.

Here they found all their companions lying about on the grass enjoying themselves, but all impatient to be off.

They leaped up, somewhat inclined to upbraid Rupert and his companions.

But at sight of the huge stew-pot they burst into a laughing hurrah, and in a few moments they were all on their way towards the woods.

To most of those standing round, the appearance of the laughing, merry boys was a subject of pleasure.

But not to two who watched them.

Bob and Giles had followed them, or rather, had come a short cut across the fields.

They knew that the lads would have to go a considerable distance along a lonely road to reach Peutland Woods.

Here, even in the daytime, scarcely anyone was to be met.

Here, therefore, there was a chance of being able to kidnap the one they sought, if they could not destroy his life.

But they were foiled.

A dozen boys were not easily to be disposed of, and so, with many a deeply muttered curse, the murderers passed into the tavern to drink.

The happy boys now hurried away as fast as possible, and it was not very long before they were in the woods.

Preparations were made for dinner.

Rupert lit a fire, the materials for the "gipsy stew" was got together, and soon the fragrant mess was swinging from three stout sticks placed firmly in the ground.

The stew and the fire was then left in charge of two of the younger boys, and the others went off in search of nests and various other errands which delight the hearts of boys.

But a special occurrence claims all our attention.

It was arranged that when the dinner was ready Rupert should call the lads together by a bugle call.

At about three in the afternoon the welcome sounds were heard, and the boys at once began flocking in.

The cloths were laid upon the ground, kept down by heavy stones at the corners, and were soon covered by the various articles necessary for the consumption of the good things.

What an aroma it was to be sure that ascended into the air of that pleasant afternoon.

Quickly all were busy with knives and forks and spoons, the teachers willingly joining in the feast.

Presently the assemblage became conscious that they were not alone.

A number of tall, gaunt figures came gliding up among the trees.

They did not advance as far as the dinner party, but only leaned against the trees and looked on.

After a moment the boys recognised them, and a grin of merriment went round the circle.

The newcomers were none other than the lads of "Hungry Hall," a school close to their own.

They, too, had a holiday.

At least, those who were able to be let out.

The ones who would not "blab" secrets.

They, too, had a picnic.

Such a one!

They had brought their dinner with them, consisting of bread and scrape and an onion each.

"Light, easily carried, and wholesome," said Dr. Carver, their master.

Poor fellows!

It was cruel for them to smell the fragrant aroma which came from the dining-room, as the Blakesley Hall fellows called their piece of velvety turf, cruel for others who had any hearts at all to see their gaunt and eager looks.

"What's to be done?" said Ship Ahoy. "They look so starved that I cannot eat my dinner."

"Let's give them some," said Rupert. "We have plenty."

So the haggard, pale, and starving schoolboys were called forward.

They were not in any way shy.

Such feelings as that had disappeared long ago.

With rapid steps indeed they advanced, and understanding that they were invited to join the feast, they threw themselves on the grass near the more fortunate lads.

The "hungry army" had come to the woods under the leadership of the ushers Small and Meekly, who, having partaken of their dinner of bread and cheese, had thrown themselves on the velvet turf a little distance off, to doze off their weariness and hunger.

Presently they missed their boys.

Up they leaped in fear.

Where could they have gone?

Had they fled?

If they had, how dread would be the anger of Carver!

But they stopped presently.

In their search they had smelled something.

The fragrant aroma had reached them too, and they dashed forward.

Only to pause in wonder.

The sight before them passed all their ideas.

At first they were angry.

Then their stomachs asserted the mastery, and they "sniffed."

"Sniff, sniff, sniff," and they entered the charmed circle too.

At Hungry Hall very little distinction was made between pupils and teachers.

In fact Dr. Carver and his family were the only persons in the establishment who were ever indulged in what was a proper amount of food.

The doctor was a fat man—a man of very large size indeed, considering his height.

His wife was a person of similar build, while his two daughters were remarkable for their robust proportions.

In fact, it was a common joke in the neighbourhood that they *would* have their food on threats of exposing the system on which the school was kept.

So Messrs. Meekly and Small, smelling such a delicious aroma as never for a very long day had been smelt within the precincts of Hungry Hall, could not find strength of mind to resist it, and began to draw near to the rustic feast.

The tutors of Blakesley Hall Academy felt naturally inclined to burst with laughter.

But they manfully resisted the inclination, and, in a most gentle and polite manner, invited the half-starved men to join them.

Small and Meekly put the best face on the matter.

Both sat down with bland and genial smiles.

But their efforts to be calm were very lame.

The " wolf " within them was aroused, and it was not until their hunger had in some measure been appeased that they were able to join in any connected conversation.

The boys of Hungry Hall were meanwhile rattling along at an alarming pace.

" They'll create a famine a-board," whispered Ship Ahoy to one of his companions as he saw one of the " hungry army " swallow at one mouthful a piece of meat large enough to choke him.

" Yes; I never saw anything like it," said Rupert. " I wonder how they can exist in this half-starved state. Look at that boy, there goes a sausage at a mouthful. Oh, Lewis! see that pale youth yonder, with the intellectual eyes, can't he put away boiled beef? "

" Yes, they are like cormorants."

" The head master ought to be ashamed of himself," cried Rupert. " I only wish he was near at hand, that we might give him a general hiss."

" Oh, you don't know him," said Ship Ahoy, " or you'd never say that. He'd stand a hundred broadsides without flinching—bullet head, goggle eyes, red hair, florid, puffed-out cheeks, thin sarcastic mouth—altogether a most unprepossessing fellow, and one who would only nurse an insult, and not dream of resenting it at once. That's Dr. Carver."

As he said this, a general titter arose from the surrounding company.

The cauldron containing the gipsy broth or stew, which was Rupert's special make, and which was to be eaten as a last *bonne bouche* before the dessert, was suspended on its three sticks beneath the branches of a large tree.

As Rupert rose to see to it, he became conscious of something above the cauldron, and looking up, he saw a fat, podgy, red-haired figure suspended among the branches.

He guessed intuitively who this must be; but after one comprehensive stare he took no further notice of the apparition.

" Now then, boys," he cried, " the stew is done; up with your plates."

It is needless to say that the cauldron was not large enough to contain any very large quantity for each boy after the drain that had been made upon it before.

But still it was very nice as a taste of what can be done in an *al fresco* way.

During the distribution of good things, the red - haired podgy party among the boughs overhead, had been doing all he could, making indeed frantic efforts, to keep himself from falling.

At length, just as Rupert was about to ladle out the last drop of soup, there was an ominous crack.

Our hero at once dodged on one side.

Just in time.

For the portly form of Dr. Carver, having cracked the bough, came headlong down, right into the cauldron, upsetting it, and sitting down in a boiling hot pool of greasy liquid.

This was an awkward moment for everyone present.

The boys of Blakesley Hall Academy, being under no restrictions, burst into a side-splitting roar of laughter, which echoed merrily through the forest glades.

The " hungry army " having new life instilled into them by the unusual supply of food, felt an unaccustomed sensation of hilarity, and when the doctor fell a titter ran through their ranks in spite of themselves.

As for Dr. Carver himself, the word " rage " is hardly strong enough to express the fury within his breast.

As he raised himself from the ground, he, for an instant, glared round him defiantly and furiously, like a bated animal.

Then he wiped from him as well as he could the greasy stains which thickly besmeared his clothes, and addressed Mr. Tobias Lyttleton, who, by the exercise of immense self-command, was able to speak now, and listen without betraying the merriment which was fairly convulsing him internally.

" What is the meaning of this scene, sir? " he cried. " I address myself to you, as you appear to be in charge of these boys."

Tobias bowed and smiled amiably.

" And we have, I believe, often had the pleasure of meeting before," said he.

Dr. Carver stared.

" Was this man chaffing him? "

" I think not, sir," he said.

"Oh, indeed, yes!" said Mr. Lyttleton, sweetly. "I have often met you in the streets of the town, when our respective schools have been promenading for health."

Dr. Carver glared.

"Ha!" he cried; "then you are responsible for this disgraceful scene?"

Tobias Lyttleton, alias Long Toby, was by no means a coward.

In spite of his leanness, his muscles were strongly developed.

He had a wrist like steel, and a mind insensible to fear.

So he smiled tauntingly.

"Well," he said, "these matters affect different minds in different ways. Mine I hope is a well-constituted mind, and consequently I experience nothing but pure delight in the contemplation of these boyish enjoyments. This is my birthday, and on such a day they do exactly what they like, provided always they keep within the bounds of propriety."

"Indeed, sir," blustered Dr. Carver; "then you think it is within the bounds of propriety to induce my pupils to act in a rebellious manner towards me?"

Long Toby's smile now became broader.

The boys had finished their meal, and fancying that Dr. Carver and Mr. Lyttleton were enjoying a little chat amicably, they had gone off with a "whoop—halloa" into the recesses of the woods for a game of hide and seek, while Messrs. Small and Meekly had hastened to hide their diminished heads.

So Mr. Lyttleton had a chance of talking freely to Dr. Carver.

Both he and Dr. Walton had a great dislike, and in fact a loathing for this man.

"Rebels, do you call them, sir," he cried, laughing. "Why surely you know the old adage—'While the cat's away the mice will play.' And this time the cat was positively up a tree."

This allusion to his late undignified post of observation in the branches of a tree made Dr. Carver furious.

"How dare you, sir, insult me," he cried, putting up his red, puffed face threateningly. "Haven't I a right to do as I like? What has it to do with you if I like to climb a tree to enjoy a book in warm weather?"

"Ha! I did not know you had dropped a book," said Tobias, with provoking calmness. "I apologise. I made a great and grievous blunder. I had thought that you had posted yourself there to watch the proceedings of your poor half-starved scholars."

For an instant Dr. Carver stood aghast at this direct accusation.

"You impertinent vagabond!" cried the vulgar fellow. "You look yourself as if you could crawl up the barrel of a gun. How dare you insult me?"

Tobias threw his umbrella and book on the grass.

Then he glanced round him.

Not a boy was in sight.

Now was his time.

He advanced to the master of Hungry Hall, the cruel destroyer of young lives, and seizing him by the nose shook it violently.

"I have long wished for this opportunity," he said, "you glutton. Now I give you the choice of two things. Apologise to me at once, or I will thrash you and fling you into the ditch."

Dr. Carver was a strong man and a blusterer, but the calmness of Long Toby made him doubt.

"What, sir?" he said, in an undaunted voice, though his heart began to fail him, "you ask me to apologise, when you have pulled my nose?"

"Yes. And will thrash you if you don't," replied Tobias, taking out his watch. "If you have not apologised in five minutes your punishment may be said to be self-inflicted."

Dr. Carver hesitated.

He glanced at his adversary and measured him mentally.

Certainly Tobias was not a starveling, though he had called him so.

What was to be done?

The time was nearly up.

The watch already trembled in the nervous hand of the usher. He began to advance, his face white, his eyes set.

Discretion seemed the better part of valour.

"Well," stammered Carver, drawing back, "of course, if I have been hasty—if circumstances have misled me—I beg to apologise for——"

"Cur!" cried Lyttleton, whose closed hand fell, baulked as it were of its prey, and turning his back he walked off.

This was gall and wormwood enough for the fat master of the Hungry Hall.

But fresh humiliation was behind.

As he glanced with vengeful eyes after the retreating figure of the man whose iron will had conquered him, he saw peeping from behind the trunk of a large and wide-spreading oak the laughing face of our hero Rupert.

There was a roguish twinkle in his merry gipsy eyes, and it was evident to Dr. Carver that he had heard and seen all.

The hate which shot from the greeny orbs of the master of Hungry Hall would have been enough to make Rupert's heart sink within him.

But he saw it not.

All he thought of was that the abominable man who starved his scholars had got the worst of it, and with that his generous heart was content.

Not so Dr. Carver.

As Rupert went off, laughing at him, with a hop, skip and a jump, the schoolmaster muttered to himself—

"Ah! my boy, if ever I get you into my power won't you suffer for your eaves-dropping insolence. You shall be sorry that you ever were born."

He little knew himself how soon his own evil wish would be accomplished.

For the present he satisfied his irritation of mind by hastening home, bullying his wife and daughters, and on the return home of Messrs. Small and Meekly, giving them notice to quit at the end of a month.

This was all very little in the way of revenge.

Deep in his breast there remained the hungry longing for vengeance against Lyttleton and Rupert.

However, events were playing into his cruel hands.

The boys—"hungry army" and all—were disporting themselves in the woods to the top of their bent.

Never before in their existence had the boys of Hungry Hall enjoyed themselves so fully.

But Rupert little dreamed of the cloud hanging over his head.

The two men who had addressed him as he made his purchases of Mrs. Grigson had lost no time in making their way in search of the principal "villain of the piece."

And so, while the careless boys were enjoying the merry sunshine and their breezy gambols in the woods, an evil spirit was stalking amongst them.

For, even while they were enjoying their banquet, Hugh Blacklock was watching them, in search of the boy whose life he hoped to ruin as revenge against Reuben Pendarven.

Disguised so effectually that no one would have known him, this recreant gipsy had observed all the proceedings, and, hidden behind the ample concealment of a large oak tree, he had observed the furious look of hate which the master of Hungry Hall had cast at Rupert when he discovered his knowledge of his disgrace.

In an instant his mind was made up.

He had *carte blanche* from his employers for any villainy.

But when he had quite satisfied himself of the position of affairs, he at once made his way in the direction of Hungry Hall.

He was almost breathless with astonishment when he found that the place was situated really on an island—really cut off from all other habitation by the rapid waters of the arm of the sea where Ralph had nearly met his death.

He had thought that it was a mere figure of speech to say that it was surrounded by water.

"Why, this spot seems made specially for the job," he muttered. "Once here, he will never see a friendly face again. I'll see to it at once."

And, without hesitation, he engaged a boat and was rowed over to the island school.

Rupert was now in great peril.

CHAPTER X.

THE HERMIT'S ROCK.

TOBIAS LYTTLETON was at all times a generous-hearted man, and he was so pleased by his interview with the master of Hungry Hall that he entered into the games of the Blakesley Hall scholars with the zest of a youth of fourteen.

Dr. Walton was one of the good old-fashioned schoolmasters who did not pretend to be looking always upon the dark and severe side of nature.

On this occasion he had taken Mrs. Walton and his only daughter, Sylvia, out for a day's pleasure.

He had privately intimated to Long Toby, moreover, that he intended taking them to the theatre, so that he would leave it entirely to the discretion of the usher what time the boys came home.

So, as Lyttleton was peculiarly joyous, he suggested an al-fresco tea.

"We'll have tea out here, if you like, boys," he said, addressing an admiring group. "You can no doubt buy some bread, and butter, and eggs from yonder farmhouse; and as for a fire, you, Rupert, have proved an adept at that. Don't do this purely on my suggestion. I only thought you would prefer it to a formal tea at the academy."

The boys unanimously shouted their delight.

Long Toby provided the money.

Rupert, Ship Ahoy, and three others went off to the farmhouse.

The others foraged about for wood and so forth for the fire, and these being procured, amused themselves with various games.

Presently our hero came back successful with his schoolmates, laden with bread, beautiful fresh butter, eggs, and watercresses fresh from the beds.

Such a repast again!

But boys have wondrous appetites.

The kettle was hung over the blazing fire, the cloth relaid, and as if no dinner had ever sent its attractive aroma through the forest glades, the scholars once more set to work.

Everybody seemed in happy and joyous spirits.

Only one person tried to mar the pleasure.

It was just six o'clock when everything was cleared away and packed up, and the things returned to the farmhouse.

Long Toby stood with his watch in his hand, glancing round at the faces of the boys.

"It does not get dark until eight o'clock," he said, "and Doctor Walton has told me to use my own discretion in regard to the time when I took you back to school. Most of you, I expect, have learned your lessons in advance, but those who have not, or who are tired, can stroll quietly home. I am going to remain until seven o'clock, so that those boys who want another romp in the woods can remain here and return home with me."

"I think I shall go back to the academy now, sir," said Ralph Pendarven.

Throughout the day he had been ill at ease.

Rupert had been the presiding genius.

The boys had followed his lead, had watched with interest the manner in which he had prepared the gipsy meal, and had elevated him at once into quite a social hero.

Ralph was jealous of all this.

His hatred of Rupert had never abated since the day of the fight, and it had been increased tenfold by the self-sacrificing act which had made our hero his rescuer.

Mr. Lyttleton was by no means a short-sighted man.

Through all the years of his tutorship he had carefully studied youthful character.

He knew all about the fight, its commencement and culmination, and he gauged rightly the feeling which prompted Ralph.

"Very well," replied he, "you can go, certainly. Now, my boys, those who wish to go back to the school can walk with Master Pendarven. Those who are going to remain can run off again and meet me here at seven. Not a minute later, mind."

Only a moment's hesitation.

"Well, I'm off into the woods, for one," cried Rupert.

And off he went.

Ralph was left alone.

He coloured crimson, so painfully indeed that Long Toby pitied him.

"You are in a decided minority, Master Pendarven," he said, smiling. "If you don't want to join your schoolmates, you can remain here with me, if you like, and I will lend you one of my books."

"Thank you, sir," said Ralph, "but if you do not mind, I will go back to the school house. I do not feel very well."

"Go, by all means, then; do not let me detain you, Master Pendarven," said Long Toby.

Then he added to himself, as Ralph, with a murmured "Thank you" moved away—

"Better in health than temper, I fancy, my boy. I can't make out all this. I feel convinced there is some mystery in regard to these two boys. There is one thing certain, however, I'm Rupert's friend in everything. I feel certain he is true and honourable to the backbone."

Rupert found himself presently detached from the others, with Ship Ahoy and Lewis Allenby for his only comrades.

Most of the lads were tired out after the day of revelry and feasting.

They had had cricket and running matches, and had climbed the trees, and all kinds of things in the way of boyish excitement, and now they desired a little more quiet recreation.

Suddenly an idea struck Rupert.

A memory, as it were, came to him.

"I say," he cried, halting, "let's go to the Hermit's Rock."

"What's that?" said Ship Ahoy.

"A big stone, I fancy," replied Rupert, laughing. "But I'm told that it is a most curious spot. They say that it was the home of a hermit for many long years, and that, owing to some terrible news that he heard from abroad, he cast himself from a rock overhanging the hut into a deep pool in front of his dwelling. But let's go and see. I know where the place is."

"Lead on, Macduff then," cried Ship Ahoy. "I'm game for anything in the way of fun."

"I don't know that it's much fun," said Rupert, "but I've no doubt it will be interesting, if, indeed, it does not prove to be dangerous. But if there be danger British boys will never flinch from meeting it. This way, lads."

The path led down first into a deep dell, over little running streams, and then up again suddenly into dense plantations, through which it was difficult to make their way at all.

Up, up, up.

The path seemed ever ascending.

"Why, we shall be on the top of the mountains directly," cried Lewis.

"Yes, and then down again into the deeper depths," said Rupert.

"That's good," cried the comic boy, "it'll be all the more easy to get along. *Facilis*, you know, *descensus Averni.*"

"Ah," cried Rupert, "a fine of three bottles of ginger beer for quoting Latin. I'm not sorry, I'm dying of thirst."

So, jokingly, they hastened up to the spot where the hermit's house was situated.

It was surrounded by an almost impermeable hedge.

It was dusk now.

A very lonely hour to approach so still and solemn a place.

The rays of the sun shot upwards now, and tinted the clouds with rose colour.

But in the midst of the trees and natural hedgerows there was a calm dulness as it were, a heavy suggestive silence.

To the other boys it was rather a risky adventure.

But to Rupert it was a mere matter of course.

He had been accustomed ever since he could remember to roam about the forests by night, and there was nothing new in thus making a late approach to an old ruin.

So he plunged forward at their head, and they at length stood on the edge of the Hermit's Pool.

It was a grim, dark, desolate spot.

The water was perfectly still and glassy.

Round it the reeds nodded.

Over it was a risky-looking bridge.

On the other side was the tumble-down wooden structure which had for so many years served as the home of the hermit, and above it, hanging as if threatening each moment to fall, was a huge square piece of rock jutting out from the surrounding ground.

"Why is it called the Hermit's Rock?" asked Ship Ahoy.

"Ah, you seem to know all about it," cried Lewis Allenby, "so tell us."

"Well, I can only say," replied Rupert, "that from the little I have heard, the hermit, whoever he was, fancied he had committed some heinous sin, and as an expiation of this he used to go up on the top of that hanging rock and fast for forty-eight hours together."

"Ho, ho!" laughed Lewis Allenby, "he'd have made a capital usher at Hungry Hall."

"And so," proceeded Rupert, "he continued this peculiar style of living until age told upon him, and one night, after his fast, he seems to have fainted from exhaustion, and rolled over the edge of the rock into the pool."

"And was drowned?"

"Yes. Once in there always in there," said Rupert, "for it is bottomless. At any rate no one has ever yet been able to fathom it."

"So much for the legend," said Lewis, looking at his watch; "but it's now a quarter to seven, and if we are going to explore the hut, or even have a look at it, I fancy we shall have to be quick."

"I don't like the look of that bridge at all," said Ship Ahoy. "But as others have done it before me, I don't see why we should be afraid."

"We must be careful though," said Rupert. "Let me go first. I'm the best swimmer, if the old thing does give way."

"Here goes," he added.

And placing his hand firmly on the balustrade of the bridge, he began creeping over.

However, it was not so unsafe as they had imagined.

They all contrived to get over it without any mishap, and stood presently in the room where the strange old man had spent so many lonely and melancholy hours.

It was a small square room, with a cupboard, a table, and a chair.

There was not a vestige left of any utensil he could have used.

But there was a little place in the back wall which attracted Rupert's attention, and this, upon being examined, proved to be a doorway.

Pushing this open, our hero peered into the darkness beyond.

It was darkness, too.

Utter, profound, solemn.

"Hush a moment!" cried Rupert, to the boys, who kept wandering curiously about; "I want to listen."

Both stood still.

Scarcely breathing, Rupert thrust his head into the utter gloom.

A strange sound, drip, drip, splash, splash, came to him in the silence.

"That sounds like the sea," he thought; "how I wish we had more time."

But it was useless hoping.

The adventure was bound now to come to an abrupt termination.

But of this he was determined—

He would return alone and try to ferret out the mystery further.

Something in that dismal dripping of water, and the surging sound beyond, seemed to beckon him on to further investigation.

It connected itself in some way with the island school.

"Past seven," said Ship Ahoy. "'Bout ship, and make all sail for port."

And so, leaving behind him what to him would have been the best part of the adventure, he followed their lead, passed out of the hermit's hut, crept over the crazy bridge once more, and was soon standing by the side of Mr. Lyttleton.

The latter was in a wondrous good humour.

"Well, boys, you are pretty punctual, considering all things," he said. "Now let us hasten home and to bed. You will sleep without rocking to-night, I think."

"But I shall dream, sir," said Rupert, "for I really think this is one of the happiest days I ever spent in my life."

"I am glad indeed to hear that," returned Mr. Lyttleton, "as it is my birthday."

"Can I ask you a favour, sir," said Rupert, eagerly.

"If it is in reason at all I will grant it," said Long Toby.

"It is only this, sir," said our hero. "I have a great desire to revisit the hermit's hut, and I don't know how I can do so unless I can obtain special leave. So, sir, when next you want anything over in Ambleside, may I go over instead of Allenby?"

A flush—a very faint one—rose to the cheeks of Tobias Lyttleton at this.

There was a tender little secret connected with his messages to Ambleside. A gentle face awaited him there, a face which would always bless him by its sunshine some day when his purse was well enough filled.

"Certainly," he said; "the day after to-morrow I will send you over to Amble-side. You could, of course, return by half-past four if you chose, but you can have till half-past five. That will give you abundance of time."

Rupert's face glowed with joy.

It would not have done so had he only known the result of the adventure.

But why should he have foreseen any evil in so simple a thing?

He thanked Mr. Lyttleton heartily, and when that night he lay upon his comfortable bed, he dreamed visions in which the boys of Hungry Hall, and mysterious hermits, and cousin Reuben, and Hugh Blacklock were mixed up in a most hobgoblin manner.

CHAPTER XI.

RUPERT CONTINUES HIS ADVENTURE AND DISCOVERS MORE THAN HE EXPECTS.

DURING the next day and a half nothing particular happened at the school.

At length the hour arrived.

Tobias Lyttleton took him out into the playground, and speaking somewhat nervously, said—

"Here is a letter, Rupert, that I desire delivered to Miss Jessie Rudleigh. You will see her address on the letter. There is no answer, but—but—perhaps she may send a message."

He placed the letter in Rupert's hands as he spoke.

"And I may remain out until half-past five?" said Rupert.

"Yes, according to my promise," returned Long Toby. "I have told Doctor Walton that you are going to Ambleside on an errand for me."

It was with good spirits indeed that Rupert set out.

The great object in view was to get over the ground as quickly as possible, and so now at a quick walk, now at a trot, now at a run, he made his way to Ambleside.

The object of his search was soon found.

Everyone knew Jessie Rudleigh, the pretty daughter of the poor curate, who had worked away his life in the service of the parishioners, and whose child was now in the humble position of companion to the vicar's daughter.

She was a fair-haired, blue-eyed girl of some nineteen summers, looking almost too merry and light-hearted for the sober, pedantic teacher of five-and-thirty.

But love is blind.

He simply worshipped her. She respected and bowed down to him as a superior being.

Rupert paused not to think of anything of this kind.

He ate the lovely fruit given him by Jessie, carefully preserved her tiny note in the breast-pocket of his jacket, voted her a "jolly nice girl," and then went off in high spirits in the direction of the woods once more.

The hermit's hut looked for less strange and mysterious in the sunlight than it did on the evening of the holiday, when he had visited it in the gloaming.

It almost seemed as if it had lost some of the romance which had surrounded it on that night.

But there was the mysterious inner door which had to be investigated.

He had provided himself on this occasion with some small torches, candles and lucifers, and so when he had once more crept across the crazy bridge, he lit one of the former articles and glanced round him.

The place seemed different now.

Before it had looked dull and gloomy, now he could see every rent in the wooden walls, every cobweb that depended from the roof, every dirty nook and slimy track of animals.

He hastened quickly from the ruinous scene into the next room, and with beating heart opened again the little door.

Then he listened.

He had not been mistaken.

He could hear plainly the drip, drip, and the dull plash of the water.

Cautiously he raised himself to enter, for the opening was not flush with the floor.

He could not yet, even with the aid of the torchlight, see whither he was going.

His foot, gradually placed down on the other side, found wherewithal to stand on, but as he displaced some stones or rubbish they fell.

A dull thud from a wondrous distance below told plainly that he was standing upon the edge of a well, or some deep fissure in the rocks.

There was nothing in any way unprecedented in all this.

He knew Cornwall well enough to be aware that there were the most extraordinary places on its coast.

Huge caverns, connected by rocky corridors, formed by the hand of nature.

This might be one of these, or it might be one of the tremendous fissures which must have been caused by some internal struggle of the elements.

Whichever this was, how could he cross it to pursue his adventure?

How, indeed, could he venture to let go his hold on the woodwork, standing as he did on the edge of an unknown abyss?

By degrees, however, his eyes became accustomed to the darkness.

The light of the torches seemed to dive into the gloomy recesses, and search out and dissipate the black shadows.

And so at length he was able to make out that he stood on the edge of a yawning, well-like abyss, across which a rude plank bridge was flung.

Rupert did not act with any foolhardy rashness.

He raised his light in every direction, so as to "take his bearings," as Ship Ahoy would have said, and so that his sight also might get accustomed to the peculiar obscurity.

Then cautiously he began to make his way across the bridge.

Great care was necessary.

There were no hand-rails, and the boards "giggled" as he crossed them.

But he curbed his impatience, and in a few moments he was on the other side.

Here he found himself in an old vault, built heavily of stone, evidently the work of hundreds of years previously.

Then a memory came to Rupert.

He had been told that in ages gone by an abbey had existed on the rocks beneath which the hermit had built his hut.

He was no doubt now in the long disused vaults of the sacred edifice.

There was a chance, consequently, of his being able to walk on firm land.

However, he walked very cautiously.

At any moment he might come upon a pitfall as bad as that one which he had just had to cross.

Presently, as he was advancing, he heard a strange sound.

It seemed like voices.

Eagerly he paused and listened.

The sound came again, dull and mysterious, from the depths of the vaults beyond him.

A doubt entered his mind.

Should he retreat or advance, or should he conceal himself while the others went by, and thus discover perhaps the real secret of the vaults?

To retreat was certainly to give up the adventure.

So he glanced round him in search of some place of concealment.

There was not much difficulty in finding this.

Almost opposite the place where he was standing was a large alcove, with some loose pieces of waste timber near it.

Into this he at once slipped, and dragging some of the timber in front of him, waited.

Nearer and nearer came the voices, but the speakers walked very slowly, as if they were carrying a heavy burden.

Nearer and nearer in the darkness— for Rupert had extinguished his light— until the red flicker of their torches could be seen, preceded by the steadier illumination of a large lantern.

As they approached, he saw there were three men.

"RUPERT'S ARMS WERE SUDDENLY PINIONED FROM BEHIND

One of the men was holding a lantern and a torch, while the two others were bearing a body between them, and torches in their disengaged hands.

They went slowly to the edge of the huge pit.

"Now, then, Bill," cried one, "heave him in. My wrist is pretty well cramped. One—two—three!"

And with a swing they flung the body over the edge, where, after a time indeed that seemed awful to Rupert's eager ears, a dull, sickening, splashing thud told that it had reached the bottom.

"He's all right," said another of the gang, whose voice seemed familiar, but whose face was not visible to Rupert in the strange glow. "Let's be off; I'm sick o' this place."

"Well, the air do get down one's throat like," said the lantern-bearer. "Here, take a nip o' this."

And he handed a flask of spirit to his companions, after prudently taking the first draught himself.

The two others having disposed of the liquid with evident relish, they all crossed the bridge of planks.

Then came something which inspired terror even into the brave heart of Rupert.

As soon as they had crossed the plank bridge the two men stooped down, while the other held aloft the torch, and dragged the woodwork away.

They did not throw it down into the pit, but pulled it inside the aperture in the back wall of the hut.

This was terrible.

Of course he could not, dared not, cry out.

The men were evidently engaged in the crime of murder.

What would they do with one who had witnessed their actions?

There was only one answer to that.

They would kill him and hurl him without mercy to the bottom of the abyss.

So he remained quiet, even though his heart told him that he was being cut off from humanity.

Who could hear him, out in that lonely part of Pentland Woods, no matter how loudly he might call?

The only hope he had was that Tobias Lyttleton, knowing his intention of visiting the hermit's hut, would institute a search there, and that he would be found at last, even if it was late at night.

This comforting reflection would have had but little strength within him, had he but known that shortly after his departure for Ambleside, Tobias Lyttleton received a letter stating that his eldest brother was dangerously ill in London, and desired to see him.

While Rupert, consequently, was lying in the alcove hiding from his enemies, Long Toby was dashing away to the metropolis.

But our hero knew nothing of all this.

There was one consolation, and that was that he knew that here must be means of walking for a long distance, as the men who had thrown the body into the abyss had carried it along for some distance without encountering any obstacle.

A bright idea, therefore, at once struck him.

"I will explore the place while I am waiting," he thought. "Surely they will bring lights if they come for me, and when I see them I can shout."

So he relit his torch, gave way to a little shudder as the black, yawning mouth of the abyss discovered itself to him, and then cautiously proceeded to follow the path which he supposed had been traversed by the men.

Of course his movements were but slow, being regulated by the evenness or unevenness of the ground.

But at length he reached a spot beyond which he could go no further.

There was for a few yards an incline, and at the bottom of this was a wooden door, set in two formidable square pilasters, and—locked.

The soil, however, was soft, and there he could see the imprint of recent footmarks.

"I am finding out this mystery, at the risk, however, of my own life," he thought. "Here I must be content to wait until my friends come to rescue me. Then I will endeavour to persuade them to aid me in the search."

With this reflection he proceeded back to his original post of observation, and waited.

While here his thoughts kept wondering at the probable meaning of the scene which had just occurred before him.

Do what he would, he could not help connecting this affair—this casting away of a body, and the recent locking of the big door—with the school on the island.

Could it be possible that there was a subterranean way to this horrid school ?

Did they add murder to the starving of their scholars ?

The more he thought of this the more he felt convinced that this must be the interpretation of the whole affair.

Time went on.

He glanced at his watch.

Half-past six.

How the time had flown.

Well, it was no use despairing yet.

He would only now have been missed, and it would take at least half-an-hour to organise and bring a relief party.

Besides, why should they think of being so prompt ?

They would not search for him perhaps until dark.

So he must perforce be patient.

Rupert had been in a great many strange adventures, but never perhaps in one which promised so unpleasant a conclusion.

It was awfully lonely, and still and drowsy down there.

Now and again he shouted aloud.

But no answer came save the echo.

But drowsiness would steal over him.

He tried all he could to battle against it, but in vain.

Presently the feeling overcame him entirely, and he went off into a pleasant slumber.

How long he had slept he knew not, when he was awakened by a hot glow on his face, and as he opened his eyes the light of a lantern nearly blinded him.

"Well, of all the extraordinary finds, of all the extraordinary bits of good luck, I'm blest if this ain't about the most curious," said a familiar voice. "A hundred pounds earned without a try."

"You're sure he's the boy ?" said the man's companion.

The other chuckled.

"Sure, yes; he's the very identical, and no mistake," replied he; "give us the barney."

Rupert did not understand their slang.

But he knew he was in danger.

"Let me get up," he said. "My limbs are stiff lying here."

"They're likely to be stiffer before long, my lad," said the man, whom he now recognised as "Bob," the one to whom he had given the money for tobacco. "We can't accommodate you at present, in spite of past favours. There, don't be rusty; it's best to be quiet. We don't want to hurt ye. All we want is to give ye up to yer father, Hugh Blacklock."

Hugh Blacklock !

Great heavens ! what did it all mean ?

Had he gone mad ?

"My name is not Blacklock," he said. "It is——"

But he never finished the sentence.

A handkerchief saturated with some powerful soporific was pressed over his nostrils, and he lapsed into unconsciousness.

When he again awoke he was in a dormitory.

A pleasant room, with clean linen, and, indeed, everything scrupulously exact.

Where was he ?

That was the first thought that came into his aching head.

He was not well acquainted enough with the rooms in Blakesley Hall Academy to tell whether he was there or not.

All, therefore, he could make out of the whole affair was that he had fallen asleep, had an awful dream, being frightened into unconsciousness, and been found and brought home to the school by Long Toby.

He sprang up at once and approached the window, the blinds of which were drawn down.

He pulled these up.

Then he fell back with a gasping cry.

The truth was revealed to him too suddenly and terribly.

The windows were barred, and all around the building where he was the sea flowed placidly in the bright light of a summer morning.

He was at Hungry Hall.

In the power of the man who, unknown to him, had sworn such a deadly oath of vengeance against him.

He gave one glance round him, saw his clothes, hurried them on, and then began battering at the door.

"They have caught me," he cried, all his gipsy blood rushing wildly from heart to head, "but can they keep me ? I would prefer death to a prison."

CHAPTER XII.

IMPRISONED AT LAST—WHAT IS THE NEXT MOVE?

OBSTINACY is one thing, resolution is another.

There is as much difference between the two as there is between bounce and real courage.

When Rupert found at last that all the bawling, shouting, and banging was useless, he gave over and sat down to think, after dressing himself properly in case of emergencies.

What was to be done?

Evidently he was in the hands of those who were too powerful to contend with in the ordinary way.

Whatever he did would have to be done by cunning and adroitness.

His passion had been great when he had attacked the door, but he had exhausted it, and now, in his calmer moments, he began to invent all manner of schemes of escape.

Boy-like, he indulged in a good many romantic ideas.

Conjectures of the wildest kind floated through his brain, and after all came to nothing.

Many boys would have wept under such circumstances.

But not Rupert.

The manner in which he had been saved by his cousin Reuben out of the very jaws of death seemed to tell him that he was reserved for better things than to be the victim of such a foul death-monger as Dr. Carver.

He was in the midst of these reflections, looking out meanwhile on the island and the water which encircled it, when he heard the key turn in the lock, and the door opening admitted a boy. Rupert knew him at once.

He was the boy with the thin yet handsome face and intellectual eyes who had, as our hero had expressed it, " put away " such a quantity of beef during the feast in the woods.

He measured him now, not intellectually, but physically.

" I could seize him, take the keys from him, kill him if I liked," thought Rupert; " but of what use would that be?"

His defiant mood had gone.

Strategy had come to his rescue.

" Well," he said, seeing that the lad had a jug, a plate, and a piece of bread with him, " have you brought me my breakfast?"

" Yes," half stammered the boy; "you musn't blame me for anything. I'm sent up here with your breakfast, and every door is locked after me, so that if you took this key away from me it would be no good. You could only get out into the passage, and the windows of that are barred."

" What makes you say that?" said Rupert, laughing.

" I saw you looking at the key."

" Ah! I hope I'm not a fool," said our hero. " I might have looked at the key, but I know as well as you do what useless nonsense it would be to think of possessing it. I should be no nearer liberty. What is this? Oatmeal or pig's wash?"

" Oh, it's beautiful to what we have," said the boy; " we don't have it half so thick as that, and the piece of bread is twice as big."

" I don't wonder you look starved," said Rupert; " but I'll try and eat the bread and swallow this wash, for I'm dreadfully hungry. Won't that schoolmaster of yours catch it when my friends hear of it!"

" Ah!" sighed the boy, " we all say that; but time proves what nonsense it is. There is no chance of your friends ever knowing that you are here."

" My cousin—I mean my father," said Rupert, catching up his words quickly, " will soon discover it and fetch me away."

" You think so, but you don't know what to expect here," he said; " wait for a week or two, then you'll know better."

" A week or two," cried Rupert, contemptuously. " A few hours or a day at most would be too horrible to think of."

His mind could not yet grasp the idea of a sojourn at " Starvem Hall."

" I daresay you do think it is horrible," said the boy, with a shudder, " but you've no idea yet how horrible it is.

Why, bless you, your friends may think you are here, may feel convinced you are here, and might come here in search of you. They'd be treated with every politeness, and be shown all over the place, but they would never see you."

" Why ? "

" Because there are secret places where you could be popped at a moment's notice. Have you done breakfast ? "

" Well, I've washed my mouth out as the horses do," said Rupert, laughing. " I suppose it would be sacrilege to ask for more ? "

" I don't know about the sacrilege," said the lad, " but you wouldn't get it."

" Well, you can give my compliments to Doctor Starvem——"

" Starvem ! Is that what people call him ? "

" Yes ; and well he deserves the title. Give my compliments to Doctor Starvem, and tell him that if he has a loaf and a few bloaters, or some nice bacon, such as we have up at Blakesley Hall, I shall be glad. But tell me first what is your name ? "

" Leigh Glindon."

" What a nice name ! How long have you been here ? "

" Four years."

" Four years in prison ! What a weary time. Wouldn't you like to escape ? "

Glindon looked around him as if he were really afraid that walls had ears.

" Escape ! Yes, I should. But there is no such thing except when you are dead."

" Ah, I see," said Rupert, " they've so reduced you that you have no energy left to fight for yourself. Well, while I've got a little remaining I shall make a fight for liberty. Will you come too, or, rather, will you help me ? "

Glindon shrugged his shoulders incredulously, as if treating the idea as a mere absurdity.

" What is your age ? " asked Rupert.

" Seventeen."

Our hero started in astonishment.

Certainly Leigh was tall and so forth, but his childlike face was totally unlike that of a lad of the age he mentioned.

" Good gracious ! " cried Rupert. " I had no conception that you were so old as that. You don't look as old as I do. But I won't chaff you. It isn't fair. If things go roughly with me, I shall be as lanky and have as little spirit in me as you have ; but they've got to take a lot of good roast beef and plum-pudding out of me yet before they make me like you. Glindon, I won't talk like this any more if you'll only say you'll escape if I get you the chance."

" Escape ! yes, that I will," said Leigh, with a ring of enthusiasm in his voice that Rupert had never heard before, and he took our hero's firm hand in his and pressed it.

" That's jolly," said Rupert. " Now I've got a chum to work with me I'll do wonders. How long can you stop here talking ? You'll be wanted in school, won't you ? "

Leigh Glindon laughed heartily at this.

" Oh, as for school," he said, " nobody ever troubles about regular hours here ; but this is Thursday, and on Thursdays we never are bothered about lessons until about midday. Doctor Carver goes somewhere on Wednesday nights where he always gets too much to drink, and no one thinks of lessons until twelve o'clock."

" What is the time now ? "

" Only nine. I can stop another hour."

" Very well," said Rupert ; " but have you had your breakfast ? "

" Long ago," returned the boy, " and forgotten it."

" I have money with me," said Rupert. " The rascals who attacked me did not take that from me. Isn't there anyone on the island who can be bribed to get proper food—to bring it in secretly from the town ? "

" Yes, there is," said Leigh ; " that is if you like to pay exactly double price."

" I don't mind that if we are certain to get it," said our hero. " Who is it ? "

" A boy—half-witted they say he is—called Bob Dolly," said Leigh. " He's a comic customer, but if ever any of us do get hold of a few pence, we always find him honest."

" Perhaps he might be persuaded to take a letter to the post."

" No, not the least chance of that," said Leigh. " He knows all about that. He is positively the only one who could take such a thing, and if he were bowled out he would be accused, and he guesses what sort of punishment he'd get."

" Well, well, provisions will keep up

our spirits," returned Rupert; "and now tell me something about the school, so that I may plan the escape on which I am determined, even at the risk of life itself!"

As Leigh remained silent, Rupert asked—

"Is there a playground?"

"Yes, a large one," replied Leigh.

"High walls, I suppose?"

"Yes, with spikes on the top."

"Ha! then that proves," said Rupert triumphantly, "that there must be means of escape other than you think. If not there would be no precautions taken in regard to the spikes."

"The walls of the playground abut on the arm of the sea in its deepest part," said Leigh Glindon. "It is built on the rock, so that even if anyone succeeded in climbing it and got down on the other side he would be drowned."

"If he couldn't swim," said hopeful Rupert.

"Swimming would be of no use," said Leigh. "It is the deepest, swiftest, and most dangerous part of the river. Even large boats avoid it."

"Well, never mind. We'll find some means of escape," said Rupert. "Am I to go down to school to-day?"

"I don't think so."

"Why?" he asked.

"You're to be broken in first."

Rupert's face flushed at this.

"What do you mean?" he cried.

"You're too strong and well, and so on, to mix with the other boys yet," said Leigh Glindon, with a sickly smile. "Doctor Carver is afraid you might breed dissension, or lead to a riot in the school, and so you won't be introduced till he has, as I have heard him say to Mr. Meekly, touched the head through the stomach."

"Well, he won't touch my brain through my stomach if I can help it," said Rupert. "You had better go at once and send Bob Dolly on his errand to the town. I feel starving."

"It's no good feeling like that," said Leigh. "He won't be going just yet, and then he won't be back before night or late in the evening."

"Then I shan't have anything all day?"

"Only regulation food," said Leigh; "when Bob does come, however, you

may depend on my coming to you at once."

"You seem to have the run of the place."

"Yes; because they don't feel afraid of my escaping," said the boy, with a faint rush of colour to his cheek. "I have no friends except those who sent me here to starve and get rid of me; and with no money, and no one to go to, they don't fancy it's likely I should try and get away."

"You shall have money and friends, too, if you only aid me to escape," said Rupert, "and now be off, and try and send Bob Dolly soon."

He gave Leigh the money, shook his hand, and in a few moments was again alone.

It would be uselessly tedious to describe this day.

It passed on dreary wings indeed.

At three o'clock Leigh brought him some bread and cheese, but dared not stop longer than to tell him that he had despatched Dolly on his provisioning expedition.

After this our hero saw Bob Dolly, a tall, thin, crooked-back lad, about eighteen, rowing with long, swift strokes across the rough water.

Then, at six o'clock, came a scanty basin of gruel, and he was told to go to bed.

"I shan't undress, Leigh," he said, in a voice which made Glindon experience a sudden emotion of fear. "I don't know what may happen to-night yet."

"I don't quite understand you," said Leigh.

"You're coming again with what Bob Dolly brings," said our hero, "and you'll stop and feast with me."

His blood had begun to boil with rage.

Instead of famine causing him to be down-cast and weak spirited, it roused up all the fiery blood in his veins, as it would have roused his evil blood had he possessed any.

He had formed a wild scheme of wresting the key from the hands of Leigh Glindon, and forcing his way through the outer door to face the foes he knew nothing of.

But this wild spirit soon passed away.

He knew that by what he proposed he would be bringing Leigh Glindon into trouble, and that of course he did not desire to do.

So he calmly watched the grey of the evening descending over the sea, and then, when darkness came, he threw himself on the bed to think.

He had forgotten to speak about lights.

Surely Leigh would have the sense to ask Bob Dolly to get some candles.

Thinking of this, of his cousin Reuben, of his own strange life, of the scene in the cave, wondering how much longer it must be before he could claim his own and punish the assassins of his father, he at length fell into a sound sleep.

CHAPTER XIII.

A FEAST AT HUNGRY HALL.

WHEN our hero awoke again, he found that a bright light was shining in the room, and that something had been placed up at the windows to prevent any such unusual illumination being seen out at sea, or on the other bank of the river.

On the only stool belonging to the chamber was seated Leigh Glindon, while on the common deal table was a large basket.

Leigh was looking more ghastly pale than usual.

Perhaps it was the light of the candles.

But Rupert preferred to think it was exhaustion.

He rose at once from the bed.

"Halloa, Leigh!" he said in a subdued voice of welcome, "you've come then?"

Leigh smiled.

"I try," he said, "never to break my word."

"And is that the basket containing the banquet?"

"Yes; and a goodly banquet it is," said Leigh, as he undid it; "you must contrive to hide some of it away, for Bob Dolly can't go to the town every day."

It was a mass of things which Bob had bought—cakes, a small flask of wine, some fruit, and last, but not least, some cold boiled beef, some cheese, and two loaves.

"He's a sensible fellow," said Rupert. "Let's begin at once. I'm hungry."

The two boys waited no more.

Drawing the table noiselessly up to the bed-side, they at once began on the banquet; such a one as Leigh Glindon had not set his eyes on for many a long day.

He did not attempt to disguise his appetite, and consequently did not speak until he had satisfied it, washing it down with a weak mixture of wine and water.

"Well," he said, when he at length put down his knife and fork, "thanks to you, Rupert Clifford, I have had the first real meal here which I have seen for a long time. I hope I shan't be ill. I've got such a dreadful pain in my chest."

"You mustn't go to bed just yet," said Rupert laughing, "or you'll die of indigestion. Let's talk."

So the two lads went on comparing notes as before until the small hours in the morning, when they gripped each other by the hand and parted.

Next day much the same routine was gone through.

Rupert had carefully preserved his provisions, and with the abominable fare provided for him at the school, he was enabled to go through the day without feeling in any way faint, and at the same time keep something towards the next morning.

On this morning he was summoned to the schoolroom.

Such a schoolroom!

Whitewashed walls, splashed everywhere with ink, rude forms, barred windows, admitting but a feeble light, through facing towards the walls of the other wing.

And such a crew of scholars!

Emaciated, pale, furtive of eye and slinking of mien, they formed a terrible school—a school presided over by Silenus and two starved satyrs.

Leigh Glindon looked on this morning a striking contrast to the others.

He was still pale and gaunt of course.

But there was an unusual light in his

eyes, and an unusual jauntiness in his manner.

As for Rupert, with his ruddy face and well-knit, well-developed form, he was just like a fish out of water.

The doctor gave him one piercing glance.

Evidently he thought that the discipline he had undergone would have cowed his impetuous spirit.

But he was wrong.

The pride of the Pendarvens still burned and glowed in Rupert's dark gipsy orbs.

"James Johnstone!" cried Dr. Carver, in a loud voice.

No one moved.

Rupert stood quietly leaning one hand on one of the broad deal tables.

A frown gathered on the face of the principal.

He rapped angrily on his desk with his ruler.

"James Johnstone, I say, come here!" he cried; "I wish to speak to you."

Still no one moved.

Mr. Meekly, who with Mr. Small had been reinstated in the graces of Dr. Carver, on expressing his sorrow for his great delinquency in eating something when they had a chance, was busy chalking some numbers on a huge slate preparatory to some lesson in arithmetic.

Dr. Carver grew red with anger.

He was not used to be thwarted in any way.

"Mr. Meekly," he said, "bring me that new boy Johnstone. We must see that he is made an example of, if he presumes to show want of discipline like this."

Mr. Meekly, with no show of alacrity be it said, approached Rupert.

"Excuse me, Master Johnstone," he said, addressing our hero somewhat deferentially in memory of the delicious stew with which he had been indulged at the woodland picnic, "but perhaps you are slightly deaf. Doctor Carver, your new schoolmaster, desires to speak to you."

Rupert made no reply.

Mr. Meekly plucked him gently by the sleeve.

"Pray, come, Master Johnstone; if you make a scene it will be bad for every-one."

This was said in a gentle and confidential way.

Rupert shook him off.

"If you are addressing me by the name of Johnstone, you are acting under some delusion, of which I am very glad, as I shall not, when you know who I am, be detained here. My name is not Johnstone, but Rupert Clifford."

Mr. Meekly turned to Dr. Carver.

"The lad says that his name is not Johnstone, but Rupert Clifford," he said.

Dr. Carver rose, arming himself with a formidable bludgeon, for it was neither a cane proper nor a stick, but an immense bamboo.

"What do you say?" he cried, planting himself before Rupert in a vulgar attitude of contempt and defiance. "Your name isn't Johnstone?"

"No, it is not."

"And what may it be?"

"Rupert Clifford."

"Oh, indeed!" mockingly. "Very well. Now, Master James Johnstone, you have been brought here and placed under my care by your father, Mr. Robert Johnstone—a very worthy man—and your uncle, Mr. Horace Johnstone, also a very worthy person, and you have been left entirely to me. They told me that I might find some sign of this delusion, but take my advice, don't give way to it. Set to work, learn your lessons, keep your mind fixed upon them, and you'll soon get rid of all the unpleasant things that are now preying upon you."

Rupert listened to this long harangue with folded arms, and a smile of contempt wreathing his lips.

"My name, sir," he said, when Dr. Carver had finished—"my name is Rupert Clifford, son of Colonel Gerald Clifford, of the Larches. I was placed by him at Doctor Walton's—Blakesley Hall Academy. When out on a walk the day before yesterday, I was rendered insensible by some ruffians in a place called the Hermit's Hut, and when I woke I found myself in your school, from which I now demand my instant release."

Dr. Carver shook his head, and glancing over gravely at Mr. Meekly, tapped his forehead significantly.

"Ah, Mr. Meekly," he said in a gentle voice, "I fear this is a case for the detention ward. His mind is evidently a little affected."

"I would not proceed to extremes unless he becomes violent," said the usher quite gravely.

Of course it was his *role* to play into the hands of the master.

"Well, well, we'll try him again," said the master, gravely. "Come, my boy; the Latin class is about to commence. Join it, and let us see how far you are gone in your classics."

"No," replied Rupert, firmly. "I am determined to do nothing in this house until you have brought me face to face with my father, or you have shown me a letter from him to you that he desires me to remain here. Doctor Walton is my schoolmaster, not you; and I cannot talk of anything else than my instant release from this house of starvelings."

Dr. Carver grew livid with rage.

All intermediate business was over now.

It was war to the knife.

"Come to your class," he shouted, furiously.

And he flourished his bamboo.

"I have no class," said Rupert.

"This is beyond endurance," he yelled. "Mr. Meekly, bring me the triangle. Leigh Glindon, help Mr. Meekly."

A defiant look was in the eyes of our hero.

From experience he knew nothing of the word "triangle" as applied to punishments.

But his common-sense told him pretty well what it must be.

He waited calmly—at least, with outward calmness.

Within he was raging like a furnace.

In a few minutes the usher and Leigh Glindon returned, bearing a wooden machine, which, when placed in position, was firmly fixed in the centre of the floor in the shape of a triangle, with rings above and rings below for firmly fixing the victim.

Rupert's heart beat wildly at the sight.

He was a good and brave boy.

But a boy is only a boy after all; and he could not avoid a little sinking of the spirits as he contemplated the fate which might be his.

However, he resolved to be as brave as he could.

"You see, Master Meekly," said Dr. Carver, in a tone of suppressed rage, "this is not a case which we can treat as one of lunacy. It is sheer insolence and insubordination to cover a natural propensity for laziness. Up with him."

Rupert no longer stood with his arms folded.

They were straight down at his side and his hands clenched.

"If anyone attempts to hoist me he will repent it," he said.

Dr. Carver made no remark.

He was inwardly boiling over with intense fury.

He saw that the eyes of all the hungry boys around were fixed upon him, and he knew that now or never was the time to ensure his discipline.

Mr. Meekly, too, was greatly excited.

He was under the unpleasant delusion that he was about to be asked to hoist Rupert and attach him to the triangle.

Not so.

Dr. Carver never dreamt of it.

He knew well how little the weak and half-starved usher would avail against the strong and well-fed lad from Blakesley Hall Academy.

Even Mr. Small was away and not able to assist.

However, Mr. Meekly's troubles were soon over.

Dr. Carver made a simple sign to him, which Rupert did not observe, and the usher slid away and passed out of the room.

Apparently Leigh Glindon knew at once that this meant some evil to Rupert.

He tried desperately in the face of all to put Rupert on his guard.

In vain.

Dr. Carver began to talk against him in order to direct the attention of our hero to anything except what was going on.

Rupert was deceived thoroughly in this way.

"One more chance I give you, Master Johnstone," said Dr. Carver. "If you will beg my pardon, and come to your class I will forgive you, as you are a new boy and seem rather excited. If not, as I must preserve discipline in my school, I must inflict a very severe chastisement."

"Nothing will alter me, sir," said Rupert. "The only respect I owe you is what is due to a man older than myself. That respect I do not deny, but as a schoolmaster I owe you none, as I have been kidnapped here, and I have demanded my freedom."

While he had been speaking treachery had been going on—treachery which Leigh and the other fellows saw without daring to raise a finger to warn him.

Meekly had re-entered the room with a tall, broad-shouldered, hulking ruffian, who was evidently not on the starvation system.

Just as the word " freedom " left the lips of Rupert, his arms were suddenly pinioned from behind, and his wrists were thrust into the springs of the triangle, which clicked to like hand-cuffs.

He had only just time to kick out and plant one blow in the stomach of his unseen adversary, and then his legs were also pinioned.

" Well done, Freeman," said Dr. Carver, who had noticed how the kick had taken effect upon his factotum's stomach.

" I don't call it well done," growled Freeman, as he rubbed the injured part. " I only wish I had the thrashing of him myself."

Dr. Carver smiled complacently as he turned up the wrist of his right coat-sleeve.

" No doubt," he said ; " but that is a pleasure I reserve to myself."

And in another moment Rupert Pendarven, our hero, received the first blow which he had not had a chance to return.

His eyes were fixed on Dr. Carver as he r ised his bamboo to strike.

Never did the schoolmaster forget their expression.

It was not an evil glance.

There was no evil in Rupert's nature.

But there was a concentrated warning as it were—a look which plainly said—

" You are doing me a cruel and unmerited injury, and I warn you that it will neither be forgotten nor forgiven."

The blows were heavy and brutal, for fierce passion gleamed from the wicked eyes of the man, but Rupert felt very few of them.

His mind and body seemed to succumb before the humiliation, the shame and the pain.

He gra dally became unconscious, the blows seemed as if falling on a numbed body, and then all was darkness.

When he awoke he was once more in the gloomy turret chamber.

He was undressed and in bed, and his body ached terribly from the brutal blows he had received.

But he at once sprang out of bed.

The flask of wine which Bob Dolly had brought he had left half full, and this he hoped to find in order to take from him the exhaustion caused by the brutal beating.

It was getting dusk when he found himself in his bed, but the pain of the blows was still strong upon him.

It was evident, in fact, that he had been cruelly ill-treated, even when he was in a state of unconsciousness, for his flesh was cut—big wheals could be traced everywhere, and bruises were beginning to appear—black and blue—all over him.

If they had found his wine, they had also found his provisions, and, what was of still more consequence to him, his money.

But he found to his delight that everything was just as he had left it.

This, of course, as he discovered afterwards, was owing to Leigh Glindon, who pretended to be the friend of Dr. Carver, and the enemy of Rupert.

He affected to resent " his upstart ways," to repeat all his talk " about escape and other nonsense," and so thoroughly disabused the mind of Dr. Carver of any possible collusion between them, that he gave Leigh the office of waiting upon the recalcitrant new scholar.

The wine, which Rupert found untouched and drank off at a draught, did him an immense deal of good, and gave him strength to eat a few biscuits, after which he was able to snatch some refreshing sleep.

Rousing himself at last from this, he found himself not alone.

Leigh Glindon was with him, calmly reading by the light of a flickering taper.

" How are you, dear Rupert ? " he whispered, as our hero moved uneasily, and then opened his eyes.

" Very sore and ill."

" You were very imprudent."

" I can't help my temper," returned our hero. " I am determined that he shall not break my spirit. He shall kill me first."

"He will, I fear," said Leigh, "for he is a man without a single scruple, and will go on brutally ill-using you until you die or give in."

"Then I shall die," said Rupert, quietly, "for I shall never give in. I don't think he'll have so good a chance again. Forewarned is forearmed."

"You have time to get up your strength," said Leigh. "You are to be kept to your room for two days."

"And will Bob Dolly be able to go over the water to-day?"

"Yes," said Leigh, with a smile. "Are you getting hungry again?"

"Well, I have nearly exhausted the provisions," said our hero; "but that is not the thing. I want some wine and a good stout cudgel."

"What for?" asked Leigh in astonishment.

"To escape with," said Rupert. "I won't risk telling even you my plan, for fear your heart might fail you and spoil all. What I want is for you to promise that the instant I show you the means of escape you will follow my lead."

"Yes," said Leigh, "though I fear I shall only be a burden to you. Here, drink up your gruel, Rupert, and let me go. We mustn't have long interviews now, or I shall be suspected."

In a few minutes Leigh was gone, and Rupert was left to meditate upon his plan of escape—a plan which was destined to create such a scene and such a change at Hungry Hall, as even he little dreamed of.

CHAPTER XIV.

IN WHICH OUR HERO DOES A DESPERATE DEED.

How Leigh Lindon contrived to persuade Bob Dolly to such a thing it is hard to say.

However, it was certain that he used his influence to marked effect, for the next evening not only the provisions and the wine arrived, but a fine strong ash stick, cut fresh from the woods.

Rupert smiled as he saw and handled this.

"To-morrow, Leigh," he said, firmly, "I shall die or escape."

"That can't be," returned Glindon. "Your time is not up until the next day."

"Never mind," said our hero; "it will be to-morrow or not at all. I've seen the little house where the boats are kept, and I think, now I've mapped out the part of the island I can see from my window, there ought to be no difficulty in reaching it. Once let me get on board a boat, and I'll give anyone on the island a good race for it."

"But you've got to reach the boat," said Leigh. "Four doors to pass through, and the house is so arranged purposely that anyone attempting an escape would have to go through the schoolroom."

"I know that," said Rupert, "or

rather I guessed it. Dr. Carver is not the sort of person to leave loopholes of escape for any one. But that won't affect me. It will rather help me in my plan than otherwise."

"You might tell me safely," said Leigh Glindon, who, to confess the truth, was bursting with curiosity. "You know well that I should not betray you."

"I know that well," said Rupert, taking his hand, "but if I were to tell you, Glindon, it would really spoil all. You must be content to wait until I explain all, or rather, till you see all. Then take advantage of what you see, and act at once. And now let us have a feast."

"I can't stop," said Leigh, though he eyed the good things wistfully.

"Why?"

"It would be unsafe, after all that has happened."

"Then leave me just enough for supper and breakfast, and take all the rest with you."

Glindon shook his head.

"No, no," he said; "that would never do."

"Then eat a mouthful or two and be

off," said Rupert. "I'll have your breakfast all ready for you in the morning, and a nice drop of wine, and then —victory!"

Leigh ate some cold beef and bread as quickly as he could, drank some wine and water, and was off.

A dim glimmering of what was about to happen was now in his mind.

He saw its dangers, and fully realised them too.

But he would not draw back.

Life in the island school was intolerable, but the idea of life on the mainland was simply hopeless, without even the shadow of a friend.

Now, however, things were far different, and he hailed with pleasant anticipation the coming struggle.

Even the small quantity of proper food he had eaten had given him more power and vigour.

And so now, having had a fill of good food, and some very fair wine, Leigh Glindon felt a new being, and quite equal to any emergency.

Next morning dawned.

Rupert ate his breakfast early, waiting for no gruel.

At ten o'clock appeared Leigh Glindon, pale with excitement.

"Have some breakfast, old man?" asked Rupert.

"No," said Leigh, in a tremulous voice, "I can't eat. I'll have some wine, though, if you have any."

"Yes; I kept your share," said Rupert. "I knew that you would want something to keep your courage up."

Leigh gladly drank what was in the little bottle—good port wine.

"Now," said Rupert, whose ruddy cheeks had somewhat lost their colour, "give me the key of this door."

And he flourished his ash stick with playful threatening.

"Oh, but——" began Leigh Glindon, with a look of horror.

"There are no 'buts' in the case," said Rupert, calmly. "If at the last moment you have turned coward,. I shall take the key. You are older than I am, Leigh, but I am the stronger, and now I feel the strength of a dozen within me. Come, old boy, the key."

"They will kill me," said Glindon, mournfully.

But he handed over the key.

"They won't have the chance if you are brave," said our hero, confidently. "Follow me, and do as I do. Now, Leigh, you will see that I shall do nothing rashly. Tell me, in the first place, what I have to face outside this door."

"Nothing. You only cross an empty passage, and the same key opens the door opposite," said Leigh.

"And then?"

"Outside the door are Messrs. Meekly and Small. It used to be only one of them, but since the triangle business both are sent. You see, Rupert," added Glindon, who had really been thoroughly roused—"you see you are regarded as a desperate character."

"Well, and when we have disposed of them," said Rupert, confidently.

"Then you descend the stairs and have to go right through the school-room."

"Well, I am going to rush out upon these two miserable beings who take his money to help in the starvation of others," said Rupert. "Then I shall make a dash downstairs to the school-room, and make a rush for liberty."

"And I?"

"You must do as I do," said Rupert. "I shall turn the key upon the ushers, and unless they can force their way through iron bars, they will certainly be unable to escape until long after we have made good our way across the arm of the sea."

"Go on and prosper."

Rupert's words were stirring his blood as his blood had never been stirred before.

"Now, Leigh, then," said our hero, "and let not your heart fail you."

He opened the bedroom door, passed across the corridor, opened the next door, and stood face to face with Messrs. Meekly and Small, who were talking earnestly.

For an instant the two men of little names and little natures stood aghast, and during this instant Rupert, followed by Leigh Glindon, strode to the door.

Then, horrified at their own inaction, the ushers dashed forward.

Leigh stood resolute, and Rupert, flourishing his formidable stick, cried—

"I warn you to advance no further. I have no desire to do you any personal violence, but I am detained illegally here, and I am going to take my freedom, even at the risk of your lives."

For another instant the men looked doubtful.

Then, remembering that their wretched living, and perhaps their lives were at stake, they rushed forward.

The ash stick struck Meekly right across the face, bringing him to the ground in a moment, while a well-directed blow from Leigh sent Small staggering away.

Then, the door being opened and the key reversed during the first moments of hesitation, the two boys darted through and locked it on the other side.

"Now for old Starvem himself. I do not fear him," said Rupert, as he put the key in his pocket. "I shall rush in, you must follow, snatch the key from the door, and open the one opposite. If there is any very great uproar, I shall strike out right and left."

Everything was very quiet in the schoolroom except for the sound of a boy crying vigorously.

The doctor had just administered a cruel blow with the ruler on his knuckles for not remembering something which he had never been taught, telling him not to be obstinate and imitate the foolish boy upstairs, who was doubtless weeping his heart out by this time at his own folly.

Just as he made this remark with evident relish, the door was flung open, and two forms appeared which made him imagine for a moment that he had gone mad, or that two wild Indians had made their way into the school.

Rupert plunged in, dusky red of face, and flourishing a stick, and Leigh, whom the excitement of partial success had deprived of his pallor, came boldly in behind him.

"What is the meaning of this, rascals?" cried the exasperated schoolmaster, dashing to the door through which Rupert and his friend desired to make their escape.

"The meaning is plain," said Rupert, "and I am not going to waste time by further talk. If you don't let me go quietly through that door I shall force my way through, so if you value your life, let me pass, villain."

Carver eyed him aghast.

He was a strong man.

Rupert was only a boy.

He rushed to his desk and procured his stout bamboo.

"You young rascal!" he cried. "I'll teach you to rebel."

And with a face crimson with anger, he rushed at Rupert.

This was just what our hero desired.

"Quick, Glindon! Open that door," cried Rupert, as with upraised stick and flashing eyes he confronted the doctor.

An ominous kicking against the upper door showed that the ushers were "up and doing."

In an instant Leigh advanced to the door and unlocked it. Then he waited.

But not for long.

If Rupert had had the worst of it he would at once have interfered.

But as it was, it was most prudent to wait near the portal for fear of sneaks.

Rupert was not getting the worst of it.

As the schoolmaster dashed at him, intent upon striking him a furious blow, however disastrous, he dodged aside and struck Dr. Starvem a blow on the cranium that made it rattle again.

The blow was well directed and heavy.

"Help!—some of you boys!" gasped Dr. Carver, the blood starting down his face.

No one stirred.

They liked it, and accordingly pretended to be afraid.

Another blow aimed recklessly by the old ruffian, and an answering one again on the old villain's head, followed by a thrust from Rupert catching him in the stomach.

"Bread — and — water — for — a — month!" gasped Carver, "if no one helps me."

"They won't fear that," said Rupert. "They don't get much better now. Let me pass, rascal!"

"Go to Freeman. Tell him to look for the boats, Smiles," gasped the doctor, holding his head between his hands.

And while Leigh was too excited to stop him, a boy, so small and thin that he gave one the idea of a clothed skeleton, glided between his legs and ran away.

There was no time to be lost.

Victory was within sight, and they must grasp it.

Leaving the door slightly ajar, Leigh Glindon sprang forward, and catching the schoolmaster by the back. of his clothes, threw him on his face.

"Now, then, Rupert," he cried, "no revenge! Quick—let's escape, and we are safe."

Rupert only paused one moment to give a contemptuous look at the prostrate man, and then the two boys bounded away.

The door was closed—the key taken away.

They were even now in the free air and glorious sunshine.

"Hurrah!" cried Rupert. "You acted like a brave gentleman. Come on! Let's lose no time. Now for the boathouse."

"Freeman's there," cried Leigh Glindon excitedly; "and that sneak, Smiles, has gone to put him on his guard."

"Then we'll put him on his back," laughed Rupert.

But his laugh was of short duration, for as they rushed forward they saw Freeman standing at the boathouse door, gun in hand, and ready to fire.

Our boys would have been more than human had they not been alarmed at the sight of the man Freeman in such a position.

Rupert knew already his ferocious nature, and was quite certain that he would have no compunction in carrying out any brutal orders given him by his master.

The fall of old Dr. Carver, the paltry tyrant of Hungry Hall, meant the fall of Freeman too, and consequently he was ever on the watch to preserve his master's interests.

"Stop there, you boys," he cried; "where are you going?"

"To the mainland!" shouted Rupert. "We want a boat."

"Have you an order from Dr. Carver," said the man, advancing as the boys retreated.

"No; but we are going to take a message for one of the tutors," said Rupert.

"Ah! you young reptiles," cried the man, "you think you can deceive me, but you're wrong. Stop, I say, or I fire! Mind, I never miss."

"Now, then, Leigh," said Rupert, in a firm, almost stern undertone, "now, then, for life's sake jump with me. It's a

choice now between death by starvation and death by being shot."

"Or drowning," smiled Leigh, in a ghastly way. "I'm ready. I'll escape or die with you, Rupert."

And as the man raised his gun to his shoulder, the two boys leaped together into the water.

If it had been an ordinary river into which they had plunged, there would have been no danger in the height of the bank from which they leaped.

But in this spot the river swirled and rushed round jagged boulders, and coming sharply down with a rushing tide, the water here lashed itself into mad fury, throwing up hissing waves to the very edge of the high bank, and then hurtling out again with a roar.

The man with the gun stood aghast, looking at the plunge.

"By Je-rusalem!" cried he, "that's a leap and no mistake. Why, it's death for them. I don't surpose either on 'em 'll ever come up to the top again."

But he was wrong.

In a few moments both of the boys reappeared far out in the stream.

They were being rapidly borne away to sea.

As he saw them, Freeman raised his gun again to his shoulder.

"Ah!" he said to himself, "there they are, after all. It's a pity to wing 'em, they're such brave youngsters. But needs must when the devil drives. I've got more respect for my neck than to let 'em go."

Of course this only took a second to think.

Then he fired.

But Rupert, even in the water, had his eye on him.

Leigh was very faint, and colourless, and despairing.

But Rupert was brave and spirited as ever.

The very fact of escape seemed to give him a new lease of life.

"Dive—he's firing," said he tersely.

Leigh Glindon had no strength to dive.

He dropped as it were, while Rupert went down like a fish.

When they rose to the surface they were so far round the bend of the river, and so little above the swirling water, that Freeman could see nothing of them.

"I think I've popped them off, or one of them, at any rate," he muttered, as he ran along the bank; "but I must try and make sure, or old Carver 'll raise the very deuce."

He could not run very far in the same course taken by the lads, because the shore of the island went round at this point in the form of a semi-circle, and at the very furthest part where he could stand in safety, he could see nothing of the lads.

"If either of 'em is shot," he said, "it's pretty certain they will never survive when they reach the bar."

The bar was truly a dangerous spot.

When the water was low you could see almost across the whole mouth of the river a long row of black rocks like teeth.

Towards these the boys were being rapidly hurried, and not a boat of any kind was in sight.

Just as Freeman was thinking of returning to the boathouse and getting out a large boat in which to follow up the two fugitives and recovering their bodies, Dr. Carver came running up with Messrs. Meekly and Small.

The principal was, as may be supposed, in a furious rage, and blood running down his face.

He had only just recovered from the effects of the stinging blow he had received from Rupert, and had had to burst open the upper door in order to let out the imprisoned ushers.

"Well," he cried, as he came up panting for breath, "have you shot the young rascals?"

"I don't know. I fired and, I think, missed."

"Cowardice, as usual," said the master, savagely; "but where are they? What's the use of standing there like a dazed fool? Tell me what has happened."

"Well, you see," said Freeman, quite composedly, "you don't give a fellow much time to tell you anything. But if you'll listen, I'll explain."

"Go on, then."

In a few minutes Dr. Carver knew all.

"Then if they're drowning out there," he cried, "if their dead bodies are found there will be the deuce to pay. We must get out the large boat and pull down with the tide at once. You, Mr. Meekly, had better see to the school; get the boys in order, give them a holiday, and promise them extra food. You, Mr. Small, come with me. You can steer, and I and Freeman can row."

Without waiting for more the latter hurried off, and had soon got the largest boat out.

Despite its large dimensions it floated beautifully in the water, and when propelled with the tide by the strong arms of Dr. Carver and Freeman, it went on at a spanking pace.

There was no sign, however, of either of the boys.

They seemed to have vanished.

"I expect those young scamps have pretty well settled themselves," said Freeman, as they rested on their oars.

"If they're drowned and carried right off to sea so much the better," growled Dr. Carver, "then we can say that they got out a boat against my wishes and were drowned. Now then for the bar. Softly, Mr. Small."

The water was low and there was extreme peril, but exerting himself to the utmost, the little man shot the nose of the boat between two jagged teeth of rock, and after one wild leap it rode gently and easy on the bosom of the sea.

But not a sign of the two boys could be seen anywhere.

The principal and the others searched every spot eagerly.

But in vain.

"They're drowned sure enough," said Dr. Carver, "and as the tide is running out so swiftly they are no doubt carried right away. At any rate, it is no use remaining here any longer. We had better get back at once."

"That's more than we can do," returned Freeman. "The tide's still running down, and we should be swamped if we tried to pass between the rocks yonder."

"What are we to do, then?" said Carver, helplessly, and wiping the spots of blood from his face.

"We must row up to Seaborne, or cruise about until the tide serves."

"Let us pull away to Seaborne," said the doctor. "Hoist the little lug sail, and we shall not be long getting there. We may perhaps hear some news of the runaways."

So the little lug sail was set, and the nose of the boat was turned towards Seaborne.

"THE SKINNY FINGERS SHOT FORWARD, AND BILLY UTTERED A CRY OF TERROR."

CHAPTER XV.

RUPERT AND LEIGH ONCE MORE—DEADLY PERIL—WHAT OF THE PUNISHMENT?

MEANWHILE Rupert and Leigh had made their way as best they could across the river.

With the strong tide that was flowing it was utterly impossible to be certain about reaching a given point.

But there was one projection, with a low bank, and coarse grass and reeds growing on its edge, which both regarded with eager hope.

If they could only succeed in reaching this they would be able to clutch hold of a good strong purchase, and draw themselves up on the shore.

Striving hard, they at length contrived to force their way into the current which set for that part of the shore, and everything was going on swimmingly when Leigh Glindon began to lose strength, and rolled over like a helpless ball at the mercy of the tide.

And then Rupert heard the awful cry—

"Help! I've got the cramp!"

Cramp! and in such a tide as this, rushing headlong to the sea.

Rupert knew the peril of his friend, and he knew also the danger to himself.

But he was a boy whose mind was high above the idea of yielding to a mere instinct of self-preservation.

He would not in fact give a thought to the idea of rescue unless his friend who had fought thus far with him was rescued too.

So he turned at once, and battled as well as he could in the direction of young Glindon, who had gone down twice, and seemed preparing for the third and fatal descent.

Rupert, however, was there in time, and keeping as far as he could from the wild kicks and grasps of his friend, who by this time knew not what he was doing, he caught him by the hair of his head, and began dragging him with him to the hoped-for haven of rest.

It was perilous work, for Leigh Glindon was strong in his death struggles, and every now and then, as he writhed his body nearer to his brave preserver, it seemed as if he would clutch him in his deadly embrace.

Again and again it seemed as if it was inevitable.

But by dint of great risk and resolute courage, by patience also and forbearance, our hero contrived to reach the shore, where, clutching the reeds, he remained for a moment to get breath ere he landed.

Then, knowing that every moment's immersion in the water was full of peril to his friend, he contrived to drag him ashore.

The cramp fortunately had not reached Leigh's stomach, or he would have taken no further part in this story.

It had only attacked his legs, and he was able to speak.

By dint of rubbing violently, and then running as fast as he could, he was soon enabled to get back the use of his limbs.

Their actions were concealed from Freeman by a small clump of densely-growing trees, and as soon as they began to run they found themselves diving down into a valley.

So while the savage boatman and the old master of the Starving School were rowing and sailing in quest of them, they were lying wrapped up in blankets at a cottage not very far from the banks of the arm of the sea, while a boy was sent off post haste to Blakesley Hall Academy to give information of Rupert's whereabouts.

It was not long before Dr. Walton himself made his appearance.

He looked very grave when he heard of the adventures through which Rupert had passed.

"There is no doubt," he said, "that that was a murder of which you witnessed the end in that cave behind the hermit's hut. But how and by whom he was murdered I am at a loss to think. In regard to your detention at Doctor Carver's academy, Colonel Clifford will no doubt understand its meaning better than I do, and I shall at once send for him."

He wrote a letter at once at the cottage, while the boys' clothes were drying, and went to the village to post it.

By the time he came back Rupert and Leigh were dressed ready to go to the school, for the water in which they had been immersed was salt sea water, and was not likely to give them cold, even if the clothes were not thoroughly aired.

They set out accordingly for the academy.

Both boys seemed quite recovered from the effects of their perilous swim, and indeed appeared as if it had improved them.

They had had some warm milk and a little brandy given them by the woman at the cottage, which had sent a healthy glow through their frames, and the quick walk to the school caused them to arrive with cheeks red with natural heat.

"I would advise you to say nothing about this matter in the school," said Dr. Walton, ere they parted, "for you do not know how your father will act or will wish you to act in the matter. He may prefer to keep the whole affair quiet"

"Very well, sir," said Rupert, "I will do as you wish me, but how am I to account for my absence? The whole school knows that I have been away against my will, and that a search was made for me."

"Yes, they know that much," said Dr. Walton, "but that is no reason why they should know more. You must put them off. Tell them they must not ask you for particulars."

Rupert smiled.

"I am afraid our boys are very inquisitive, sir," he said, "but I will do my best."

He was quite right.

He was welcomed in the playground as a hero of romance, and was plied with questions innumerable in regard to the adventures he had gone through.

But he preserved a resolute silence.

"I have gone through some funny scenes," he said. "I admit that, and perhaps some day I shall be able to explain it all. At present it only concerns me and my father the colonel, and so I cannot tell you anything."

So he stopped them at once.

The boys talked a great deal together, and there was the usual amount of scandal, and Ralph Pendarven sneered, and said all manner of unkind things.

But Rupert was resolute.

Jeers and coaxings were alike useless; and the thing was regarded as a mystery which only time would elucidate.

On the third day arrived Reuben under his pseudonym of Colonel Gerald Clifford.

He remained closeted with Dr. Walton for a very long time, and from the grave look upon his face it seemed to Rupert that the worthy schoolmaster had received some confidences which he did not expect, and which had considerably enlightened him as to the behaviour of Dr. Carver.

At the end of the interview our hero was called up into the room.

He was received kindly by both, but with an unbounded show of affection by Reuben.

"My boy," he said, as he pressed his hand warmly, "I feel almost grateful for this incident, as you have not suffered any injury. It seems to me to be a warning to us both to proceed in our good work until the end without fear. It seems as if Providence were specially guarding you through all dangers, in order to work out the punishment of those who have proved such terrible and unscrupulous enemies."

"And what are you going to do?" asked Rupert.

"Well, my boy," said Reuben, who acted admirably the fatherly character, "I have told your worthy master here that until I am able to establish a certain matter, I cannot make as much fuss about this disgraceful affair as I should like. But I am going to see Dr. Carver myself, and without in any way compromising Dr. Walton, I shall give him a punishment he richly deserves."

"When are you going?"

"As soon as I have made a necessary arrangements," said Reuben. "I think I may say to-morrow morn without fail. I want you to accomp me, and also Master Leigh Glindon."

Rupert's face gleamed with delight.

"I know Leigh will be pleased," said he, "at the very idea of looking upon Dr. Carver's face as a free boy."

OR, THE MYSTERY OF A DARK NIGHT.

"Ay, and to see his punishment, my boy."

And so saying, he took an affectionate leave of Rupert, a warm one of Dr. Walton, and departed.

Rupert waited eagerly for the coming of the next day.

Reuben was busy all day in the village, spending money and seeing a number of people.

Next morning, about ten, he arrived at the school, and as previously arranged with Dr. Walton, our hero and Leigh Glindon were at once ready to accompany him.

They went across the pleasant fields until reaching the banks of the River Dart, before it discharged itself into the arm of the sea, they found a boat waiting for them with four powerful men at the oars.

"Jump in, my boys," cried Reuben, quite gleefully. "I promise you that before we have done with Dr. Carver he will be sorry indeed that we paid him a visit."

CHAPTER XVI.

THE SCENE AT HUNGRY HALL—A STRANGE RETRIBUTION.

It was eleven o'clock at Hungry Hall.

Dr. Carver had met with some reverse of fortune, or something of the kind that morning, for his face was fiery red, and proclaimed that he had applied for comfort to the whisky bottle more often than usual.

He was in an uncompromising humour.

The unfortunate members of his skeleton school had done their best in every way to please him, and yet it was useless.

He quarrelled with their manners, their voices—with anything he could fall foul of—and their manners and their voices were deplorable indeed, considering that he had dragged them away from their breakfast before it was half done.

Breakfast!

Save the mark!

A cup of weak oatmeal, and two thin slices of bread.

"I tell you what," he was saying, just as the clock was striking eleven, "that I won't stand any more of this. I never looked upon a more beggarly lot of idiots in my life! If you can't behave yourself properly, I will thrash the whole school. I'll show you who's master here."

These last words were shouted out at the top of his voice.

And they were answered in a way he little expected.

"That's just what I've come to see," said a voice.

And the door opening admitted Reuben Pendarven.

No one would have imagined from his quiet—and, in fact, his pleasant countenance—that he had come on such an errand as he had done.

Dr. Carver, however, took no notice of his expression of face.

He was struck dumb, as it were, by the insolence of a man daring to come into his establishment, and even into his very schoolroom, without being announced.

"Who are you, sir?" he cried, advancing slightly.

But he paused as he saw entering behind the intruder the forms of Leigh Glindon and our hero.

"What, may I ask,'" he added, quickly, in a voice almost choked with rage, "what is the meaning of this most unwarrantable intrusion?"

"Well," said Reuben, closing the door, "I can most readily explain that, the more so that I know that I am standing in the presence of a most contemptible coward."

This was terrific to Dr. Carver in the presence of the entire school.

"Have a care, sir," he cried, "how you insult me in the presence of my scholars. I will have you ejected from the premises if you do not leave them at once."

"I came for the purpose of insulting you," said Reuben, "and the more people that happen to be present the more consonant it will be with my feelings. In the first place, I desire to know the meaning of your disgraceful outrage on my son here, Rupert Clifford."

"I do not know any one of that name," returned Dr. Carver.

"Strange! after he has been a scholar in your school. Let me introduce you. This is my son, Rupert Clifford, who nearly lost his life through your brutality."

"I know that boy only by the name of James Johnstone," replied Dr. Carver.

"Indeed! Will you kindly tell me then who placed him here?"

"What if I refuse?"

"I will horsewhip you before all the school."

"Oh, indeed!" said Dr. Carver, livid with rage. "Have a care, or I may chastise you."

"Well, we will run the risk of what you say," replied Reuben; "only I warn you I think the best thing you can do will be to apologise. I do not say this in any spirit of braggadocio. I simply tell you what I mean, and that is, that unless you at once apologise for your brutal and unwarrantable behaviour to my son, and to his friend, Leigh Glindon, I will thrash you before the whole school."

"Indeed!" said Dr. Carver; "and, pray, may I ask why, if I have committed the illegal acts of which you accuse me, you do not at once apply to Captain Carlyon, who is the nearest magistrate, and ask him to commit me to prison, or something of the kind?"

"That is my affair," said Reuben, contemptuously. "But I have one very good reason, and that is, that I do not wish to drag my ancient and honourable name into court in company with such a disreputable one as yours. But I am wasting time. My object in coming here is to humiliate you as much as possible before the boys whom you starve and ruin. Down on your knees, you vagabond, and beg my pardon humbly, or I will give you such a thrashing as you have never dreamt of."

As he spoke these words, he drew from beneath his coat a stout horsewhip.

Dr. Carver turned nearly purple.

He knew, rather than saw, that his pupils were gazing at him with an expectant, and an almost delighted look.

"Thrashing! you confounded vaga-

bond!" he said, seizing his formidable ruler. "I'll break your head."

"The most advisable thing you possibly could do," said Reuben, "if it lies in your power. Once more, will you apologise?"

"No."

"Then take that."

And raising his whip with a sudden jerk he cut Dr. Carver over the head.

With a yell of rage the infuriated schoolmaster dashed at him with uplifted ruler.

Reuben was far too accustomed to ash sticks, and so forth, in the woods to bother about a little piece of oak of that kind.

And consequently the attack was not of the slightest avail.

The blows from the heavy riding-whip continued to descend like hail, and the ruler, quickly wrenched from the hand of the man who was reeling about under the unexpected chastisement, went crashing through a window.

I say unexpected, for Dr. Carver never dreamed that there was such nerve and strength in the wrists of that slim gentleman who was so calm and quiet.

Slash, slash, slash! went the whip on the shoulders of the master.

It was useless to cry out.

No one came to his rescue.

The boys stood by passively, no matter how he yelled for help.

"Call Freeman," he shouted, as he was forced to his knees.

"Freeman is safely in custody of my men," returned Reuben, quietly, to this remark, though in a very loud voice so that he should hear it during the repeated castigation. "Don't trouble yourself about him—apologise."

Dr. Carver had by this time nearly lost all heart.

The lashes had descended mercilessly, his sides and shoulders ached, and his head felt bursting.

"Yes," he stammered, "I apologise."

"Before all your school?"

"Yes, before all my school."

"Rise then, coward—villain!" cried Reuben; "be assured I have not done with you yet. My tongue for the moment is tied, and I cannot do by you as I should wish, but the day will yet come when I shall be free to do as I please, and then I will answer for it that a terrible punishment will overtake you."

As he was speaking, Dr. Carver had struggled to his feet and staggered towards his desk.

His hair was roughened, his face in streaks of white and red, and his clothes all in disorder.

He clutched the desk as he reached it, and glanced back vengefully at Reuben.

"Do you think," he cried, furiously, "that I shall ever forget or forgive this? Do you fancy that this brutal assault will pass by unpunished?"

As he was speaking his trembling hand, unobserved by Reuben, was softly gliding into the half-open drawer of the desk.

"I do not suppose you will forget it," said Reuben. "I hope not, but—ah—assassin!"

Assassin truly.

For, as Reuben was speaking, the master of Starvem Hall had drawn a revolver swiftly from his drawer and fired.

The ball whistled perilously near to the head of our hero's devoted uncle.

But Rupert was equal to the occasion.

As he saw the pistol levelled he sprang forward and caught the arm of the schoolmaster.

But too late to stop the ball.

"You young imp, take that!" said the infuriated man, and he aimed a furious blow at Rupert.

Our hero, however, dived and avoided it, and, as he did so, caught Carver between the legs and threw him on his back.

The revolver flew out of his hand, and Reuben, picking it up, threw it through the window after the ruler.

Then catching Carver by the collar, he administered another good thrashing, and then motioned to Rupert and Leigh to come with him.

As they reached the door, he turned and addressed the scholars.

"If, boys," he said, "I had the power to better your lot, I would. At the present moment my hands are tied, and I can do nothing. Of money I could give you in plenty, but you would not be able to spend it. But be assured that what I can do I will do to rid you of the rule of that cowardly tyrant yonder."

As soon as they had gone, Mr. Meekly and Mr. Small, who had been kept outside by one of the village "roughs," rushed in.

In their inmost hearts they were inordinately delighted at the punishment received by their principal.

But, of course, they professed the utmost concern, and with their assistance he was presently conveyed to his bedroom without having to go through the degradation of being seen by his wife or daughters.

"Meekly," he groaned, as he got between the sheets, "and you, Small, listen. I'll double your salary ("He can afford it, considering what we get," thought they), and I'll—I'll see that in future you have plenty of food. But swear that you will help me in having my revenge."

Neither Small nor Meekly felt at all revengeful against Reuben.

He had simply done what they would have liked to have done themselves long since.

Only that they dared not, and so they swore.

"What do you wish us to do?" asked Small.

Carver groaned.

"I should like to kill them both," he growled, "but the law does not allow it."

"You do not generally wait for the permission of the law," suggested Small.

Dr. Carver took this in quite a different sense from what was intended.

He imagined that Small was hinting at the propriety of defying the law, instead of reminding him of the hideous things which had been done in that island prison.

"No, and if you compass the destruction of this Rupert and his supposed father," said he, "I will make your fortunes."

Meekly looked at Small, and Small looked at Meekly.

Assassination for money was not in their line.

But they were afraid to show how shocked they were for fear they might offend him.

"We must think of it," said Small. "It is a thing too serious to dispose of in a moment is the fearful crime of murder."

Doctor Carver was in too much pain

from his castigation to be very sure in his calculations, so he said—

"Get me some Irish whisky, Small, and you Meekly, go and see where Freeman is."

Meekly went off at once to do the bidding of his master.

In reality he knew pretty well what had become of Freeman, for he had seen the landing of the little crew, and was aware that he was utterly powerless to move.

But he was not prepared for the object which he saw.

He found Freeman dripping like a drowned rat, and blood all over his face.

He had attempted to do very much the same thing as his master, but his kind intentions had been nipped in the bud.

One of the stalwart rustics whom Reuben had brought with him had caught him in the act of presenting his gun at the latter and had seized him.

A wink was enough to the others, and in an instant the man who had attempted Rupert's life was thrown into the river.

Strong hands were near, and ready to pull him out of course.

But still when Mr. Meekly arrived the boatkeeper was a most deplorable object.

"Freeman," said the usher, "Doctor Carver wants you."

"Then he'll have to want, and you tell 'im so," growled Freeman. "I've had about enough of this 'ere place lately, and if I'm going to have much more of these 'ere games, I'd rather cut it altogether."

Reuben heard these words as he prepared to enter his boat.

"He's an abominable villain," he whispered to Rupert, "but I think he would be of great service if kept in his proper place. Suppose we bribe him over?"

This was made easier by what followed.

"Shall I tell the doctor," said Mr. Meekly, "or shall I wait here until you are ready?"

"Tell him what you like," growled Freeman, "it doesn't matter to me. I'm going to take a boat and go over to the mainland."

"And when will you return?" suggested the usher mildly.

"Ah, there's no saying that!" said the boatkeeper. "You see, I've taken in a large drop of water, and it'll take a good drop o' rum to mix with it, so I may be late like."

"There's room here in our boat, Freeman," said Reuben. "Jump in, if you like, only be quick."

Freeman hesitated but a moment.

Then he turned jeeringly towards Mr. Meekly.

"Tell Doctor Carver I'm gone for a trip with the strange gen'leman what come about the boys. P'r'aps shan't be back until to-morrow."

And with a malignant grin he entered the boat.

"He is a strange being," said Meekly to himself, as he walked away. "I don't see that Doctor Carver's done anything specially to put him out of temper, except bully him. Well, well, I suppose he goes, as the servant-girls say, to 'better himself.'"

"Rupert," whispered Reuben to Rupert, as they glided out on the surface of the water, "I think we have scored high against your uncle to-day."

"How, Reuben?"

"All this is his doings,' said Reuben. "He will see that he is defeated step by step."

"Yet, Reuben, he will see that we are obliged to work in the dark."

"Yes," said Reuben smilingly, "boring towards the sunlight."

CHAPTER XVII.

A NEW BUT SHADY ALLY—LEIGH GLINDON'S WISH.

As soon as they had landed on the other side, at no great distance from Blakesley Hall Academy, Reuben dismissed his rustics.

He gave them money in addition to their promised reward, and they went away delighted.

They had expected a rough time of it,

and instead they had had simply the amusement of ducking Freeman.

"Be's ye wanting us again, mister?" said one of them, grinning broadly.

"No, not at present," replied Reuben, with a smile, "but perhaps in the future I may find something for you to do. Now, Freeman, although you tried to blow my brains out——"

"No, I didn't do as bad as that," said the man sheepishly. "I'm sure——"

"There, say no more about it now," returned Reuben. "Meet me at the 'Falcon Inn,' at Seabourne, to-night at eight o'clock, and I'll explain something to you. Here is some silver, but don't drink too much, or our interview will be of no avail."

And without waiting for thanks, he moved away.

".How degrading it is to me, Rupert," he said, as they walked on, "to be compelled to lower myself, as it were, to the level of these men! How I hope it will not be for long!"

"I hope not, indeed, Reuben," said our hero. "I feel as if you were doing too much for me. After all the years you have toiled and slaved for me, I begin to wish to make some return. The only one I can make is to persuade you to give up so perilous a task, and retire with me to some other part of dear old England, where you can set me to work at something which will enable me in some way to pay you for all your devotion."

Reuben patted him on the head.

"No, Rupert," he said "I remember the past, and the solemn vow I swore to your father—no, no, boy! Hand-in-hand we began, hand-in-hand we'll go on."

They had reached at this moment the cross-roads.

Here Leigh Glindon paused.

Fortunately for Reuben and Rupert he had not heard their conversation.

He, in fact, had been too wrapped up in his own miseries, his hopeless future and his viewless past.

"Excuse me, Rupert," he said, "will you explain to your father that I must part from you here, and I have taken courage to ask a great favour of him."

"A favour of me, my boy," said Reuben, with an amused smile.

"Yes, sir," replied Leigh, flushing;

"I must leave you here, and I have no where to go to. I have no friends. I do not even know who placed me at the school on the island. So, as I must go somewhere to get work, will you kindly lend me a few shillings to make a start with, and I will honestly repay you."

Reuben did not laugh now.

He took the boy by both hands and shook them warmly.

"Leigh," he said, "you are a good and a brave young fellow. You have befriended Rupert manfully, and as you have no friends, you must allow me to act as your guardian until we can ferret out your real position. Until then you must go to Blakesley Hall School, and do your best to learn and look after Rupert. After all that has happened he needs as much protection as he can get. Don't refuse. Some day I'll tell you how to repay me tenfold."

Leigh did not refuse.

But he was too overwhelmed to say much.

He stammered forth a few words of thanks, and then taking Rupert's arm walked on.

The afternoon was very pleasant.

So it was towards evening when they once more entered the academy.

Dr. Walton was astounded at what he heard.

"You have made a most desperate enemy," he said.

"Yes, I am aware of that," replied Reuben. '"But he is only one added to a long list, so I am not afraid. I must ask you, however, to keep a more careful watch over Rupert than ever. I fear he will need it.".

"Take every care of yourself, my dear boy," said his cousin, as they parted at the school-gate. "You will require every precaution."

"Be not afraid, dear Reuben," he said. "I will be cautious for your sake, though I do not believe that Ralph Pendarven knows anything about the matter."

"Nor I, Rupert," replied his cousin. "It is not very likely that he would be entrusted with the secret that his father is an assassin. Good-bye. May Heaven be your protector!"

"Good-bye, dear Reuben."

And so, with a warm hand-clasp, they parted.

Things went on pretty much the same as usual at Blakesley Hall Academy.

Leigh Glindon had been taken into the school at the request of, and under the guardianship of Reuben, *alias* Col. Gerald Clifford, and had created some degree of interest among the scholars.

His face was not a common one, and many of the boys at once recognised him as one of the Hungry School which had feasted with them in the woods.

How he came at the academy was a mystery.

"My friends thought it better I should be here," he said when questioned. "I know no more. I do not pry into matters that do not concern me."

It was Ralph Pendarven whom he addressed, and that worthy looked unutterable things.

But Leigh, whose appearance was wonderfully improved, did not look by any means the kind of adversary whom Ralph would like to tackle, and so he had to grin and bear the insult as best he could.

But we must pass on to other incidents.

For some time past it had become evident to all the boys that a thief was in the house somewhere.

Not a thief who purloined valuables, such as watches, or rings, or chains, or clothes, be it said.

No.

It was a paltry thief, who stole cakes and sweets, and so on.

A council of war therefore was held in the dormitory.

In Rupert's room the boys were considered to be beyond suspicion.

"There is no doubt there is a thief in the place," said Rupert, "but the thing is to catch him."

"That may be easier than we think," said Ralph. "The thefts have only taken place very recently."

And he cast an insulting glance towards Leigh Glindon.

"Perhaps you have taken the things yourself," said Rupert calmly, "as you know so much about them."

He had long since ceased to care what he said to Ralph.

And he would not stand by and see his friend grossly insulted.

"Be careful what you say, Clifford," cried Ralph, with flushed face. "I'm not obliged to put up with your insults."

"Don't let's quarrel," said Ship Ahoy. "Avast there, I say. Let's anchor in peace, and stow our jawing-tackle while Rupert gives us his ideas."

This speech restored the boys' usual light-heartedness, and Rupert said—

"Well, I don't say that I have any very special thing to propose. The only idea that really suggests itself to me is that we should resolve ourselves into a kind of detective force, and keep on the watch for a week. This day week we'll meet again and report progress."

"But if anyone finds him out in the meantime?" said Leigh.

"Then let him out with his name at once," said Rupert, "otherwise we will keep silence, and work—each in his own groove."

This was unanimously agreed to.

Well, the week went by.

The boys kept to their compact.

Not a word was said in regard to the business on hand.

Perhaps there were a few mysterious looks and words.

But that was all.

At length the eagerly expected evening came.

All went to bed as the hour struck to the minute.

The door was fastened after a good look-out had been taken outside, and then Rupert, standing on a chair, said—

"Gentlemen and schoolmates, I can save you a great deal of trouble by stating at once that I have discovered the thief."

"Discovered him!" repeated many eager voices.

"Yes," said Rupert, "I have. It is no other than Bill Bradford, the page."

A universal exclamation of astonishment greeted this statement.

"What—Buttons?"

"Yes, no other than Buttons I caught him in the act."

"But how? Oh, do tell us all."

"I will," said Rupert. "In the first place I had no suspicion whatever of Buttons.

"I began yesterday to fear that we should all be made fools of.

"But as I came up the stairs from the basement, I saw a form suddenly dart from the open door of a room, and rush through the entrance to the playground.

"I knew him at once.

"It was Bill Bradford."

"Did you clap on all sail and pursue e pirate?" said Ship Ahoy.

"No," said Rupert, laughing. "I was going to, and then I thought it was better to cast anchor, as you would say, and think.

"At last I came to the conclusion that I would put something for him to take, and so I posted off to my box and got some cakes."

"El Dorado found at last!" cried the comic boy, cutting a caper on his bed.

"Yes, I got the cakes," said Rupert, not heeding the interruption, "and placed them in a bag just by the side of the schoolroom door, as if they had been dropped there in a hurry.

"After this I got behind the door and kept as quiet as a mouse.

"Presently I heard the sound of approaching footsteps.

"The witching moment had come."

"Ha, ha," laughed the comic boy, "quite a romance. What journal are you going to send it to?"

"Please shut up," said Rupert, laughing, "or you'll never hear the end. What's the use of a thrilling story if you don't hear what happens to all the characters?"

"All hands aft, if you're going to make a disturbance on the quarterdeck," said Ship Ahoy. "Silence!"

And silence it was.

"Well, to resume," said Rupert, "you see I must tell you all, for, to a certain extent, you are his judges, and consequently, you are bound to know all about it."

"Quite right. Steer ahead," said Ship Ahoy.

"I heard the footsteps then," continued our hero, "and then they stopped outside the half-open door.

"I crept closer behind the door.

"He pushed it slightly open, and glanced round.

"Of course the more he pushed the more he concealed me.

"'Ha!' he grinned. 'Unexpected plums are always good.'

"And then he picked up the bag.

"'Have you got anything nice there?' I said in a hollow voice.

"His back was turned to me, and he started with an 'Oh,' facing me now with a cake in his mouth, and the bag distended with good fare.

"'Never mind, Buttons,' I said. 'Give me a bit.'

"'Yes, here's a cake, Master Clifford,' he said. 'They're awful good. I found 'em.'

"And I think he was going to make me any amount of promises, when I heard a heavy tread.

"'We must bolt,' I said. 'Here's Mr. Lyttleton or the doctor.'

"And he bolted.

"Now, boys, having told you this much," said Rupert, "I'm going to tell you how to give him such a severe punishing that he will never forget it."

CHAPTER XVIII.

BILLY BRADFORD GETS A SHOCK.

WHATEVER the proposition was that Rupert proposed to his schoolmates for the punishment of Bill Bradford, it received approbation among the boys in the dormitory, and all details were left in his hands.

Whatever these details were they evidently included a visit to the kitchen, and a long "confab" with the cook, and the other servants.

There he experienced a little difficulty.

But a little persuasion, and a little "palm oil" was at last successful, and everything having been properly prepared and arranged, Bill Bradford was left to his own sweet devices.

Rupert was quite right in pitching upon him as the thief.

His mania was for food.

Nothing in the shape of comestibles was safe against him.

"All was fish that came to his net."

Bill Bradford coming into the kitchen "on the pick," as the cook would have expressed it, found her asleep in the easy-chair near the fire.

Bill looked everywhere around.

Not a sign of anything in the way of food was visible.

Disgusted he turned away, and with his lamp in his hand, he proceeded towards the stairs to go on a voyage of discovery in the upper part of the building.

To do this he had to pass the pantry door.

"Gracious me! What's that?" he cried, involuntarily. "Oh, my."

Well might he make an exclamation of some sort.

The pantry door was open.

Never had such a chance been in his hands before.

His mind was made up.

But first he must reconnoitre.

He went back on tiptoe towards the kitchen and peered in.

All was still.

At least with the exception of the peculiar tune to which Anne the cook-maid sent her pigs to market.

"I'll chance it!" he said.

And drawing the door gently to after him, he proceeded towards the pantry.

The key was in the lock.

He took it out, placed it on the inside, entered and fastened himself in.

"Now for a feast."

Placing his lamp on a niche destined for the purpose he glanced round him.

The prospect was indeed a tempting one.

On every side was nothing but the food which was Billy's "god."

Newly-baked loaves of home-made bread, tempting butter, biscuits, jams, marmalades, sugar, juicy joints, cheese —many of the jars open.

"My!" cried Bill, seizing a large spoon, and driving it into the jam-jar. "That's prime."

With his mouth full of the succulent preserve, he looked about him to see what should be his next delight.

He ate a few biscuits by way of keeping his stomach in tone, and then applied to the marmalade.

This was delicious.

At least so thought Billy Bradford.

"Well I never!" he spluttered, gulping down a goodly mouthful of the preserved orange, "what carelessness to leave the door open. They'll never suspect me, for I've never let them see I like jam. They'll remember leaving the door on the jar, because they'll miss the key and think of it, and so the boys will be accused. Never mind, they wouldn't get the sack and I should."

A large tart had now disappeared.

This did not seem in any way to appease the appetite of the gourmand.

Increase of appetite grew with what it fed on.

A taste here and a taste there ; and then he espied a bottle of ginger wine.

In an instant this was seized, and being conveniently uncorked, was raised eagerly to his lips.

A goodly draught warmed his stomach and revived his spirits.

"I wish I could eat everything here that's open," he said, with a deep sigh, " but I suppose that would be impossible. Dear me, I shall never have such another chance. That jam's lovely. I don't think it could hurt me to have just a little more."

The boy who, with his greediness and his libations, began to feel very strange, took accordingly another large mouthful of jam, when, just as he held the glass jar on the edge of the shelf, a hollow groan was heard.

Smash went the jar. Such a smash too.

The hair of Billy Bradford began to rise on ends.

His puffy cheeks grew pale.

"What could the sound be?" was his first thought.

The second thought was—

"If that crash is heard—what am I to do or say?"

He stood listening intently.

Then, as no one seemed inclined to come in quest of the disturbance, he pulled himself together, took another draught of the ginger-wine to rouse up his lost courage once more, and sat down on a stool."

"Well, I wish I hadn't heard that horrible sound," he said, half aloud. "It's made me tremble all over like. I ought to be off now and leave the door open, so that when they come in and find the jar smashed, they will think it is the——' '

"Devil!" said a deep and hollow voice.

"Oh, Lor'! oh, Lor'!" cried the boy, leaping up, "someone calling——"

"Old Nick!" cried another voice.

And then a dim, phosphorescent light began to show itself through the pantry, and the lamp went out.

"Prepare for judgment," said a horrid whisper in his ear.

And something clammy touched his cheek.

The boy shuddered and uttered a choking cry in his terror.

"Oh, dear, oh, Lor'! What can it all mean?" he groaned.

And then, with tottering steps, he began making his way towards the door.

But at this moment a white form, a ghostly, ghastly form, began to rise slowly from the floor.

It was not possessed of any particular contour.

It was far more like the "shapeless mass" in Byron's "Manfred."

It rose slowly and glidingly, while gibbering sounds seemed to hover around in the air.

When it had apparently reached its full height, it raised a horrid long skeleton hand, and the same icy whisper said—

"Seize the thief!"

The skinny fingers shot forward, and Billy Bradford, uttering a cry of terror, shrill and piercing, fell to the ground.

In an instant the lamp was re-lit, the ghost cast off the white garment with which it had been enveloped, and revealed the grinning features of the comic boy, while Rupert, our hero, rose from another corner.

If they had indulged in their laughter they might have roused the page-boy too soon, and so they repressed their merriment, but it was a matter of great difficulty to do so.

However, they somehow succeeded, and were able to survey by the light of the lamp the absurd object which lay extended on the floor.

He looked, of course, as if some horrible accident had occurred to him.

The jam was plastered on his head, and intermingled with his hair, and had smeared itself all over his neck and a part of his collar.

"It's all right," said Rupert; "things couldn't have happened better. Where's the red ink?"

Lewis quickly whipped this out of his pocket.

"There you are," he said, "as right as ninepence. Shall I do the deed?"

"Yes, only let the cold stuff wake him up," said Rupert; "be careful, and I'll hold the light."

As he threw the rays of the lamp on the insensible lad (insensible now from the effects of the wine) Lewis Allenby besmeared the victim's face and hands with the ink so as to resemble the "out-pouring of the life stream," as he termed it.

When he had completed his task Billy Bradford did look a strange object.

No one coming in on the instant would have doubted that he had met with some terrible accident.

"I think it is all right now," said Rupert; "let us go. He seems to be getting restless."

So out they crept.

They took the lamp with them, and with all the ghost materials they took their way upstairs.

They were determined that they would give no one the chance of discovering them, and they knew that their plan had succeeded.

After awhile Billy Bradford roused himself.

His senses coming back to him, he slowly raised himself and glanced around.

All was in utter darkness.

"Where am I?" was his first thought. "I hope I ain't in prison."

He put his hand up to his head, which ached very badly.

Of course he instantly encountered the mass of jam—clammy, sticky, and wet.

"There's been a haccident," he cried. "I've been and broke my 'ead, I expects."

Then he slowly rose, and groped about for a light, but of course his efforts were in vain.

His heart began to beat wildly with horror, his limbs were weak and tottering, and his stomach was afflicted by a dull aching pain.

"I have had some awful fall," he groaned, "and cracked my nut. I must try and get into the kitchen, at any rate."

Slowly, and feeling his way by painful

degrees, he at length reached the kitchen door and peered in.

Anne, the cookmaid, was still sitting in her place near the fire.

"Anne," cried the disconsolate lad, as he made his way towards the sleeping girl.

The boy's voice roused her at once, and she looked up with her big, good-looking, sleepy hazel eyes.

Only for a moment did she glance in the direction of Billy Bradford.

Then she uttered a shrill shriek of horror, and rushing to the bell-pull that communicated with the servants' bed-rooms, tugged at it vigorously, crying as she did so—

"Heaven's sakes! don't come near me. I can't a-bear blood, and never could. Oh, dear, oh, dear! what have you been a-doin'?"

"I feel nearly dead," groaned Billy, subsiding, jam and all, into a chair, for his stomach began to feel in terrible pain.

"Yes, but what 'ave you been a-doin'?" reiterated the girl.

"I don't know," groaned Billy.

He did not exactly know what to say.

He was aware, of course, that sooner or later the discovery must be made in regard to the pantry thefts.

But he had no fear of being accused.

He had a fixed idea that he had split his head open, and had injured himself internally, but of the fact that his head was simply smeared all over in jam he was utterly ignorant.

As he mused upon his peculiar position, and rapidly became more and more in pain, the sound of hurrying feet was heard, and the other servants came rushing in.

The cook, a jolly, middle-aged woman, stood for a moment wrapped in astonishment, and then burst into a roar of laughter.

"Why, bless me, Billy, what 'ave you been doin'?" she cried; "putting your head in a jam pot?"

"Jam pot?" said Billy, indignantly, though the words made him tremble, and caused him to become much worse internally, "I don't know nothin' about jam pots. What I does know is that I've bin and knocked my brains out."

"Never giv' ye any credit for any, Billy," said Jemima, the housemaid;

"howsumever, if them's brains, they're a very curious colour."

"Look in the glass," said Mrs. Adams, the cook, giving him a hand-glass.

Billy's eyes goggled more than ever when he saw the figure he cut in the mirror.

What could he say?

"But I am bleeding at the neck somewhere," he said; "look at my collar."

"The very best red ink," said Mrs. Adams. "I begin to suspect something, girls. Don't let this fellow go. I'm going to the pantry."

It is doubtless thoroughly understood by my readers that Mrs. Adams was in the secret of Billy Bradford's punishment.

It was she, of course, who had purposely left the pantry door open.

Rupert and his confederates provided the tempting jars of jam and marmalade, and the ginger wine.

But Mrs. Adams was in her way a very good actress. She uttered a cry of horror when she saw the jam and glass scattered about the floor, the marmalade half eaten, and the ginger wine half drunk.

She called all the others to the scene of the disaster.

"The young reptile!" she cried, as the other servants came in. "The thievin' young varmint. I'll pay him out for it."

And she rushed back to the kitchen, where she had left Billy Bradford.

He was bad enough when she quitted the room, but now he was writhing on the floor in awful agony.

"I hope those boys haven't gone too far," muttered cooky. "I must see Dr. Walton."

She did so at once.

As agreed upon, the whole story was told.

Although the worthy schoolmaster laughed at first, he looked serious over the fact of Billy's great agony.

"Well, Mrs. Adams," he said, "I certainly think this punishment serves the boy right. But boys are not very good hands at administering medicine, and perhaps they have overdone it. I must come down and see."

On his way down he went into Rupert's room.

"Master Clifford," he said, "I know all your arrangements for this evening, and I am not prepared to say that you have not acted perfectly right, but I am afraid you have put too much jalap in the jam, and so forth."

"I hope not, sir," said Rupert, whose cheeks were tingling at being interrogated on the subject, although he may be said to have expected it. "We acted, as we thought, for the best. The robberies have been going on for a long time, but we didn't want to complain to you, sir, so we thought we would try and cure him ourselves."

"Just tell me the whole affair, and how much jalap you placed in the jars."

Rupert told him.

"Dear me!" exclaimed the doctor, with an amused smile. "The boy will have to take to his bed for a day or two. There is no doubt of that. But serve him right. He ought to be discharged at once."

"Oh, no, sir, don't do that," said Rupert. "That is what we didn't wish to do. Bradford is very obliging and willing, and we don't never lose money or anything of that kind, but when we couldn't keep a cake or a biscuit or an orange, we thought we'd punish him ourselves."

"Just so," said the doctor. "I think now I'll go and see him."

He descended at once.

But no Billy Bradford was to be seen.

He had disappeared suddenly.

And when next time he was discovered, he looked very much like the ghost that frightened him.

Next morning he was quite unable to get up and perform his duties, but Dr. Walton took the opportunity of seeing him and explaining the meaning of the "dosing" he had received.

"Of course," he said, "it will be a warning to you in future."

And Billy Bradford promised that it would, and in this promise all firmly believed.

CHAPTER XIX.

IN WHICH A NEW BOY IS INTRODUCED INTO THE SCHOOL, AND A NEW PERIL ARISES FOR OUR HERO.

DR. WALTON was in his study and the boys out at play, when the sound of wheels grating over the broad, gravelly road roused him from his somnolescent reading of an old classical work.

Going to the window, he saw approaching a lumbering vehicle of the hackney coach type.

"Some new boy, I expect," he said. "Bless me, yes; I forgot. A Mr. Hardwicke said he was coming here with his son some time in June."

He saw a man and a boy descend quickly and come up the steps.

Presently the bell rang, and in a few moments a servant appeared at the study door to summon the doctor.

He went down, as usual, all smiles.

The person who had brought the boy with him was a man somewhat under forty years of age, with black hair, a swarthy complexion, eyes like dark beads, and a broad and heavily-built form.

His nose was apparently spoiled by continuous battles, and his mouth was concealed partially by his beard and moustache.

His companion was a boy about sixteen.

His hair was ashen, his complexion a dull, freckled yellow, his eyes round and yet snaky, his nose a pug, his mouth coarse and heavy, his ears abnormally large.

His figure and way of moving about was what could best be described as "lollopy," but yet there were evidences of latent strength.

Dr. Walton, surprised out of his usual decorum, paused a moment before he spoke.

The awkward pause was broken by the elder visitor.

"Doctor Walton, I presume?" he said, bowing deeply.

"That is my name, sir," replied the principal. "Pray be seated."

The stranger did so.

"You have brought me a new pupil, I presume?" added Dr. Walton.

"Yes. You had my letter, I suppose. My name is Hardwicke."

"Yes; and this young gentleman?"

It almost choked the schoolmaster to utter the words.

"This is Joshua," said the man. "You see his education has been greatly neglected."

"Just so."

At which Joshua grinned.

"Yes," pursued Hardwicke, "he is not my son, but my nephew. None of us are up to much as regards education and that kind of thing, but when my brother died and left me this 'ere lad he made me promise that I'd see arter him. Tisn't because I'm ignorant like myself that I need bring up my nephew the same."

"Not at all."

"Well, so I've brought Joshua here," continued the man. "We've made a goodish bit of money one way and another, and so cash will not stand in the way of his getting on. What are your terms—parlour-board, of course, you know?"

"Well, my terms are rather high, Mr. Hardwicke," the doctor said. "You see, we endeavour to the utmost of our power to keep the academy select, and I never take any young gentleman without the most special references."

Mr. Hardwicke smiled blandly.

"Certainly—excellent plan," he said. "Here are my references. One you will see is from the Reverend Doctor Craig, vicar of this parish, and the other is from Mr. Hubert Pendarven, of Pendarven Abbey."

Dr. Walton started visibly as his visitor said the last words.

He knew that some mysterious connection existed between our hero Rupert and these Pendarvens of the Abbey, and to have such a peculiar scholar foisted upon him by a reference from Mr. Hubert seemed a strange coincidence indeed.

He took the references, however, and perused them.

Nothing could be better.

There was no possibility of refusal.

So he brightened up.

"Ah," he said, "these are very satisfactory, very—couldn't be better. When does the young gentleman desire to begin his studies?"

"At once," said Mr. Hardwicke. "I have brought his trunks with me."

There was no getting out of it.

He must, under all the circumstances, accept the lad into the school.

"Very well," returned he, putting on his usual blandness like a cloak, which he had for a moment set aside. "I shall be most happy to introduce Master Joshua to the school. Meanwhile, here is a list of my terms."

Mr. Hardwicke took the printed form, and saw that the terms for parlour-boarders were a hundred and twenty guineas per annum.

"Ah, a good sum," he said, producing his purse—a very large leather affair— "keeps out the people you don't want."

"Just what it doesn't seem to do," thought Dr. Walton.

"Here are sixty guineas—half a year in advance."

"Thank you," said Dr. Walton, somewhat taken aback by the munificence of the vulgar party against whom he had taken such a dislike. "I will make you out a receipt."

"And Joshua," said Mr. Hardwicke, turning to the boy, "while we are speaking of money, here are three sovereigns for you. When you want more you know where to write to."

"Right you are, nunkey," said the lad, with a grin.

Mr. Hardwicke rose, bade Joshua "good-bye," told him to be a good boy and keep his wits about him, shook hands with Dr. Walton, much against his will, and then departed.

As soon as Hardwicke had departed the schoolmaster asked Joshua several questions, with a view to ascertain if he knew anything at all.

He did, if slang is anything.

He was ignorant, low and brutal in his general conception of things.

And it seemed a despairing sort of affair dreaming of making anything of him.

"You don't seem to have been taught anything," said Dr. Walton. "Didn't you ever go to school?"

"Yes, but the chap never learned me nothin'," replied the hopeful scholar.

"Dear me, what ignorance!" said the horrified principal. "What on earth have you been spending your time on until this age?"

"'YOU SHALL NEVER LEAVE THIS ROAD ALIVE!' CRIED FRED.'"

"Barge-boats and coal heavin', and so on," said the boy, "but that didn't pay, and I was goin' to take my hook to London, when Mr.—I mean Uncle Joe— picked me up and gave me these 'ere new togs, and told me I was to go to school, and be made a scholar."

"Your father is pretty well off now, I suppose?" said Dr. Walton, who felt a cold perspiration breaking out all over him at the thought of this boy mixing with his young gentlemen.

"Don't know; 'specs he is," said Joshua, with a broad and evil grin. "He's abroad somewares—got a Government berth."

"Ah," thought Dr. Walton, "then he can't be much like his brother."

But he said aloud—

"Well, my boy, I suppose you want to get on as well as you can."

"Oh, yes, sir."

He said this seriously.

Perhaps he thought he had done enough grinning for the time being.

"Then be advised by me," returned the doctor. "Nearly all my scholars are educated, and it will be bad for you if they find that you have been so neglected."

A heavy, brutal scowl passed across the brow of Joshua Hardwicke, disfiguring it sadly, and imparting to it an evil look, which almost made Dr. Walton shudder.

But it went away as swiftly as it came.

"I understand what you mean," he said; "they'd jeer me like, and try and make me feel uncomfortable. Never fear. I'll keep as quiet as I can. But, Lor', sir, you needn't be in no flurry. I'll soon learn."

This was said with a cheery vulgarity which under other circumstances would have been amusing.

But it made Dr. Walton shiver.

"Just stay here a moment, Master Hardwicke," he said, for he had had just about enough conversation with his new scholar. "In a few minutes you shall be introduced to your young friends."

And he quitted the room.

"I'll let Lyttleton have the job of introducing this uncouth cub to the scholars," he said. "Dear me! what could have possessed the vicar to have recommended me such a pupil?"

The thoughts of the youngster who rejoiced for the nonce in the name of Joshua Hardwicke—whatever his real name might be—were of a far different nature.

He threw himself down in the capacious arm-chair, and surveyed the surroundings with the air of a connoisseur.

"This is prime," he said to himself, as his eyes fell upon the well-matched furniture of the reception-room, the paintings, and the glass, and the china —"this is prime. I think I'll make my job as long as I can. Only think of this turning up just at the very moment when I thought I should have to make a flit. I wonder what sort of a chap this is that I have got to keep my eye on. Expect I'll be able to wollop him if he turns rusty."

Just at this moment Rupert, sitting on a piece of wall which overlooked the lane leading to the town, saw the man Hardwicke being driven away from the schoolhouse.

He recognised him at once.

It was Hugh Blacklock.

Of course our hero knew nothing of what had happened in the schoolhouse.

What could he want with the doctor?

There was one thing certain: Hugh Blacklock was his enemy.

Yet what was he to do?

He dared not make known his fears to Dr. Walton, because he knew not how far Reuben had confided in him.

No. He must wait and watch.

Meanwhile Tobias Lyttleton came up to the room where Joshua was sitting.

"Good afternoon, Master Hardwicke," he said, as he entered. "Doctor Walton tells me you wish to be introduced to your schoolfellows."

"I do that," said the youth, not troubling to move from the easy position he had assumed in the chair.

Tobias had been told a good deal by Dr. Walton.

What he saw was worse.

"Come along, then, with me," he said. "Your schoolfellows are all in the playground, and I can introduce you to them at once."

Up jumped Joshua.

"I hope they're jolly coves," he said. "You ain't a bad old sort yourself from the look on ye."

Long Toby reddened.

"I think I shall give notice to leave,"

he said to himself. "It will be only hastening things on a little. This way, Master Hardwicke," he added aloud.

Dr. Walton, well concealed behind the heavy curtains of the dining-room which overlooked the recreation grounds, watched eagerly the reception accorded by his scholars to the new-comer.

His eyes were fixed upon the playground. He saw Tobias Lyttleton issue forth from the house and introduce Joshua to a group of astonished schoolboys.

Then he saw Joshua describe what is known in street phraseology as a "catherine wheel," and heard his coarse and dissonant voice exclaim—

"Here I am, boys."

Then he saw him pull up right in front of Rupert, and stand as if petrified with surprise.

"Danger to Rupert Clifford! I knew it—I knew it!" cried Dr. Walton, half aloud. "But I will watch over him."

CHAPTER XX.

TURNING THE TABLES.

THE advent of such a peculiar scholar as Joshua was quite an event at Blakesley Hall Academy.

"Whatever can be the meaning of letting such a fellow as that into the school," was the general thought. "Doctor Walton must be very hard up."

It did appear strange indeed.

But the first surprise over, the scholars began to enjoy the joke.

"Well, and who are you?" asked the comic boy. "Is your lordship the son of King Copnetua, or are you a relation of the young lady of lowly birth who so struck his fancy?"

Joshua Hardwicke glanced at the speaker in astonishment.

And then with a bellow of laughter he cried—

"Don't talk Chinee, let's have a game o' marbles. I aller's like marbles 'cos I wins."

"Oh, you allers wins, do you," cried Rupert, who had very little conception of what the advent of this rough and vulgar boy meant to him. "Well, come and have a game with me then."

"Right you are," said Joshua.

And he at once pulled from his pocket a large bag, which was found to be well supplied with alleys and marbles, and bonsors, and so forth.

"What do you play for?"

"I don't know what you mean," said Rupert, "we play for marbles here."

"Oh, we play for money in London," said Joshua, producing some cash—loose silver and coppers.

"Ah, we don't gamble here," said Rupert. "We come here to learn manners as well as Greek and Latin. If you contracted such a bad habit as that of gambling in London, you'll soon get out of it here."

And he walked off.

"Well, he is a queer un," said Joshua. "Are all you fellows as soft as that?"

A general chorus of laughter followed this appeal, and Ralph Pendarven said—

"I fancy you've come to the wrong place here. You'll have to mend your manners before you get on at this establishment."

For a moment Joshua felt abashed.

So he said in a humble voice—

"I'm sure I'm very sorry if I've been a sayin' or a doin' anything wrong. But I'll try and do my best. Is your name Ralph Pendarven?"

"It is," cried Ralph, starting.

Joshua's greeny-snaky eyes glistened.

"I'm on the right scent already," he thought.

"Well, I have a message for you from a friend," said Joshua.

"A message for me!" exclaimed Ralph, in disgust at the very idea of having the remotest connection with such a being as Joshua.

"Yes, can you give us five minutes?"

"Be quick about it then," said Ralph. "I want to join the lads at play."

"It is only this," said Joshua. "A person who can tell you a great secret, a real down-right one, wants to see you to-morrow for a few minutes. Only remember 'mum's' the word."

"Where does he wish to see me?" asked Ralph, all his boyish curiosity aroused.

"Anywheres you like," said Joshua.

"Who is it, and what is his name?" asked Ralph. "I don't like seeing mysterious people."

"Ah, you're mighty particular I expect," said the other. "I'll tell you his name, but I don't think you'll know him any the better when I do. He's a party by the name of Blacklock."

"Blacklock!" cried Ralph, slightly changing colour. "Yes, I do know a person of that name well. He is a gentleman who is very fond of hunting, and often comes to my father's place."

Joshua grinned.

"Well," he said, "I don't know so much about his being a gentleman, that's just as you like to say, but he's the chap as wants to see ye about three o'clock or later on. He leaves it to you to name the time and place."

Ralph felt somewhat mystified.

Should he go or not?

"Why cannot I see him openly?" he asked. "He could call at the school, and I am sure Doctor Walton would not object to his seeing me at any time."

"Ah, but ye see this 'ere's a private affair, and he don't want anyone to see 'im," said Joshua. "He says it's werry much to your advantage."

Ralph was aware that there was some mystery connected with his family.

And perhaps there might be a message from his father.

"Yes, I will see Mr. Blacklock," he said. "I will be in the plantation at the back of the grounds at five o'clock. Just yonder, where the beeches are."

"Right you are," said Joshua; "he shall get a message from me fust thing in the morning. And now for Rupert! What crackjaw names they do have to be sure. Why can't they be contented with plain Josh or Bill?"

With this reflection he proceeded hurriedly in the direction of the spot where Rupert was talking to some friends.

They were engaged, in fact, in arranging about a boating match, which was soon coming off on the river Arrow.

"Can I have a word with you?" said unabashed Joshua. "I shan't detain you long—as the hangman said to the convict."

Rupert eyed him in disgust.

"I hope you will not," said Rupert. "Is it anything very particular?"

"It is, or ought to be to you," returned Joshua, "but it can keep."

And he turned away.

Nobody seemed to take any notice of him.

He had succeeded in making himself obnoxious to all the boys who had yet seen him by his manner.

Joshua, however, seemed proof against everything.

He went away, sat down on a mound a short way off, and watched the group of boys.

"If he won't listen to me," said he, with a spiteful intonation in his voice, "I'll make him smart for it, 'cos I'll tell all I know before the other boys."

But he was not offered the chance.

After the boys had settled their arrangements for the coming boatrace, Rupert strolled towards the new boy.

Joshua sat still and did not offer to rise as our hero approached.

He resolved to let Rupert open the ball himself.

The gipsy schoolboy lost no time in doing so.

"What is it you want to say to me?" he said. "I can't see that you have anything private to say to me."

"Yes, I have," said Joshua. "You're blessed with a short memory, and I'm not."

"Out with it, then," said Rupert, somewhat angrily, for he was one who hated concealment, and was anxious that everything should be fair and above board.

"Don't you remember me?"

"I do not."

"Well, I do you."

"When did you meet me, then?"

"At Hadley Fair."

Rupert flushed slightly.

Joshua saw that he had touched a chord of memory.

"Ah, you remember, I see," cried Joshua. "Well, two years ago, I was at Hadley Fair and a boy struck me with a stone, and you prevented me from giving him a good hiding."

"Certainly, I remember it all now," said Rupert. "You had been annoying the boy by throwing water over him, and by many other things, and then, because he complained of it, you set upon him like a brute beast. And so I stopped you at it, just as I would do again."

"Oh, you would, would you ?" said Joshua, looking down from his height contemptuously upon the lesser form of Rupert. "I don't think you'd find that pay. I've had a good many hard knocks in the world since the time when I saw you, and I've got in the way of giving them back."

"I'm not in the least afraid of you," said Rupert. "You'll find that I'm not to be brow-beaten, no matter how big my enemy may happen to be."

Joshua laughed.

"It takes you such a long time to say 'who's afraid,'" he cried. "But I ain't a-talking of that particular, though I daresay as I could hold my own with anyone who tried his games on with me. No, if you're a-going to stick yerself up as everybody, why, I knows a secret about you, and I shan't be off telling it."

Rupert laughed.

But he felt uncomfortable.

His life at Blakesley Hall Academy had not been so rosy that he need be regardless of everything that seemed to threaten him.

"Well, tell away," he cried, "there's no secret that I mind you telling."

"Don't be too sure of that," replied Joshua. "In the first place your name isn't Rupert Clifford."

"What is it, then ?"

"It's Rupert Lee, or somethin' of that sort," returned the boy. "You're only a gipsy. Why, I knew ye quite well when you were livin' about the fields and lanes."

Rupert reddened.

"If I chose to be with the gipsies it was quite of my free will," he said. "What does it matter to you ?"

"I don't say it does, but it matters to the other boys, I'll be bound," replied Joshua sneeringly.

"They wouldn't care one way or the other," returned Rupert. "They know that when I came to this place I was a well-educated gentleman, and so it doesn't matter to any one of them where I got my learning."

"Oh, I don't know," said Joshua; "they seem to me to be a jolly lot of prigs, and just the ones who'd round on you if they knew you'd been really followin' the caravans all yer life. Howsomever, I ain't forgotten that 'ere day at Hadley Fair, and if I can only find the chance of having my revenge, you make your mind up I will."

Rupert smiled at this.

A new idea had sprung into his brain.

So little accustomed was he to the meaner forms of revenge, that it had not occurred to him before.

But now it would have to be a case of diamond cut diamond.

"You say I am here on false pretences," he said.

"Yes."

"Then my answer is, so are you false and villainous."

This was a hit for Joshua.

But he only coloured a little.

"How's that ?" he said.

"You are here under the name of Hardwicke."

"Yes."

"You are supposed to be the nephew of Robert Hardwicke."

"Yes."

"That was Hardwicke—your uncle—that brought you here in a hackney carriage this morning."

"Of course it was."

"Then," said Rupert, "you're telling me falsehoods, and are here under false pretences, for whatever your name may be, it is not the name of the man who brought you here. His name is Hugh Blacklock."

"I don't know what you mean," said Joshua, confused. "You didn't even see him."

The words were uttered deliberately enough.

But it was evident that Rupert had hit the right nail on the head.

"Oh, yes, I did," returned our hero. "I saw him as I stood on the ruined wall yonder—saw him leave the school and come by me in a hackney carriage. I know him of old as a vagabond—an enemy of my father and of myself—and I shall be on the watch."

This was turning the tables with a vengeance.

Joshua felt for the moment beaten.

He knew, however, that he had had

carte blanche given him to carry out his evil designs against our hero, and consequently the only thing to be done was to wait and be on the alert.

"Do as you please," said Joshua. "I shouldn't ha' never spoke, only you rounded on me directly I came into the school. I wasn't grand enough, ye see, for the likes of you—a gipsy boy."

And seeing a light come into the eyes of Rupert, which, in spite of his own

size, he didn't like, he turned on his heel, and went quickly away.

"He's sent here as a spy, or worse," thought Rupert, "but I'll be even with him."

"He's mighty cheeky," was the inward idea of Joshua, "but I shall soon take him down a peg or two. He isn't everybody if he is the heir to some coin. Well, he won't be heir much longer, or live much longer, if my plan's all right."

CHAPTER XXI.

THE MISSING CERTIFICATE—FRESH PERIL FOR RUPERT.

MEANWHILE, before we proceed to describe further the machinations of Joshua and Hugh Blacklock, we must turn our attention to another character in our story, whose actions were destined to destroy to a great extent all the plans of the latter.

We allude to old Frost, the grave-digger of Merton, the place Reuben once visited in search of the missing certificate.

One day, somewhat like a fortnight before the arrival of Joshua and Hugh Blacklock at Blakesley Hall Academy, a storm of some considerable violence was raging over Merton Heath.

On this night, about nine o'clock, the cottage contained only the old grave-digger.

As a rule his daughter was with him, a jolly, buxom girl about twenty-five.

On this evening, however, she had gone over to the town to see a relation, and would not be back until the morning, and the old man had taken the opportunity of looking over his papers.

"Ah!" he said, as he opened a dingy old box and spread some papers out before him. "I shan't have much solid coin to leave Annie, but I'll leave her what's as good as money. I couldn't carry out the game while old Enoch was alive. But I've succeeded in my revenge. I swore that he should never have the benefit of the possession of this document, which he would not share with me. And yet for myself I've never used it."

He read over the names as if triumphing in their perusal.

"Miles Orford and Jane Manser,

Horace Pennethorne and Elizabeth Woodby, Richard Pendarven and Mona Lehman. Ha, ha! that's it. Wouldn't somebody I know give thousands to have this to destroy it? And wouldn't someone else give thousands to get it to clear his mother's name?"

All the time that he was thus soliloquising aloud, and arranging and re-arranging the papers, a man's face had been glued against the window without.

Amid the howling of the wind the old man had not heard the approach of anyone, and so this stranger, whoever he was, had watched every movement, and as the table was close to the window he could see plainly that the piece of paper was part of a register.

He could scarcely tell the name, but the few letters "Pend" that he could make out brought back to him a conversation which he had had with Tom Frost years ago.

An evil light came into his eyes.

"Ah!" he cried, "I expect I shall be able to make capital out of this."

And he knocked at the door.

The old man did not at first hear him, but at a second summons he started up, and grasping the paper almost crushed it in his desire to conceal it.

"Who is there?" he cried.

"It is I—Fred Frost."

A change at once came over the face of the old man.

It was a look of relief, but still he did not evince any great pleasure.

"All right, Fred," he cried.

And with no very good grace he made his way to the door and opened it.

The man, who now entered, was about eight or nine and twenty, with red hair, a face expressive of stolid determination.

He shook old Tom Frost's hand heartily.

"I hope I'm welcome, uncle."

"Certainly, my boy. Have a nip of rum," said the old man, who seemed to look upon the advent of the intruder as quite a necessary evil.

"That I will, uncle," said the new-comer. "I'm drenched to the skin, as you see. I haven't seen such a wild night as this on Merton Moor for many a long day."

"It's many a day since you've been across it, my boy."

"Yes, and I was in a great hurry, too," said Fred. "I shouldn't have called now only I saw a light in the window, and I knew you were up. I never thought you were so busy though."

"I was knocking a long time at the door, and finding that you didn't come to open it, I looked through the window and saw you looking at that page of the old register that you told me about a long time since."

The old man glanced uneasily at him.

"You saw the page of the register?"

"Yes," said Fred, "and I saw the letters 'P-e-n-d.' It reminds me of the name of the person you spoke about. Pendarven. That's it. It comes to me plain enough now. What are you going to do with it?"

"Ah, that's a question," said the old man; "yes, that's a question. The thing is, Fred, can I trust you?"

"I hope so, uncle," said the man cheerily, as he drew up his chair to the table by the side of the other. "Try me. You told me a long time ago that there was a secret in regard to your relations with the Pendarvens, which might some day prove of use to you in a monetary way. Can't I help you with it?"

"Well, I don't see how you can," said the old man, "leastwise, except in so far as you can come with me to old Merton Church to-night."

Fred stared at this.

"Well," he said, "that's a curious start, and no mistake. Why, it's nigh on two miles to the church, and the wind and the rain's enough to knock ye down."

"Well, look ye here," said old Tom, "this 'ere page of the register that we're a-talking about contains the marriage certificate of Richard Pendarven, once of Pendarven Abbey, to Mona Lehman, a gipsy girl. Hubert Pendarven would give a jolly sum of money to get it to destroy, and others would give a jolly sight more to get it to prove their right to the property."

"Well, there it is," said Fred. "Why don't ye go and get the money at once?"

"I can't. Old Maltby stole the page from the book, and I knew it, and I stole it from him, and so I ain't going to put my head in a noose for any man."

In vain Fred explained to him the folly of this.

In vain he showed him that in one case (that of Hubert) no questions would be asked—the man would be glad enough to get the paper at any price—and that in the other gratitude would prevent anyone from hounding down an old man who was doing such a service.

Tom Frost was obstinate.

"He knew he had done wrong," he said, "but he'd escaped them 'ere hand-cuffs all his life, and he wasn't going to help anybody to put 'em on now."

"Then what's your idea, uncle?" said Fred, seeing that all endeavours at persuasion were in vain.

"I'm going over to the old church now," said Frost, "and I'm going to put the page back in the register. Nobody will be any the wiser, and when I'm dead and gone, Annie can give up the confession that I carry about in my pocket here and get the reward."

"Well, uncle," said Fred, into whose mind a strange idea had stolen; "as you've made up your mind to all this, and won't be persuaded to my way of thinking, I'll do everything I can to help you in your little plan. Let's be going."

In a few minutes the two men were ready, armed with a couple of good thick sticks, and well primed with rum.

The night had not by any means improved.

The wind was howling wildly, and the rain coming down in torrents.

But neither of the men paid any heed to the warring of the elements.

On they went, until after a long and

weary journey they reached the old church of Merton.

It was a grand old building—one of the true Norman type—a solemn one at any time, even in the bright glory of the sunlight, but at night, specially dark and sombre.

Neither old Tom Frost nor his nephew, however, paid much heed to this fact.

They were used to graves and their inhabitants—accustomed to traverse the cities of the dead in all weathers and at all hours, and so, without hesitation, they swung open the iron gates and passed along the gravelly path.

Reaching the church gate, Frost took out some keys and at once opened it.

Within, as they entered, all was wondrously sombre and still.

On ordinary nights, when the moon shone, belts of light came in through the diamond-paned windows, and fell in variegated patches on the floor.

Now, not a ray fell anywhere.

Taking a large lantern from his pocket, however, the old gravedigger led the way to the vestry, the door of which he opened.

"You're a knowing old card, uncle," said the younger man. "How did you manage to get these keys?"

"I took Roger Maltby's long ago," said old Tom, "and I pretended I'd lost 'em down an old shaft, and so he had a new set made."

The vestry lamp was now lit, and a dim, religious radiance illumined the sacred chamber.

Then the two conspirators proceeded to examine the volumes, until they came to that which should have contained the certificate of Richard Pendarven and Mona Lehman.

It took but a few minutes to discover it, turn over the pages, and replace the missing one.

Tom Frost did not gum it in.

He simply loosened several other pages in the same way, and then put the volume back in the spot whence he had taken it.

"Why didn't ye gum it or fasten it in somehow?" asked Fred. "They may think it's a forgery, being stuck in loosely like that."

"That's just the reverse, ye see," said Tom Frost. "If it 'ad been gummed in

they might have suspected something, but now I've pulled out several pages and left 'em loose, it don't look anything particular."

As he said this, a low rumble was heard above their heads.

"Hark! What's that?" said the old man, clutching Fred by the arm.

"It sounds main like thunder," said Fred. "We'd better be off if we don't want to be caught in a fearful storm."

The old gravedigger was trembling now like a leaf.

He had at all times a horror of thunder and lightning, and now that he was engaged in a transaction which was on his part very shady, he feared them all the more.

He quickly closed the door of the church, and they were soon making their way as quickly as they could across the fields.

Nearer and nearer came the flashes of the lightning and the booming of the thunder, and more and more did the old man tremble.

At length he paused a moment.

His face, as Fred saw it by the flashes of the electric fluid, was ghastly in the extreme, his eyes supernaturally bright, and his body trembling as if he had the palsy.

"Come, come, uncle," said Fred, "for heaven's sake pull yourself together, or we shall never get home."

"Ah!" shouted the old man, as if seized with a sudden frenzy, "I shall never see home again! The lightning! On such a night as this I once robbed a dead body of its gold rings. Ugh! Fred, save me."

A terrific flash had dashed from one side of the horizon to the other, jagged and terrible, lighting up the wild moor with its stunted trees, and falling with dazzling effect on the windows of the old church of Merton, bringing out in sombre relief the quaint figures which everywhere ornamented it.

With a shriek of horror the old gravedigger flung his arms aloft, and dropped on the drenched ground.

"What's up now, uncle?" cried Fred. "You'll about freeze if you lie there."

There was no answer.

The old man lay like a log mid the rough long grass and weeds, and Fred, kneeling down, turned the light of the lantern upon his face.

The awful truth in a moment flashed upon him.

His uncle was dead.

He felt his heart.

It was still.

"Well, here's a go," thought Fred; "the lightning has killed him. What am I to do now? If I carry him home, Annie 'll think I've murdered him, or, at any rate, there'll be suspicion, and I shan't be in a very good position to refute it. No, I must leave the old man here. He's dead, and the storm can't hurt him. To-morrow must see me at Pendarven Castle with the certificate. Now for the confession, and then the keys."

The former he found, and tore in a hundred pieces.

"Now for the keys," he muttered, gleefully.

And he began to search diligently everywhere.

But in vain.

They were nowhere to be found.

"No matter," muttered the man, "I must go to Pendarven Castle without the page, as I should have done if the old man hadn't died. Good-bye, old man, I'll look after Annie. I'll come back rich and marry her off-hand."

And as he fled away in the darkness of the night, Rupert Pendarven little knew what a fresh and perilous cloud was darkening the horizon of his life.

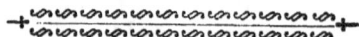

CHAPTER XXII.

AT THE OLD CASTLE ONCE MORE.

FRED FROST had come into the neighbourhood of Merton without a farthing in his pocket.

But he did not leave it so.

When he found the confession in his uncle's pocket and destroyed it, he found also old Tom Frost's purse, which he placed in his pocket, and discovered to contain about five pounds' worth of silver and gold.

So he obtained a bed where he was not known; and on the next morning, after an early breakfast, he quitted the inn, and took the coach to Ardrey, close to Pendarven Castle.

He did not propose going there in the daytime.

People engaged in the peculiar style of business that occupied the mind of Fred Frost at that moment prefer the darkness to daylight.

At length, however, evening came, and with an eager step and a resolute heart, he made his way towards the castle.

Knowing as he did that what to him was a fortune depended on that night's work, he was careful.

He had acted, too, with a calm deliberation worthy of a better cause.

He left not a letter, a card, or a piece of paper on his person by which he could be identified in the event of any untoward incident.

All documents, etc., he carefully concealed in a spot in the woods near at hand, which it was unlikely that any one save himself would think of searching, and with the exception of the relics of his five pounds, his pockets were empty.

His appearance did not certainly impress the servant who opened the gates of Pendarven Castle with any great idea of his importance.

There was nothing absolutely shabby about him, but he looked loose and baggy, and entirely a different sort of person from the usual visitors.

"What name shall I say?" asked the man.

"I am certain that your master would not know it," said Fred, loftily, as he drew from his pocket a tiny note. "I fancy that if you give him that, however, you will find he will see me at once."

The man, with a muttered, "Very well," turned him over to the watchful eyes of the under keeper, and proceeded towards the inner gates.

The note contained but a few words—

"The bearer of this note has important information to give to Mr. Hubert Pendarven touching a certain marriage certificate of which he has been in search."

Hubert Pendarven was sitting in his study writing some letters when the note was brought to him.

He read it with some surprise.

"Marriage certificate!" he said. "What does the man mean? Unless old Roger deceived me, that bugbear has gone long ago. But perhaps it will be as well to see him. Just as Ralph is rising into manhood, to see him ousted by the son of that gipsy woman would be bitter indeed."

These words, of course, were inaudible to the stately servitor who stood waiting at the door.

"Admit this man. Bring him up with as little fuss as possible. I don't like to refuse to see him, as he is the son of a poor friend."

"Yes, sir, I'll bring him up quite quiet."

In a few minutes Fred Frost was ushered into the presence of the master of the castle.

Hubert Pendarven gazed for an instant with intense earnestness at his unexpected visitor.

He was a villain himself, as we know, a villain of a far deeper dye than ever Fred Frost would have stooped to have been.

But still, he recognised craft and low cunning in the aspect of the red-haired man before him, with his ferret eyes, sly expression, and heavy mouth.

He saw that he would have to oppose villainy by villainy.

"Good evening, sir," said Fred, twirling his hat, but looking smiling and undaunted in the presence of the master of the house, who sat staring at him with a cold, haughty, insolent regard. "I hope I'm not interrupting you at a busy moment, for my news will keep; only I fancy what I've got to say will be interesting to you."

"Ah!" said Hubert Pendarven, "and profitable, you think, to yourself, else I should not have had the honour of this visit."

Fred was by no means abashed or insulted by the manner of Hubert towards him.

He only grinned.

His was a nature not easily rebukable, and knowing the character of his host,

he, without any great stretch of imagination, considered himself his equal.

"Just so," he said; "case of mutual benefit. However, I'm not one to push my services on anybody. I daresay the other side will pay as well as you."

This was a stubborn, vulgar nature, which Hubert saw it would be very difficult to combat.

So he said with a grim smile—

"It would be better, I think, to state your meaning, and the purport of your visit, before going into the question of sale and barter."

"Just so," replied Fred. "The whole affair lies in a nutshell, and so it is absurd, as you say, to beat about the bush. You are seeking a certain marriage certificate."

"There you are wrong, I am not."

Fred rubbed his hands genially.

"In that case," he said, with grave politeness, "all I have to do is to apologise for my intrusion and go."

"Pray tell me before you do so," said Hubert, "what marriage certificate it is that you fancy I am interested about?"

As Hubert said this Fred started.

"What's that?"

He fancied that he had heard a sound at the door, and leaping from his seat he dashed it open, regardless of the presence of the master of the house, and saw retiring from the landing the unmistakable outline of a human form.

"Who is there?" he cried, in a voice which echoed strangely down the broad old staircase.

But no answer came, and the figure disappeared suddenly.

Fred returned into the room with unmistakable signs of annoyance on his face.

"You don't teach your servants good manners, Mr. Pendarven," said he. "There are eavesdroppers in your house."

"Eavesdroppers!" said Hubert, sternly. "Whom did you find outside there?"

"The man who let me in."

"Are you certain?"

"Yes, as far as I could tell in the moonlight on the staircase," said Fred. "At any rate, I saw a man sneak away from the landing and go down. Of course it is nothing to me, only I should think our business could be transacted better without a third party."

"Certainly," said Hubert. "Speak in a lower tone, and suppress as many names as you can. If I can only discover who this person is who was listening, I will punish him severely."

"Well, as far as I can see, I had better let you know how much of the affair I am acquainted with, so that you will be able to see at once how far the document I speak of is valuable."

"Just so."

"What I know, then, is this," said Fred Frost. "Many years ago a little boy was missing from the castle on the same day that his father was basely murdered. That boy was the supposed heir of this place. In fact, between you and me, he *was* the heir, Rupert, son of Richard Pendarven."

He paused to observe the effect of his words.

There was absolutely none.

Hubert had heard these words said to him so often one way and another that he was perfectly callous on the point.

"Well?" he said.

"That boy," then pursued Frost, "being the real heir, some one you know had an interest in proving that his father and mother were never married, so he bribed a parish clerk to abstract the certificate of the marriage from the register and destroy it. The man did abstract it; but he did not destroy it, but concealed it."

Hubert started to his feet.

"The villain!"

"The words come strangely from you, Mr. Pendarven," said Fred Frost, with a smile; "but at any rate he concealed it, and it was stolen from him by my uncle."

"An honest confession."

"If I were an honest man, or if you were one, I shouldn't be here," said Fred, coolly.

Hubert's cheeks flushed.

"Come, come," he said, "no insolence. Proceed with your story."

"Well, this certificate my uncle kept in his possession until last night, and then he made a written confession, which was to be left to my cousin as legacy, so that she could make money out of you after his death.

"This confession is no longer in existence, as I destroyed it after my uncle died suddenly in a fit on his return home from the church, where he had replaced the marriage certificate."

"Replaced it!" cried Hubert, excitedly, roused out of the usual calm. "I have but to see old Maltby, and——"

"He is dead, too," said Fred, calmly. "I only discovered it to-day."

"But I know the church well," said Hubert. "Your information is most valuable. I have but to go there with a trusty companion, and the thing is done."

Fred Frost smiled.

"But you see the register is not at Worlingham Church," he said. "That is where Maltby had you."

"What do you mean?"

"Exactly what I say. Richard Pendarven and Mona Lehman were not married at Worlingham Church."

"Where then?"

"That is just the secret that I wish to sell you," replied Frost, "or, rather, I will undertake to get you the page of the register and bring it here for a certain sum."

"No, no," cried Hubert. "No, no; I must accompany you, else how can I guard against forgeries?"

"All right," said Fred. "And now comes the figure."

"Name it."

"Well, in such an affair as this, it would be useless attempting to mince matters," said Frost. "You are a rich man. You have a son whom you desire to inherit this property. At any moment, if I chose to speak, I could impoverish and disgrace you. You do not suppose, then, that I should name a small sum."

"Name it, then."

"Twenty thousand pounds."

Hubert Pendarven felt back in his arm-chair aghast.

It was a daring demand.

"You must be mad," he cried, jeeringly.

"Not a bit of it. As sane as you are," said Fred. "The sum I ask is a very large one for me; but it is nothing like a year's income for you. However, there are two sides to the question—two sides who will pay, yours or another's."

"And what sum do you want down?" asked Hubert.

"Five thousand pounds, and an acknowledgment from you in writing that you are aiding me in the matter—that I am your agent. A paper, in fact, confessing the fraud. Otherwise how am I safe for the other fifteen thousand?"

"You offer a most preposterous proposal," said Hubert Pendarven, "which I refuse at once. Why, if I consented, you would have me entirely in your power, and could sell me at any moment to my enemies."

"It is for you, then, to make a proposal, Mr. Pendarven," said Frost. "In case you do not think it worth your while, I can see what Rupert and his cousin say."

"A truce to threats," said Hubert, "they are but waste of time. Let us understand one another properly. I cannot think of this proposition in an instant. I must have time to consider. Let me see you here again to-morrow night about this hour, and I will try and arrange everything. I cannot prolong the interview now."

"Very well," said Frost, "I will be here."

And in a few moments he was once more on the outside of the castle.

"I think I've sprung a gold mine," he thought, as he left the castle grounds. "The old boy will hardly like to refuse me what I ask. If he only gives me half, I can go back to the old place and ask Annie to marry me, and I can buy a farm and settle down happy, without any more bother on my mind."

With which idea he dived his right hand deep down in the pocket where he could jingle his five pounds, and passed away in a direction where he could spend some of it.

On the road to the inn there was a small public-house, and here Fred paused for a time.

It was an inn of very bad repute called the "Red Moon," and frequented by gipsies, tramps, and other persons of doubtful character.

But there would have been no danger if he had kept sober.

Fred Frost's appearance, with the exception of his bounceable manner, was certainly not that of a man possessed of wealth.

Fred liked company, however.

Instead, therefore, of having a glass and then pressing onwards towards the village inn, the "Horn of Plenty," he chatted to the landlord, invited him to drink, got into conversation with people at the bar, and finally began, as the vulgar expression has it, to "flash his money about."

It was just before this part of the episode that a man entered—a man about fifty, with two children.

He looked haggard and woe-begone, and when he called for half-a-pint of beer and a crust of bread and cheese, Fred would insist upon paying for a pot of the best, and standing substantial refreshment also for him and the young ones.

The man accepted the offer, and lounging near, surveyed Fred with a critical eye.

Upon such a frail thread hung Rupert the gipsy boy's fortune at this moment!

While Fred was talking and showing his money in a pretendedly accidental manner, the man listened carefully to every detail, and when he declared that he must "hurry up, or he would never reach the 'Horn of Plenty' by closing time," the tramp went out.

No one observed him go.

Indeed, with the meal which had been given him, all interest in him and his children had died out with Frost.

Fred Frost said "good-night," had "just another toothful," and went out into the open air, which at once commenced its usual practice of making him intoxicated.

He had only half-a-mile to walk, but it was a dark and lonely road.

He went on whistling until suddenly a man darted out into the middle of the road and stood before him.

Fred drew back and clutched his thick stick.

"Well, old man," he cried, "what's the matter with you? Do ye want some more beer? Don't sell it out here on the road."

Something gleamed swiftly in the uncertain light.

It was a long knife.

"It's no use talking like that, governor," said the tramp, surlily. "You saw me just now up at the 'Red Moon,' and I'd got two children with me. Them two are the only things in the whole world I've got to love, and they've been starvin' and dyin' afore my face day after day."

"Come, old man, draw it mild," said Fred. "I can't listen to sermons; if I do I shall never get to the 'Horn of Plenty' before it closes."

"Look here, young man," said the old tramp, "look here. I'm not in the humour for joking. I saw your hand full of silver to-night up at the 'Red Moon.' Give me half of it, and I'll let you go. If you don't, I'll take your life and all the money you've got."

If Fred had not drank such a quantity of bad liquor, he might have driven a bargain with this man, in view of his dishonestly won fortune.

As it was he raised his stick.

"Get out of my way, you old dotard," he cried, "or it will be the worse for you. It will be your life lost, not mine."

For answer, the tramp suddenly raised his left hand and threw a stone which he had concealed, while, as Fred staggered back under such an unexpected assault, the assassin dashed on him with his knife.

Of course the nephew of the grave-digger was unprepared for such a thing as this, and taken off his guard, he was only able to aim a feeble blow at the man, who was thus desperately determined to mend his fortunes.

This took but little effect, and he felt at once the burning rush of the cold steel into his chest and dropped his stick.

"You villain!" he murmured, as he grappled with his foe, "you shall never leave this road alive if I only get the upper hand of you!"

"Nor you, if I succeed," panted the tramp, as Fred's strong fingers grasped his throat.

And so on they fought, swaying to and fro, wrestling with fearful energy, the tramp finding opportunities ever and anon to inflict a wound with the knife he grasped so strongly.

Loss of blood soon told on Fred Frost.

He began to sway to and fro, and at length releasing himself by a mighty effort, he contrived to strike one heavy blow at the tramp's head.

This, however, seemed only to have the effect of enraging him, and springing forward, the tramp drove the knife up to the hilt into his victim's breast.

Fred grasped at the air convulsively, and then fell heavily over on his side.

At this instant the heavy galloping of the horse patrol was heard, and finding that his victim lay perfectly still, the assassin dropped his knife and began to search his pockets.

In a swift and practised manner he transferred the money to his own person, and then, seizing the knife once more, he dashed into the dense plantation at the side of the road, and scrambled as hard as he could through the tangled trees and brushwood in the direction of a deserted barn, where he had left the two children for whom he had committed the hideous crime.

The wretched creature whom he had left in the road was not yet dead.

He lay there for some minutes stunned and senseless.

Then a terrible reaction came—a sense of his own loneliness, of the crime which had led to it, of the despicable thing he had been about to do.

A confused memory of Hubert Pendarven floated through his brain, a knowledge of his own wickedness, a dread of its punishment, and then an intense longing entered his heart to find Rupert and Reuben and do an act of justice.

Remembering a flask which he always carried in his pocket, he sought it with eagerness, and finding it, drank its contents off at a draught.

Thus temporarily revived, he began to call out at the top of his voice—

"Help! murder! help!"

And then, by the exertion of almost superhuman efforts, he began to drag himself along the road on his hands and knees.

He had yet a quarter of a mile to go before he reached any human habitation, and there seemed little chance of his getting there.

However, he hoped by continually shouting at the top of his voice to attract the notice of some chance wayfarer, especially as at no great distance he had to cross at right angles the high road to the market town of Marborough.

So, halting every now and again to shout loudly, he crawled on, growing rapidly weaker and weaker as he progressed.

At length he reached the cross roads.

He heard the sound of cart wheels, and as they approached he cried in a louder voice than ever—

"Help! help!"

The extra exertion, however, was too much for him.

As the words left his lips, and went echoing over the road and into the woods, the blood bubbled up into his mouth from his wounded chest, and he swooned away.

The market-men coming up on their slow cart soon afterwards found him lying in the roadway weltering in the red life stream.

"I heard him cry 'help!' surely," said one of them, as he bent over him with his lantern, "but he don't look now as if he'd ever cry out again."

"No; there's been murder here. He's dead," said the other.

Which way would this affect our hero Rupert—for good or for evil?

Time will show.

But the shadows are thickening deeply, and the perilous clouds gathering, and a crisis, one way or the other, must come.

CHAPTER XXIII.

RALPH PENDARVEN'S INTERVIEW WITH HUGH BLACKLOCK IN THE SCHOOL PLANTATIONS—A FRESH EXCITEMENT IN STORE.

WE must, in the natural sequence of our story, return to Blakesley Hall Academy.

Ralph Pendarven did not look forward with any pleasure to the coming interview with Hugh Blacklock.

He hated mysteries.

He had discovered, and more particularly of late, that his own life was full of them, and he would gladly have cast them utterly aside and sailed forth in the open, straightforward light of day.

But he felt compelled, nevertheless, to keep the appointment he had made.

He began to be quite assured that there was something more underlying what he had heard about Rupert than he knew of.

For this reason he was anxious to meet this man, hoping that he would at any rate learn something in regard to his antecedents and prospects.

So, at the appointed time, Ralph made an excuse to leave his companions, and with an anxious heart he proceeded in the direction of the rendezvous.

Hugh Blacklock was already waiting.

He was pacing to and fro anxiously, but meditatively, slashing the grass and wild flowers with his whip.

He looked up eagerly as Ralph approached.

"Ah, Master Pendarven," he said, "I am glad you have come, for my business is of great importance, and I must return to the castle to-night."

"I did not like coming, Mr. Blacklock," said the boy; "but as I was told it was something in regard to the property, I resolved to do so at any risk. Do not keep me long, however, or I shall get into trouble."

Hugh paused.

He scarcely indeed knew how to commence what he desired to say.

"I won't keep you long," he said. "Come and sit on the trunk of this tree, and I will explain everything as shortly as I can."

The boy said nothing, but sat on the tree trunk as he had been requested.

"You see," said Hugh Blacklock, "you are the reputed heir of the castle."

"Yes, Mr. Blacklock, I am the heir of the Pendarven estates," replied Ralph, haughtily.

"I don't know so much about that," said Hugh. "That is a question which I expect will have to be settled in a court of law, unless certain things are done. At any rate, I have been for a long time a great friend of your father's, but we have fallen out over a little matter of detail."

"Does this concern me?" asked Ralph.

Hugh smiled grimly.

"It does," replied the other, "because I am going to tell you a secret which has been kept from you too long."

"If it is one of my father's secrets I would rather not hear it."

Blacklock was angry at the boy's persistence.

"All these cursed Pendarvens have

the devil's own temper," said he to himself.

But aloud he cried—

"No, it is not your father's secret, it is your own. So you had best listen. If Rupert Pendarven lives you are a beggar."

Ralph's lips quivered, and a strange presentiment of evil entered his mind.

But his temper came to his aid.

"I say again that this folly that you are talking can have nothing to do with me. True or untrue it concerns my father, not me. If there is a battle to be fought he must fight it, not I."

"You are absurd," said Blacklock, "and I shall tell you, very briefly, therefore, why I come to you and not your father; and if, when you know all, you refuse to do as I say, then we can consider that this interview never took place. Pray listen."

"Proceed, sir," said Ralph, with a stern kind of doggedness.

"In the first place then," continued Ralph Blacklock, "I have quarrelled with your father about terms, but I don't want to quarrel with you. It may be an ugly thing to say, but you are no more the heir to Pendarven that I am. The boy you know as Rupert Clifford is your cousin, the legitimate son of Richard Pendarven, your uncle, and Mona Lehman. Now, until this lad is got rid of, your position is simply nothing."

"Got rid of!" cried Ralph, indignantly. "I don't know what you mean."

"Not what you fancy I mean," said Hugh, with a knowing movement of the head, "though, of course, if he were to die, all this worry and mystery would be over for ever. No, what I intend you to understand is this: that Rupert Clifford must be got out of the country; he must disappear, and that can easily be arranged without any real injury to himself."

Then bending forward, he hissed in Ralph's ear—

"He must be got rid of or you will be a beggar."

Ralph looked up and asked haughtily—

"Well, and what have I got to do with it? I can render no assistance."

"Very much," replied Blacklock. "On a certain night—you sleep, you see, in the same dormitory—you can leave your window unlocked. You can give the gipsy boy a draught prepared by me, which will make him sleep heavily, and in the middle of the night, when you are all asleep, he will be carried off without anybody ever being the wiser."

"And why, since you have an emissary in the school, who is not apparently very particular," said Ralph, "why do you ask me to do some dirty action which my father refuses to have anything to do with?"

"There are three reasons," said Hugh, in a voice which seemed strangely stern to Ralph. "In the first place, your father has quarrelled with me, and I wish you to sign a paper giving me a certain sum when you are of age; secondly, Joshua, whom you call my emissary, is not one of those who sleep in your dormitory; and, thirdly, when you know that the girl I loved was taken from me by the protector of this Rupert, the real and bitter truth, I fancy that you will be the best ally I could have."

Then after a moment's pause he said—

"Now listen to me again."

And bending down, he whispered something in the boy's ear.

It was not a very long story, but as he listened, his cheeks blanched, and his eyes retreated, while dark circles formed round them.

The boy moved not, spoke not, while the man repeated his cruel words, the story of the murder, which had been done at the old abbey some fifteen years before by his father.

Hugh Blacklock caught him by the wrist, as he finished speaking, and peered evilly into his face.

"Now," he cried—"now that you know all, will you not aid me in kidnapping this boy, the cousin of my deadliest foe, he that robbed me of the girl I loved, the one who stands between you and your inheritance?"

But he spoke his words to the winds.

Ralph Pendarven had fainted.

Could his father be a murderer?

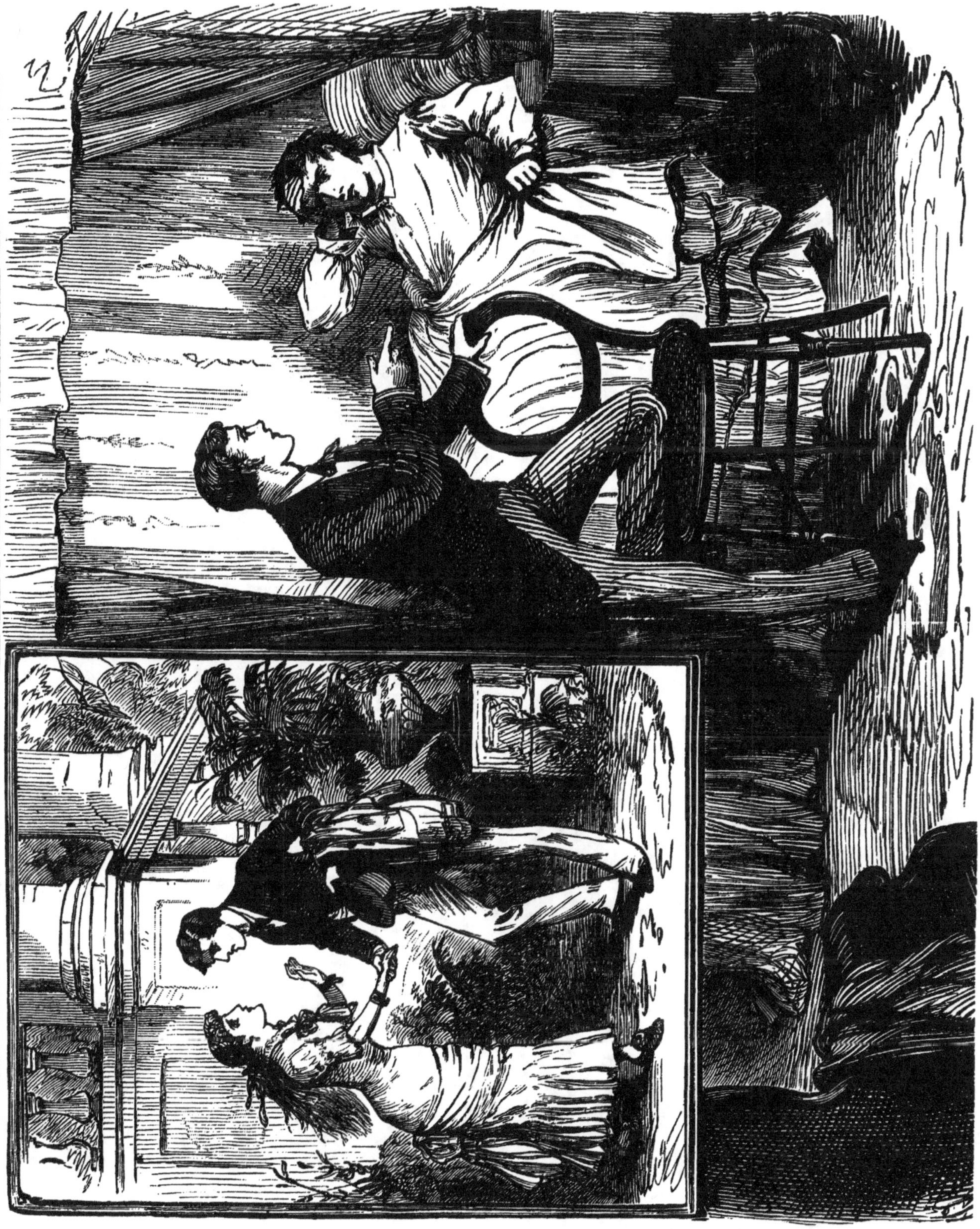

"'YOUR PLAN TO DESTROY THE LIFE OF RUPERT WAS FOUND OUT   CRIED LEWIS.''

CHAPTER XXIV.

A STRANGE REVELATION—THE COMING BOAT RACE.

IT was some time before Ralph Pendarven recovered from the effect of the sudden and unexpected communication made to him by Hugh Blacklock.

He had, as we have said, gone off into a dead swoon, and for a moment or so he was so white and still that it seemed to the gipsy as if he had gone off altogether.

But it was not so.

Presently, when Hugh Blacklock had chafed his hands and poured some brandy down his throat, Ralph opened his eyes and glanced around him.

At first there was a look in his eyes as of one awakening from a dream.

Then, as his eyes fell upon the face of Hugh Blacklock, the look changed to one of stony horror.

As soon as he had sufficiently recovered he rose, without uttering a word, and began to totter off.

"Where are you going?" cried Hugh Blacklock, in surprise.

"To the Academy."

"But you have not yet answered me."

"About what?" asked Ralph, pausing.

"You know all now," said the gipsy, "and you are aware of the terrible shadow of the hangman that broods over the house of Pendarven."

"Yes."

"And you refuse to do as I wish—to give me a paper entitling me to a certain sum when you come into the property?"

"Yes."

Hugh laughed jeeringly.

But he felt very uncomfortable.

He had failed with the father through his hot and ungovernable temper—he had now failed with the son.

"Well," he said, "I think you are very foolish; however, if you insist on having your own way, you must have it. I must go to the other side and try and make terms with them."

"Perhaps you had better," said Ralph, with pale lips. "It seems to me that they have the best right to it—according to your story."

The last words were a revelation to Hugh.

His bronze-tanned skin turned yellowy pale.

"Why, don't you believe me?" he said.

Ralph turned upon him with rigid form, blazing eyes, clenched hands.

"No—a thousand times no!" he said. "Do you expect me to believe from the lips of a vagabond that my father, whom I respect, who has always behaved to me with such kindness, is a murderer, a common assassin? Blacklock, gipsy, rascal, I leave you to do as you please. I will have nothing to do with it."

And with these words he walked away.

Ralph Blacklock muttered a curse between his teeth, and for a moment seemed puzzled as to what course to pursue.

Then he hastened after Ralph.

"One moment, Master Pendarven," he said.

The boy paused and glanced at him in contemptuous anger, but he did not speak.

"Remember the schoolboy that was found dead in the wood? That crime is also on your father's hands. Now all I want to say is this," cried the gipsy, "that if ever you have need of me, you will find me always by writing a letter to the post-office at Smaleton."

And he turned and went away.

This was exactly what Ralph wanted.

Boldly as he might stick up for his father, his mind was in a whirl when he considered the words of this man.

What in fact was he to believe?

Could it be possible that the terrible accusation which this gipsy villain had made against his father was true?

Could it be that he—Ralph Pendarven—who had always held his head so high, was the son of a murderer?

Could it be that this lad—this Rupert Clifford, whom he had so insulted, whom he had deliberately made his enemy—was the true heir to a property held now through bloodshed and murder?

The thought was fearful.

Yet what was he to do?

The first thing, of course, was to write to his father.

From him he could not keep so terrible an accusation.

Of course it could not be true.

But if it were?

So, doubting and fearing, at one time discarding the notion as absurd, the next moment wondering if it could be the fact, he occupied his time in pacing to and fro until dusk came on, and he knew that it was time to return to the school.

As he did so there was only one fear in his heart.

And that was that he would meet Rupert.

There was a haunting dread in his mind.

However, there was no help for it.

He must return to the Academy, and accordingly, with a heavy heart, and a feeling of desolation as it were pervading him, he made his way through the hedge of the plantation and entered the dusky playground.

The very first person he met was Rupert Clifford.

It was as if fate was against him.

"Ah, Pendarven!" cried Rupert, "we've been looking for you everywhere. We have been making arrangements for the boat race."

The friendly way in which our hero spoke to him went to his heart.

What if it were true? His father a murderer to gain Rupert's wealth.

The haunting thought would come back.

"Oh," he said, rousing himself by a great effort, "I hope that you have not settled it all without me?"

"Oh, no!" replied Rupert, somewhat surprised at the tone of his cousin's voice, and struck, too, by his altered manner and pale, careworn face; "no, you couldn't fancy we could do that!"

"Well, how far have matters gone then?" said Ralph, trying to assume his old manner.

"Why, we are to meet the Cameronians to-morrow in the five-acre field," said Rupert, "you and I, and Lewis, and Ship Ahoy, to arrange about the terms and the day."

"Good. Our side isn't chosen yet, is it?" asked Ralph.

"We only want two."

"And how about practice?"

"Oh, we shall have as much chance as the Cameronians," said our hero; "and you know Doctor Walton will be sure to give us some afternoons to ourselves the week before the race."

Chatting thus, the two passed on towards the schoolhouse.

Every soft inflexion of Rupert's voice went like a dagger into the heart of Ralph.

He saw in a moment what a generous mind was possessed by this young rival in learning and fortune—how ready he was to be friendly and to speak as if nothing had happened between them to disturb their companionship.

In very truth, Rupert never gave Ralph credit for having anything to do with the villainies against which he and Reuben found it so difficult to battle.

He might indeed know that he was not properly the heir of Pendarven Abbey, or that there was at any rate some flaw in the title of the inheritance.

But in regard to the awful deed which handed the fortune over to Hubert, our hero did not believe that his schoolmate knew anything.

Little did he fancy what an awful revelation had been made by Hugh Blacklock.

"What time to-morrow are we to be in the five-acre field?" asked Ralph.

"About five."

"Good; we will go up there together," said Ralph; "but I hope that Joshua won't be of the party."

"He says he can row 'splendid,' said Rupert, laughing, "and when I asked him if he'd been practising on the barges he got very wild."

"I shall refuse to row in the eight if he is in it," said Ralph.

Rupert looked surprised, and he certainly felt so.

He knew perfectly well that Joshua and Blacklock were in some conspiracy against him, and that Ralph was supposed to be going to be a party to it.

Why this sudden change against Joshua?

Was it because of a quarrel?

What if Ralph were deceiving him after all?

Yet, no.

The disgust and anger on the face of Ralph was too thorough to be acted.

"If you do, so will I," said Rupert. "It seems a shame that the boy should be allowed to be in the school. He's a perfect cad. He can't help being un-educated, and all that, but he's a thorough low-minded brute."

"Ah!" said a voice close to his elbow, "you must not be uncharitable."

Rupert started round.

It was the voice of "Long Toby," the usher.

"I'm not uncharitable," said Rupert, "but you do not know what an un-bearable cur he is, sir."

"He has had no opportunities of cultivating himself like you two," said Mr. Lyttleton; "if he had he would no doubt have taken advantage of them. Some of these rough lads grow up to be accomplished and, at any rate, successful men."

"Ah, sir," said Rupert, with a smile up into the teacher's face, which dis-armed his words of what might have seemed impertinence, "you are speaking now of what may be *in futuro*. I think he is a brute *in presenti*."

The tutor's face twitched with merri-ment at this grammatical pun.

"Ah, Master Clifford," he said, "fun is all very well in its way, but it must not be allowed to stand in the way of solid reality. Of course, if Master Joshua makes himself so thoroughly objectionable, as you all seem to say, we must look after him."

Next day the boys were off at the appointed hour to the five-acre field to meet the Cameronians, who were the pupils of a school in the neighbouring town of Samborne, kept by a Scotch gentleman of the name of Cameron.

They were nice, gentlemanly young fellows, and Rupert was in a fever of excitement for fear Joshua should make himself a nuisance and disgrace the school.

But they had an unexpected pleasure in store for them.

Joshua did not put in an appear-ance.

A strange thing, in fact, had hap-pened.

He had received a long letter from Hugh Blacklock, which had considerably disconcerted him.

In it was explained in brief the result of the interview between him and Ralph.

"The whole thing is quite rotten to the very core," he said, in conclusion, "and we must commence over again. So meet me in the plantation to-night at five, and I will explain a new plan of operations."

Hugh Blacklock's plan was a terrible one.

Both Rupert and Ralph were now in his way.

His idea was this—

Rupert, Ralph and Hubert being got rid of, Reuben became by law the next heir.

His plan must be to dispose of the whole lot.

And then?

A new Reuben must be found, some-one who could come forward and per-sonate the long-outlawed cousin.

To his clumsily villainous mind this scheme presented no great difficulties.

He had no compunction; he feared no attack of remorse; he was despe-rate.

But as Joshua was evidently to be easily moulded to his purpose, and had absolutely become established in the school, he conceived it best that he should carry out his original scheme of treachery, while Hugh proceeded to get rid of the older victims who stood so inconveniently in the way.

While the other boys, therefore, were talking innocently enough of the coming boat race, and arranging plans for mutual enjoyment, Joshua was listening to the villainous words of Hugh Blacklock, and greedily drinking in the promises of wealth which fell from the lips of the tempter.

CHAPTER XXV.

A DEMON'S SCHEME.

IT was managed between the lads that on the day appointed there were to be eight races.

The third was to be the eight-oared contest for the championship of the two schools, and all the others were between individuals or pairs.

Curiously enough Ralph and Rupert were coupled in the last race against two of the very best of the Cameronians.

At any other time the former would have been very angry at this arrangement.

But on this occasion Ralph felt no such feeling.

The interview he had had with Hugh Blacklock was rapidly changing his nature, and his mind was fairly dazzled with horror at the bare uncertainty in regard to that terrible winter's night.

"I am glad we're going to row in the same boat," he said, "for I've not the slightest doubt we shall win."

"We shall have to practice together, then," said Rupert; "we don't want another ducking."

Ralph flushed a little at this.

It brought to his mind what had happened so long ago, when Rupert, the one whom he had been taught to regard as his enemy, had saved his life.

"Yes, I remember the last one, and you may depend upon it, I do not want another like it. But we must certainly take a good spell at practice, and then we're not likely to be in danger."

That night Ralph slept but little.

His dreams were haunted by continued visions.

Hideous forms kept continually chasing him to and fro, and driving him into dangerous places, where in horror he awoke and sprang up in bed with a cry.

In fancy he saw the murder of his uncle, the flight of Reuben, and the murder of the king of the gipsies in the dark woods.

The boy's mind was racked by doubts and fears.

He had written to his father, asking to be sent for home for a day or two, in order to hear explanations of the terrible story of murders he had heard.

But even this failed to give his mind relief.

For pressing on his brain continually was the thought—

"What if this story of crime be true?"

*   *   *   *

Time sped on.

Preparations were made actively for the coming boat race.

Practice was indulged in continually.

During all this time Joshua took little heed of what was going on.

At least apparently.

He gave out his intention not to join in any race but the "All Comers."

Yet often in the evenings when the other lads were not there, he made his way down to the boat-house, and, after remaining there some time, could have been observed out upon the dusk-darkened waters of the Arrow, pulling steadily and vigorously.

The boys laughed at this.

But Joshua took their jeers all in good part.

He was playing for high stakes in his mind but the result meant murder.

At length the day arrived.

A splendid day it was too.

One "specially fitted for the occasion; got up on purpose," as Lewis said.

The sky was pure cerulean blue, save for the presence here and there of a few fleecy clouds, not dense, but only like tiny puffs of white smoke, which served to show up more plainly the exquisite colour of the rest.

The sun was consequently pouring down in uninterrupted glory, though a pleasant breeze was blowing, and serving to render this pleasant summer's day the more endurable and refreshing.

The meeting of the two clubs and their respective friends and adherents was to take place in the five-acre field.

On the margin of the Arrow, near the winning post, where a red flag waved over the waters, fixed to a punt moored in mid-stream, was a large marquee, where the principals of the respective schools were seated with their friends.

At about twelve o'clock the field began to fill.

It was the day's outing.

Pretty indeed did the graceful girls of Merton look as they wandered about on the green velvety turf.

Presently, as the clock struck twelve, a gun was fired.

This was the signal that the sports were about to commence, and consequently all began to flock towards the big marquee.

Then the boys of the two schools arrived, and at sight of them the band struck up "See the Conquering Hero Comes."

At length the boats were brought up, and the crowd lined itself along the banks under the shade of the wide-spreading oaks.

All was excited anticipation.

The first two races were not shared in by those who were to take part in the big race of the day.

The most inferior of the boys were picked out for these small affairs, but still as they were pretty well on an equality the races were by no means devoid of interest.

While these were going on Leigh Glindon, among others, strolled off to look at the boats which were reserved for the future contests.

Leigh was not one of the eight.

He was kept back for a sculling race with one of the bigger boys among the Cameronians, and he was anxious to have a look at the boat which was to carry his little red and white flag.

As he neared the boat-house, nestling among the trees on the borders of the creek, he fancied he heard a noise as of a hammer and chisel at work.

"That sounds funny," said Leigh to himself. "I wonder whose boat he's tinkering up? I hope it isn't mine."

Of course he imagined that it was the keeper of the boat-house at work.

So, hoping for the fun of finding out a secret, he approached cautiously and peered through one of the wide cracks which were to be found all round the boat-house.

He started back in astonishment as he did so, and could scarcely restrain a cry.

But he did so, and bending down again observed narrowly the movements of the worker.

No wonder was it that he was surprised.

The worker inside the boat-house was none other than Joshua.

With a mallet and a chisel he was doing something to the bottom of a boat which had a blue flag floating at the stern.

He knew the colour in a moment.

It was that chosen by Rupert for the sculling race, which was to be the last but one of the day's events.

"Ha, ha!" thought Leigh Glindon, "so you think you'll give Rupert a ducking for the way he snubs you. All right, my boy. I think that I've a plan to spoil your little game."

He only imagined, as he said, that Joshua was having a bit of fun (a cruel bit be it said) with our hero.

He never dreamed that his design was in reality a deliberate attempt at murder.

He was so delighted at the idea of spoiling what he thought to be a cowardly action, that he resolved to conceal himself and wait as long as ever Joshua did, even if he had thereby to forfeit his chance of competing.

However, he did not have to remain long in suspense.

Joshua came out in the course of another ten minutes, glanced cautiously round him, and then, darting swiftly behind the trees, reached the back of the large marquee, and then sauntered into the midst of the company, where, amid the excitement, the merriment, and the general enjoyment his arrival was unnoticed.

Leigh Glindon, as soon as he was sure that "the enemy" was out of sight, crept round to the entrance and crawled in.

What he did when he was in there we shall not pause here to tell.

That will come out in due time.

Whatever it was he came out with a flushed and merry face, and walked in the direction of the big marquee with every sign of pleasure and satisfaction on his countenance.

Leigh Glindon was a very different person now from the boy who had escaped from the tyranny and starvation of "Hungry Hall."

He was naturally of a good constitution, and his frame was strong and hard, even during the old terrible days of no food.

Now he had developed into a stout, robust-looking lad.

When he approached the company he was full of excitement at the idea of something which had occurred to his mind in regard to the bit of fun he had planned against Joshua.

All was bustle now.

The two eights were looking well and trim, the Blakesley Hall crew in blue caps, the Cameronians in red.

Every boy seemed up to his work, and as they took their seats nothing save a confused murmur could be heard.

But when at length they went off with a fine burst, there was a simultaneous roar of voices, handkerchiefs and hats were waved, and everyone settled himself or herself to watch and enjoy the contest for the silver medal, the possession of which entitled the winners to the title of Champion Eight in that locality.

The course was from the winning post to a barge moored out in the centre of the stream opposite a spot named Denman's Corner, then round the barge and back to the post again.

It was a good spin, and the time ordinarily occupied was a quarter of an hour.

Both eights seemed in good " fettle," and the race throughout was well contested.

Little by little the Blakesley Hall boat, however, began creeping to the front.

Only a very small advantage, however.

As they neared the barge they were about half a length in advance, and then taking the turn in a far more graceful and effective way than their opponents, they increased their advantage to a length.

As the little blue flag was seen fluttering merrily in the breeze so far ahead there was a loud shout of applause.

On came the boats.

The excitement becomes intense.

The race is really a splendid one.

The Cameronians, rowing bravely, put on a good spurt, and lessen their adversaries' advantage perceptibly.

" Steady, boys, but pull strong," says Ship Ahoy, the coxswain of the Blakesley Hall boat.

They increase their stroke one.

The others endeavour to do likewise.

But in doing so they get " straggly."

The flag on the summit of the winning post flutters gaily only a short distance ahead.

The Blakesley Hall boys are rowing as one man.

The throng begins to see the winner.

" Bravo, Blakesley Hall ! "

" Steady there, Cameronians ! "

" Keep it up, Blue ! "

" Go it, Red ! "

These and other remarks are roared out indiscriminately, the crowd press perilously near to the water's brink.

Another two minutes, then a roar of applause ascends towards the blue vault of heaven.

Blakesley Hall has won by two lengths !

It has been a pluckily-rowed race throughout, and while the victorious crew land, amid shouts of welcome and approval, everybody congratulates everybody else, the band strikes up once more " See the Conquering Hero Comes," the conquerors are muffled up in soft comforters and given warm coffee, the defeated crew, " beaten but not disgraced," come in for a good share of public favour, and then all settle down for lunch and a good hour's rest.

For most of those present the great event of the day is over.

For Joshua the great event is to come.

How great he little knew.

CHAPTER XXVI.

THE BOATRACE DAY (CONTINUED)—JOSHUA'S TRAP AND WHO FELL INTO IT.

ABOUT two in the afternoon another gun was fired and the racing commenced again.

The first was a four-oared contest in which Rupert and several others of the crew did not take part.

"I'm glad of this rest, Leigh," said our hero to Glindon; "that was a good pull."

"'A good pull, and a long pull, and a pull all together' that was, I think," said Leigh. "It was a splendid race."

"Well, it was a stiff one," returned Rupert, "and if I had not had this rest I shouldn't have been able to go in for the sculling match."

"Ah! by the way," asked Leigh, "does that come off before the pair-oared race?"

"Yes."

"I see it all now," thought Leigh. "By the dirty trick he has attempted Joshua hoped to prevent Rupert from joining Ralph Pendarven in the pair-oared race. The miserable sneak!"

He did not, however, give full vent to his ideas.

He passed it off, in fact.

He did not wish to tell anything for fear of losing the chance of punishing Joshua for his dastardly scheme.

"You're in three races then to-day?" he said.

"Yes," returned Rupert, smiling, "and a sorry exhibition I shall make of myself in the last one, I expect."

"Oh, I don't know that," replied Leigh; "at any rate, win the one-oared race. I want to see you conquer all by yourself. You know what I mean, not in a boat where there's anyone else to help you, but entirely by yourself."

"Dear old Leigh," cried Rupert, "you are always wishing me good luck."

"Do I not owe everything to you?" said Leigh smiling.

"And I? Could I have escaped from that hideous Hungry Hall if you had not been there to help me?" said Rupert; "but come, Leigh, give me another sandwich. I know it's bad for my chance to eat, but I can't help it. I'm as hungry as a hunter."

In a few minutes after this the wager boats were drawn out of the boat-house, eight in number.

There were eight competitors, in fact, Rupert, Ship Ahoy, Leigh Glindon, Joshua, and four Cameronians.

With intense anxiety Leigh watched the manning of the light craft.

He thought that perhaps Joshua might find out his bit of fun at the last moment and spoil it.

But no.

Joshua entered his boat unsuspectingly.

In his wildest dreams he could never have imagined that he had been seen when engaged in his diabolical work in the boat-house.

The eight boats were alike in size.

Everyone of the boys was eager and excited.

None more so than Joshua.

His murderous scheme seemed to him to be on the very eve of accomplishment.

He had bored a hole in the bottom of the boat which was to be used by Rupert, or rather had chiselled round a square of woodwork so artfully that the continued pressure of his foot would break it open, and the water would rush in too quickly to render aid of any use.

He knew nothing of course of the cleverness of Rupert in swimming.

The gun went off once more.

Far away rolled the echoes over the woods, echoes which were soon lost in the uproarious applause which greeted the starting of the eight competitors.

They started well.

And a very picturesque sight they were as they rushed onwards.

Joshua was strong.

He had, moreover, had considerable experience on the Thames.

And so early in the race he began to show in front.

"You see," said Tobias Lyttleton, smilingly pointing to the big boy, whose raw-boned hands clutched the sculls so vigorously, "you see, the much despised boy is showing you the way to do it."

Joshua had "aped humility" with Tobias Lyttleton.

Poor, simple Long Toby was easily taken in.

But Ralph Pendarven and the others were not so easily duped.

"Yes, sir, I see he is going ahead," said Ralph, to whom the words were addressed; "it is the preponderance of matter over mind."

The usher laughed.

But his merriment was short-lived.

What was the matter with Joshua?

His boat suddenly came to a dead stop, although his sculls were being worked furiously.

He was too far off to see his face, whether it was red or white.

But they could see he was in trouble, for he caught hold of the sculls with the right hand, and waved the left, while his voice came faintly across the waters, shouting for—

"Help!"

The other competitors took no notice of him.

Their business was to win.

Joshua had been leading, our hero second, Ship Ahoy was third, a Cameronian named Amhurst fourth, the others coming along in a bunch.

As Joshua's skiff seemed to stop, the others went by with a rush.

Then there was a loud outcry, and the former (boat and all) disappeared beneath the swiftly-running stream.

CHAPTER XXVII.

A NEARLY FATAL CRIME.

RUPERT, and those who were with him in the race, were too near the winning-post to take any notice of the upset of Joshua's wager boat.

So while one of the boatmen put off to endeavour to save the lad who had so strangely gone down, Rupert, amid deafening cheers, came in at the head of the competitors.

It was a very popular victory, and everyone exulted to the utmost.

But there was a great crush and pressing forward, and just as the voice of the throng went upwards towards the blue heavens in a roar of triumph, there was a loud cry of alarm.

The crowd in pressing forward had infringed upon the wooden landing-stage, which was only a very frail and temporary affair, and one of the foremost in the assembly, a little girl of some fourteen years of age, was cast headlong into the deep water.

For a moment the crowd was so paralysed by affright that no one offered to render aid.

A thrill of anxiety had gone through them when Joshua had met with his mishap.

But they had regarded it as one of the natural accidents which occur on such an occasion, and when the boat put off to the rescue they felt satisfied.

Now, however, it was different.

The sight of the beautiful girl seemed to suggest such utter helplessness that the breasts of all were filled with consternation.

But, if others hesitated, there was one there, who, in such scenes as these, never dreamed of drawing back.

This one was Rupert.

He saw the little white form being carried away on the breast of the stream, and in an instant, before anyone else could make up his mind, he had kicked off his rowing shoes, and was swimming rapidly away in his drawers and jersey.

Again a roar of applause greeted him, and one of the boats—that of Leigh Glindon, was rapidly turned in the direction of the brave swimmer and the little white speck which he was endeavouring to save.

It was a time of great excitement.

As the young girl was being carried out rapidly by the tide, the boat which had put off to save Joshua was returning with that individual, insensible, and with his arm broken.

Rupert had reached the young girl just as Leigh Glindon shot up to the spot with his wager boat.

Others had followed as soon as they could do so, and when our hero had once clutched the white-robed form of the insensible girl, and succeeded in supporting himself by holding lightly to the side of the tiny craft, he was fairly surrounded by friends.

Of course such boats were not of a kind which was very useful in such an emergency as this.

But Leigh Glindon was not deterred by any idea of danger.

He gently and cautiously took the fair and fragile burden from the arms of Rupert, and placed her before him on the wager boat.

One of the Cameronians assisted our hero to assume a like position on his outrigger, and then both began to row slowly towards the shore.

They were greeted, as may be imagined, most enthusiastically.

But a surprise awaited Rupert.

He had little idea whom he had saved.

He knew that the girl was pretty.

That was all.

However, when he landed, dripping like a Newfoundland dog, a gentleman of some sixty years of age hurried up, and eagerly scanned the features of the young girl.

Another and younger gentleman was by his side.

The latter proved to be a doctor.

He examined the young girl cursorily, and felt her pulse.

"She is in no way hurt, Sir Charles," replied Doctor Stanton. "Give her some slight stimulant, and let her be carried to some neighbouring house, where she can be put to bed. You will find no harm will come from her involuntary bath."

As this was said the young lady was carried towards the marquee.

But the father's gratitude was not to be deferred.

"Where is her rescuer?" he cried, looking anxiously round.

Rupert was standing modestly back.

He was soon brought forward, however.

Sir Charles caught him by both hands.

"You are a brave lad—a very brave lad," he cried. "Seen lots of brave deeds in my time. Never seen anything cooler or better. Haven't time to thank you now—must look after Gladys. But you must come and see me, Here's my card. Welcome any time. What's your name?"

"Rupert Clifford, sir."

"Ah! very good name," pursued the old gentleman. "Come soon."

And away he sped.

Rupert glanced at the card as his new and eccentric friend left him and ran in the direction of the marquee.

"Sir Charles Alreston, of Alreston Towers."

The name was quite unfamiliar.

Yet still it seemed to open up a new field of enterprise.

When Rupert once more went out into the open air he saw not far off an excited group of boys.

With them was Dr. Walton.

"What is the matter?" asked Rupert, eagerly.

"We are speaking of Joshua," said Ship Ahoy.

"Is he very bad, then?"

"Yes; but Leigh Glindon's been telling the doctor something about him —something that's made the principal look very solemn," said Ship Ahoy. "I think he's been up to larks."

Rupert pressed forward towards the spot where Dr. Walton stood.

"What's this about Joshua? Is he very bad?" he asked of Leigh Glindon.

It was the doctor who answered.

"Yes, he is," he replied, emphatically, "and likely to be worse; and, if your friend is correct, it serves him right."

"What has he done, then?"

"Well, he has, I fancy, been trying to commit a murder, though I must own that his object in doing so is not quite plain."

"Shall I explain, doctor?" said Leigh Glindon.

"Certainly."

Leigh did so.

Rupert listened anxiously, and with cheeks that turned slightly pale.

He knew Joshua's object, if they did not.

At that moment Ralph Pendarven came up and shook him heartily by the hand.

"I have heard of the danger you have been in," said he, "and I am sincerely glad you have escaped."

He little knew that he too was marked out by the young murderer for death.

And at the end of the day a greater surprise than all awaited Rupert.

But of this in its proper place.

The two-oared race was a surprise to everyone.

After the exertions of our hero, it was not certainly expected that he would be able to hold his own in another contest.

But he did.

The race was a splendid one.

Perhaps during the whole of the day not one battle had roused such eager excitement all round.

And when it ended in the triumph of Rupert and Ralph the enthusiasm was positively wild in its nature.

And then the surprise came.

Victors and vanquished— Blakesley

Hall fellows and Cameronians — assembled in the big marquee.

Dr. Walton rose to speak.

"Gentlemen of the Blakesley Hall and Cameronian Rowing Clubs," he said, "I have a message for you. I have to announce that Sir Charles Alreston, of Alreston Towers, has invited you to spend a day with him."

Loud cheers followed.

"Yes, gentlemen," he continued, "and on your parts Doctor Cameron and I have taken it upon ourselves to accept the invitation."

Again deafening cheers.

After the refreshments had been disposed of in the big marquee, the company dispersed themselves over the field to enjoy themselves as they listed.

Every boy retired to bed that night highly satisfied, and if the others did not it was no one's fault but their own.

Joshua recovered his senses as night came on.

But he was very bad.

He awoke to consciousness, or a semi-consciousness, just at dark.

He was not in the dormitory.

A small room had been apportioned to him in another part of the house.

"What's up?" he said, in a low voice.

He could see no one in the room, but he hoped that even his faint voice would rouse someone to come to him.

It did.

Lewis, the comic boy, had been detailed off to watch.

At the sound of Joshua's voice he crept to the side of the former's bed.

"Did you speak?" he asked.

"Yes," said Joshua, not recognising him in the dusky light. I said 'what's up?'"

"There's not much up," returned Lewis. "I think that you are considerably down."

"Oh, I know where I am now by your foolish jokes," said Joshua. "I thought I was in a police crib."

"Where are you, then?"

"At Blakesley Hall."

"Right. And why did you think you were in a police cell?"

"I didn't say 'a cell.'"

"What, then?"

"A crib."

"Don't know what that means."

"Ah, you ain't a 'fly' chap at all," returned Joshua, with faintly-expressed contempt. "I feel precious sore. What's been and happened?"

"Your boat was swamped."

"Well, but how did it happen?"

"Oh, that's gammon!" cried Lewis. "You know well enough."

"I don't," replied Joshua.

His mind, in fact, was dazed.

But at any rate he had no conception that his villainy was found out.

"Well, to begin with, your little scheme was found out," said Lewis.

"What scheme?"

"The one to murder Rupert Clifford."

Joshua raised one hand feebly to his head.

"Don't say such things to me," he cried. "I believe you know I'm light-headed, and are trying to make me worse."

"Oh, that's very well," returned Lewis. "I daresay it's a good game to pretend ignorance, but it won't wash here. We all know it."

"Well, if you all know it," growled Joshua, "I wish you'd give me a little of the information."

"All I've got to say is that your plan to destroy the life of Rupert by cutting a hole in the bottom of his boat was found out by one of our chaps."

"You're talking Greek to me," said Joshua, in a low voice; "but go on."

"Well, Glindon saw you cut the hole, and having done so, he waited patiently until you were gone and then he altered the flags and the position of the boats. So you thought Rupert's boat was yours, and so came to grief instead of him.

"And," said Lewis, by way of addition, "I'm jolly glad of it, for it serves you right."

"Ah," said Joshua, moving painfully, "you're a spiteful lot, but I'll be even with you some day."

"Then it won't be in this school," said Lewis, "for it strikes me you'll be expelled."

"Expelled! With the vicar's recommendation! Not much. But let's leave off talking nonsense. I feel faint, and want some kind of nourishment."

"I'll go and ask," said Lewis, leaving the room, "but it's very late."

Lewis came up presently with some

beef-tea and a message that the surgeon would see him early in the morning, that he was to drink a draught the medical man had left for him, and that if he wanted anything he was to ring the bell.

Then Joshua was left to the enjoyment of his own evil thoughts.

CHAPTER XXVIII.

A STRANGE DISCOVERY—A NEAT WAY OUT OF A DIFFICULTY—THE DAY AT ALRESTON TOWERS.

ON the morning after the unpleasant affair on the river, Dr. Walton made his way straight towards the house of the Rev. Caleb Buckthorne.

The rector received him in the kindliest and most affable manner, though there was just the suspicion of an amused smile playing around the corners of his mouth.

"I am delighted to see you, Doctor Walton," he said, as he shook the learned principal heartily by the hand.

"I am sure I am very much obliged to you, Mr. Buckthorne," he said. "I thought you would be angry with me, as the person who has been misbehaving himself is a special favourite of yours, or rather I should say a *protégé*."

The rector laughed.

"My dear sir," he said, "somebody has been making game of you. This Joshua something or other I never heard of in my life."

The doctor drew forth the recommendation, upon the faith of which he had taken Joshua into the school, and handed it to the clergyman.

The latter read it, thought a moment or two, turning somewhat pale as he did so.

"This must be a forgery," he said. "I know nothing of it."

Doctor Walton told his story.

"Well," said the rector, when he had heard all, "what are you going to do with the young vagabond?"

"Send him off, of course," cried Doctor Walton, indignantly. "I'll write to this abominable impostor of an uncle of his, and tell him to send a conveyance for him at once."

On returning to the school, the first visit he paid was to Joshua's room.

The surgeon had been, and had given the lad some stimulant, which had the effect of rousing him and strengthening him.

So Doctor Walton resolved not to delay the necessary communication.

"You entered my school with a forged recommendation, and you will leave at once."

Now this was something that Joshua was not prepared for.

"Forged!" he cried.

"Yes, forged," said Doctor Walton. "I am about to write to your uncle, and ask him to send a conveyance for you."

"Very well, sir," said Joshua meekly.

What else could he do?

He was for the moment helpless.

"I am glad you quite understand me," said Doctor Walton. "In the meantime, you shall have every attention."

And he left the room.

"Well," said Joshua to himself, as the worthy schoolmaster passed down the stairs, "I think before I go I shall be able to do a very good stroke of business. In the first place, I must sham illness in order that I may not be packed off until my arm is well. Then as I mean to cut all connection with Blacklock and his schemes after I've got some money out of him, I'll make a clean sweep of everything I can lay my hands on here. I ought to be able to make a clear hundred pound over the job. And then, off to Ameriky."

The next day he began his "shamming sick," as the soldiers say.

He pretended to be in agony in his head and in his broken arm.

The doctor examined him.

There was no apparent reason for pain.

Still the boy's face expressed the most horrible agony.

He writhed in the bed, refused everything except that kind of nourishment which doctors dignify by the name of "slops," and consequently everyone, though sorely puzzled, gave in that he must be very very ill indeed.

So for the time Joshua triumphed.

Meanwhile the other boys went on in their usual way.

Rupert, in spite of his generous nature, in spite of his coming happiness, could not bring himself to visit the suffering lad.

Deep in his own heart he knew the evil plan of which he had so nearly been the victim.

He was aware that Hugh Blacklock and Joshua had planned his death.

This he was compelled to keep secret.

Doctor Walton imagined that the tampering with the boat was due only to spite or an evil propensity for mischief.

Rupert knew it was attempted murder.

Time fled on leaden wings for those who were included in the invitation to Alreston Towers.

But at length it came.

It was real holiday weather.

When they reached Alreston Towers, Rupert's eyes wandered eagerly over the lovely sward.

There was only one thing he was anxious for.

That was to behold the sweet face and the fair form of the young girl whom Providence had ordained that he should save.

But she was nowhere to be found.

Another thing made his heart beat with an unpleasant feeling.

The Cameronians had arrived before the Blakesley Hall fellows, and he could see that they were wandering about the velvety turf with several female companions.

By the time Rupert had reached the lawn he received the kindly greetings of Sir Charles Alreston.

And in a few moments he saw how foolish he had been to doubt his own good fortune.

For tripping from the house to greet him specially came the sylph-like form of Gladys Alreston.

From that moment his happy day began.

CHAPTER XXIX.

GLADYS' SECRET—RUPERT ACCEPTS A MYSTERIOUS MISSION.

DURING nearly the whole day Rupert and Gladys remained together, or at any rate near one another.

They were attracted by a strange, sweet magnetic influence.

Even when Rupert was boating, the fair young girl (upon whose face was such an expression of strange sadness) was on the bank watching him.

The same at cricket, and when the merry youngsters assembled on the terrace in the falling darkness to witness the fireworks, Rupert and Gladys stood talking together.

But as Rupert turned towards her once he saw that tears stood in her eyes

"What is the matter, Miss Gladys?" he said. "It seems strange to see tears in your eyes."

"It does to you," she replied, "but it is not strange to me. It is very rarely that I feel disinclined to shed tears."

"What is the matter, then?" asked Rupert ingenuously.

Gladys smiled.

"That is a secret, the keeping of which makes me unhappy, but which, nevertheless, I am bound to keep."

"Then I will ask no more," said Rupert.

The first dance of the evening after the fireworks the two young people footed together.

They were engaged for the second, but when Rupert looked round for her she was gone.

Rupert went into the open air, leaned over the balustrade of the terrace and indulged in a reverie.

Suddenly this was broken by the sight of a little figure running swiftly across the wide lawn.

Then after a pause, as if it was cautiously looking round, it ran swiftly towards the house.

As it neared the terrace Rupert felt sure that he recognised it.

It must be Gladys.

What could it mean?

What mystery could she be involved in at so tender an age?

He crept back into the shadow and waited.

Presently—just at the bottom of the steps which led from the terrace on to the wide paths—he heard loud sobs.

He could bear it no longer.

In a boyish way he had conceived a deep love for this sweet young girl.

So without further hesitation he ran down towards the spot whence the sound came, and found Gladys weeping bitterly.

"What is the matter?" asked Rupert, in a gentle voice.

The girl was so utterly surprised by his sudden speech that she uttered a sharp cry of dismay and leaped back, as if detected in the commission of some crime.

"It is only I—Rupert Clifford," he said. "Don't be alarmed at me. I will go away if you wish it, but it would be my dearest wish to help you, if it lay in my power."

The young girl hesitated.

"I don't know what to do," she said. "I feel almost mad."

"Pray, Miss Alreston, if you are in any trouble, trust me. I am only a boy, but I have been trusted with many a secret, and I know I have never betrayed any one. Pray have confidence in me."

The girl seemed suddenly to rouse herself and take a resolution.

"Yes, Rupert Clifford," she said, "I will trust you. I have great need of a friend."

"Then pray do not delay," cried our hero, eagerly.

"Not now," said the young girl. "I dare not stay out longer. I shall be suspected."

"Then what am I to do?" asked Rupert.

"Tell me where I can meet you to-morrow?"

"At what time?" asked our hero.

"About five."

Rupert thought a moment.

At any rate he would come.

Of that he was resolved.

The only question was where.

A moment's consideration and it was decided.

"Do you know the cross roads at Lamondby Point, just a mile from the school?"

"Yes, I know it well," said Gladys. "I will be there. And you will really come?"

There was a joy in her voice which he had never heard before.

"Unless I lose my life between this and then I will be there," said Rupert.

"I shall be grateful to you all my life," said Gladys; "but you do not yet know what I want you to do for me. It may be something you will not care for."

"We will talk of that to-morrow," said our hero. "I think now we had better return to the ball-room for fear our absence should be observed."

He had his arm round her waist to help her up the steps as he spoke, and very happy he felt just then in his boyish love.

The young girl felt an indescribable yearning towards this lad.

She glanced up brightly into his face.

"Do you really care for me?" she said, archly.

The boy lover glanced down into her eyes, and with a sudden impulse bent down and kissed her.

"You naughty boy!" she cried, pushing him away, "you mustn't do that again or I shall be very cross."

Rupert looked very demure.

"I'm very sorry if I've offended you," he said. "Perhaps I'd better not come to-morrow or I might offend again."

Our hero was very young.

But he was a good diplomatist.

Gladys' lip trembled and a tear trickled down her cheek.

"Now you are going to be unkind and cross and ungenerous as everyone is to me," she said; "so I've made a mistake after all."

"No, you've not," said Rupert, still holding his arm round her waist, "only you seemed so lonely and so pretty and good that I couldn't help kissing you. I'll never offend any more."

Gladys laughed up into his eyes.

"Perhaps I was wrong," she said, "in being so hasty."

And so as they passed along to the banqueting hall Rupert took one more, which was returned to him; and, as far as their youthful comprehensions went, they were "lovers" before they re-entered the ball-room.

"Gladys, let us join the dancers," he said; "it will mystify them regarding our absence."

"Yes, but my eyes are such frights with crying."

"Your head ached till you cried, and you went out on the terrace."

"You naughty boy; you will teach me to tell fibs."

"I think from what I saw I am telling the absolute truth," returned Rupert.

And they joined the dancers.

When "good-bye" time came, Rupert was shaken most vigorously by the hand by her father, and a little packet was left in his palm.

"That," said Sir Charles, "is a little memento. Don't look at it until you get home. Whenever you do look at it hereafter remember how bravely you behaved the other day, and try to be as brave again."

He pressed the boy's hand again.

But though Rupert was pleased at this, there was something else he longed for.

Without a "good-bye" from Gladys all would indeed have been hopelessly miserable for him.

It came, however, just as he was expecting that he would not see her again that night.

As he stepped down the marble steps leading to the grounds, dolefully enough, but in advance of the others, the little well-known white figure came hurrying up from the shadows, and said—

"Good-bye, Rupert. Don't forget to-morrow evening."

The little ripe red lips were put up temptingly near his, and he kissed them heartily.

"Good-bye, and heaven bless you," he said in a voice of real emotion. "Some day, when I am a man, I'll tell you what good you have done me by this kiss and the trust you have placed in me. You have made a man of me now, given me a mission to fulfil, and—but there. Gladys, years hence I may tell you all I feel, I cannot now."

He pressed Gladys' hand, bade her good night, and having bade adieu to Sir Charles and the others, he was presently *en route* for Blakesley Hall.

"Sly dog, that Rupert Clifford," said Sir Charles, "making up to my girl! Wish he was older. Good family and all that kind of thing, I believe; and money too."

This was addressed to Dr. Walton with a dig of the ribs, as the boys were filing off across the grounds.

"Yes," said the schoolmaster, "his father, or his adopted father, or whoever it may be, is rich. The lad has money of his own, and he is of higher birth, I verily believe, than any of us imagine."

And so they parted.

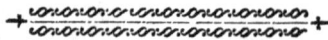

CHAPTER XXX.

DISGRACE—A DESPERATE VENTURE.

"Can I have permission to be absent from school from half-past four until six this evening, sir?"

The words came clear, distinct, resolute, but respectful from the lips of Rupert, our hero.

Dr. Walton looked at him in surprise.

"You astonish me, Master Clifford," he said, somewhat sternly.

"Why, sir?" asked Rupert, still with due respect, though he gazed full in the face of the pedagogue.

"Why!" exclaimed Dr. Walton in astonishment; "you ask why! Was not yesterday a whole holiday?"

"Yesterday's holiday, sir, had some-thing to do with to-day's failure," said Rupert, quietly. "We had a thorough twelve hours' enjoyment, and it tired us out, and——"

"Ah! that may be," returned Dr. Walton; "but pray tell me why you desire this leave?"

"It is for a pure matter of business, sir."

"Business! Is it to meet your father?"

"No, sir."

"Is it for any business which your father has asked you to transact for him?"

"No, sir."

"Then I decline to let you go."

"'WHAT ARE YOU DOING HERE, GLADYS?' CRIED SIR CHARLES."

"Only this once I ask it, sir," pleaded Rupert. "I will not ask such a thing again. You do not know how much depends upon it."

He saw Gladys in his mind's eye as he spoke; her eager joy as she reached the trysting-place unobserved, her despair and misery as she found that he was not there.

His generous heart rebelled against the picture, and his fiery gipsy blood too rebelled against the authority of Doctor Walton in such a case as this.

"No, it is of no use for you to plead," said the schoolmaster. "I see in your manner signs of rebellion which must be checked. Besides it cannot be important."

"It is so important," returned Rupert hotly, "that I would almost risk expulsion from the school by going counter to your wishes than not go at all."

The doctor fired up at these words.

In fact he was fairly aghast.

"Master Clifford," he said, "I am very much surprised at your conduct. Go to your room—your dormitory—at once, and do not show yourself out of it until to-morrow morning. And then I shall expect you to have learned by heart —accurately—fifty lines of Virgil."

Rupert had by this time completely lost his head.

"Very well, sir," he said, with white lips. "Yesterday a petted hero, to-day a culprit, sentenced to solitary confinement and an imposition! *Sic transit gloria mundi!*"

And before Doctor Walton could say another word the boy had left the room.

Rupert, meanwhile, hurried to the schoolroom, selected his Virgil, and then made his way up to his dormitory.

What was he to do?

His heart rebelled against what he thought the tyranny of Doctor Walton.

He rose and looked from his window across the playground, over the meadow, and along the pleasant lane.

He could see almost to Lamondby Point, where he had appointed to meet Gladys.

He took out his watch.

It was now half-past four.

Just time to meet Gladys at five.

The thought inspired him with a desperate courage.

He would go.

He took his cricketing hat out of his box, put it on, and glided down the stairs.

He met no one.

An exultant feeling arose in his heart.

The gipsy blood, which coursed in his veins, ran riot as it were with pleasure at the idea of such a short time even of freedom.

He cautiously crept to the door which opened out upon the playground.

Out then into the latter, across the meadow, over the ruined wall, and along the lane.

He had escaped.

He went along at such a rapid pace that he arrived at the rendezvous long before his time.

He glanced along the pleasant lane, in which he knew that Gladys Alreston was bound to come.

His heart would scarcely have been so light had he known what was happening at that moment at the school.

About a quarter of an hour after the successful flight of Rupert from the Academy, Doctor Walton remembered something which he especially desired to see him about.

"Tell Rupert Clifford I wish to speak to him," he said to Leigh Glindon.

"Where is he, sir?" asked Leigh.

"Up in the dormitory."

Leigh, wondering why Rupert should be in disgrace so soon after his triumph, went upstairs at once to the sleeping chamber.

He searched everywhere, but no Rupert.

The schoolmaster said nothing when he heard that Rupert was nowhere to be seen, but a heavy frown settled upon his face.

"Rupert's in for it this time, and no mistake," thought Leigh Glindon.

CHAPTER XXXI.

GLADYS' CONFESSION—RUPERT TAKES THE OFFICE OF CHAMPION—A MOST UNEXPECTED FINALE.

It was with a glad and a fastly-beating heart that Rupert saw advancing along the lane the form of Gladys Alreston.

She was attired this time not in white, as he had seen her on the two former occasions, but in black velvet and white lace.

The little fairy looked exquisitely beautiful in this, with her golden hair falling in waving masses over her dark-clad shoulders.

A pretty flush of health was on her cheek, a bright sparkle in her eye, and her lips were rosy red.

In a few moments their hands had met in a close warm pressure.

"You good boy!" she said, flashing bright glances at the handsome lad. "You are punctual."

"Yes, I tried to be in time," he said, ruefully.

If she only knew at what a sacrifice.

"You will think me a strange girl," she said, "to come to you for advice and help, when I have so many others older and stronger around me. But I cannot trust one of them, and I am certain I can trust you."

"Be quick, then, and tell me, Gladys," said Rupert. "I have but little time, and Doctor Walton is very unreasonably angry to-day."

"I will not keep you long, Rupert," returned the girl. "I'll tell you my meaning as briefly as I can, and then explain the service I want of you.

"I am the eldest child known to those friends of my father's who live in this neighbourhood.

"In fact, I am the supposed only child.

"But this is not the case.

"I am the second child, and have a brother, Reginald Alreston, a tall, handsome fellow, six years older than I am."

"He is twenty-one, then," said Rupert.

"Yes," replied Gladys, "and he was very high-spirited. Even as a boy he was so.

"So when he got into some scrape in London and applied to my father to aid him, he was refused.

"This was two years ago.

"Of course, I did not know much about it at the time, but I was told by one of the servants what a scene there was when Reginald came down to see his father.

"There was an awful quarrel, and after a time my brother left the house, and swore he would never enter it again.

"But times changed.

"He kept his word until two weeks ago, when he wrote to say that he was dangerously ill; that he had supported himself as best he could by drawing, but that now his hand was helpless, and that he must ask his only protector to aid him.

"My father tore the letter in two, and returned it without a syllable."

"Dear me!" said Rupert, in sorrowful surprise. "He was so generous—so kind to me."

Gladys smiled.

"Ah," she said, "you saved his favourite child—his only one, as he calls me."

"It is a strange story," returned Rupert.

"Alas, Rupert, you do not know how hard and cruel my father can be."

The shadows were deepening, time was flying, and still Gladys had asked him nothing.

She seemed anxious to go on with the story of her troubles.

"Gladys," he said, taking her hand tenderly, "you must not forget that I am but a poor champion. Some day, if you only consent, all my time, my heart and my service shall be yours. Now I am but a schoolboy at the mercy of my master. Pray tell me how I can serve you, and at any risk I will do it."

The young girl heaved a deep sigh.

"You have reminded me, Rupert," she said, "what a selfish being I am! What I want you to do is this. In this purse are fifty pounds in notes. I have saved the money from time to time, thinking that Reginald might be in trouble. I want this money sent to him.

I have no conception how to do it. I dare not trust anyone at Alreston Towers. Will you send it to him for me, Rupert?"

"Yes, of course I will, Gladys," replied the boy, delighted at the confidence reposed in him; "but you must trust me also with his address."

The girl flushed.

"Ah," she said, "I had forgotten that. Of course I must. It is a very poor place, I fear. Poor Reginald! Here it is. No. 3, Marver's Rents, City Road, London."

"Would you like me to send it by post, or would you like me to take it?" asked Rupert, with wonderful coolness and self-possession. "You would, I fancy, feel so much more satisfied if you knew that I had placed the money in his hands."

"Oh, yes," replied Gladys, brightening up. "I should indeed feel more safe and satisfied. But how can you do so? How can you get away?"

"I will manage all right," he said, cheerfully. "I can't get away until to-morrow, but I will start early—say nine. I can be in London at one o'clock. By two o'clock your brother shall have the money. But how shall I let you know that all is right?"

"If you undertake it, I know all will be right," said the little maiden; "but you can leave a note for me here in this hollow tree. I shall come for it in four days. Tell dear Reginald that he has my best love, and if his illness becomes dangerous, he is to send to me and risk everything."

"You quite depend on me, Gladys?" he asked, as they paused at the bend of the road.

"Yes, quite," said the young girl; "but I must now say good-bye."

The words trembled on her rosy lips; her face was turned upwards towards his, and he bent down and kissed her.

Then like a frightened fawn she fled away along the lane.

Rupert paused a moment ere he turned, that he might watch the sylph-like figure of the sweet young maiden until it disappeared round the bend of the lane.

"Heaven bless her!" was his murmured prayer, as he wheeled round and prepared to proceed schoolwards.

But a loud cry escaped his lips, and he staggered backwards as he did so.

For there, angry, pale, and threatening, stood before him the schoolmaster, Dr. Walton.

"Well, sir, and what have you to say for yourself?" he cried.

Rupert was pale and distressed.

But what was he do?

"I am very sorry to have disobeyed you, Doctor Walton," he said—"very sorry. But I told you when I asked you for leave that I had a great reason for desiring it."

"I am aware of that," returned the schoolmaster, more angry than ever, "but you must know that a schoolboy is not his own master, and must conform to the rules of his academy, no matter what personal inconvenience it may subject him to."

"I know that, sir," said Rupert; "but in this case, it is not my personal convenience that I have been studying, but someone else's. Even now I find it necessary for me to write a letter to my father and post it at once. So I must ask leave to go to the town."

"And pray why do you wish to go to Melton when you can post the letter at the school?" he asked.

"Because it is most important," said our hero. "It is, in fact, a matter of life and death, and I want to receive an answer early to morrow."

"Very well," said the schoolmaster, "you can go. I will go with you. Just remember this. I know there is some mystery overhanging your life. I know that there is often a necessity for you to communicate privately with your father, or I would not permit it. I shall also write to him explaining your behaviour, and asking him to suggest the means of preventing its recurrence."

"Very well, sir," said Rupert. "I am grateful to you for permitting me to go to the town. We shall only be a very short time gone."

"Yes, we will start now," said Dr. Walton; "but on the way I shall expect you to explain why I find you here with Miss Gladys Alreston under such peculiar circumstances."

"That I cannot explain, sir," said Rupert, quietly.

"I will ask you no more questions then," said Dr. Walton, who now felt irritated beyond the expression of words. "I must leave all to your father."

They went on silently together for some time.

Presently they reached Melton, and the two letters were despatched.

Rupert's was one requesting Reuben to ask him up to London the next day, and that of Dr. Walton was a request that when convenient "Colonel Clifford" would honour him with a visit.

The next day Rupert presented himself to the doctor, saying—

"I have to ask for leave to go to London, sir."

The doctor looked at him in utter amazement.

Had the boy taken leave of his senses?

"Well, certainly, Master Rupert Clifford," he said, "you are acting in a most strange manner. What right have you to ask me?"

"It is by my father's wish," said our hero.

And he handed in a letter.

It ran thus—

"DEAR RUPERT.—Tell Doctor Walton that I do not answer his letter, because I think it will be wiser to see him in regard to the whole matter. As regards yourself, it will be best to go up to London as soon as you receive this. You know what station to go to.

"Yours in haste,
"G. CLIFFORD."

Dr. Walton was utterly surprised.

"How long do you suppose you will be absent?"

"Only till to-morrow night, sir."

"That will do then," said Dr. Walton. "If you are late take a fly from the station. Under the circumstances I do not think it exactly safe for you to be about after dark."

It was a responsible journey for a young lad to take, but he was in no way daunted when he reached the London terminus.

He remembered well the direction given to him by Gladys — Marver's Rents, City Road—and he soon reached it.

The entrance was a narrow archway of grey stone, and the pavement had a look as if it had been worn out by the continual shuffling of weary feet.

The schoolboy, fresh from the pleasant air and generally joyous surroundings of the country, was naturally somewhat loth to enter such a place, but he summoned up his courage at last and knocked at number three.

In an instant he was surrounded by an admiring group of youngsters of both sexes, some shoeless, some with boots, but all with dirty faces.

"Is Mr. Darlington in?" was Rupert's inquiry.

That was the name by which Reginald Alreston was known.

"Oh, yes: Mr. Darlington," said a bare-legged girl about twelve, "he's in 'cos he can't go out. You'll find him in the third floor back."

Rupert lost no time in going up the squalid staircase and knocking at the door.

A faint voice said—

"Come in."

And the lad boldly entered and advanced to the bedside.

He saw there a face which at once obtained his sympathy.

It was so like that of the sister, whose generous little heart had sent him on the mission.

"I hope you do not think me intruding," said the schoolboy.

"No, I am glad to see new faces," said Reginald, "and yours is one that I like. But it is, indeed, a mystery to me why you are here. What is your name?"

Rupert hesitated.

"I am at present called Rupert Clifford," he said, "but I may some day lay claim to another name. My name, however, is no guide. I come from Miss Gladys Alreston, of Alreston Towers, with a letter."

The face of the sick man, before so pale, became suffused with a rosy tint of excitement, as with eager eyes he began to read the precious missive.

Then tears came into his eyes.

"Dear little Gladys — dear little sister!" he said. "Ah, Mr. Clifford, you don't know half how good she is."

Rupert flushed now.

"Oh, yes, I think I do," replied he.

"Well, she has saved my life this time," said Reginald; "that is to say, if things are done on the spot. But I have no one here whom I care to trust. If you will aid me to dress, and also could fetch me a little wine, I think I could find strength enough to get out, and with a cab I could reach some lodging in a more respectable neighbourhood."

"I will fetch the wine first," returned our hero, "then you will be better able to dress."

And without further demur he quitted the room, and in a few moments appeared again with the needed refreshment.

Reginald took a long draught of wine, and then ate with evidently little appetite a few wine biscuits.

He seemed revived, however, and said—

"I daresay you wonder at seeing the eldest son of Sir Charles Alreston, of Alreston Towers, in such a place as this," pursued Reginald.

"Yes, but I have heard a little about the matter from your sister."

"Not all," said Reginald. "Before you leave London I will enlighten you a little as regards the real state of affairs. But this place makes me feel degraded. My first act must be to quit it."

Reginald, with our hero's aid, was not long in dressing himself.

"I wish," he said, "that you would do me one more favour."

"Certainly."

"Go next door, ring the third bell, and a little old man will come to you. Tell him I want to see him, and that I am going to pay him his rent. He'll be up here like a shot."

Rupert was off at once to the door of the next house.

As Reginald had told him, it was opened by a curious little old man, who stared in a most wondering way at the well-dressed young gentleman who thus unexpectedly appeared before him.

"What is it?" said the old man, rubbing his hands together.

"Mr. Darlington wishes to see you in order to pay his rent.

"I will come at once, sir."

He was astounded when he saw Reginald dressed, but he had sufficient presence of mind to merely say—

"I am glad, sir, to see you up."

"What is the amount of your bill?" said Reginald.

"I have it here, sir," he said (old Commins he was called in the court); "the bill has been made out some days. Two pounds ten, sir."

"There is your money; give me a receipt."

Reginald pointed to pen and ink.

The man did as requested, and pocketed the money.

"If ever I can do you a service, Mr. Darlington, in any way——"

Then Reginald thundered forth—

"Yes, you can do me a service. Some day, when my father and I are reconciled, let him know how you robbed me of my money while I had it; how you let me lie in sickness in this wretched room when it was all gone; how you jeered at my wants, laughed at my starvation, made game of my poverty; and how, coward and dotard, you cringed to me when at last the money came to fill your hungry pockets. Go!"

"One moment, Mr. Darlington," said the old man, in hoarse accents, and as he spoke he caught at the back of a chair, looking at Rupert. "I didn't quite see the face of this 'ere young gentleman before, but as I've seen it plainly now, may I ask is his name Pendarven?"

Rupert's face flushed.

But he did not betray himself.

"My friend's name is Clifford," said Reginald, "not Pendarven."

"And yet I am not mistaken," said old Commins. "I will swear that. If you should run across a party named Reuben Pendarven, tell him I want him, and I can do him a service."

These words were bewildering to Rupert. What could it mean?

"You take me aback," he said, after a moment's consideration.

"Then you do know the name?" asked the old man eagerly.

Then he continued—

"If you know where Reuben Pendarven is, he will thank you for your information," and with these words he left the room.

It was not long before, leaning on the arm of our hero, Reginald made his way downstairs into the dingy street.

A cabman was directed to drive to Brompton, where Rupert soon found lodgings for Reginald.

Then, despite all our hero's requests that he should rest first, he said—

"I must tell you why you see me in this wretched state. It is of no use trying to delay my confession, if confession it can be called."

Rupert saw that Reginald was far too weak and excited to stand contradiction.

"The story is a very short one," said Alreston, "it is merely the old one of a father's sternness and a son's disobedience. My father desired me not to go into the army. I went. My father relented and wished me to marry a rich heiress in order to show obedience to his wishes.

"I refused, and wedded a young girl of my own choosing, beautiful, good, but poor. My wife, my Rose, was indeed good and kind to me.

"But bad times fell upon us.

"I sold out of the army, took a situation and lost it; then I lost my wife, and after her death everything went wrong.

"I went down, down the ladder, until I arrived at the position in which you found me to-day.

"Once only I wrote to my father, and that was enough.

"My request, which was only for money to emigrate, and never return, was refused, and after that I had no courage to ask again for aid.

"Again and again, I have heard from dear Gladys, and now she has saved me; and I have a chance once more. But what will bring back the past? What will give me my Rose, my love, my wife?"

As he said the words his head fell back, and when Rupert sprang forward with a cry, he saw that the face of his new friend had an impress as of death upon it.

This seemed a pretty end to his adventure.

CHAPTER XXXII.

RUPERT'S MISSION—THE TRUTH AT LAST.

IT was quite impossible for Rupert to leave Reginald Alreston in the condition in which he now was.

When he recovered from the swoon into which the memory of his old love had cast him, he was in no mood or condition to say more.

The doctor, whom the frightened Rupert had summoned to his side, had pronounced talking quite out of the question, and so, telling him that he was to keep himself very calm and quiet, and he would soon be well, he quitted him, "leaving him," he said, "in good hands."

In this dilemma, and knowing he was due at the school on the next evening, he wrote to his cousin and told him the whole story.

"I know that anything wrong," he said, "you would not aid me in. But in this matter I appeal to you. All I wish you to say for me is that I am in town by your full consent and wish."

By the same post he wrote to Doctor Walton, saying that he was compelled to remain in town, but that a letter from his father would explain all.

This, of course, was satisfactory to the doctor, though very mysterious.

However, Rupert had gained his point.

He had performed Gladys' mission, and was able, at any rate for a time, to remain to take care of the brother.

On the following day our hero received a letter in which Reuben told him that he had written to Doctor Walton.

At the same time he thanked Rupert for the information he had given him about old Commins.

On the second day Reuben arrived.

He had called at Reginald's place to see Rupert before he paid his visit to old Commins.

"If I prove my innocence now, my dear Rupert," cried Reuben, "after all these wretched years, it will be through you."

"When are you going to see Commins?"

"To-night, and if I find that he has any information to give me which will enable me to resume my own name, depend upon it I will lose no time in making my way down to the neighbourhood of Pendarven Abbey. Then, Rupert, you can assume your own name, and——"

"Stay!" said our hero. "Be not

rash, dear Reuben. "Remember your vow to vindicate my mother's honour. Until that is done I cannot assume my name.

"You are right, Rupert," said Reuben. "So I long to see this old villain Commins. By the way," he added, "you must be with me for a few hours this evening."

"Yes," returned Rupert, "I can leave Reginald for a time."

To the Gipsy Schoolboy and his cousin this visit to the man Commins seemed to open up a real prospect of good in the future.

"I feel certain," said Reuben, as they hastened on, "that directly I succeed in establishing my innocence you will find your proofs, and be recognised as Master of Pendarven."

Rupert laughed.

But yet a bright flush came to his cheeks.

"Here we are at last," he cried, as they came to the dingy archway. "I will take your note to the old man, and we can wait for him at the 'Clarendon,' as you propose."

Old Commins was surprised when Rupert gave him the note.

"I will be round at the 'Clarendon' in a few minutes," he said. "Mr. Pendarven did quite right in not coming here; it would not be safe."

Rupert and his cousin were soon seated in a very pleasant parlour, and the old man was not long in following them to the place.

But what a change had taken place in him!

The man was dressed in a black frock coat and waistcoat and plain drab trousers.

His hair was brushed up in a way that suggested alarm; but his voice was bland, and his smile placid.

"Glad to see you, Mr. Reuben Pendarven. Do you remember me?"

Reuben regarded him intently.

"Well," he said, doubtingly, "I never knew anyone of the name of Commins in my life, and yet there is something about you which seems strangely familiar."

"Ha, ha!" laughed the old man, "that's just it—just it! But we must recognise one another somehow, or we shall never be able to do successful business."

"Give me some clue, then."

"An old lawyer's office in Gray's Inn," said the man. "An office on the second floor; a young man of the name of Reuben Pendarven, who had overrun the constable and wanted to borrow money very often; an old clerk of the name of Tom Croft who used to sit in the outer office and admit the visitors. Doesn't all this suggest anything?"

Reuben's face lit up suddenly.

A ray of memory had broken in upon him.

"Why, yes, it does," he said. "You are Tom Croft."

The old man laughed.

"That's just it," he answered. "I am."

"You know everything, then," said Reuben, at length, "and wish to sell your knowledge."

"Yes; and now let me explain all," said Croft. "The first time that I became acquainted with you, Mr. Reuben, was when you came to borrow a thousand pounds, and the governor, Mr. Mat Lewis, said, 'He's as right as a trivet, Tom. Don't make a fuss when he comes. Bring him straight into my office. He'll be one of our best customers, or I'm a Dutchman.'

"Well, you proved so.

"All the loans you had were paid off to the moment.

"Well, the time came, as it always does in these matters, when your father became angry at your extravagance, and refused to pay any more.

"You begged Mat Lewis to lend as usual, and he declined.

"A week after a cheque was discovered to have been forged for five thousand pounds on Mat Lewis.

"This was the exact sum which you had asked for, and by a chain of the most convincing circumstances the guilt was brought home to you. Is it not so, Mr. Reuben?"

"Yes, yes!" cried Reuben Pendarven, impatiently. "I know all this, but I want to know how it was done."

"That is what we are coming to," said the clerk. "In the office with me was a young fellow named Jack Loftus, who knew your affairs quite as well as I did, and had evidently made more of a study of them.

"Well, he and a man called Tim

Delany forged the cheque and got the money.

"They stopped in the office just the same, and never flashed their money about, or drank or did anything to excite suspicion, and then another five thousand cheque was floated, supposed to be signed by your father.

"Then, of course, suspicion fell on you.

"Tim and Jack paid a man to swear that you had enticed him to help you. They swore that you had tried to get them to go in for the swindle with them, and then to make matters worse you ran away.

"Perhaps it was natural.

"But it wasn't any less foolish for that."

"And you," interrupted Reuben, hotly; "what finger had you in this villainy?"

"I am here to tell the truth and to make money, if possible," returned Commins, smilingly, "but listen.

"I'd overheard what had been said between Tim Delany and Jack Loftus, and a good bit that was said to the other man, Jim Dowton, and I swore I'd tell the whole game if they didn't give me some money, and always keep me posted up where they were.

"They consented.

"How could they help it?

"They gave me a lumping sum, and I left the employment of old Mat Lewis as soon as I thought it would not excite suspicion; then I settled down as a rent collector at Marver's Rents after I had spent all my money, and here I am."

"And what is the first move to be?" asked Reuben.

He spoke with no disguise of the contempt he felt.

"Jim Dowton will turn Queen's evidence against the other two. I shall see him to-night and promise him—'no prosecution and a hundred pounds.' Tim Delany is dead, but I know where Jack Loftus is to be found, and as he's done me a dirty trick, why I shall pounce on him at once."

"But Mat Lewis—is he alive?" asked Reuben Pendarven.

"Yes, and strange to say he never really believed you guilty. He always had just the same idea as I had and have now, and that is that your uncle Hubert paid these men to get up the whole affair."

Reuben started at this.

He rose abruptly.

"Well," he said, "I will give Jack Loftus in custody for the forgery on my father. I hope Mat Lewis will prosecute also. I will meet you here again to-morrow night."

And so they parted, Tom Croft remaining to drink success to his expected good fortune, and our hero and Reuben proceeding to their lodgings.

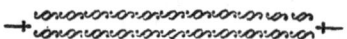

CHAPTER XXXIII.

RUPERT STARTS AGAIN FOR SCHOOL, AND JOSHUA SETS TO WORK.

RUPERT'S presence was no longer required in town.

"Well, Rupert," said Reuben, on the morning after the interview with Tom Croft, "I don't think I need detain you in London any more. I hope that your friend, Miss Gladys Alreston, will be pleased with you."

"Yes, I should hope so," said Rupert, with a slight flush. "I will leave early in the morning. Gladys told me that she was in the habit of having walks by the river, and so I shall run the risk, and get up near the house and wander along by the water's side."

"Why not write?"

"All her letters are opened for fear she should correspond with Reginald."

"Ah! well. Go down by the last train to-night."

Rupert's heart was full of pleasurable feelings when he did go, for not only could he tell Gladys now that she had sent in time to save her brother's life, but bear to her the glad tidings that Reuben had found him a good position, which would keep him as a gentleman until the time when Sir Charles' heart melted, and he came into his fortune.

On the same day which saw Rupert

on his road Jack Loftus was arrested and taken before the magistrate.

Next morning Hubert Pendarven, sitting at breakfast at Pendarven Abbey, saw in his daily paper the account of the examination.

He looked astonished and fearful as he read it.

But he trembled, and his lips grew white as he read one paragraph.

"In answer to the magistrate the prisoner said—

"'I plead guilty, your worship, but I was paid to do it by Mr. Hubert Pendarven, of Pendarven Abbey.'"

The paper fluttered from his nerveless hand.

"Well, well," he murmured, "this is a catastrophe indeed. What made this rascal stop in England after all and be caught like a rat in a trap? What can be done?"

He rose and paced the room impatiently.

Then he paused.

"Something must be done," he said. "I must go to London and try and settle matters. Heavens! if this is only the beginning of the end—if through this the whole horrible story comes out!"

With a shudder, he took a decanter from the sideboard, poured out a tumblerful of wine, and drank it off.

"Whatever I do I must not give way before my people," he said, "but if all fails, I must fly or kill myself."

Meanwhile we must return to the school.

The evil-minded Joshua was perfectly well now.

The time for action had consequently arrived.

About ten o'clock everything was quiet at the school.

Joshua crept out of bed, and approaching the door, listened eagerly.

It was all so still that one could have heard a pin fall.

The boy's heart leaped with an evil joy.

He had studied the cruel and dishonest part he was to play, and he was now well prepared for it.

With his boots slung by a string round his neck, he began to creep down the stairs until he reached the first floor.

On this floor was the little room which Doctor Walton used as a private study, and where he kept his money.

He had made a survey of this place, and was acquainted with every nook and corner in it.

He peeped first through the keyhole to see if any light was there.

All was still and dark.

He opened the door gently and peeped in.

"All's well," muttered the rascal.

Then he entered on tiptoe and stole gently across the room.

The money, as the dishonest young rascal was well aware, was always kept in a little box in the bureau that stood in the corner.

Like many other professional men, Dr. Walton was very careless, and the key was in the lock.

With an evil smile, Joshua opened the bureau.

Yes.

All was right.

There was the tiny cash box.

His hand was already upon it, when a sound startled him.

The sound of a door being opened.

He hastily and noiselessly closed the bureau, and crouched down by the table.

But he took one precaution.

Even in that short time he locked the bureau and took the key out.

The door opened just as he concealed himself, and Dr. Walton himself entered the room.

"What in the name of all that's horrible brings him here?" thought Joshua, whose heart, which lately beat with delight, now sank to the very lowest ebb. "I suppose the old chap takes it in his head to snooze here, or something of that sort."

Dr. Walton, in fact, did not seem in any hurry.

He sat down calmly in his armchair, lit his pipe, and closed his eyes.

Slowly, after a few moments, Joshua crawled from beneath the table.

But as he was about to make his way towards the bureau, he noticed for the first time an intense heat.

It seemed to come from the landing.

And then, as he glanced towards the door in wonder and dismay, he beheld small coils of smoke coming from beneath it.

A horrible idea entered his brain.

He was hemmed in.

The place was evidently on fire, and

if so, there were but two courses open to him.

In the first place to confess his presence to Dr. Walton.

In the second to be burnt to death.

He crawled nearer the door to see how far the danger had extended.

He opened it gently.

The doctor never moved.

One glance out showed Joshua what had happened.

The schoolhouse was on fire.

Only a moment he hesitated.

Then he made up his mind.

He would creep out, then rush into the room, rouse the schoolmaster to a sense of his danger, and while the worthy man was out of the room, he would commit his wicked act of theft.

He had no time left for more reflection.

Rising from the heated floor, he made a dash into the room.

"Doctor, doctor!" he cried.

The schoolmaster sprang up.

"What is the matter?" he cried.

"Quick, sir," returned Joshua, "the house is on fire. This way."

The unsuspecting doctor made a spring for the door.

Joshua sprang for the bureau.

The key was in an instant turned in the lock, his hand seized the cash box, and leaving the bureau open, he made a dash for the window.

It was fastened with a patent fastening, and he could not open it.

Thief and coward as he was, he was trapped.

*   *   *   *

Meanwhile we must return to Rupert Pendarven.

Coming down to Melton-on-the-Sea by the train, as was arranged on the night of the arrest of Jack Loftus, he put up at the "Lord Warden Hotel."

At seven in the morning, Sir Charles Alreston, feeling restless, wandered out into his grounds.

The graceful river ran at their extremity, and to this he made his way.

He was by no means a happy man.

Obstinacy had been his bane all his life through.

He had love for his eldest son.

But he would not give in.

Reginald had run counter to his wishes.

Going down to a point known as Melton Edge (in consequence of some old boundary), he sat down, and leaning against a tree, contemplated the rapidly-flowing river.

Presently he became aware that he was not alone.

He heard voices near him.

A familiar name too—Reginald.

Carefully and noiselessly, Sir Charles parted some of the small branches at the side.

This enabled him to see the speakers.

To his astonishment he saw Gladys sitting on the grassy bank, with her head resting on the shoulder of Rupert Pendarven.

She was weeping, and our hero's arm was around her waist.

The first emotion in the heart of Sir Charles was intense anger.

"Do not give way," said Rupert gently to the girl. "Reginald is better now, and in good hands. He will soon recover all his old strength."

"He is coming near us, too, you say," returned Gladys.

"Yes, soon," replied Rupert. "And, perhaps, when your father knows all, he will relent."

"Yes, when he hears of his starvation and misery," said Gladys.

The baronet's cheeks grew pale.

"Starvation!" he muttered. "I didn't know the boy had come to that. I must listen to more."

CHAPTER XXXIV.

THE FLIGHT OF GLADYS.

"CHEER up, Gladys," said Rupert, after a moment; "your brother will suffer no more privations, and some day the sight of his only son may arouse a long-forgotten love. Never despair, Gladys."

The young girl smiled up at him.

He had his arm still round her waist, and by an irresistible impulse, he bent and kissed her.

"The young rascal!" cried Sir Charles.

And with the agility of youth he sprang through the bushes and confronted the astounded pair.

Gladys, with a startled cry, leaped to her feet, and for an instant, seemed as if she was going to cling to Rupert for protection.

Rupert, on his part, turned very pale, and stood glaring silently at the angry old man.

"What is the meaning of this, Gladys?" he said. "What are you doing here at this time in the morning with one of the scholars from the academy? Are you not ashamed of yourself?"

"No, I am not ashamed of myself," said Gladys, respectfully, "because I have done nothing wrong. My meeting here this morning with Master Rupert Clifford was purely accidental."

"Well, we will continue our conversation elsewhere. With your friend here I will continue it at Blakesley Hall Academy."

And without so much as another look at our hero, he took Gladys by the hand and strode away.

"Good-bye, Miss Alreston," said Rupert.

"Good-bye, Rupert," said Gladys.

"Ay, it will be good-bye," said Sir Charles, angrily. "What do you mean by exposing our private affairs to an utter stranger—a boy, who will tell everyone? But I shall take good care you do not have much chance of seeing him again."

"How?"

Gladys trembled.

"You will not remain at home."

A wild look came into her eyes, and she turned deadly pale.

"Not remain at home!" she cried. "You cannot mean that?"

"I do mean it," said Sir Charles.

On reaching the Towers, Gladys was about to walk away to her own apartments.

But he stopped her.

"Understand," he said, "that I am going to Lady Denmore's to-day, and the companion she chooses will have to take the place of a mother to you."

And he left the room.

When Sir Charles reached home, Gladys was waiting for him in the drawing-room.

But without a word to her, the baronet pulled the massive bell-rope.

In a few moments Mrs. Bassett the housekeeper made her appearance.

She expressed no surprise at being called, but simply said—

"Do you want me, Sir Charles?"

"Yes," replied the baronet, calmly. "A lady is coming this evening as chaperon to Miss Alreston. Until then you will see that my daughter has no communication with anyone—in fact, she had better keep her room."

That evening Mrs. De la Poer, the new chaperon, arrived.

She was a lady about thirty, a widow, and had evidently moved in good society.

Gladys was at once sent for.

But she was nowhere to be found.

Sir Charles heard with horror that her window was found open, and that her travelling clothes were gone.

A letter was on the table, which the baronet read in silence and then destroyed.

That evening, at the "Lord Warden," just before he set out for the academy, Rupert received the following note—

"DEAR RUPERT.—Good-bye. I have run away. Don't think me ungrateful for all your kindness to my brother because I have not told you my address. I have a great reason. Write to Reginald and tell him all.

"GLADYS."

Young as he was our hero was able to see the gravity of the step which the young girl had so suddenly taken.

All the way to the school her vision haunted him, helpless and alone, after all her delicate culture.

Yet what could he do?

CHAPTER XXXV.

JOSHUA'S PERIL—THE DENOUEMENT OF THE PLOT.

MEANWHILE Joshua saw with horror the fix which his own villainy had placed him in.

The fire had a good hold of his part of the house, at any rate, and there he was stuck, helpless, between two perils.

He could not escape through the windows, which were securely latched, and on the other side the red and scorching flames lapped between him and freedom.

Doctor Walton, driven back into the room by the force of the flames, saw him.

"What are you doing here now?" he asked. "Quick, we must go out by the window!"

"I have tried, but I cannot open the fastening," said Joshua.

"Let me try," cried Doctor Walton.

He hastened to the window, leaped upon a chair, and in a few moments had undone the patent fastening.

When the window was thrown open, there was a greater roar of flame on the landing, and a rush of smoke beneath the doorway.

Joshua, at the bidding of Doctor Walton, glanced down from the window into the darkness below.

"Can you jump that distance?" asked the doctor.

The lad hesitated.

It was at least sixteen feet to the ground.

"Is it hard earth below?"

"I don't know what you call hard earth," said the doctor. "If you are afraid let me go first."

Joshua still hesitating, the schoolmaster drew himself up on the windowsill, and seizing the ivy which clung to the old wall, began to lower himself down.

In a few moments he had reached the ground.

"Now, then, Joshua," he cried.

"I'm coming, sir," said the lad.

But the words were said in a very quavering and doubtful sort of voice.

He got on the sill, made a feeble clutch at the ivy with his trembling fingers, and then let himself go.

In an instant a fearful cry rang out on the night air.

The ivy had given way, and he was precipitated headlong to the ground.

The one cry was all that escaped his lips.

When he reached the ground all was still.

The doctor had disappeared.

When he had shown Joshua the way to safety, he at once dashed round to the front of the house, hoping, at any rate, to find someone whom he could despatch in search of assistance.

When he reached the front door, he found an excited throng of persons assembled.

Servants, pupils, and others, were mingled together in one talkative and eager crowd.

A shout of delight ascended in the night air, as they recognised the schoolmaster, and to his surprise his wife flung herself sobbing on his breast.

"Oh!" she cried, "thank Heaven you are safe."

"My dear wife," cried he, disengaging himself from her fond embrace, "pray do not distress yourself about me. Think what danger they must be in upstairs."

"No, no, dear husband," said Mrs. Walton, "all danger is over now. All our fears were for you."

"You bewilder me," said the schoolmaster, "pray explain."

She did so.

The heat and the suffocating fumes had roused nearly everyone in the house, and all had escaped but Joshua.

"Joshua was in my room and escaped with me, but I don't see him," he cried; "he may have missed his hold of the ivy and fallen; let us go round and see."

Accompanied by Long Toby, and one or two of the head scholars, Doctor Walton hastened round to the ground below the study window.

They held lanterns in their hands now, so that they could see everything very readily.

And as they approached the spot where

Joshua had fallen they saw someone kneeling by another's prostrate form.

Hurrying up and casting the light full in the face of the kneeling figure, Doctor Walton started back in amazement.

It was Rupert.

"You here, Rupert Clifford," he cried.

"Yes, sir," replied our hero. "I was entering by the front gate, when I heard a faint moaning cry, and hurrying to this spot I found Joshua. He is dead. He died with that moan, I believe."

They knelt round the quiet figure and examined it.

Rupert's words were too true.

As they lifted him from the ground something heavy fell from his pocket.

"What is that?" cried the doctor, as he stooped to examine it. "Bless me! My cashbox! Well—well. His sin has found him out!"

His part of the evening's tragedy never transpired.

Of course, though advertised for, no one ever appeared to claim Joshua's body.

Doctor Walton had money in hand for his schooling.

And so he was buried quietly in the country churchyard; and the scandal which had threatened the school was averted by silence.

CHAPTER XXXVI.

A WHOLE HOLIDAY—FARMER POPGUN'S PIPPINS.

ON the next day when the boys were assembled in the schoolroom, after prayers had been said, Doctor Walton addressed them.

As he did so his voice was broken with emotion.

"We are all—you and I and my family—very much upset, naturally, by the events of last night, and I propose, therefore, that we do not take any lessons to-day. I give you a whole holiday. The page boy will bring out your provisions, and I trust you will enjoy your holiday."

The day was soon disposed of.

One party chose a game of cricket; another a row on the river, while another party, under the leadership of Rupert and Leigh Glindon, agreed upon a party to the Gipsy Knoll.

It was a wild romantic place, much affected by pleasure parties from all parts, and had been called Gipsy's Knoll from time immemorial, in consequence of some event connected with a tribe of gipsies who had resided there years ago; and been mixed up with some awful crime.

To this spot then we will accompany Rupert and his party, who went off joyous and full of fun, little dreaming of the results which would follow that simple picnic party.

Their meal was despatched with all manner of jokes and laughter.

"We only want some of Farmer Popgun's pippins for dessert now," said Leigh Glindon, "and we should be all right."

He would not have said this had he been aware that a tall man of unmistakable gipsy origin was leaning behind a tree near them, and listening to every word they said.

"Ah!" cried Ralph Pendarven. "Farmer Popgun's pippins are a well-known nicety. Let's pay him a visit."

"Stop a moment, young gentlemen!" said a stern voice.

The scowling looks, and the rude appearance altogether of the man who had so unexpectedly obtruded himself, was by no means pleasing to our boys.

Now the reader must not imagine for a moment that the worthy tiller of the soil, whose patience and property they were plotting against, was really named Popgun.

Nothing of the kind.

His real name was Brandford.

But he possessed a blunderbuss.

It hit a good many things sometimes, but not those intended to be hit by its owner.

He had a most magnificent orchard, where grew the pippins which were the talk of the vicinity and the special temptation of every schoolboy.

Real golden pippins.

Suffice it that our boys, who were no better and no worse than others, had made up their minds to have a taste, and consequently they were by no means overjoyed at discovering that they had been overheard.

They regarded the tall swarthy gipsy with anything but friendly looks, as he strode into their midst.

"Well," said Rupert, looking at him steadily, "what if you have heard all?"

"I'm going to put a stop to your little game," replied the man.

"Oh, you are, are you?" said Rupert. "How are you going to do it?"

"I shall go and inform Farmer Brandford," he answered.

This was straightforward with a vengeance.

The boys looked utterly disconcerted, with the exception of Rupert, and the man laughed loudly.

"I thought you'd sing small at that," he said. "I want some 'bacca and ale, and a penny or two to spend, and I know I'll get it up at the farmer's if I go and tell him."

"But you won't go," said Rupert, in a whisper.

"Why not, pray?"

"Don't you know I'm romany rye?" (a gipsy gentleman.)

The man eyed him intently.

"You look romany," he said, "but I've been taken in before. What's your name?"

Rupert advanced a step or two, and whispered the name.

The man started.

"Were you with the King of the Gipsies?" inquired the man.

"Yes, with Reuben, when Lee had died after making him king."

"Can you patter?" (talk gipsy language,) asked the man.

"Yes."

"Then answer me in romany, so that these boys can't hear," he whispered. "Where is Reuben?"

"Why do you want him?" asked Rupert doubtfully.

"For good. You are right to be careful," said the man; "but tell him that Carter Smith, of Lee's tribe, wishes to see him. If you are the baby that was brought on that stormy night from Pendarven Abbey, I've got something to tell him that'll be good for him and you, too."

"I am that boy."

"And Miriam Lee—where is she?"

"She has long been Reuben's wife."

The man smiled.

"Ah!" he said. "I expected that."

"But where have you been that you have not heard this?" asked Rupert. "It is all known to the tribes."

"Yes, I have no doubt; but I have been away abroad," said Carter Smith, "travelling with some of our tribe. I have only returned to England two weeks. But you will tell Reuben?"

"Certainly, and I will meet you again," said Rupert. "But the boys are looking askance at us. Write to me and say where I can see you next Wednesday, which is a half-holiday."

"You are at school then?"

"Yes, at Blakesley Hall, not far from here."

"All right."

And the man began to move away.

"You are not going to tell Farmer Popgun then?" cried Reuben, with a wicked smile, and in ordinary English.

"No, not now," said the gipsy. "I'll go and get you a bushel, if you like."

"No, no! that would be downright robbery. We are only going to have a look round. *Cashgar bok!*"

"*Cashgar bok* (good luck)," replied the gipsy, and without taking any notice of the other lads he stalked away.

"Now, boys," said Rupert, "let's go on, if you're coming."

The farm of Farmer Popgun was not far from the picnicking ground.

On arriving at length at the hedge which formed the boundary of the grazing-field our boys did not hesitate.

Entering the field by a wide gap in the hedge, they found the cattle resting amid the tall grass.

The animals took no notice of them, but hung their sleepy heads.

"We're in luck," said Leigh Glindon. "I've heard that some of those long horns of Farmer Popgun's are not the sweetest tempered."

"I hope they've had nothing to ruffle their serenity to-day then," said Rupert, "for those horns could transfix you like an elephant's tusks."

The orchard wall was reached.

The ditch was dry.

At one point the wall leaned inwards, and a fissure ran upwards to the summit.

"'MEEKLY TOOK THE BULLOCK BY THE TAIL, AND HUNG ON LIKE GRIM DEATH.'"

They had provided a "rope," consisting of handkerchiefs knotted together, to be held for the assistance of the others by the one who reached the top first.

Rupert volunteered, and was soon on the summit.

He held down the rope, which Leigh Glindon seized and scrambled up.

Then he took the handkerchief while Rupert dropped to the ground, and so on till all were over.

The boys glanced round furtively on all sides.

Not a human being was in sight.

"This way," said Leigh Glindon. "I've been here before, and I know how to reach the golden pippin tree by the shortest route."

The golden pippin tree was soon reached.

All were served, and each had two or three apples in his pockets in a very short space of time.

Then an adjournment was made to a quaint and picturesque corner of the orchard, where grew a famous plum-tree.

This was a most strange old spot.

As the boys approached, walking tip-toe over the moss-grown ground, they heard the unmistakable sound of voices.

Rupert by a sign called a halt.

Then he crept forward on his hands and knees, and peered through the long grass and reeds, and so forth.

The sight which met his eyes was one which astonished him.

Seated on the natural piece of lawn, with their backs resting against the brickwork of the disused well, was a couple of lovers.

The man had his arm around the waist of a demure-looking little damsel about eighteen, but as her companion's face was bent towards hers, it was at first impossible to recognise his features.

Presently, however, as he turned, startled by a slight noise, Rupert could hardly repress a cry of astonishment.

He knew the face at once.

It was that of Mr. Meekly, one of the ushers at Hungry Hall.

Rupert turned and beckoned to his comrades, making them understand by gestures that they were to approach as he had done—that is, on their hands and knees.

They did so.

Rupert rapidly wrote something on a piece of paper.

Then he gave it to Leigh, with instructions to pass it round.

Our hero waited until all the boys had read it and nodded in token of assent.

Then he glided away.

CHAPTER XXXVII.

THE LOVERS' SURPRISE—AN UNEXPECTED DENOUEMENT.

WITHIN a few minutes after the boys had read and approved of Rupert's note, a complete cordon had been drawn round the two lovers.

The tottering wall of the orchard, tall and blackened, was in front of them, while the boys formed a semi-circle.

They had crept quite close up now, and could hear every word spoken.

"My dear Susie," said Mr. Meekly, "I am so happy now you have consented to a flight and a speedy marriage."

"I dread what father will say," replied the girl.

It was most amusing to observe the difference of voice.

The boys could hardly help laughing at the shrill treble of Meekly and the stout, hearty one of Susie.

"Oh, his anger will vanish," said Meekly, with a feeble squeeze. "I feel overjoyed at the prospect of making you my own. You will be sure to be able to bring the little box of money?"

"Oh, yes," said confiding Susie.

"I would never dream," pursued the tutor, "of asking you to aid in our elopement, only you see I cannot get any cash until I go to my uncle's in London."

"Ah, he's going to pawn his watch to live on," said Ship Ahoy, in a low tone.

"Don't mention it," said Susie. "All I have is yours."

"Excuse me, my dear," exclaimed Mr. Meekly, hesitatingly, after a short pause, "but did you— er —think of— er —bringing—the—er——"

"Ah, the sandwiches," cried the girl.

Oh, yes! Poor old dear! How you must suffer in that horrible place!"

No sooner did Mr. Meekly see the sandwiches than the love business was quickly and entirely suspended.

He sat to with a will.

Susie looked on with placid pleasure.

To her Meekly was a model man.

He was certainly not very bad-looking, in spite of his leanness.

But, of course, he was weak and haggard through the continued misery at Hungry Hall.

It was not long before the usher had devoured his bread and meat.

Then the fond girl produced from her pocket a small bottle containing brandy.

This Meekly drank at a draught.

Then he was a new man.

He embraced Susie with fervour.

"You are a dear, good girl," he said, "and I will reward you for your kindness when we are married."

At which Susie simpered, blushed, and was about to answer, when a loud voice near said—

"I say, Leigh, hurry up away from that plum-tree."

"What for?"

"Farmer Brandford's coming. Mr. Carver is with him. They're searching for Mr. Meekly, the usher."

The effect of these words was immense.

The girl gave a little shrill cry, and clung to her lover.

But the lover was not at all inspired by this appeal to his feelings.

He looked collapsed.

Every bit of real strength, and every bit of "pot courage," too, seemed to have oozed out of him.

"Let us fly!" cried Susie.

"Yes, let us fly," said Meekly, stammering; "but where?"

"Anywhere out of this dreadful place."

"Well, then, you'd better go one way, and I another," said Meekly. "If we are found together, all is lost."

"Yes," said Susie. "Good-bye till to-morrow."

"Yes, to-morrow; and then—oh!"

The exclamation was not called forth by any rapturous anticipation, but by sharp physical pain.

A very hard and indigestible pippin had struck him in the eye.

Rupert had not forgotten his visit to Hungry Hall, or the way in which this usher and the other had truckled down to keep him in that abode of starvation and villainy.

As Meekly cried out, Susie fled.

She did not wait to see how affairs stood.

She only thought that her lover had been suddenly assaulted by her father.

Dashing towards an opening in the hedge, she was about to crawl through, when she encountered the handsome, laughing face of Leigh Glindon.

She drew back with a cry.

Turning to seek another opening by which to make good her flight, she saw Meekly on his knees, with his hands over his eyes.

He appeared to be babbling forth some inarticulate appeals for mercy.

No one was near him, and close by, within reach of his hand, was his own heavy stick.

In the midst of her fear she laughed.

"He's a coward," she muttered, "and he shan't have me, or my money either."

As she spoke, Leigh Glindon again stood before her.

He was six months older than she was, tall and handsome.

"Don't be frightened, Miss Brantford," he said. "If you wish to get off before your father comes, I can show you the way. As for that miserable object, he was once my tutor, and I know him well."

The girl looked at him, blushed, and gratefully accepted his offer.

Leigh glided through the undergrowth, and at once led the way to the fissure in the wall, where there was a turning to the right leading to the poultry fields.

"I can find my way now," she said.

"I hope we shall meet again," returned Leigh. "But I hear footsteps. I think you'd better go the way I told you. If your father meets you here, you may still get in trouble. We can climb over into the cattle field, and you can get round to the farm by the road."

Susie was half beside herself with fright, and she assented.

The leaning wall was at length reached, and by dint of much struggling, Leigh at length contrived to land the buxom farmer's daughter fairly on the other side.

Then they walked across the field together.

Meanwhile, Rupert and the others were picking plums and throwing unripe apples at Meekly.

In the midst of this amusing pastime, a stentorian voice was heard addressing the unfortunate usher.

"So," cried Farmer Popgun, for it was he, "it is you who incite the boys to rob me, and come with them to share their plunder. Get up off your knees, you rascal, or I will put the contents of this gun through you?"

The farmer's threat was effective, for the reputation of the "popgun" had reached the ears of Mr. Meekly.

But now it was a case of close quarters, and damage might be done; so he sprang up.

"Oh, Mr. Brandford," said the coward, "I am so sorry, but I was led into this."

The farmer fairly bellowed his reply.

"What!" he cried. "You hypocritical scoundrel, you mean to tell me that these boys led you here?"

"Boys!" stammered Meekly. "I never mentioned boys. I was thinking of girls."

"Do you mean to tell me that you pretend not to know that at this moment you are surrounded by your schoolboys, and that I caught them stealing my plums and throwing them to you?"

"I know nothing about throwing plums to me," said the usher. "Something hit me in the eye just now."

"By Jove! if you prevaricate and don't answer me correctly," cried the angry farmer, "I'll put a bullet through you!"

"I will tell the truth, sir," said Meekly tremulously; "I was enticed here by your daughter."

Had a thunderbolt burst at the feet of Farmer Popgun, he could not have been more surprised.

"You lie, you villain!" he cried.

And discarding the "popgun," he made a dash forward with a thick short stick which he tore from the hedge.

Had he succeeded in reaching Mr. Meekly, no doubt that person's ribs would have suffered so that he would have had to proceed, or rather be carried to the nearest hospital.

As it was, the farmer's broad bulk prevented his forcing his way through the brushwood quickly enough, and taking advantage of the delay, Meekly scrambled up the wall and quickly dropped on the other side.

The farmer gave vent to an oath.

"I won't touch them boys," he said, "I'll be after him. He's the worst. Enticed by my daughter, eh? The cold-blooded, lying villain!"

He at once rushed away in the direction of a gate in the wall.

Of this only he had the key, and he at once ran thither and opened it.

As he did so, he saw that Meekly had been cut short in his wild career.

The cattle had placed a cordon round him.

They had waltzed towards him from all quarters when they saw him running, and thus hemmed in he feared to move.

The farmer advanced.

"Now then, you rascal," he said, "tell the truth, or I'll put so many shots in your legs, that all the surgeons in Melton will be a month extracting 'em."

"I swear it was Miss Susie, your daughter," cried the sneak.

Then the boys, peeping over the wall, saw Farmer Popgun take deliberate aim, and from amid the smoke that followed, there came a terrible cry.

CHAPTER XXXVIII.

IN THE POND.

THE schoolboys naturally expected that being so near his intended victim, Farmer Popgun had this time succeeded in winging his adversary.

The scream seemed to intimate that he had done something desperate, but when the smoke cleared away, however, a most laughable sight presented itself.

Mr. Meekly was half-kneeling, half-sitting, on the grass, with his hands pressed to his ears, while an unfortunate cow was standing near at hand, with her head evidently riddled with shot, for the blood was pouring from it rapidly in many places.

The farmer now made a dash for Meekly.

But the cattle were in a wayward mood.

The advent of so many strangers, and the firing of the "popgun" had so demoralised them, that when the farmer came rushing down towards them, they eyed him defiantly, and waited his approach, instead of as usual walking quietly off.

Just as the farmer came up the usher, finding that no attack was made upon him, took his hands from his ears, and leaped up ready for a run. But as he did so, he turned to see if the coast was clear, and came face to face with his foe.

For an instant he hesitated.

It was only an instant, but in that short space of time he saw that the farmer was unwieldy, and possessed especially of a large corporation.

So he resolved to try his legs against those of his adversary.

Regardless now of the cattle he made a dash for freedom.

And away went the farmer after him.

The cattle seemed only to have been waiting for this.

With a loud roar and a toss of the head, three or four of the longest horned ones began to rush after the fugitives at a terrific pace.

The first victim was Meekly.

With a snort of apparent delight the animal nearest to him stooped its head as it reached him, and catching the little man by the seat of his breeches with the tip of its horns it flung him high in the air.

As usual the bullock paused to catch him.

But it had just missed its aim.

Instead of falling on its horns the usher alighted on its back, and the animal, startled by the unexpected weight, started off at a good pace, and began to career wildly round the field.

At the same time old Popgun, having been thrown too, came down with his back to the bullock's head, and had to cling on with his arms round the animal's neck, and his legs firmly fixed on both sides like Mazeppa.

In this position they began dashing hither and thither amid loud and continued applause from the delighted boys.

"Let's join in the fun, boys," cried Rupert, "The bullocks won't hurt us, and I know the old fellows can't catch us."

The boys consequently lost no time in scrambling over the wall.

In a few minutes they were in the field.

The other cattle seemed highly amused at the spectacle before them.

They stood with their heads forward, and their tails wagging, glancing at the peculiar scene.

The bullocks with their burdens went round and round the field, snorting and bellowing, and tossing their heads, the little usher and the farmer seeing nothing of the schoolboys in their intense fright.

Their positions were soon to a certain degree altered, however.

Meekly, whose very vitals had nearly been shaken out of him by the extempore series of joltings to which he had been subjected, had collapsed, and was now hanging on to his "charger" by holding firmly round its neck, lying on his face, and clinging with his legs.

The farmer had contrived to wriggle himself round, so as to get his face towards the bullock's head.

But by this time the animals were getting fairly furious.

Unaccustomed to such burdens, they were now leaping and curveting about in their endeavours to rid themselves of their riders.

As the boys at last with a loud shout made their way into the field to the rescue, the bullocks made a sudden dash for the deep pond which lay in the middle.

"We shall have to be quick now, if we want to be of any use," said Rupert. "It begins to look serious. I don't want old Meekly to be drowned, bad as he is."

The boys ran swiftly after the infuriated animals, who made straight for the pond.

The water at the edge was not deep.

But out in the middle, where both the bullocks presently paused, the anything but pleasant-looking liquid was nearly up to their backs.

Consequently the legs of both the

unfortunate riders were completely under water.

Even this, however, was a respite.

After the furious ride they had been compelled to enjoy, even a rest half under water was not to be sneezed at.

The farmer, during this temporary cessation of hostilities, drew out a huge red pocket-handkerchief and began to mop his face.

"This is a pretty pickle to be in, all through you," he gasped, looking daggers at Meekly.

"It isn't through me; it's through——"

"Don't you say a word about my daughter again," said the farmer, "or when I get hold of you I'll break every bone in your body."

"No, no, sir," stammered the usher, "I ain't going to say a word about your daughter, sir. It's through those confounded boys, sir. And, oh, dear! oh, dear! here are a lot of them again."

"Ah," cried Farmer Brandford, "but these are Blakesley Hall fellows, and not your miserable skunks of the starving academy. They've come to help us."

At this moment our little party drew up their forces on the bank.

"What's the matter, farmer?" cried Ship Ahoy. "Got on a rock?"

"Might as well be," said Brandford, "for all the chance I have of getting off unless I go up to my neck in black mud. You'd better drive these 'ere animals out of the water if you can. I think they're pretty well worn out, and if they could be driven there I could slip off."

"All right," said Rupert, "we will have a good try."

With one accord the boys began to shout at the rear of the bullocks, who were now leisurely lapping water.

But it seemed preposterous to think that they would be able to effect any earthly good.

The animals remained stolid and stationary, except that they raised their heads and looked round.

It was getting late.

The boys were getting tired.

But the farmer thought of something.

"Throw us one of them 'edge stakes," he cried. "I'll catch un."

Rupert threw with a slow-swinging aim, and the farmer caught it with ease.

"Now, then, my beauty," he cried. "I'll make ye move."

And digging the end of the stick into the animal's side, he soon had it under way, as Ship Ahoy would have expressed it.

"Give me one, too," pleaded Meekly, in a plaintive voice.

The boys demurred.

But Rupert had a soft heart.

"I think the little man has had enough of it," he said.

And with a light swing as before he flung the stick to the usher.

The result was disastrous.

Meekly had never been on horseback, and even the substantial back of a bullock was very unsubstantial to him.

So as he reached up to catch the stick, which was very fairly thrown to him by Rupert, he overbalanced himself, clutched wildly at the air, and fell headlong into the slimy water.

A roar of laughter, loud and hearty, rose from the lips of the boys, and so startled the farmer's ponderous "steed," as it placed its feet on *terra firma*, that it paused and turned its head.

This was Popgun's golden opportunity.

And he was not slow to take advantage of it.

He at once slid down from his enforced eminence, gave the bullock a blow on the buttocks, which sent it bellowing away, and then turned to see how matters stood with the enemy.

He had, of course, beheld nothing of the undignified descent of Meekly into the black and duck-weeded pool.

And so, as he glanced round, his surprise was great to find that the usher had disappeared.

Of course his surprise did not last long.

If Meekly had remained in the horsepond for any length of time he would have been dragged out a corpse, for the water was literally thick with offensive matter, and would have choked him in a few minutes.

"Where's the usher?" he bawled.

"Sunk!" shouted Ship Ahoy.

At this moment, as the bullock, relieved of its unusual burden, began to move towards the bank, the wretched little man from the island school reappeared above the weedy surface.

He had struck a point where it was possible to stand with his head out of water, and there he remained for a moment gazing wildly round him in search of aid.

To the credit of Rupert, be it said (and all who could swim among the little party were of the same mind), he was fully resolved to plunge into the murky fluid to the rescue of the usher, if any sign of real danger was to be seen.

The horrid nature of the water in the pond, however, kept him and the others back until the last moment.

And as it happened, it was just as well that it was so.

Suddenly a bright idea struck Meekly.

He could not swim, the bottom of the pond was treacherously uneven.

What was to be done?

As the bright idea flashed across his mind he "took" not "the bull by the horns," but the bullock by the tail, and held on like grim death.

A roar of laughter naturally greeted this; and the bullock was also somewhat disconcerted.

No doubt, had the indignity been offered to it on dry land, it would have resented it by a backward kick.

As it was, it could not very well indulge in any kind of retaliatory measures, and accordingly suffered Mr. Meekly to retain his hold while it leisurely proceeded ashore.

The idea was indeed a bright one of Mr. Meekly, for the animal took him ashore, and having done so, and been released from the unusual strain upon its tail, it trotted off after its fellow in misfortune.

Now came the trying point.

The farmer and the usher were face to face.

Each looked very much the worse for wear.

But whereas Brandford was only untidy, wet and hot, Meekly was absolutely collapsed.

He couldn't have run away now if the farmer had threatened to shoot him.

But Brandford was not vindictive, although he had "peppered" one of his own bullocks.

"Look here, Mr. Meekly," he cried, as the usher stood tremblingly before him. "I don't bear malice, and as you've had a good turn of it, I'll let ye off this time without the thrashing you deserve."

"Thank you sir," stammered Meekly.

"But I warn you," continued the farmer, without noticing the interruption, "if ever I catch you round this way again, I shall thrash you so that your bones will ache for the rest of your life."

Mr. Meekly made no further remarks, but simply shuffled off.

There is perhaps nothing in the way of discomfiture so wretched and so humiliating as to sneak off, beaten, with the knowledge that a whole crowd of tormentors are at the back of you.

Every shout of laughter seems to bear with it weapons of offence.

And so felt little Meekly with a vengeance as he hurried along as fast as his legs would carry him in the direction of the high road.

His heart was, however, full of vengeance.

Satisfied he might be for the moment to get off so easily.

But deep down in his heart was a spirit of revenge.

What form his revenge should take he had not yet decided.

That he must decide upon in his calmer moments.

In the meantime the boys had come round Farmer Brandford, and, repressing the merriment which they naturally felt at his appearance, they asked him how he was and whether they could be of any further help to him.

"No thank ye, lads, and much obliged to ye," said the farmer, "but I tell 'ee what. If ye'll come up to the farm I can give ye a fine glass of cider, and if ye don't like that ye can have a cup o' tea and some cake."

The boys hesitated only a moment.

The invitation was a pleasant one.

But the time when it was given was most inopportune.

They could not very well make their appearance at the farm with their pockets crammed full of apples and plums.

"We really have not time, sir," said Rupert, "but some day we will take advantage of your kind offer, if you will renew it. Good-day, sir."

And so, with a general lifting of hats, the young rascals were off and away.

Never for a moment did the farmer suspect them.

He wished them "good-bye," and on his road home he was engaged in concocting some scheme by which he could benefit them.

"Well, boys," said Rupert, as they made their way gaily homeward, "what do you think of the day's fun?"

The answer was unanimous.

Everyone had enjoyed himself immensely, and when they reached the academy they one and all voted the holiday a success.

In the playground, when they returned, they found Leigh Glindon.

"Ah, Leigh," said Rupert, laughing, "we have been all wondering what had become of you. Did you lose your way?"

"Yes," said Leigh, with a smile, "but I found something better."

With which enigmatical reply Rupert was for the time being compelled to be content.

And thus ended a day which in sad after times Rupert remembered as the last joyous one at Blakesley Hall.

CHAPTER XXXIX.

A LESSON IN CRIME.

EVERYTHING appeared outwardly now to be tending towards the success of Rupert Pendarven.

And yet, perhaps, at this very moment, when everything seemed rosy, never had such a dark cloud threatened his future.

As my readers have seen, the unexpected revelation made to Ralph Pendarven by Hugh Blacklock had for the time made a most extraordinary change in his feelings towards our hero.

But the result of an interview he had had with his father, after sending his letter and receiving a reply, had entirely changed his nature again.

He received his son at the Abbey in his usual warm way, but his first words were sufficient to prevent any immediate discussion.

"Ha, Ralph, my boy, happy to see you," he cried; "glad you are punctual. We'll take a turn in the park and have a chat. Much better than here."

The last words were significant.

Ralph took up the cue at once.

"I shall be glad to have a stroll in the park," he said. "It will be quite a change for me."

If the boy had misunderstood him or hesitated, Hubert Pendarven would have been far better pleased.

As it was, the thought occurred to him—

"This youngster will be an ugly one to mould to my wishes. And yet, what can I do? He is my only son."

They were soon out in the park, seated on a rustic bench beneath a huge oak tree in the centre of a lawn, where there was not a chance of anyone interfering with them, or overhearing a syllable of their conversation.

"Now, my boy," said Hubert, calmly, "tell me precisely what has happened to get you into your present extraordinary state of mind. Tell me everything. Do not spare me in the slightest particular, so that I may know how to act."

The boy at once did as he was requested.

"Well, Ralph," said his father, when he had finished speaking, "tell me what is your opinion of all this?"

"I am to speak plainly, father?"

"Yes."

"Then I think that Rupert Pendarven, now called Clifford, is the real heir to this property."

"You coolly tell me, then, that I am a murderer?" said Hubert Pendarven.

"No, no," cried the boy, eagerly, "others may have done the murder and spirited him away, but he is the rightful heir."

"Do you know what that means?" asked his father, coolly.

"Yes, the loss of this property," said Ralph. "I am quite prepared for that."

"You are prepared to give up to another the estates which you have been taught to consider your own after my death?"

"Yes, for Rupert would be my friend, and he would see that I never wanted for anything."

"You are truly magnanimous," said his father with a sneer; "and pray, in this pretty little arrangement, what part am I to play?"

"I never dreamed of yielding anything, of speaking, or even hinting at anything," replied Ralph, "until the moment came when I became master of this place. After your death, father, if I live, what harm can I be doing you if I give up all to its rightful owner?"

Hubert Pendarven had kept patience too long.

He now lost it entirely.

"Look you here, boy," he cried, fiercely, as he clutched Ralph by the arm, "I will have no more of this speculation as to what is to happen after my death. Once for all, to give in now would be declaring me a felon—an assassin. It would not only be to yield up these splendid lands, this princely fortune; not only to court poverty, but to court it as the son of one whose career should have been cut short long ago by the common hangman."

The boy did not answer.

"Ruin, disgrace, disaster will meet you everywhere. You will be a beggar, an outcast, railed at and avoided by everyone. Look on the other side of the picture. You will be rich, courted, the owner of one of the handsomest estates in England. And remember that Rupert Clifford is not a poor boy. He has wealth through his pretended father, who is really his cousin Reuben Pendarven."

Ralph started in astonishment.

"What!" he cried, "the one who you told me was an outlaw and a forger?"

"Hush, my boy!" cried Hubert Pendarven, losing for a moment his presence of mind, and glancing around him as if afraid the very wind would bear the words away to some perilous point of the compass; "that turns out to be wrong. He has cleared his name of that entirely, and I am daily expecting him here. He will have to receive from me a large sum of money, and an income also out of the property of one thousand pounds."

So he went on, speciously setting forth the advantages of silence and discretion, until Ralph said, with a shudder—

"Father, you are so eager and earnest, that I begin to believe one thing."

"What is that?"

"That you must know something of my uncle's death."

Hubert Pendarven turned ghastly pale.

"What then, ungrateful boy?" he cried. "If there were any truth in such a horrible accusation, would not the deed have been done for you?"

"For me!" cried Ralph, with a shudder. "I was not born."

"Yes, you were a year old when—when your uncle died," said Hubert; "but enough of this. I will say no more. Do as you please, Ralph. Tell your suspicions to others—hand me over to justice. I have no doubt that, after all these years, it would be difficult enough to prove my innocence."

"Pray do not talk like that, father," said Ralph. "All I want is some explanation. Cannot you give any in regard to that night, and the reasons why such a hideous report was circulated about you?"

Hubert paced to and fro for some moments in anxious thought.

Then he paused suddenly.

"Well, Ralph, I will trust you," he said. "Make what use you like of my confession, if so you can term it."

"It will be of no use to me, father, except for my own satisfaction."

"It is simply this then," said Hubert. "Your uncle Richard gave me cause of grievance by marrying again, and having an heir. This heir I declared should never inherit. I paid a man to destroy all evidence of the marriage, but finding that my brother had left a will, leaving Rupert all the money, whether legitimate or not, I at once went to him to remonstrate. He was obstinate, we came to words, then to blows, and he fell, hurting his head severely against the fender and becoming insensible. Footsteps were heard at that moment, and the friends with me advised me to fly. I did so."

"And the will?"

"That matters not. If it is still in existence, Rupert can only claim two thousand a-year. The property is entailed, and you are the only legitimate heir. So you see how the insane story cropped up."

As he spoke, he saw a man-servant come out of the terrace window, and look around him anxiously.

Then perceiving two figures far off under the oak, he seemed to think that they might be the master and his son, and hastened towards them.

"Something important, I expect," said Hubert Pendarven, and he hastened forward to meet the domestic.

The man handed him a letter, which he broke open anxiously.

As Hubert read it, a sickly grey colour stole over his face.

"Ah," he said, "this is most impor-tant, Ralph. I meant you to stop a day or two. But I see I must leave for London to-night. We will dine early, and I will drive you over to the station. All right, Thomas. Tell the boy to wait. I will send a reply, and he can post it."

And as the man started off, he hastily followed.

A letter was a simple thing to upset the boy's mind, but still he had a pre-sentiment that it meant fresh misery and disaster.

CHAPTER XL.

HUBERT PENDARVEN SHOWS THE WHITE FEATHER.

AFTER a hurried luncheon, Hubert Pendarven drove his son to the railway station.

The letter he had received was from his lawyers, and had evidently upset him greatly.

It had run thus—

"Pray come and see us. Matters must be arranged at once between your-self and Reuben Pendarven. Nothing can be gained by delay, and from all we can see much may be lost."

These significant words had their due effect.

The express train which dashed at headlong speed through meadows and villages was all too slow for him.

On reaching the office of his solicitors, he found both the partners, Owet and Merrifield, there ready to receive him.

They wore very grave faces.

"Good morning, Mr. Pendarven," said Owet and Merrifield in a chorus. "We are glad you came up at once. You see your position is one of great nicety, and we may almost say danger, and it will be necessary to act with promptitude and without hesitation.

"You really talk so enigmatically, and so mysteriously that you quite alarm me," said Hubert, with a sickly attempt at a laugh.

"Well, you see," said Mr. Owet, "we have been lawyer and client for such a time that I feel a kind of diffidence in speaking plainly. It is such a very delicate matter. You are aware," he added, "of what your cousin accuses you?"

"Yes."

"You know he has proofs."

"Yes."

"Can you confute them?"

Hubert Pendarven was now very pale.

"This is a cross-examination, sir," he said, somewhat bitterly.

"Well, no," said Merrifield, smiling; "it is what I would rather call an examination in chief. It is absolutely necessary that you should thoroughly understand your position, and also necessary that we should know how far you can refute the accusations made against you."

Hubert bowed assent.

"The case is simply this," said Merri-field. "Reuben asserts that the case—the false case got up against him years ago—was arranged by you, that the per-jurers were suborned by you, and that he can positively prove the fact in the same way as he has undoubtedly proved his innocence."

"It is false," said Hubert, savagely.

"Just so," put in Mr. Owet; "but then the point is, how are you going to prove it?"

"I don't know. It is all such a time ago that I cannot think how or where I could get evidence on the subject at all," replied Hubert.

"That's just it," said the lawyer. "We can't defend you with no defence."

"Whom have they got on the other side? What witnesses, I mean?"

Mr. Owet read the list.

Hubert's face changed visibly as he listened.

"He has a whole array of enemies against me, then," he said.

"Yes; it looks very serious," replied Merrifield; "but tell me, Mr. Pendarven, have you any objection to an interview with Mr. Reuben Pendarven ?"

"For what purpose ?"

"To see whether you can come to any arrangement with him."

"Well," said Hubert, "there is, of course, one arrangement that has to be made, and that is an important one. My cousin Reuben must have all his money returned to him in full—I mean the money of which he would have had the use if he had not been out of the way."

"A very large sum to disburse, you will find," said Owet.

"That matters not," said Hubert. "Whatever my other faults may be, I am not wilfully extravagant. I have abundance at my bankers to meet all his demands. In fact, I have saved up against the evil day that might come."

The lawyers did not question the honesty of this remark.

They merely bowed and said—

"That is a very good thing. Mr. Reuben is here at this moment, or should be. He wrote to tell us to expect him."

Hubert rose and glanced at the lawyers somewhat angrily.

"Is this a trap ?" he said.

"We never trap our clients," said Mr. Owet, "and more than that, there's no occasion for you to see Mr. Reuben unless you please. It is entirely a matter for your own judgment and discretion."

"I will certainly see him," said Hubert. "Prepare him, if he is here, for an interview at once."

Mr. Owet whistled through the pipe which communicated between his room and the clerk's office.

The answer came back quickly—

"Mr. Reuben is here."

"You would doubtless like to have your interview in private ?" said Merrifield.

"Certainly."

"Then step this way."

He led Hubert into an inner chamber.

Here he left him for a few minutes to his own reflections, and then the door was once more opened, and a tall, military-looking figure entered.

These men had not met for many years, but each recognised the other at once.

There was no pretence of hand-shaking or other sign of welcome.

Each understood the other too well.

Reuben knew that he was face to face with the man who had ruined his young life, and felt too that he was gazing at the assassin of Richard Pendarven.

Hubert, on the other hand, was aware that he was in the presence of an uncompromising foe.

Striding forward till he stood within a foot of Hubert, Reuben, looking sternly in his face, said—

"So we meet again at last, Hubert Pendarven."

Hubert's voice was husky as he said—

"Yes; it is eighteen years since we met."

"It is false," returned Reuben, fiercely ; "we met sixteen years ago."

"Where ?" asked Hubert. "If it was so, it must have been a very trifling occasion, for it has quite escaped my memory."

"It may have been a very trifling occasion to you," said Reuben, "but it was a most terrible one for me. It was on the night when you and your confederates murdered Richard Pendarven."

Hubert started back, and stood facing Reuben with clenched fists.

"What mad insult is this ?" he cried. "Have a care over your tongue."

"I have no reason to fear you," said Reuben—"you have great need to fear me. I have not come now, however, to speak of the murder of Richard. That will be proved all in due time. What I came here for is to speak of the money due to me, and also to ask what steps you propose taking in regard to the dastardly way in which you suborned witnesses against me in the dark days gone by."

"All that has to be proved," said Hubert, trying to put a bold face on matters.

"It requires no trouble to prove it," said Reuben ; "everything is ready, and unless you come to terms at once you shall be prosecuted without further notice."

"And what terms are they ?"

"If you will consent to acknowledge your nephew, Rupert Pendarven, and place him in possession of his rights—

that is, of Pendarven Castle and the fortune appertaining thereto—I will agree to forego this prosecution," said Reuben.

"A very pretty offer," sneered Hubert.

"But a much prettier punishment," said Reuben, "disgrace and imprisonment, for conviction is absolutely certain."

"And then this absurd story of assassination, and so forth, sixteen years ago, would be confessed to be a falsehood."

"I know nothing of that," said Reuben. "Suborning to perjury is one thing, murder is another. Nothing but flight can save you from the results of that."

Hubert paced the room excitedly for a few moments.

His sin was certainly finding him out now.

And what could he do?

No fresh crime would have power to rescue him now from the consequences of the old one.

There were too many persons in the secret.

"Well," he said, as if coming to a sudden conclusion, "you must give me till to-morrow to decide."

"Very well."

"Will no compromise do?"

"I do not think so."

"You are acting on your own responsibility?"

"Not entirely."

"How can anyone be helping you in such a matter?"

"Rupert's heart is even now beating wildly at the mere prospect of being able to track the murderer of his father," replied Reuben, eyeing him sternly.

"Of that I am resolved not to speak," said Hubert. "I shall put it to my lawyers to tell me if I am compelled to put up with such atrocious calumnies. I will let you know to-morrow if I am able to effect a compromise. At any rate, I must have till then.

"And now," he added, "what amount is it that you require?"

"Thirty-six thousand pounds!"

It was a large sum.

But Hubert did not even wince.

He knew exactly what it meant.

Simply the annual sum of two thousand pounds, which had been due to Reuben for eighteen years.

"You demand no interest then?" said Hubert, curiously.

"Not a farthing from such as you."

Hubert writhed under these words.

But what could he do?

He certainly would have found it a useless game to have struck his enemy.

"Very well," he said, "I will say no more. You have the game in your hands now, and it seems to me that you mean to play it cruelly. If I give up Pendarven Castle to Rupert, I am a ruined man."

"But you save your life," said Reuben, coolly, "for no one would oppose your flight. I for one would not, for the sake of the family name."

Hubert waited for no more.

He seized his hat, and with the words "you shall hear from me to-morrow," he was hurriedly leaving the room when Reuben said—

"One moment, sir; the thirty-six thousand pounds."

"You can have a cheque now," replied Hubert. "I have my book with me, and will write it at once. You can draw the cash to-day. It is all yours. I have not touched a farthing."

The cheque was quickly written out.

Reuben examined it, saw that all was correct, and then Hubert once more passed through the door and into the lawyer's sanctum.

"Well," said Mr. Owet—"well, how did you get on?"

"Just as I expected. I have given him a cheque for thirty-six thousand pounds."

"Bless me! Would he not take it in instalments?"

"Certainly not," cried Hubert, impatiently. "I never dreamed of suggesting such a thing. In this matter I prefer paying at once—I have a reason."

In a few minutes all was settled.

Then a whispered conversation took place.

A large cheque found its way into the hands of the two lawyers, and Hubert at last quitted the office.

"Curse that infernal fellow!" he muttered, as he leaped into his hansom cab, and drove to his hotel. "He has got the whip-hand of me now, and no mistake. But I can live for revenge yet."

Next day passed.

And the next.

Then, finding not even so much as a line from Hubert, Reuben wrote.

Still no answer.

Leniency to one whom he thoroughly believed to be a murderer was not to be dreamed of by Reuben.

So as Hubert had broken his word, he determined to wait no longer, but proceed to Pendarven Castle himself.

CHAPTER XLI.

ANOTHER QUARREL—RALPH CHANGES HIS MIND.

It was the day after that on which our boys at Blakesley Hall went on a "foraging" expedition, as they called it, to Farmer Popgun's orchard, that Rupert was walking slowly along a narrow, leafy, pleasant lane leading from the town to the school.

He had not met a soul on his road to the school.

He paused a moment at the bridge over the Lea—a tributary of the Arrow—to think, and the bright sun and the balmy breeze, and the wondrous stillness of everything, brought to his mind vividly the last time he saw Gladys Alreston.

The only difference was that then it was morning and now it was evening.

Poor Gladys!

Where was she?

What was she doing?

How was it that she had never written to him?

Well, he must be patient and bear these misfortunes.

He roused himself from his reverie presently with a sigh.

"Ah, well," he murmured, "it's no use dreaming. That will make the time pass all the more heavily. Ha! who is that coming up along the cross-road? Why, Ralph Pendarven, as I live. I shall have a companion back to the school after all."

He advanced quickly.

"Well, Ralph," said Rupert, in a cheery voice, "where have you been?"

"On business."

"That's rather a short answer," said Rupert, laughingly.

"Yes; I don't like telling my affairs to anyone when there's no occasion," replied Ralph, mending his pace.

The gipsy schoolboy could not understand this.

His blood rose at it.

"What is the matter?" he cried.

"I'm not well. I've got a head-ache, and want to be alone."

He said this with such a look upon his face that Rupert knew at once that it was untrue.

"I am sorry to see you so cross with me, Ralph," he said. "I thought we had come to be such good friends."

"You thought wrong, then," cried Ralph, angrily. "You know very well that it isn't natural for us to be friends."

"Not natural?"

"No."

"And why?"

"Because I know you to be not Rupert Clifford, but one who claims to be my cousin, and the rightful heir to Pendarven Abbey."

"Well," interrupted Rupert, "what if this were true? What if——"

"Oh, that is not all," interrupted Ralph, passionately; "not only are you and your supposed father (who is your cousin) trying to turn me out of the inheritance which I have always been taught to believe unalterably mine, but you try to fix upon my father the burden of a terrible crime."

Rupert turned pale at this.

It was the first time such a subject had been mentioned between them.

"It is a strange subject to speak about," he said. "If what has been told me is true, why then your father will have to stand a terrible trial. But his fault is not yours. You will not suffer——"

Ralph would not permit him to properly express himself.

"I would not suffer?" he interrupted furiously. "If my father is disgraced, shall I not be disgraced, too? If my father was proved to have committed a fearful crime such as you falsely accuse him, should I not have for ever the brand of Cain upon my brow?"

"But we are not discussing that now," said Rupert. "It is merely a matter of money and right to an estate. I have never brought it up to you, remember. An allusion to it has been from you. Let it not be mentioned again between us yet. We are still only boys, and we must await the course of events. Give me your hand, Ralph, and let us be friends as before. Whatever others do cannot be your fault."

Ralph rudely repulsed the hand proffered to him.

"Keep your hand to yourself," he cried. "I didn't know you had turned coward and milksop."

Rupert reddened with anger, and he sprang forward with clenched fist.

"If you say that again, or anything like it, I shall certainly punch your head!" he cried fiercely.

"I do say it again. You tried to get out of all this, and pretend friendship simply because you are a milksop and a coward."

In an instant he found it necessary to defend himself.

Rupert was as good as his word, and a blow, aimed at Ralph's head, would have sent him reeling into a noisome ditch two or three feet deep, where he would have effectually quenched his ardour.

But he parried the blow skilfully, and prepared for a good defence.

The boys were taller, stronger, and more active and accustomed to fighting than they were when they first went to Blakesley Hall.

And so the combat went on with immense spirit.

Blows were rapidly given and exchanged, and damage done.

In a remarkably short space of time both had received severe contusions.

Ralph had a black eye, and had bled profusely from the nose.

With hats off, ruffled hair, and discoloured linen, they looked a pretty pair.

But it was soon to be seen that Rupert was getting the best of it.

Gradually he drove his adversary back towards the ditch.

He did not do this purposely.

He had no idea, in fact, of ending the fight in this ignoble way.

But in his anger, and in the excitement of the combat, he did not notice it.

Just on the edge of the ditch presently Ralph slipped.

He tried to save himself, and fell on one knee.

Rupert paused.

"Have you had enough?" he said.

"No!" cried Ralph. "Before I've done with you I'll kill you!"

He sprang to his feet as he spoke these words.

Rupert drew back appalled.

The face he looked upon was literally convulsed with passion.

It looked hideous.

And Rupert saw, too, that he held in his hand a large, jagged stone.

He shuddered as he thought of this, and compared the present moment with those awful moments years ago at Pendarven Abbey.

If ever there was murder in the eyes of anyone it shone now from those of Ralph.

"Coward!" cried Rupert.

And he made a sudden leap forward.

But he missed.

Ralph dodged him, and in another moment the jagged flint was hurled.

If it had taken effect where he intended it, it would have disfigured our hero for life, for it was aimed full at his face.

But it did not.

Rupert, by avoiding it, received only a wound, a slight one too, on the side of the head.

Then, with a cry of anger, he sprang forward.

He dealt five or six blows in rapid succession.

So rapidly, in fact, that it was almost impossible for Ralph to see them coming.

Again and again they fell on forehead, ear, or nose, until at length, when trying to avoid a blow, Ralph slipped over the edge and fell headlong into the black and noisome water.

And there Rupert quitted him, saying—

"A proper place for such a villain!"

There was not enough water for him to drown himself in, and consequently, as there was no danger, our hero left him to get out of his plight as best he could.

Though flushed, excited, and exhibiting signs of maltreatment, Rupert was resolved to say nothing of the occurrence unless Ralph did.

Accordingly, when he reached the school, he went straight up to his room, and revivified himself before he paid a visit to Mr. Tobias Lyttleton.

Ralph, meanwhile, was in a state of great uncertainty.

If he told the truth in regard to the plight he was in, he stood more in fear of ridicule than anything else.

Rupert might be punished, but it would be a slight punishment.

So he resolved to say nothing and bide his time.

Surely some chance would come for revenge, and it was not long in coming.

Not a word was said by Ralph in regard to the thrashing he had received from Rupert.

He declared that he had been attacked by tramps, and so it all passed away, and no one knew anything about the renewal of hostilities between the cousins.

About a week after the chance came.

The usual fortnightly assault-at-arms was to take place in the riding-school, and Rupert and Ralph were two of those who were set down to fight a duel with foils.

When Ralph knew this an idea instantly leaped through his brain.

If the tip, or cap, was knocked off the foil, how easy it would be to run his adversary through the chest as if by accident ; and it was with this murderous idea that Ralph looked forward to the contest between them.

At Blakesley Hall Academy the boys were taught everything that would render them brave and strong men.

There was a riding-school—not a large place, be it said—but one where it was quite possible to have a short canter.

This at times was utilised as a gymnasium, and at others as a drill-room.

A regular drill-master, a corporal in an Irish regiment, named McDermot, was employed at the school, a man who took a pride in his boys, and was delighted at nothing so much as when he saw them marching down Melton High Street.

"Divil a bit o' difference twixt them and the regulars," he would say, as he stood outside the door of the "Melton Arms," cigarette in mouth and cane in hand, watching the school as it was marshalled down the street by Doctor Walton.

Well, it was drill-day.

Or rather the day of examination in drill.

Among the couples who were to have a duel with the foils were Rupert and Ralph, as I mentioned.

Eagerly did Ralph look forward to this meeting.

But when the two took their places with others in the riding-school, he seemed as calm as anyone would be under the circumstances.

In his heart, however, there was raging an eager longing for revenge.

And he had adopted a brutal method of achieving it.

Coming into the riding-school before the other boys, but after he knew that the drill-master had examined all the weapons, he had deliberately broken off the button.

The foil was neither more nor less, consequently, than a rapier.

Of course his intended victim was quite unsuspecting.

He never dreamed of such an act of cowardly vengeance.

So the battle began cheerily.

Rupert was quite a master of fence.

At this game, and at single stick, he had again and again practised when among the gipsies, and he was the head of the gymnasium in consequence.

The special pet of Jim McDermot.

The fight went on for some time very evenly.

But at length the superior skill of Rupert asserted itself, and Ralph was rapidly driven back.

Through all his advantages and disadvantages, however, he kept one thing in view.

And that was the chance of pinking Rupert in the side.

At length it came.

By luck rather than good judgment he directed a sudden lunge at his adversary close over the region of the heart.

But our hero's hour had not yet come.

As Ralph lunged he somehow caught his foot and fell forward, his foil pinning Rupert by the shoulder to the wall.

But at the same time punishment overtook him,

"'THE THING'S GOT TO BE DONE, OR I'LL TURN EVIDENCE MYSELF,' CRIED BLACKLOCK."

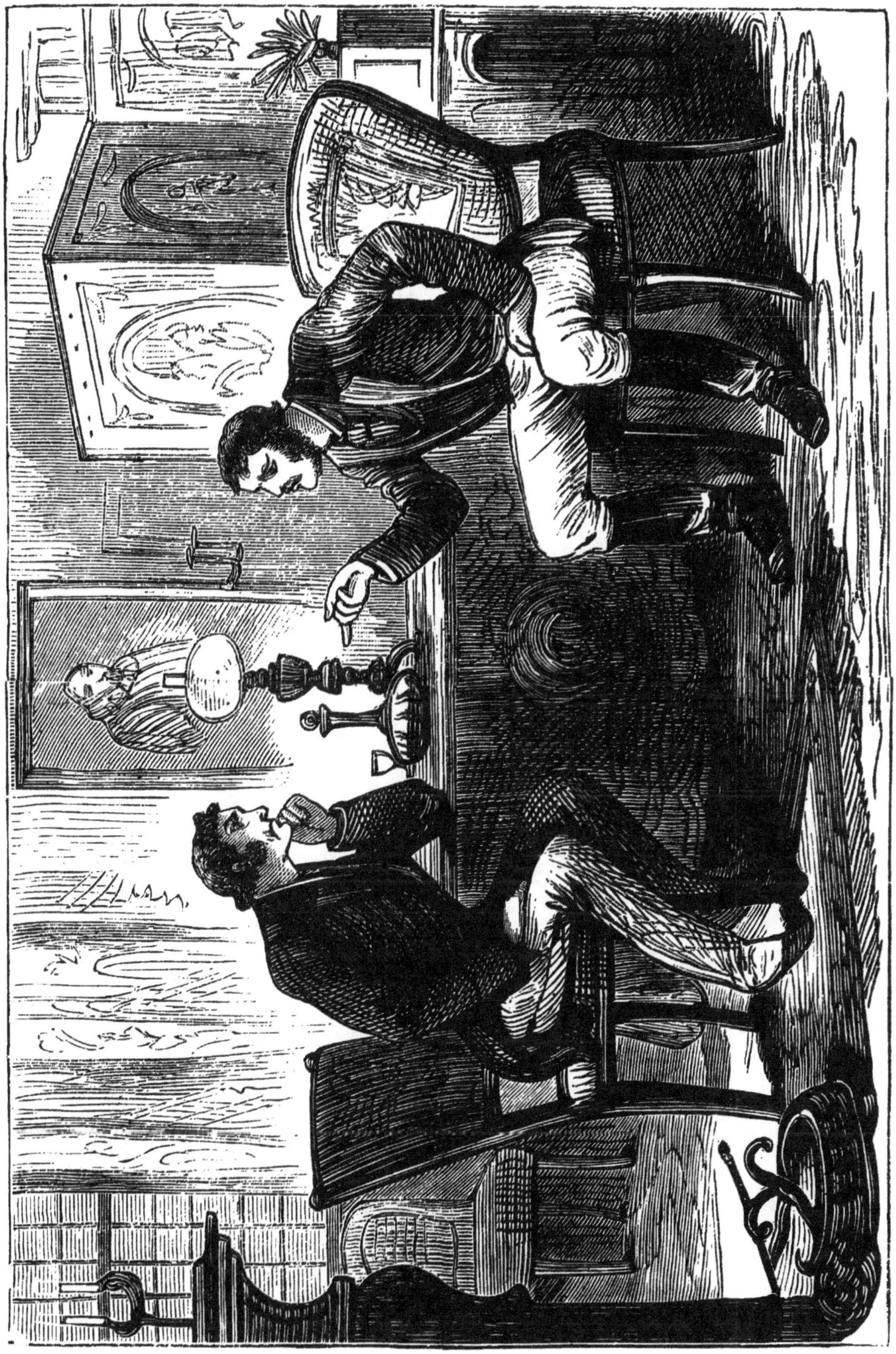

In falling with such force, the foil broke in his hand, and the part of the steel which still quivered in the wood caught him on the side of the head, inflicting a horrible wound, and absolutely tearing away part of the scalp.

The cries of pain which involuntarily escaped the lips of both Rupert and Ralph brought the drill-master and the boys rushing in a body to the spot.

Both Rupert and his enemy were very badly injured.

The extraction of the foil from the wound was a most painful operation, but our hero suffered it without flinching.

Ralph was lying fainting on the floor of the riding-school.

The wound which he had received was a most awfully painful one, the skin and flesh being wrenched away.

There was no doubt that his punishment was the worse of the two.

"Shure, and this is a most extraordinary affair," said McDermot. "I can't make it out at all, at all."

"The button is off the point, sir," said Ship Ahoy. "It doesn't take much accounting for."

"But how did it come off, that's what I can't make out," said the Irish drill-instructor. "Faith, and it was meself examined every one of the foils before the game began, sure."

He examined the foil again.

"I can't see how that could have broken off so near the top by merely a thrust straight at the wall. It looks like foul play."

"So it does," said Ship Ahoy; "and when Ralph Pendarven's better I mean to inquire into it. By the way, sir, if the button was knocked off just at the moment of the fight, it must be here on the floor somewhere now."

But, as my readers are aware, it had been removed before the fight.

There was no proving this, however.

No evidence, of course, could be adduced.

But in the minds of everyone there was an uncomfortable feeling that there had been some wicked deed in contemplation.

In regard to Rupert he could only think one thing.

He knew that Ralph entertained bitter spite against him.

What, then, if murder ran in the blood?

What if this attempt on his life was a planned thing?

For that it was an attempt there was no doubt in his mind.

How should he act?

How resent it?

Without, in fact, any absolute proof, how could he cast such a thing in the teeth of his natural enemy?

At any rate, do as he might, he knew that he was in greater peril than ever.

CHAPTER XLII.

NEARER STILL TO THE END.

ON the day after Ralph had attempted to take his cowardly revenge upon Rupert, Reuben Pendarven paid a visit to Blakesley Hall.

He had determined that neither he nor our hero should longer go on under false colours.

But at the same time he resolved to do nothing to prejudice Ralph.

Little did he think how very small a quantity of forbearance and sympathy he was worthy of.

Doctor Walton received Reuben with much cordiality.

He had a great liking for Rupert, and his supposed father too, and was always glad to welcome the gipsy king.

"I am come to-day on a curious errand, doctor," he said, after the first greetings were over, "to make a confession which will no doubt astound you."

"A confession," said Doctor Walton. "You will never make me believe that you have done anything to need confession."

"Well," said Reuben, smiling, "in the way you mean, perhaps, I have not. But I have in another, because I have obtained your friendship and esteem under false pretences."

Doctor Walton looked grave.

"Pray explain."

Reuben calmly told him the whole of the Pendarven story without reservation.

The worthy schoolmaster listened with a very grave face indeed.

It was a terrible story as we know.

"I pity you and Rupert from my heart," he said; "but what of the other? What is to be said of him?"

"Do you mean Ralph?"

"Yes."

"I do not wish to harm him," said Reuben; "all he has done may have been forced upon him, but at any rate, everyone knows that he is not responsible for his father's misdeeds. I must ask you, however, to watch more keenly over the life and interests of Rupert than ever."

"I will."

Reuben and he parted on wonderfully good terms.

The former avoided any meeting with Ralph Pendarven.

He saw Rupert, got the boys a half holiday, and then without any hesitation made his way towards the school on the island.

Hungry Hall would seem to be the very last place in the world where he would have occasion or desire to go.

After what had happened there, a visit might seem a perilous undertaking.

But Reuben appeared to have no fear.

He took a boat, rowed over alone, and was soon in the presence of that august personage, Dr. Carver.

He rose at once in a fume of anger.

"How dare you intrude yourself upon me?" he cried.

"Why should I not?"

The tone and the manner were most provoking, considering that the interview took place in the schoolroom.

"Have you forgotten the infamous manner in which you behaved on your last visit?" roared Carver.

"I remember that you received from me exactly what you deserved and asked for," replied Reuben; "but I did not come here for the purpose of exposing you again before your scholars. I wish for a short private interview in regard to the re-appearance of one Carter Smith, a gipsy, from whom I have obtained most valuable information."

He looked straight into the pedagogue's face as he spoke.

The face of Dr. Carver became absolutely livid.

"Ah, that alters matters," he cried, with an attempt at being genial—a very stammering attempt be it said. "I will dismiss the school, and we can have the interview you desire in my private room."

Reuben simply inclined his head in token of assent.

"You can rise and play, you boys," said Dr. Carver, with a majestic wave of the hand. "This way, Mr.——"

"Pendarven," put in Reuben.

Dr. Carver started.

But he made no remark until they reached his private room.

"You quite surprise me," he then said. "I have always understood that your name was Colonel Gerald Clifford."

"Yes, you were perfectly justified in doing so," replied Reuben. "I had reasons for keeping my identity a secret, and of that—now that you know that I am Reuben Pendarven — you are thoroughly aware."

Doctor Carver glanced at him with a blustering look.

"Well, pray come to the point," he said. "I don't see why my time should be wasted. I do not care particularly whether you are Reuben Pendarven or not; or whether you have been aggrieved or injured in any way. All I want to know is your immediate object in coming here?"

"I fear your memory is somewhat defective," said Reuben, "so I will remind you of a few little matters, which may refresh it. Did you know my uncle, Richard Pendarven?"

"No."

"Doctor Carver, you lie!" thundered Reuben, fixing his gaze sternly on the doctor.

"Sir!" cried the schoolmaster, "you are taking a gross liberty."

"Not so. You are false in everything, even your name."

"What mean you?"

"I mean that your name is not Carver, but Hepburn."

The pedagogue was silent.

"You do not deny that," said Reuben.

"I do," replied Carver, faintly.

"As you would deny anything which

would be against your evil purposes," said Reuben; "but since you deny that, I will not ask you individual questions, but simply make a statement.

"On a certain night one winter, seventeen years ago or nearly, Richard Pendarven, my uncle, was murdered at Pendarven Abbey.

"Those who entered the Abbey, headed by my other uncle, Hubert, were named Carter Smith, Ebenezer Holmes, and James Hepburn.

"I do not say that when they entered the house they had any preconceived idea of murder.

"They went to steal a will, no matter what the resistance might be.

"The resistance was great, and you helped in the crime.

"Yes—you! Do not attempt to deny it.

"You did not succeed in destroying or, indeed, in finding the will.

"But you did worse. You found the marriage certificate, proving the union of my uncle Richard with Rupert's mother, and you destroyed that, so that we have been unable to find the church."

"And pray, after all these assertions, what do you want with me?" said Doctor Carver, in a faint voice.

"That matter rests entirely with you," said Reuben.

"How?"

"It is very simple. If you refuse to confess that your name is Hepburn, and that you had a hand in the murder at Pendarven Castle, I shall simply lay the matter before the magistrates, and you will be arrested. If, on the other hand, you like to give evidence against Hubert Pendarven, you will get off scot-free, or at any rate, with a nominal term of imprisonment."

Doctor Carver knew not what to do.

To give in was ruin. Yet resistance did not seem of very great use.

"You must permit me to say, Mr. Pendarven," he said, after a pause, "that you have taken me utterly by surprise. I must really consult my lawyer before I attempt to do anything in the matter."

"Consult your lawyer to ascertain whether your name is Carver or Hepburn?" cried Reuben. "Well, in that case no more need be said. You must take your course, and I must take mine."

He rose as he spoke and approached the door.

"Very well," said Doctor Carver. "I deny entirely everything you assert. I don't know, in fact, what you mean, and consequently I will say 'good day.' My lawyers are Messrs. Fitchet & Co. of Melton."

"Be it so, then," said Reuben; "but you will repent the hour when you refused to take my advice."

When Reuben had really quitted the place, Doctor Carver leaned his head on his hands, and was for some time buried in deep reflection.

For a few moments he doubted whether it was prudent even to permit Reuben to leave the island.

But how could he well prevent it?

Reuben, he was well aware, was not the person to be careless enough to venture there without being thoroughly armed.

No!

There was only one thing to do.

That he knew when Reuben had spoken about given information.

That one was flight.

At first he thought of letting the ushers into his secret; but after all he decided that it would be best not to trust anyone.

He had just received the quarter's money for his pupils, and accordingly, he was pretty fairly provided with funds.

No hesitation, accordingly, should be allowed to interfere with his plans, and he at once prepared his family for flight.

All the explanation vouchsafed to the astonished ushers was that he had just received news that a relation was dying, that he desired to see them, and that they would be absent a week.

The ushers were to see that the school went on as usual during their absence.

Within the hour, Carver, *alias* Hepburn, was on his road to London, after writing to Hubert Pendarven and explaining all.

On the same evening he was on the way to Paris.

CHAPTER XLIII.

BLACKLOCK SPEAKS HIS MIND—A DIABOLICAL PLOT.

THE letter which Hubert Pendarven received from Doctor Carver considerably upset that gentleman's peace of mind. And no wonder.

The web seemed gradually closing round him.

Who could expect anything else from his antecedents?

Those who sow the storm must expect to reap the whirlwind.

Yes, so it is. Men see the evil lives, the wretched results of crime.

But they take no heed.

Hubert, when he had taken part in that murderous scene at Pendarven Abbey, expected, fool that he was, that no remorse would follow.

He was cruelly wrong.

It followed on the instant.

When he had left the Abbey behind it began.

The awful face of his brother seemed gleaming out of the darkness, and phantoms of all manner of hideous shapes hovered around him.

These never left him.

Day and night he saw them.

When he stood by his wife's death bed, they seemed to mock and laugh at him.

And now the phantoms had taken real shape.

The confession of the forgers had placed him in a terrible position.

Every moment he was expecting Reuben and the officers of the law, and when he received Carver's letter, and found that his much injured nephew was in the immediate neighbourhood, he felt as if nothing short of flight or the commission of some fresh and awful crime would release him from his incessant dread.

Reuben once out of the way, he would be safe from the punishment which would inevitably follow the proof of his having been guilty of subornation of perjury.

Meanwhile, there was another person who had much the same notions in his head.

This was Hugh Blacklock.

If his master was found guilty of one crime, it seemed to him a natural consequence that the discovery and the punishment of the greater crime must follow.

And in this discovery and punishment he would inevitably be included.

Very late, therefore, on the evening when Doctor Carver's letter reached Hubert the ex-gamekeeper was announced.

Hubert grew pale.

The coming of this man always brought something evil with it.

But yet he could not refuse to see him, and in a few moments they were closeted together.

An evil scowl was on the brow of the gipsy keeper.

" Well, Blacklock, sit down," said his master, with an attempt at geniality, " and tell me what has brought you here so late."

" Bad news for both of us."

This familiar style of talk was habitual now.

And though Hubert liked it not, he could not resent it.

" Ha, what is it?" said he. " It seems I get little good news anywhere now."

" You're right; but this is worse than all. You know a man called Carter Smith?"

" Yes; why ask me such a question?" said Hubert.

" Well, he has turned up."

" I know it."

Hugh Blacklock looked incredulously at the speaker.

The well-acted calmness of Hubert Pendarven deceived him.

" You take it very coolly," he said, " but I happen to know that it is no light matter. Carter Smith has seen Reuben. He has told him all, and before twenty-four hours are over our heads we shall be in gaol unless something is done."

" What can be done?" said Hubert " I know you are telling me the truth, as I have heard from another source— from Hepburn."

Blacklock turned deadly pale.

"Hepburn!" he cried. "I thought he had gone to Australia, and died years ago. Such was the report."

"Ay, and I paid him well to go out," said Hubert, "but nevertheless he cheated me. Some foolish fancy brought him back to England, and with my money he set up the school on the island of which we have heard so much. He is the Doctor Carver of such unenviable notoriety."

"Well?"

"He has written to warn me. My nephew Reuben has been there. He has told him that he intends to proceed against me, and offered him pardon if he would turn evidence against me."

"And Hepburn?"

"He refused. He was far too frightened of a public exposure to remain, and so he has fled to France."

"That is one thing good. But Carter Smith, what of him? He has the dying confession of the fourth man."

"He too must be disposed of," said Hubert. "The question is how?"

This was said gloomily.

And yet he knew when he spoke the answer to his own question.

Hugh Blacklock was not so squeamish.

He came to the point at once.

And somewhat roughly too.

"Well, look here, Mr. Pendarven," he said, "there's no use in beating about the bush. The thing's got to be done, or by Heaven I'll turn evidence myself."

Hubert looked angry.

"I don't see any reason to talk in that manner," he said. "You have always found me ready to fall in with your plans, and this is a mutual affair. You may depend upon my going in for it heart and soul. Tell me what your plan is?"

"It is very simple and easily explained," said Blacklock; "that is if there are no listeners."

"No; I think not," returned Hubert. "I don't fancy anyone in this house troubles himself enough about my affairs to listen. But you can satisfy yourself by looking, if you like."

Blacklock did so.

Everything was perfectly still.

There seemed no chance of any eavesdropping, so returning to his seat, after locking the door, he continued—

"In the first place, Hubert Pendarven, let us thoroughly understand one another. I don't like this game of going about with my neck in a noose, and it appears to me that while Reuben and Rupert live, I shall be always in danger. All the plans you have proposed and had carried out, have turned out to be stupid failures. In the first place, another boy gets killed in his place; then Joshua is sent to the school, and makes another bungle. What I want done is to be right down straightforward."

"Well, out with it."

"I will. Reuben is not far off. This very night he is lodging at the 'Lord Warden' hotel. To-morrow morning the gipsies of his tribe and mine come here and will camp in Blaynton Wood. At night-fall he will visit them. When he returns towards the hotel we must meet him."

"We!" cried Hubert, with a start.

"Yes," returned Blacklock; "I don't want any more second-hand work. What is to be done now must be done by ourselves."

"You say must," returned Hubert; "but what if I refuse?"

"You'll have to take the consequences," replied the outcast gipsy; "for if you do I shall certainly give evidence against you. You know the old saying about self-preservation, etc. I'm just of that kind of opinion; and if you're going to fight shy of——"

"No, no," said Hubert, "pray explain; I'll join you in anything."

"Ah! that's business," cried Blacklock.

And without further to do he bent forward towards him, and explained his plan.

It was a most diabolical one; but still, Hubert, as he heard it unfolded, seemed to take comfort from it.

His eyes sparkled, though his cheeks grew pale; and he muttered—

"Well, it is a desperate deed; but still, I see no other way. It seems to me that you are right."

"Right! There's nothing else to be done," returned Blacklock. "To-morrow evening meet me at eight o'clock by the stile that leads across the five-acre field of Farmer Joyce. It's as dark as pitch up Rose Lane, where the trees arch over, and we can hide there till Doomsday without being seen."

"Good. I will be there; and when this is all over I think I shall try to sell the estates and leave England."

"What, man!" exclaimed Blacklock, "after fighting for them as you have; after wading through blood for them, sell them to another! No; I'd stick to 'em now."

"I cannot," said Hubert. "At any rate I shall try to quit them. They seem haunted. The walls seem pictured with horrors; and—but there, we will not discuss it now. If I sell them there will be plenty of money; and Ralph can do as he pleases if I fly the country."

"Ah! That's a bad game," said Hugh Blacklock; "I'd never do that for anyone. No; I'd stick to the old walls, and brave old Nick to the last."

"Well, we will see how matters turn out," said Hubert, as he rose; and going to the cupboard brought out some spirits and glasses.

"Here is a drop of something to give you courage. And, by the way, I wish you would go to the 'Lord Warden' in the morning, and see if you can see anything of Reuben; find out all his movements, who he has with him, and so on. Perhaps he has the young cub with him; and so we can make short work of it."

"Yes, I've thought of that," said Blacklock; "I'll come round in the afternoon to the paddock, and we can take a stroll and talk where no one can see us; and as I'm very low in the pocket, I'd be glad if you'd give me a cheque for a couple of hundred. When this job's done, I want to go over to Ireland on business."

"I wish you'd break your neck by the way," said Hubert to himself.

But he was outwardly most gushingly friendly.

He wrote out the cheque at once; and after a few more words, Hugh Blacklock took his leave.

He went whistling away down the wide avenue of the Abbey; and away through the plantation to the road, and then on light-heartedly towards town.

No one meeting him would have imagined that he was anything but a happy, well-to-do man.

He had long ago discarded the dress which had stamped him as a keeper on the Pendarven estates.

Dressed in an easy style, as a gentleman farmer, and walking with a firm though jaunty air, he was just the opposite in appearance of what he was in heart.

No one meeting him in the lane would ever have dreamed that black and foul murder already lay heavy on his soul, and that even then his brain was plotting the commission of more crime.

CHAPTER XLIV.

THE NEXT DAY—THE RENDEZVOUS—THE MURDER.

HUBERT PENDARVEN and Hugh Blacklock met next day as arranged in the paddock.

"Well," cried the former, seeing that the latter was joyous in his demeanour, "well, how have you fared?"

"Very well. The two are at the hotel."

"That is good. Anyone with them?"

"No one."

"Why does he delay coming here when he knows so much?"

"That's just it," said Blacklock, "that is why I look so satisfied. If we had not decided upon our scheme, we should have found some visitors here whom we should not have relished. In fact I believe that Reuben has collected nearly all the information he wants, and that he is only waiting for the arrival of some one from London to fall foul of us."

"I can't see much reason for joy in all this," said Hubert gloomily.

Blacklock burst into a hoarse laugh.

"Why, you've got no idea of revenge," he cried. "I've been wishing for this hour ever so long. I swore seventeen years ago to have vengeance on Reuben, and it's come at last."

"I can't quite understand you," said Hubert; "during all these years it seems absurd to think that you could not have swept him from your path and mine, if you had sworn to take his life."

"The same applies to you."

"Not at all," said Hubert Pendarven. "I have been so haunted by the memories of that night of horror, that I have sworn not to imbrue my hands in blood again. Nor would I join in such a scheme now, were it not that I feel in mortal fear every moment of what may happen."

"Your scruples have been those of a haunted coward then," cried Blacklock. "I have had none, but I have failed for want of opportunity. Now we have a chance of wiping off the face of the earth the only two beings we really fear, it is to be hoped that you will not lose courage at the last moment."

"Not I," replied Hubert; "you need have no fear whatever."

"Good! I must take your word for it, although years ago you were not so brave."

"I was younger, and less bitterly in earnest," replied Hubert. "Then I sinned to obtain a fortune; now I shall sin to avoid the hangman."

"Everything is ready," added Blacklock. "When you meet me at the stile, I shall be provided with everything necessary—masks, pistols, and a good stout dagger each."

"Be careful where you procure them," said Hubert, timidly.

"Have no fear. Do you think I want to fix the halter on my own neck? No, no; the weapons I have chosen have long since been forgotten by those to whom they belonged, and have no maker's name on them."

They parted presently, after a few more words, and did not meet again till night.

After a day of feverish anxiety—a day in which he was never at rest, and started almost at his own shadow— Hubert Pendarven set out for the rendezvous.

He was well primed with spirits.

Not enough to make him unsteady.

But enough to set his blood coursing madly through his veins; to confuse and inflame his brain; to deaden conscience and awake revenge.

What a walk that was through the black wood!

Every moment he paused to listen.

The wind seemed to have whispering voices.

Moonlight rays forcing themselves through the dense foliage here and there, appeared to him the spectres of the murdered, waving white arms at him.

The rustle of the bushes was their hissing laughter.

Shuddering and shivering he went stumbling on along the rough path, and, for the first time in his life, experienced a sensation of joy as he saw the figure of Hugh Blacklock leaning against the stile.

It was a weight off his mind to have even this unmitigated villain as a companion.

Anything was better than darkness and solitude, with the memory of his crimes behind him, and the prospect of another crime before him.

"Is that you, Blacklock?" he cried, in a wavering voice, speaking merely for the sake of something to say.

"Ay, my brave master," said the exkeeper, sneeringly. "Why, your voice is as unsteady as an old woman's with the ague. You're late, and there's no time to be lost, so I hope you'll pull yourself together."

"Yes, yes, I'm all right," said Hubert. "Give me the mask and weapons."

The keeper at once handed him his pistols, his dagger, his mask, and a cloak which comfortably covered up his person.

Then, when each had imbibed another draught of brandy, they stepped into the road, and began walking quickly in the direction of Blaynton Wood.

Meanwhile, we must return to Reuben and Rupert, the object of the two assassins' deadly purpose.

When Reuben quitted the school on the island, and the presence of the murderer who had so long concealed himself from justice, he went straight to the "Lord Warden" hotel, and sent for Rupert.

"Tell your master," he said, "that I require you for a time with me, and that you will not be able to return to the school for some considerable while."

Little did Rupert, when Reuben sent him this missive, imagine what the duration of this absence would be, or what terrible events would cause it.

He was surprised himself at the letter.

An absence again after the week he had spent in London was a most unexpected thing.

But still, he was glad to go.

He found Reuben at luncheon.

"Well, my boy," said his cousin, after he had grasped his hand warmly, "there is no use putting off any longer the exposure of Hubert Pendarven. I have such proofs now in my hands that it is only waste of time to defer it. Perhaps, when he finds he is run to earth, he will make a confession that will put you in possession of your rights."

A flush of joy overspread the face of Rupert Pendarven.

"Ah!" he said, "that, of course, would be the means of clearing my mother's name."

"Yes, certainly."

"Then tell me exactly what it is you propose," said Rupert; "I am all anxiety to know."

"In the first place, then," said Reuben, "I am collecting my witnesses. Carter Smith, who knew the man who made a deposition before a magistrate in America. Then the gipsies who were in the camp on that fatal night, and heard from Lee, their king, the story of the murder. Then I, too, have my evidence, and before he can rebut all this, Doctor Carver will be in custody too."

"Why, what has he to do with it all?" asked Rupert, in astonishment.

"He turns out to be Hepburn, another of the four assassins. He has fled, I hear; but the officers of justice are after him. When he is caught, and Hugh Blacklock, we have the whole of them. One of them will be sure to turn evidence against the others; but I do not suppose that Hubert will dream of letting it go so far. When he hears of the approach of the officers of justice, he will deliver up his ill-gotten wealth and fly."

"That would be better than exposure; but still, my father's death calls for vengeance," said Rupert. "How can we forego it?"

"Perhaps heaven may forestall us," said Reuben, gravely; "at any rate, this evening we go to the gipsy encampment to arrange matters. I shall be glad to see some of the old faces."

"So shall I," said Rupert. "I cannot help feeling some of the old spirit in me. I long to be off and away into the green woods, to sleep once more in the tents of the tribe, and take my meals out under the clear canopy of heaven."

"Ah, you must give up all those ideas," said Reuben. "Remember that you are the head of a grand and ancient family, and you will have to settle down on your estate like the 'fine old English gentleman.' I shall be glad indeed when all is settled."

In the evening, when they were about to start for the gipsy encampment, Rupert noticed a strange change in his cousin.

There was a sad and grave expression on his face, and a wistful look in his eyes, which our hero had never seen before.

"What is the matter, Reuben?" he said; "you don't seem yourself."

"I am all right," said his cousin, with a forced laugh, "but I have had a dream which has rather upset me. I had a snooze while you were gone down the High Street to post my letter, and I had a most horrible vision. I cannot well tell it to you, for it was so confused and unreal, but it has left a most unpleasant feeling in my mind.

"Don't go to-night," said Rupert. "I should certainly put it off till to-morrow. There is no such great hurry for a few hours."

"No, Rupert; I will not give up my idea for a foolish dream. We will go now."

Again our hero tried to dissuade him. But in vain.

And so just after six o'clock they sat out for Blaynton Wood.

It was twilight as they left the "Lord Warden."

"What a lovely evening!" said Rupert with eagerness, as they hurried on. "I long to see my old friends at their evening meal."

"They will be glad enough to see us," said Reuben, who, as he hastened on, seemed to lose some of his gloom. "Among them, at least, I know I can hope to see some friendly faces; to grasp hands whose grasp is true. The 'house dwellers,' as we are called, are not famous for the reality of their friendships, or their aversion to murder."

"Hugh Blacklock is not a very good specimen of a gipsy," said Rupert; "he is crafty, cunning, and murderous."

"There is an exception to every rule,"

said Reuben. "But here we are. See, there are the lights of the fires twinkling through the trees."

He spoke this in quite his old voice.

The very proximity of the tents seemed to restore him to his good spirits.

Presently they reached a part of the hedges where there was an opening.

Through this they went, and in a few minutes they came upon the familiar scene—the squat tents, the fires, the women cooking or sitting round the merry glow, the forms of strong, swarthy men standing about.

In a moment their appearance was noticed, and there was a murmur of greeting from all; even the women rising to do honour to their king.

For although Reuben was living away from them, he was still acknowledged as king; and it was well known that his absence had a special reason in it.

They were both the centre of an eager crowd for a few minutes; and then Reuben and Carter Smith, with one or two others, drew apart from the rest.

An earnest conference took place between them for some time; and then everything having apparently been settled to Reuben's satisfaction they returned to the fires.

Here, as in the olden days, he and Rupert sat with their wild companions to partake of one of those stews, with an imitation of which he had treated the boys of Blakesley Hall once in the woods.

It was about half-past eight that they set out upon their return journey.

Carter Smith, and one or two others, accompanied them a little way up the road; and then, bidding them "good night," went back towards their encampment.

"Your prophecy came true indeed," said Rupert; "we did get a hearty welcome."

"Yes," said Reuben; "and what is more, I've done some good business. As far as I see now, the web is closing tighter and tighter around Hubert Pendarven."

Little did he think when he uttered those words how near him were his enemies—lying in wait to betray and murder!

They had now reached that part of Rose Lane where the branches over-arched the roadway, and caused an utter and pitchy darkness.

Here and there a dim light penetrated through breaks in the trees; but even these were invisible except to those standing near.

Not a sound was to be heard.

Even the wind had lulled; and their own voices, and the echo of their own footsteps, was all that broke the stillness.

Some strange feeling was upon them as they entered the utter darkness, and they ceased speaking.

All kept quiet for about five minutes.

Then there was a sudden rush, and Reuben fell back half stunned by a tremendous blow on the head.

A similar blow aimed at Rupert by a second assailant with a heavy bludgeon caught him on the shoulder but glanced off.

When Reuben recovered he was already being attacked again by the ruffian who had struck him, and he saw that our hero was in a similar predicament.

Both Reuben and Rupert were amazed.

Beset always by enemies, they were well aware of the danger which they would run by being without weapons, so in addition to their heavy sticks they carried pistols.

For the moment, however, they were unable to use them.

The attack of their foes was so swift, so unexpected, that they were taken quite aback.

But after a minute or two they were able to hold their own.

This, however, was not suited to the plans of the murderers.

They did not desire to enter into any lengthened combat.

They had hoped to be able to stun their victims, and finish their deadly work with the knife.

Pistols are noisy things, and they feared by using them to rouse the neighbourhood.

Now, however, they had no alternative.

Their intended victims were expert in the use of the bludgeon, and it was evident from the way in which they whirled them about their heads that they would soon be the aggressors instead of the assailed.

"Keep them going," cried Hubert, close to Hugh's ear.

Then he drew back, and swiftly drawing his pistol fired at Reuben.

It was he whom he feared and hated most, and he, therefore, who must be the first victim.

The ball was well aimed.

With a loud cry of pain Reuben fell back, and a second shot sent him to the earth.

Maddened as he felt by his cousin's murder, Rupert was unable to run to his aid, or ascertain what was the amount of his hurts.

For Blacklock's strong arms whirled his weapon about like a flail.

Then, suddenly, there was another report, and Rupert was wounded in the shoulder.

As the ball sped, however, the report so near made the ex-gamekeeper start aside, and Rupert, wounded as he was, brought his stick with such force upon the head of his adversary that he staggered back.

If Rupert had been a coward he could now have made good his escape.

But he was far too brave.

Drawing his pistol, he took the best aim he could and fired.

The ball took effect, as was proved by a gasping cry from some one.

But single-handed he would have been an easy prey to the two assassins had not at this moment a strange incident happened.

From both sides of the road some dark figures bearing lanterns leaped forward with a loud shout.

The murderers did not stay to do battle with their new foes.

Dashing their sticks at the lanterns, and succeeding in smashing one, they fled away along the dark high road, and though pursued they contrived to make good their escape by plunging into one of the dark plantations.

Meanwhile, Carter Smith, who with his companions also had reached the scene just in time to save the life of Rupert, knelt down by Reuben's side, and examined him by the light of the one lantern left.

He was lying on his back, his eyes closed, his face upturned towards the over-arching trees, his features suffused by a deadly pallor, his breast smothered in the blood which had welled up from a wound over his heart.

"Reuben, our king, is dead!" said Carter Smith.

"Dead!"

What a dismal echo that word had!

Rupert uttered a wild cry of despair, and crouching near took his cousin's hand, and gazed eagerly into his face.

"Speak to me, Reuben," he cried, "pray, speak to me! It is I—Rupert."

But there was no answer.

"It is of no avail to speak to him," said Carter Smith, with kind firmness. "Let us bear him to the camp."

And so raising him up gently, they bore him away to the tents, as the old King of the Gipsies had been borne seventeen years ago.

To describe Rupert's feelings as he passed along in this dismal *cortège* would be difficult indeed.

His mind was full of mad rage and despair.

Reuben had talked once of the hushing up of the story for the sake of the old name.

Rupert had demurred to the idea then.

Now his heart was bursting with a wild craving for vengeance.

CHAPTER XLV.

ON THE TRACK OF ANOTHER ASSASSIN—SMALL CONFESSES THE SECRETS OF HUNGRY HALL.

WHILE those awful shadows of misfortune were once more clouding the life of Rupert Pendarven, we must return to Hungry Hall, the history of which had become so thoroughly mixed up with that of our principal characters.

Doctor Carver, *alias* Hepburn, had given instructions, as we know, to Small and Meekly to keep on the school on the old lines until such time as he returned from abroad.

But when they came to look over matters, they discovered that they had been thoroughly deceived, and that the principal had bolted.

Every farthing was gone, and from letters they found in his desk, they discovered that he had forestalled the quarterly payments.

There was nothing left but to close the school, and let the whole thing be exposed.

Having arranged everything, the two ushers sent for Freeman.

But he was gone too.

The bully of the school and his wife had both disappeared.

"Well, this is a nice predicament," said Small, as he tossed off a glass of the schoolmaster's strong whisky. "I must say that I never expected it."

"Never mind that," said Meekly, who was roused by circumstances into a different state of mind altogether from what he usually affected, "the thing now is, what are we going to do, as it has happened?"

"That's it," said Small. "I think we've got enough provisions to last us two days, and the tradespeople won't stop supplies just yet. Meanwhile, we had better inform the police of our suspicions."

"Police are always best left alone," said Meekly, "in a place like this. We don't want it overhauled."

"That's what I do want," said Small.

"What, to be hanged?"

"Not it," said Small. "I want revenge on the old villain for serving us this trick. We'll go and have a look round, open some of his favourite cellars, and particularly the one leading to the subterranean passage under the river. Then we'll send for the police, and say we looked over the school, when we found out that he had run away, and they'll soon be after him. We can put the youngsters in their charge, and let them have the bother, as we're left without funds."

"That's not a bad idea," said Meekly, "its best to be first in the field. If we were to run away, and he was to be brought back, we should get put in the dock with him."

The next day passed.

On the morning of the second day, they received a letter, which by some means the artful fugitive had had posted in London.

It was very brief but excessively to the purpose.

"I have gone for good. Do the best you can. Send for the boys' parents. The address book is in my desk."

"The old villain!" cried Small; "now for the police."

They went on a tour through the premises, opened every place which could possibly throw a light on anything, and then sent for the police.

The boys were utterly astounded by the turn things had taken.

Since Doctor Carver's departure they had had splendid food.

It was the policy of the ushers, of course, to give it them.

The boys knew nothing, however, of the fact that the master had fled, and they were consequently greatly astounded when they found the premises in the possession of the police.

Little did Rupert think how Meekly and Small were playing into his hands.

But they were.

Every move that the police made against Dr. Carver was forging more strongly the chains round Hubert Pendarven.

When, with lanterns held by the two ushers, the constables examined the basement of the house, they were overwhelmed with horror and amazement.

They discovered cupboards long closed, containing the skeletons of lads still wrapped in their day clothes, some stretched full length, some kneeling as they had died, praying for mercy or deliverance.

And when passing to the entrance of the subterranean passage, they paused in doubt and dismay.

The wind came sweeping from the chill chambers far away beneath the Hermit's Hut in the woods, nearly extinguishing the torches held by the two constables in front.

It looked strangely solemn and gloomy.

"Ugh! this is a shivery hole and no mistake," said one of them. "If we've found skeletons in cupboards there, what shall we find here?"

"I think it's very likely that you'll find more," said Small; "but you can't find anything worse than murder—boys starved to death, and so on."

"No, you're right. Well, come on; we can't do no good a-standing here anyhow."

So on they went along the dark subterranean way, the dull glow of the torches and the flickering light of the lanterns scarcely seeming to show them the way.

It was a long distance beneath the river, between walls reeking with damp.

Evidently at some time or another the school on the island had been used for a far different purpose than that of an academy.

No useful end would have been gained by building great subterranean ways, except to be used as a means of flight in case of attack.

"It's a rum place, too," said one of the constables. "I expect it was built years ago by some of them Commonwealth fellows."

"Yes, very likely," said Small, whose teeth began to chatter with fright, although he had often been that way before. "It's certainly not a place which anyone would be likely to build for amusement."

"No," said Meekly, "it's certainly not a place that anyone would come to if he wasn't obliged."

They reached presently the bottom of the pit, where Rupert (as my readers will remember) saw the boy flung in when he had paid his visit to the Hermit's Hut.

There an awful sight was to be seen.

Several bodies were lying about, dressed in various ways, but all evidently recently placed there.

The rats had been busy with the unfortunate victims, and, indeed, it would be only horrifying the reader to describe the whole hideous picture that was so suddenly presented to the gaze of the searching party.

"Well, this 'ere's an awful go altogether," said one of the constables. "We shall 'ave to be after him. We've seen quite enough. So we'll leave everything just as it is, and go back to the Hall; then I'll tell you what we'll do."

This was soon acted upon, and it was not long before the whole of the party was seated in Doctor Carver's study, where Small brought out the whisky.

"Well," asked Meekly, "what do you propose doing?"

"You'd better write off to the parents of these boys, and acquaint them with what's happened," said the head constable; "then you'll know better what your position is. You'd better remain here, because if you run away we shall be after you. As for Carver, we shall be after him before another hour's over his head."

"There's no knowing where he is gone," said Small. "He said he was going to Paris."

"All the more reason that he isn't going there," said the policeman. "But we haven't made a thorough search of the house yet. Maybe we'll find something that'll throw some light on the subject. You haven't moved anything in the house, I suppose?"

"Yes, we have moved things," said Small, "because we've been looking everywhere for money. But we haven't destroyed anything."

"That's as well," said the constable. "Maybe there'll be some clue to his whereabouts."

A thorough search was made throughout the house after a time, and among the papers flung down on the floor in the bed-room of Dr. Carver was an ABC guide, marked with pencil marks.

The head constable was a very acute man in his way.

"Ha!" he said, "I think we have him now. Here we are—Paris, Brussels. Yes, he's gone to Brussels. To-morrow I and a London detective will be after him. Thank you—yes, I will take another nip of whisky."

The constables, thus refreshed, took their way once more towards their headquarters, and in half-an-hour Inspector Graves (the man who had found the railway guide) was on his way to London.

Next morning all the morning papers had an advertisement offering a large reward for the apprehension of Doctor Carver, or for information in regard to his whereabouts.

We may as well complete here the rest of the story of Hungry Hall, which, with the flight of its ruffianly principal, died out of the life of our hero.

With Carver, *alias* Hepburn, we have yet to do.

But Small and Meekly, and the boys, have nothing further to do with our story.

The two former were no doubt cognisant of the awful crimes committed in the old school-house, and when everything was settled they disappeared.

No one knew what became of them, but Susie Brandford, when she heard of the wind-up of matters at Hungry Hall, was indeed grateful that she had been saved from the clutches of a despicable little villain.

The letters which were addressed to the parents, etc., of the boys, were productive of a general exodus of the scholars.

Many of the guardians were disgusted at the unexpected breakdown of their abominable schemes.

But they had no alternative but to send for the pupils when the affair was made so public, and accordingly the grim old building which had been the scene of so many crimes and so many heart-rending episodes, was left deserted.

With the last of the scholars went Small and Meekly.

Probably, had the police desired their presence, they could have put their hands on the two worthies at any moment.

As it was, they vanished from the scene.

They were not necessary for the destruction of Dr. Carver.

There were other phantoms following in his track than those of the murdered scholars, and already their skinny arms were being stretched out to clutch him.

CHAPTER XLVI.

HUGH BLACKLOCK AND HUBERT PENDARVEN ARE WITNESSES OF A STRANGE SCENE.

"HAVE you heard the news, Hugh Blacklock?" cried a voice, as on the morning of the murder in the lane the ex-gamekeeper lounged out of the "Tabard Inn."

Starting round at the sudden remark, Hugh found himself confronted by Carter Smith, the gipsy.

"You startled me," said Blacklock. "I didn't see anyone near. No, I haven't heard any news. What is it?"

"Not the murder—you haven't heard o' that?"

"Murder? No. Tell us. Come in and have a glass of ale, and tell me all about it."

The gipsy considered a moment, eyeing Blacklock curiously as he did so.

"No," he said, "I don't think I will have a drink. I'm rather in a hurry. If you're going down the lane I'll walk with you, and tell you all about it."

"I wasn't coming down the lane, but I will," said Hugh. "I was going up to the town. Mr. Pendarven's going to London to-day, and I've got to buy something for him."

"Well, the news is strange," said Carter Smith. "You know Reuben Pendarven, the one that was out of the way so long because he was accused of forgery?"

"Know him?" said Blacklock. "I should rather think I did."

"Well," continued Carter Smith, "he was murdered last night in the lane up here, and so there's an end of everything for him. It's a shame—a real downright shame—just as he's proved his innocence, and got his money back from Mr. Hubert."

"Yes, it's rather hard lines for him," said Blacklock. "But who was the murderer? Is he caught?"

"Caught?" cried Carter Smith, with a peculiar smile, "no, he's not; or, rather, not 'he,' for from the few words he spoke it seems there were two who attacked him. And there was Rupert there, too. He says there were two villains. Cowardly ruffians! But we've got a suspicion of 'em, and if the law of England won't hang 'em, gipsy law will. At any rate, it'll take revenge on 'em."

He looked very earnestly at Hugh Blacklock as he spoke, but that worthy was quite proof against anything of the kind.

"And serve 'em right," said he, as he rolled a quid of tobacco in his mouth.

" But, ye see, if the police haven't a clue to 'em, I don't see that you can have any."

" Oh, yes, we have," said Carter Smith. " We gipsies do not act on the same principles as the police. We may be wrong-headed, and may run the risk of injuring the wrong person, but we'll get at the right one somehow."

" Have you given information to the police?" asked Blacklock, with studied calm.

" No."

" Then I think you're having a grim jest with me," said the other, with a coarse laugh. " Unless I saw Reuben buried I'd never believe that he was murdered."

" You can see that if you like," said Smith. " He will be buried to-night."

" Then you don't intend to say anything about it," said Blacklock, with ill-disguised satisfaction.

" No," said the gipsy, grimly; " what we know and feel we shall keep in our hearts, and when our chance comes, we shall take all punishment in our own hands."

" I'd come into the tents, only I'm afraid," said Blacklock.

" The people won't hurt you," said Smith.

But his tone was somewhat too eager.

" No, I won't come," said the ex-gamekeeper. " I won't risk it. Reuben's wife, I know, wouldn't stand it. The way we parted, if you remember, was not of the pleasantest. I think I'll be going now. You don't want to say anything about this matter, then?"

" No."

" Very well, I'll keep my counsel," he answered. " You may depend on me. Though if I'm ever put on my oath, I can't deny you told me."

And so they parted.

Smith peered after him when they had said " good day," and Blacklock was lounging away towards the town.

" You're guilty, Hugh," he muttered, " and you're doomed. Though you're one of the tribe, you must suffer, for it is our king you have helped to slay. I

must follow you, too, for if my thoughts don't tell me wrong, you won't go to the town, but to the Abbey."

Used to the woods and fields, used to night adventures of all kinds, Carter Smith found no difficulty in following Blacklock along hedges and ditches.

He kept just sufficiently far behind the man to watch his every movement.

" How easily," he thought, as he pressed onward, " how easily could I rid the world of this villain now. In this lonely lane I could take his coward life, and no one would be wiser. But no, I must wait until the word is given, and then—who shall prevent his doom?"

Carter Smith, noiseless and patient as a sleuth hound, proved himself by no means wrong in his suspicions.

Blacklock, on reaching the stile where he and Hubert Pendarven had met just before the murder, glanced round him in every direction to see if he was followed.

Then, not dreaming of the figure which crouched near at hand, he leaped the stile, and passed away rapidly towards Pendarven Abbey.

Carter Smith still followed, until he saw him cross the grounds and make his way up the terrace steps.

Then he went back, looking on every side for signs of the evil deed of the preceding night. But except one sign, there was none.

That was on the top of the stile.

Marks of blood, where a hand had grasped.

" We have tracked the assassins," he said. " I felt almost sure before, but there is no shadow of a doubt in my mind now. No jury would convict them, because there is no one to swear to their faces being those of the villains, the cowards of last night. But I could swear the murderers are Blacklock and his master, and I could kill them without remorse."

And, eager to give his news to the tribe, he presently leaped the stile into the lane, and hurried away towards the tents.

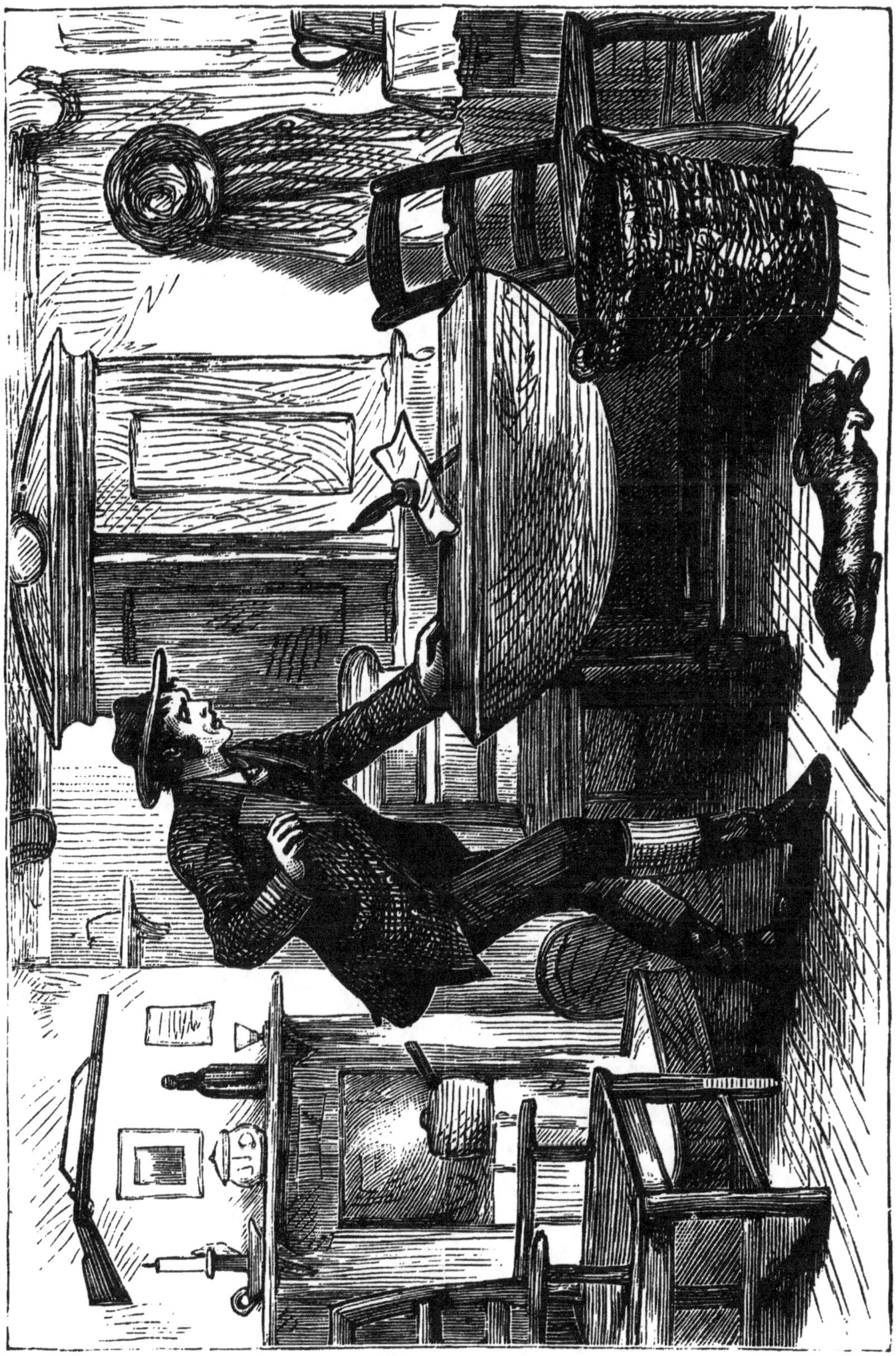

"TO THE VILLAIN'S STARTING EYES, THE WORDS APPEARED TO BE WRITTEN IN LETTERS OF BLOOD."

CHAPTER XLVII.

WHAT HUBERT PENDARVEN AND HUGH BLACKLOCK SAW IN THE WOOD.

WHEN Hugh Blacklock at length reached the Abbey, he found his "master," as Carter Smith had called him, in his private room, looking over some papers.

He looked as if he had been imbibing something more than coffee or tea to keep his spirits up; and, at any rate, he had a strange and wild look about his eyes.

"Well," he said, as he saw who it was who entered at his summons, "well, what news do you bring me—good or bad?"

"Reuben is dead."

A spasm of emotion of some kind overspread Hubert's face for a moment.

"That is well," he said, in a low voice. Then he added—

"Who is suspected?"

"By whom?"

"By those who found him, and by the police, of course," said Hubert Pendarven.

"Ah, that is the strangest thing, and perhaps not the most pleasant part of the whole matter," said Blacklock. "No one knows it but the gipsies."

"That is well," said Pendarven. "If they keep it to themselves now, they won't dare to talk about it afterwards, or they will be thought the aiders and abettors in the matter."

"I see no cause for congratulation myself," said Hugh. "When you hear what I learned this morning, you will see that they have made up their minds who did the deed, and will take the punishment into their own hands."

"Pray say on then," said Pendarven. "As you may imagine, I am all impatience."

He took a nip of brandy as he spoke, and handed one to his companion.

Anyone looking at him could tell that his calm peace of mind was gone for ever.

Even the little that was left him after the haunting visions of his murdered brother had vanished.

Blacklock was not of the same metal.

He was a coarser and more resolute villain, although his heart could not have been blacker than his employer's.

Hubert's face was worked by conflicting emotions as he listened to the words of his companion.

"Well," he said, when he had finished, "I did not see matters in your light. If we had the police and all the machinery of the law against us, I do not know how we should fare. We should be so beset on all sides, that we should not know what to do. Now we are aware who are our enemies, and can be prepared for them."

"I don't know so much about that," said Hugh Blacklock. "The gipsies are far more terrible than the law. They strike in the dark, when no one is near to restrain their arms."

"We can be secure against them, though," said Hubert, with a courage he did not feel. "But you do not speak of Rupert. He lives, of course, and is with them. He will be the one to direct the gipsies against us."

"And he will have no mercy," said Blacklock, "especially if Reuben lived long enough to give him any orders."

"Well, I'm going to see Reuben buried out of the way to-night, at any rate," said Blacklock, after a short pause. "I shall know then there's one the less to torment us, for if they once bury him, they dare not say a word more about it. I shall know what kind of vengeance to expect then."

"I'll go with you, then," said Hubert Pendarven. "I shall not feel satisfied unless my own eyes tell me that my worst enemy is beneath the earth."

"Rupert still remains."

"Yes, he is the last."

"And with his own money, and that of Reuben also, he will be a powerful one."

"No one is powerful enough or rich enough to escape a shot in the dark," said Pendarven, "and so he, as well as myself, must be on the alert."

That night, as soon as darkness came down over the earth, the two assassins once more took their way from Pendarven Abbey towards the spot where the gipsies were encamped.

It was a very dark night.

Far more gloomy than the previous one.

Hugh Blacklock walked on quite unconcernedly and boldly, although they had to traverse the very spot where the brutal scene had taken place on the night before.

Hubert slunk by as swiftly as possible, trembling at every unusual sound, and shuddering even at the whisper of the trees.

Both were masked.

Both were disguised as grooms.

It would not do indeed to be seen so near Pendarven Abbey loitering about the lanes at night.

The masks were only to be worn in the lanes and the woods, so that their faces might not show in the dim light of the lanterns borne by the burial party.

Carter Smith had not made Hugh Blacklock acquainted with the spot where the body of Reuben was to be deposited.

The only way in which this could be discovered was by creeping up as near as possible to the tents, and then by some means following the burying-party.

As they slowly neared the tents they could see the lights of the gipsies moving hither and thither.

The two spies, as they may well be termed, kept along the hedge-side until they reached behind the high trees a spot where they could behold the whole scene.

Anyone, even a stranger, could at once have seen that something unusual had happened or was about to happen.

The fires were all alight, but no preparations for a meal were going on.

The gipsies, male and female, were standing about, engaged in earnest conversation, and that too of an evidently exciting nature.

Presently all were still.

The groups broke up, and everyone took his or her place in the procession.

Then from one of the tents two men emerged, bringing a coffin between them.

Then Rupert came forth.

At that distance they knew him by his upright demeanour and his clothes.

A few words were said by our hero to those around him.

Then the procession began to move towards the very opening where Hubert Pendarven and Hugh Blacklock were concealed.

"This way," said the latter. "I think I know where they are going. I ought to, for every nook and corner of these woods is known to me."

He led the way, crawling stealthily along further into the deeply-wooded glade, and arriving at last at an open space surrounded by tall pines he halted.

They were considerably in advance of the burying-party.

But they still saw the lights advancing after them.

"They are coming this way," said the ex-gamekeeper in a low voice. "I thought I guessed where they'd bury him. This is the very spot where they've buried their dead for ever so long. Ye see, no one misses the gipsies. There's no inquiry if any of 'em disappear; and so they can put 'em under the earth wherever they please."

"I wish they'd put Rupert underground at the same moment," said Hubert.

"Ay, but there's no such luck as that."

"There could be."

"How?"

"A steady shot as he stands on the edge of the grave."

"Ay, that would do it, but it's dangerous."

"It is," said Hubert, with a sigh, in which there was a wondrous depth of agony, "it is. But is it so dangerous as leaving him alive?"

"Perhaps not. But are you armed?"

"Do I ever come out without my pistols?" asked Hubert. "No. If you have no firearms I can lend them to you."

"You may as well hand them over," said Hugh, "though I like not the idea."

"You will when you hear more of it," returned Pendarven, "but you have not much time to make up your mind. See, they are rapidly approaching nearer."

"Yes; speak quickly."

"My plan is this, then," said Hubert. "When they are lowering the body into the grave I will fire at Rupert, and then instantly at the lantern held by the man nearest to him. You fire also twice at the lights. We will not pause to see the effect of our shots, but fly straight along this avenue of oak trees. At the other end one can go one way, and one another, and to-morrow we can meet again."

And then as if to enforce his earnest opinion he clutched Hugh fiercely by the arm, adding—

"Then all our enemies are gone, Blacklock; for when Rupert and his cousin are dead what care we for Hepburn or any others?"

"True. I will run the risk," said the man.

He knew the peril of the attempt.

But he was aware also that to himself the danger was not half so great as it was to the master of Pendarven.

Hugh was a gipsy, used to the woods, and acquainted with all kinds of tricks which would never, of course, cross the mind of Hubert.

So, as he knew how the death of Rupert would clear the path before them, he agreed to this fresh and cowardly crime.

The burial party was now near at hand.

It had been compelled to wend its way slowly along, because of the irregularities of the ground, and the roots and clinging weeds that obstructed the way.

But the conversation between Hugh and Pendarven had been carried on in a swift whisper, and had not occupied much time.

The two villains, having agreed upon a signal, separated a little, so that they could fire at the same moment.

The gipsies came up to the edge of the clearing.

Here they halted, and as they held aloft their lanterns and their torches the two watchers saw that the new-made grave was ready.

Solemnly the burying party gathered round it with lantern bearers.

Two of these stood at the head of the open trench.

In the centre of these came the corpse-bearers, and on their right Rupert advanced to the edge.

Now was the time.

A slight whistle like that of a bird awoke the stillness of the night.

Then a pistol shot.

Then two more.

Hubert as he fired saw Rupert stagger and topple back.

Then as he fired again all was darkness and confusion.

Not a moment was lost by the assassins.

Away they sped in the darkness of the night.

At the avenue's end they parted.

There was a pursuit, of course.

But it was unsuccessful.

Again the two cruel and cowardly wretches had escaped.

Next morning Hugh Blacklock, dressed as usual, strolled away down the lane.

When he reached the gipsies' encampment all was clear.

The tents were gone.

The tribe had departed.

Nothing but the embers of the fires remained to tell they were there.

But when Hugh Blacklock returned to his cottage on the grounds of Pendarven he found a dagger sticking in the table of his front room—a dagger that pinned to the wood a piece of paper on which was written the words—

"To Hugh Blacklock, for himself and master.—A gipsy's vengeance never sleeps. It comes when least expected."

Hugh Blacklock trembled, and a cold perspiration broke from every pore as he read the lines on the paper.

To the villain's starting eyes, the words appeared to be written in letters of blood.

But still there was a ray of comfort in it all.

The gipsies had departed for a time, and there was a respite from fear for awhile.

CHAPTER XLVIII.

THE WATCHER AT PENDARVEN CASTLE—AN OLD FRIEND REAPPEARS ON THE SCENE.

THROUGHOUT the whole of the terrible events which had been occurring during the last few hours, no one in the vicinity of Pendarven Castle was any the wiser.

The assassins had been very particular and careful in their movements, and those whose interest it was to inform the police of what had happened, had resolved to take things into their own hands, and punish the wrong-doers in their own way.

But they did not absolutely lose sight of the transgressors.

Hubert was delighted that they had left the neighbourhood.

Yet he made one mistake.

He forgot the words of the warning— "A gipsy's vengeance never sleeps."

Nor did it in this instance.

Though the tents had been struck, and the vans had gone, and the embers of old fires had been left beneath the place where the encampment had been, there was one near Pendarven who was ever on the watch.

This was the gipsy, Carter Smith.

To him had been deputed the task of watching Hubert Pendarven and his companion in crime.

Used to the woods, his task was not only a pleasant but an easy one.

He soon framed for himself in the densest part of Pendarven Woods a little hut in shape of a gipsy's tent, and here he set up his abode.

Hidden in a little dell some hundreds of yards away from the high road, this strange abode did not lie in the track of any of the frequenters of Pendarven Castle.

A stray poacher might take it into his head to come that way by day or night.

But of such a person Carter Smith stood in no fear.

During the day the gipsy wandered about the neighbourhood, apparently always on business, but really never going far from the gates of the castle.

Not a single person entering there escaped the lynx eyes of Carter Smith.

He was a detective by nature; and no one who saw him prowling about there would have imagined for one moment that he was ever on the watch.

But so it was.

And he seemed to have his very heart in the work.

Hugh Blacklock met him once.

"Why, what on earth are you doing here alone?" he said.

"Minding my own business," he said, and turned away.

Nor would any inducements make him speak to the ex-gamekeeper any more.

At length one evening he beheld a strange figure approaching along the narrow thoroughfare from the stile to the grounds—the way by which the assassins had made their way to the lane.

The new-comer was a young man, but he seemed prematurely aged and bent.

Seeing Carter Smith he paused to make inquiries.

"This is Pendarven, my man, is it not?" he asked.

"Yes."

"I thought so," said the other, wearily, and as if making an effort to look back into an uncertain past, "I have been here before, but my memory is not as good as it has been, and I get confused."

To Carter Smith's brain there at once came the idea—

"This man is weak-minded enough to tell me his affairs if I am careful with him."

"Do you wish to see Mr. Hubert Pendarven?" he said aloud.

The man pressed his hand to his brow.

"Hubert! No, not Hubert," he answered. It is Reuben or Rupert I wish to see."

"They don't live here," said Smith, eagerly; "they are some distance away."

"But this Hubert. He will tell me where to find them."

"No. He is the enemy of Rupert. He will not tell you where he is; and more than that, it is not safe for any friend of Rupert's or Reuben's to come near this place. If you wish to give any information to either of them, you can safely trust me."

He did not think it wise to tell him the terrible events of the last week.

Infirm of purpose as the man seemed, the fact of the murder in the lane would perhaps divert him altogether from what he had at first planned.

"Very well," said the man, "let me see either Reuben or Rupert at once or I shall forget—I shall forget."

Carter Smith did not hesitate.

He had taken up his position in the grounds of Pendarven by the wish of the tribe.

But the arrival of this stranger was surely an excuse for at once deserting his post.

"Come along, then, my man," said he. "We will go to Rupert Pendarven at once. He's very ill, but he'll be glad to see you. But tell me what's your name, so that I can tell him who wants to speak to him."

"My name. Well, he won't know it, but I may as well tell you. It's Fred Frost. I'm the nephew of the old sexton at Melton."

Carter Smith's heart gave an unusual bump at this.

But he said nothing save—"All right, come along, then."

And away they went along the lane in the direction of the high road to Castleborough.

* * * *

Fred Frost!

Then he was not dead after all.

When he had been left for dead by the tramp who had robbed him in the lane, he had lain there in a state of semi-consciousness until daylight.

There he was found by some labourers going to their work, and conveyed to the infirmary.

Here he was attended carefully by the doctors, who declared him a dying subject.

However, his wonderful constitution fought against the terrible and murderous wounds inflicted by the tramp, and he gradually but slowly recovered.

His bodily strength came back to a great extent, but his intellect seemed gone for ever.

He was an excitable lunatic.

He appeared feeble and childish; so dazed that he was unable to understand the simplest things.

He was kept consequently about the infirmary to do little odd jobs, and made himself at last so handy about the place that he came to be looked on as a fixture.

The only thing that he seemed capable of enjoying was reading.

This became a mania with him.

Every scrap of printed paper, especially newspapers, was devoured eagerly by his greedy eyes. Evidently some one idea was oppressing his brain.

At length, one morning, when a few moments he had rest from his labours, he was glancing over the second column of a morning paper, when he saw an advertisement—

"In re Pendarven Estates."

He started up as these words caught his eyes with an outcry which made his companions think he had suddenly gone raving mad.

"What's the matter?" cried several voices at once.

"Matter! ha, ha!" laughed Fred Frost. "I've found it. I've found it!"

And whirling the paper frantically round his head, he rushed out into the grounds where he could be alone.

Here he calmed down, and sitting on a seat far away from the building, began quietly to peruse the advertisement—

"In re Pendarven Estates—Anyone giving information which will lead to the discovery of the marriage certificate of Richard Pendarven, of Pendarven Castle, Cornwall, and Mona Lehman, on or about the 15th March, 18—, will be handsomely rewarded on applying to Messrs. Bloxam and Bloxam, of Chancery Lane, London, or to Mr. Reuben Pendarven, the 'Chequer's' Inn, Pendarven, Cornwall."

This advertisement, slightly different in wording, had appeared in the papers for years past.

But it had escaped the notice of the sexton's nephew until now.

The name of "Pendarven Castle" seemed to rouse in him the clearest recollections.

The other names were nothing.

From the moment of reading the advertisement, it was his set purpose to go to Pendarven Castle.

The idea that Hubert Pendarven was an enemy of the rest of the family never crossed his brain.

He confided his desire to the master of the workhouse, and obtained funds to go down to the place, another more able-bodied man being sent with him.

The latter had the sense to go to the "Chequer's" Inn and make inquiries, and he learned that Reuben Pendarven had started out in the direction of the castle on a certain day and had never returned.

To the castle then he would go, and giving his companion the slip, he hastened in the direction of the place where of all others it was the worst for him to go.

Not that he had any notion of right or wrong in the adventure he had undertaken.

No.

His mind had only in it a confused idea that in some way or another some good would come to himself by a visit to Pendarven Castle.

The story of the certificate, and the strange death of the old sexton, would have yet to be formed again in his thoughts by the aid of others.

* * * *

The gipsies on quitting the spot where they had taken up their abode, did not go to a very great distance.

But they selected a place where they would be unlikely to be watched.

At about twenty miles from Pendarven Castle there was a village named Braisted, and close to this was a wood, as densely timbered as the most crowded parts of Epping Forest.

Here it was possible to conceal from view any members of the tribe whom it was desired to hide away from prying eyes.

The tents of those who did not desire to be meddled with were placed in the thickest part of the woodland, quite out of the reach of any strangers, and the other tents and vans were ranged round.

On the evening on which we again introduce the gipsy band to our readers, there were the usual fires lit, but in the more secluded part there was another fire, and round this were gathered three persons.

One of them was reclining on a mattress, with a pillow for his head.

Another was sitting by his side, while a woman was attending to a fragrant little stew which was swung over the glowing embers and crackling wood.

These three were Miriam, Reuben and Rupert.

For Reuben was not dead.

He had been badly wounded on that terrible night when Hubert Pendarven and Hugh Blacklock had lain in wait for him in the lane.

He had been given up at first for dead.

But by the gentle and careful nursing of Miriam he had recovered, or at any rate, was on a fair way to recovery.

The body which had been laid in the grave that night was that of one of the tribe who had died of old age.

While Reuben was wounded nearly unto death, and Rupert badly hurt as well, the gipsies deemed it wise not to allow their enemies to know that they had failed in their purpose.

So as the body of the unfortunate man was ready to hand, he was buried with all due honours in place of the gipsy king.

The tribe had by no means given over the idea of protecting Reuben and Rupert to the utmost of their power, and in fact, knowing the good husband he had been to Miriam and the two little ones which had been born to them—a boy and a girl—there was scarcely one of the number who would not have laid down his life for him.

When Reuben had recovered strength he was resolved what to do.

He had a most special objection to anything connected with the law.

And so until he was well he had resolved not to call in its aid.

When he was recovered, however, he was determined to allow no scruples to stand in the way of punishing Hubert Pendarven.

Reuben looked little like one who could punish anyone at this moment.

He was wan and pale, and even the exertion of leaning upon his arm seemed too much for him.

Rupert was better.

His arm had only been slightly injured, and careful treatment and fresh air had done all that was necessary to get him well.

"You're looking improved, cousin Reuben," he said; "though I dare say it will be some little time before you are yourself again."

"Yes, if my present condition is anything," said Reuben, "it will be a long time before I am like myself—if indeed I ever am. But hark! what is that?"

Everyone listened.

The sound was plainly heard of feet approaching the encampment.

"Good news coming, I hope," said Rupert.

"More likely to be bad," returned Reuben. "Our luck seems to have changed."

There was a halt of the new-comers at this moment.

Rupert started up.

"Let me creep nearer and see what is going on," he cried, "for I have a presentiment that something good is about to happen."

Reuben smiled sadly.

"Ah," he said, "I have had those presentiments before, but I do not believe in them now."

"That," said Rupert, "is only because you are ill. But see—here is Carter Smith."

"Then there is news," cried Reuben, "either good or bad. He would not come to see me unless there was something special one way or the other."

Carter Smith advanced rapidly, and it was then seen that someone was with him.

A stranger evidently.

"Good evening, Mr. Reuben," said the gipsy. "I hope you are getting on well, for I bring you news which will cheer you, yet at the same time will set you to work again right quickly."

"Pray let me know then at once," said Reuben, half rising in his excitement.

"Here's a man that knows all about the certificate," said Smith; "but you'll have to humour him. He's been suffering from some illness which has stolen most of his senses away. But if you coax him as I have done you'll learn a good deal. We will sit down here, and do things by degrees."

Smith and Fred Frost—for it was he, of course, who was the gipsy's companion —accordingly sat down, and the ale bottle was put into requisition.

"This gentleman is Mr. Reuben Pendarven," said Carter Smith, after a few explanations to Reuben, "and he's the right party for you to speak to, Fred Frost. If you had gone to Pendarven Castle all the fat would have been in the fire, I can tell you."

The change of air, the freedom from restraint, the companionship of a man who kept continually harping on the same string, had had their effect on the old sexton's nephew.

His mind, at any rate, on one subject was certainly getting clearer.

"Ah, yes—Pendarven Castle," he said. "You are not the gentleman I saw before."

"He evidently has had an interview with your uncle Hubert," said Smith.

"No, I am not," said Reuben; "we have never met before, but if it has anything to do with a certificate of marriage, it is certain you have come to the right place now. This young gentleman is the real heir to the property, and only wants that to substantiate his claim."

"Ha!" cried Fred Frost, "this is the boy who was at school."

"Yes."

"He is son to Richard Pendarven."

"Yes. But listen to me," said Reuben; "if I do not succeed now in rousing your memory in favour of my cousin, I fear we shall be as far off as ever. Do you remember the name of an old parish clerk called Maltby?"

"Yes, yes," cried Fred, excitedly, "and a man named Frost. Who was he? Who was he?"

"Steady — steady, my man," said Reuben, who was deeply excited also, but who nevertheless saw how to draw this man out. "Old Frost was the sexton, and you are his nephew."

"Yes, yes; I begin to remember," cried the man, trembling. "And Annie——"

"Ay, Annie was his daughter—your cousin—your sweetheart at Melton."

The man looked once steadily at the speaker.

Then he fell into a violent fit of sobbing, while his body trembled like an aspen leaf.

"Give him a drop of spirits if you have any," said Carter Smith. "Bring him round somehow. You've hit the right nail on the head, I think, but its unstrung him a bit."

Miriam ran to the tent and procured some brandy that was kept there for Reuben during his illness.

A small quantity of this revived Fred Frost, who shuddered, glanced round as if suddenly awakened, saying—

"I've got a desperate headache, but I seem to remember things better. Yes, I know—Annie was my sweetheart. I and old Frost, my uncle, went to the church, and he died—dropped dead in the storm. What did we go for? Ah! I know; the paper—the paper."

And he fumbled in his pockets excitedly.

Presently, tearing open the lining of his coat, he drew forth a much soiled document.

It was the letter written to Annie, written by old Frost just before his death.

His confession, in fact, of the theft of the marriage certificate from Maltby.

Reuben seized it and read it eagerly.

Then a bright flush overspread his features, and turning to Rupert, he wrung him by the hand.

"My boy, my long-suffering cousin, your troubles and trials are over now. The marriage certificate has been restored to Melton Church. All is proved."

"But, Uncle Hubert," cried Rupert in wild excitement; "does he not know?"

"He knows nothing," said Fred Frost, "He would not come to terms with me. so I left him just as I went. Only he gave me some of his devil's gold, which tempted a man to nearly murder me. Ah, bless Annie! It is her name that has restored me to reason."

"What is to be done next?" asked Rupert.

"I ought to go down to Melton at once," said Reuben, "but how can I in this helpless state?"

"No, no," said Rupert, "you cannot go. I and Carter Smith can go. Cousin Miriam can go on nursing you back to health while we are away."

"And I will go too," said Fred Frost, "if you will delay your departure till to-morrow. I feel strangely weak and ill, but a night's rest may put me on my legs again. Let us start in the morning!"

He little knew how fatal this delay would prove to all his own hopes of happiness.

"Very well," said Rupert, "that will do. If we were to start now, perhaps we should be too late to see anyone. We will be off the first thing in the morning."

Accordingly this was agreed on, and the meal prepared by Miriam being ready, they began its discussion, talking meanwhile with excited joy of the news which had so strangely reached them.

Every heart among them was light that night.

The shadows were rolling rapidly away now.

Nothing remained to be done, as it seemed, but to go to Melton, and secure the certificate and then punish Hubert for his villainy.

Even the confession of the one man who had died would be of great use.

Made as it was before a magistrate, it would have its due effect even unconfirmed by other details.

Every one went to bed happy that night.

And when the golden light of morning overspread the landscape, Rupert was up and ready.

A breakfast was hastily partaken of, and after receiving instructions from Reuben, the party of three started.

Rupert's heart was now full of eager delight.

He saw before him the realisation at last of the dream of his life-time.

At length the name of his mother was to be cleared, the truth proclaimed throughout the country, the hand of the villainous assassin stayed, and terrible retribution exacted.

CHAPTER XLIX.

THE CERTIFICATE AT LAST—DANGEROUS DELAY—AN OLD ENEMY ONCE MORE.

EVENTS had followed one upon another so rapidly, that Rupert could scarcely believe the reality of affairs as they rode rapidly away on horseback.

They reckoned that the distance to Melton could be traversed between dawn and the afternoon, even at the slowest.

But the roads were heavy with recent rains, and the horses in some places were unable to proceed quicker than a slow walk.

Thus our hero had abundant time to indulge in his reflections.

It was strange to him, as I have said, to observe how swiftly events followed one after another.

Only as it were a few hours before, the darkest time of all his life had come.

The assassins were again at work.

The friend of his whole life, the generous protector and counsellor had nearly been taken from him by the same hands which had deprived him of his father.

And now out of all this gloom and darkness had come a bright sunlight.

How he wished that his mother could have lived to see this day.

But yet he did not suffer doleful thoughts to oppress him.

The sunshine should be enjoyed by Reuben, who had sacrificed so much for him, and he would not dim it by any unnecessary dwelling on the past.

It was approaching darkness when they at length came in sight of Melton.

A storm was in fact threatening and already heavy rain drops were falling, while leaden banks of clouds were hanging everywhere around.

It was certainly a very unpromising look out.

But no one felt any oppression from the gloom.

When they pulled up at the " Melton Arms " to have a biscuit and cheese, and some of the old ale for which the hostelry was celebrated, they felt no effects from the depressing weather.

"Well, this is a pleasant reception," said Carter Smith ; " the clouds seem as if they were warning us to go back."

"Nothing would make me go back now," said Rupert. " I have come to the very verge of the discovery I have so longed for, and I am determined to retire no longer."

"No, nor I," said Carter Smith. " I have sworn to aid the king of our tribe and you too in this search, and I would lose my life sooner than fail."

"I don't fancy you'll be put to such a test as that," said Rupert, with a smile ; " there cannot be such an evil chance as that, Hubert, my uncle should know of the chance that has been made by Fred Frost here."

"I don't know about the possibility," said Carter Smith; "nothing's impossible, but it's very improbable. I should imagine he would never dream of old Frost doing such an eccentric thing as putting the certificate back in its original place."

"Well, let's be off," said Rupert, who was all impatience.

Once more they were *en route*.

Obtaining the address of the sexton (the one who had taken the place of old Frost) they soon found themselves making their way along the lane leading to the old cottage, for it seemed he had located himself there.

Frost said little.

His mind was full of one thing only.

He was thinking of Annie.

Would she be still single ?

Would she welcome him ?

The others went on swiftly, talking eagerly.

Rupert, in fact, could hardly restrain his anxiety.

No wonder he did not think of the driving rain and the threatening clouds that made the place seem as black as night.

The great secret of his life was about to be unfolded.

His mother's honour was to be vindicated, and his own position in life assured.

He was on the high road, too, towards punishing Hubert Pendarven, whom he thought of now, not as his uncle, but as the murderer of his father.

Presently they reached the little cottage.

At sight of it Fred Frost brightened up more than ever.

His memory seemed to awaken.

"Ah!" he cried, "this is the old cottage. How well I remember it! Poor old fellow! He little thought that night he was going to die so suddenly. I wonder what's become of Annie."

On the road they had obtained from him, in somewhat disjointed sentences, the history of the occurrence of that night.

From his words they had pieced together a kind of history of that night, and had, therefore, something to work on if they were to be questioned much by the new sexton.

Before they went to the door, Rupert and Carter Smith had come to one resolution.

They must not let Fred Frost appear at the cottage until after they had obtained what they required.

He would, in the first place, be looked upon as half-witted, and lay them open to all manner of questions.

In the second place, he would probably waste time in talking of Annie.

So they persuaded him to remain aloof, and not to speak of his sweetheart until the business of the day was disposed of.

The other two were received at the door by a broad-shouldered, not ill-looking man, in the dress of a navvy.

"Are you the new sexton?" asked Rupert, politely.

"Yes—leastway, I've been here some time now. Ever since the old man afore me died suddenly like in the churchyard durin' the thunner-starm."

Here was confirmation of Fred Frost's words, and Rupert's heart beat with pleasure.

"We want to visit the vestry of the old church," said Rupert, "to examine a register. Can you show us over?"

"That be the parish clerk's business," said the sexton, whose name was John Appleby.

"Yes, we know; but you see it's threatening weather, and he lives some distance off. We will pay you well, and, in fact, he is a person whom, for certain reasons, we don't want to consult in the matter. We are in search of the marriage certificate of my mother and father," said Rupert, proudly—"one which we have feared has been tampered with. So you see we are not going to the vestry for any evil purpose."

"Well, sir, I tell ye what. I'll go up with ye to the rector's house, and he'll give ye an order at once."

This was agreed on.

Rupert and Jack Appleby were not long at the vicar's.

The good man was satisfied both with our hero's appearance and explanation.

So the order and the keys were delivered, and the two hurried back to the others.

Presently all four were going in the direction of the church.

They were not long reaching the old Norman edifice, with its square tower, overgrown with ivy; and at length they had entered its sacred precincts and reached the vestry.

The sexton lit the lamps, and the volume containing the certificate was quickly taken down.

Rupert was the one to open it.

One moment of tremulous eagerness, one eager inwardly-spoken prayer, and he looked at the loosened pages.

Yes. There it was!

The long coveted paper was his.

The marriage certificate which cleared his mother's name, and made him heir to a splendid estate—which drove forth the assassin of his father, was in his hands at last.

He closed the book, when there was a sudden rush of feet along the tesselated pavement of the church.

"Hold that book, John Appleby, over yonder in the corner," cried Carter "I suspect treachery."

The words had only just left his lips when the door was flung open, and two masked men rushed in.

The intruders were disguised beyond recognition.

But Rupert and his friends had a shrewd suspicion of their identity.

They made no sign, uttered no remark, but made a sudden and simultaneous dash at the party.

Fred Frost, who was next to the door, not being so much on the alert as the others, was the first to feel the brunt of

"THE DOOR WAS THROWN OPEN, AND TWO MASKED MEN RUSHED IN."

their fury, and he fell backwards on the stone floor with a gasping cry.

The sexton was by no means a coward, but he was unarmed, and was moreover bewildered.

He knew not, in fact, how to take sides—one way or another.

Meanwhile the combatants were fighting fiercely.

Carter Smith was never without weapons.

He had pistols with him.

But he had also a huge bludgeon, and not having time to draw his firearms, he used this vigorously against the skilled swordsmen who were against him and Rupert.

There was no doubt in his mind, or in that of our hero, that the two enemies who had so suddenly appeared on the scene were Hubert Pendarven and Hugh Blacklock.

Yet it was impossible to tell to a certainty.

The wild, mad way in which they had made their onslaught, as if they were reckless of consequences, gave them no chance of speaking or of attempting to tear off their disguises.

At length, however, a new element was imported into the scene.

Fred Frost had a weapon, a stout cudgel, but he was lying on the floor, apparently bleeding to death.

The sexton presently espied this.

"Well, I don't see it's any use o' my a-standin' 'ere holding of this 'ere book," he said to himself. "I'll put it down and 'elp drive these fellers out."

He had sufficient sense to guess that the register was the prize for which the fight was being waged.

So putting the volume down safe in a corner, he leaped forward, and seizing the cudgel held by Fred Frost, he joined the affray.

Three to one in an English fight is not considered fair.

But in a conflict of this kind—with a set of murderers—six to one would not have been wrong.

Seeing Hubert Pendarven—or the one supposed to be he—draw a pistol and aim it at the head of Carter Smith, he made one tremendous blow at his head.

Had this taken effect, the end of his career would have been quickly at hand.

As it was—clumsily dealt in the hurry and strangeness of the scene—it struck him on the arm.

It was a terrific blow, and knocked the pistol from his hand.

But at the same time it had a most disastrous effect.

The shot, as the pistol fell from the hands of the would-be assassin, sped in the direction of the gipsy, and passed through his left lung.

He fell to the floor with a gasping cry.

"Don't give in, Rupert," he cried, as he lay there; "now's the most important moment of all your life."

Rupert knew this.

Without the aid of the young sexton where would he now be?

In that supreme moment how he wished for the presence of Reuben.

But he was not disheartened.

These men whom they were battling against, were the two who, of all others in the world, were his greatest foes.

It behoved him to conquer them.

And so, seeing that he was seconded by the young sexton, he paid attention only to the one whom he had to contend with, and whom he confidently believed to be Hugh Blacklock.

The other was considerably damaged by the blow inflicted upon him by Jack Appleby.

He could not use his right wrist as he was accustomed to; and so, even though the young sexton was not an adept in the art of attack or self-defence, he was able to hold his own.

Hubert (if it was he) had acted most unwisely in firing a pistol.

In a quiet hamlet such as this it would be sure to attract some notice, and though the church was some distance from any habitation, the unusual sound caught the attention of a young countryman who happened to be passing.

Running into the graveyard excitedly, he made his way to the door of the church, and with something like awe, passed along its echoing pavement.

In this place it was the custom for everything to be so quiet and solemn, that the sound of a pistol within its sacred precincts terrified him.

Nevertheless, he had courage enough to go and see what was the matter.

At the door of the vestry he paused aghast.

He had no weapon whatever, and at sight of the swords, which had been again brought into use, and were writhing about like living things, he deemed it right to rush off and seek assistance, or, at any rate, to endeavour to obtain a weapon of some kind.

But although he took no active part in the affair, his presence did good.

The masked men saw him, and the one who had shot Carter Smith, and who found the young sexton no mean antagonist, cried out—

"Hugh, the game is up. We must fly and trust to the future. Follow me."

As he spoke, he executed a rapid and brilliant pass with his sword, and Jack Appleby fell to the ground with a cry of agony.

Then, without taking advantage of the fact that there was only one adversary, Hubert, terrified at the chance of public exposure, turned and fled, crying—

"Follow me, Blacklock, if you are not mad!"

But the ex-gamekeeper, Hubert's companion in all his villainous adventures, had not the chance.

The cause in which he was fighting, and the excitement of the moment, gave Rupert, as it were, supernatural strength, and almost at the moment that Hugh's companion fled, our hero wounded his adversary in the shoulder with the sword which Rupert had dropped in his flight, and which our hero had picked up.

Instead, moreover, of getting out of his way, he took advantage of his success to put himself between his enemy and the chance of flight.

If Blacklock was out of the way, Reuben, in his present weak and helpless state, would have lost his worst foe.

For Hubert Pendarven had neither the courage nor the aptitude for creeping and sneaking about as his subordinate did in every imaginable hole and corner.

The fight between these two was a desperate one.

Rupert was wondrously skilful.

But Blacklock was endowed with tremendous strength.

Without, therefore, any cleverness in the art of fence, his sledge-hammer blows were things to be avoided.

However, fortune, which seemed to have so long frowned upon our hero, was with him on this occasion.

His fence was splendid.

His sword seemed to fly about like a living thing.

Again and again Hugh Blacklock was wounded.

Again and again, with curses strong and deep, the maddened gipsy sprang upon his young foe.

But all his attempts were in vain.

And then, seeing that Carter Smith and the young sexton were showing signs of recovering enough to renew the fight, he became desperate and wild in his strokes.

In an instant Rupert took advantage of this, and with a rapid, cut-down blow, caught Blacklock so heavily on the neck that he fell.

At this instant the sound of footsteps was again heard coming along the pavement of the church, and as Rupert stood with his sword at his adversary's throat, and his foot on his chest, the vicar and some men came rushing in.

CHAPTER L.

THE END OF THE FIGHT—HUGH BLACKLOCK CAGED AT LAST—A BITTER DISAPPOINTMENT.

THE vicar paused for a moment in utter astonishment when he beheld the scene in the vestry.

On the floor lay Fred Frost still extended where he had fallen, with Jack Appleby, the young sexton, half reclining and leaning on one elbow, and Carter Smith in a dead swoon.

Near them was Hugh Blacklock on his back, Rupert's foot on his chest, and his sword at his throat.

The floor was bespattered everywhere with blood, and everything — table, chairs, and so on—was out of place.

"What does this mean?" cried the vicar at last, advancing, and speaking in a cold, stern voice of anger.

"I cannot readily explain it," said

Rupert, throwing back his head haughtily, and eyeing the vicar boldly in reply to the thoughts which evidently occupied his mind. "I had better say at once that I and my friends here have been assailed by two ruffians, one of whom lies here, and one of them has escaped. If you will grant me five minutes without interruption, I can tell everything clearly; but I think the best thing to do first is to bind this would-be assassin, and see to the wounded."

At this moment Jack Appleby recognised some one in the little crowd of rustics who had followed the vicar.

"Hi, Joe Bradley!" he cried, "go and fetch my ropes. They're hangin' on the hook outside the church door, just opposite the newly-made grave. They'll bind him tight enough, I'll warrant."

The man did not wait to be told a second time.

In a moment he was off, and almost as quickly returned with the rope.

While he was gone on his errand, Rupert had by means of a bribe induced another of the rustics to rush off to the doctor's, and Hugh Blacklock had only just been rendered helpless by strong cords, when the village Esculapius arrived.

Fred Frost, who had never yet recovered consciousness, seemed the most serious case, and he accordingly was seen to first.

He required little attention.

He was dead.

He had fulfilled his mission, and then laid down his life.

Perhaps it was better so.

For the pretty girl who presently pushed her way through the crowd to see how Jack Appleby fared was his wife, and she was none other than Annie Frost.

Carter Smith and Appleby were not very badly hurt, and a few restoratives soon set them on their legs again.

Then, the constables having now arrived, the prisoner was walked off to the "round-house," as it was called, a little place where such desperate characters were confined at night-time until their appearance at the magistrate's the next day.

The vicar then retired with Rupert to his own house, Carter Smith and Jack Appleby going off to the "Melton Arms,"

to await his coming, and poor Fred Frost—whom Annie recognised and wept tears of pity over—being carried to the mortuary.

Rupert told his story boldly.

The time for reservation, in fact, was past.

The vicar listened in amazement.

Within the whole range of his experience, he had never been in or heard of such a scene, or in fact been mixed up in so romantic a story.

He could recognise the truth, however, when he heard it, and eagerly acquiesced in the proposition made by Rupert, which was to the effect that as other enemies were about, or at any rate likely to take the earliest opportunity to make another desperate attempt, he (the vicar) would preserve that especial volume of the register in his safe keeping, until such time as it had to be produced in public.

To this the worthy clergyman at once assented.

But he felt considerably upset in regard to another proposition, which was that perfect secrecy should be observed in regard to the story he had told him until a certain time.

"It is scarcely within my duty to give such a promise," he said.

"You need not compromise yourself in any way at all, sir," said Rupert. "You can give your description of what you saw if you are called upon to do so, but the private portion of the story need not be told."

It was a difficult thing to persuade the worthy man to do what was required.

But he at length gave the required undertaking, and Rupert left him, satisfied that the dream of his life was accomplished.

He lost no time in making his way to the "Melton Arms," where he joined Carter Smith and Jack Appleby.

On the next morning, of course, it would be necessary for him in the ordinary course to appear before the magistrates and charge Hugh Blacklock with being one of the confederates in a murderous attack on himself and friends in the vestry.

But fortunately for Rupert's wishes the worthy dignitaries of the bench did not sit until the day after.

"I shall have time to see Reuben and consult him," he said to Carter Smith;

PUBLISHER'S NOTE

pp.177-178 are missing.

"the whole affair has become so complicated now, that I would rather have his advice before I move again in the matter."

"Then we had better start to-night," said Carter Smith; "our horses have had a good rest, and we shall have an hour or two's start of the coach."

"But are you strong enough to go on a journey?" asked our hero.

The gipsy laughed.

"Strong enough! Ay!" he cried. "I've often had a wound as bad as that. But you are wounded also."

"A mere scratch," said Rupert, "which will doubtless make my shoulder ache for some time to come. But nothing to hinder me going on a journey."

"Very well then. We will have a couple of hours' rest, and be off towards home."

Strange word that uttered by a gipsy.

It meant anywhere where the tents were.

"Very well," said Carter Smith, "I'm agreeable. We will have a good supper, and some wine to keep our strength up and go."

The resolution he had arrived at was a brave one.

His wound was serious, and produced a horrible faintness at the chest.

But he was not in the least deterred.

There might be danger in following up the adventure, but he thought himself bound to risk life itself for his "king" and the "king's cousin."

Jack Appleby, whose wife was sent home with such a present of gold as she had never before in her life held in one hand, was one of those included in the supper party.

He was commissioned to go to the rector's on the following morning, and explain to him that, as the magistrates did not sit that day, Rupert had thought it best to consult his cousin before the examination, and had some hope also that Reuben Pendarven would be able to be present.

The supper, which, in spite of their wounds, the three enjoyed, was over at eleven o'clock, and Rupert and Carter Smith at once prepared to depart.

They had by this time rested considerably, and were able to mount into the saddle without difficulty.

The night was dark and gloomy, but the storm seemed to have made up its mind to blow over, and the wind was strong enough to keep off the rain.

On they went at a great speed therefore, as swiftly as they could on the muddy rutty roads, which had before impeded their progress, until, after three hours, they decided to have a rest.

The place selected for this was a cross road, in the centre of which was a piece of green with a sign-post rising from it, and a large oil-lamp at top.

Here they dismounted and tethered their steeds.

They had been resting their animals about a quarter of an hour, and were about to leap once more into the saddle, when the sound was heard of a horse approaching at full speed from the direction by which they had just come.

They both looked up at the horseman as he passed, and both recognised him at once.

It was Hugh Blacklock with his wounded neck swathed in some woollen wrap, and his left arm in a sling.

He saw the group of men and horses, seeming, however, not to trouble himself about them.

With a look of evil triumph and resolution on his white, set face, he rode swiftly on and disappeared in the darkness of the night.

"Our victory is but short lived," cried Rupert, as he leaped on his horse. "Come, Carter Smith, let us pursue him. Reuben is not safe while that villainous assassin is at large."

And so, in a few moments, they went rushing onwards in pursuit.

CHAPTER LI.

HOW ANOTHER WITNESS WAS SECURED FOR THE PROSECUTION.

DR CARVER, *alias* John Hepburn, the ex-schoolmaster of "Hungry Hall," whose inmates had by this time been distributed among their relations, much to the disgust of the latter, had (in spite of police and detectives) arrived in Paris.

It is but just to his wife and daughters to say that they were entirely ignorant of any participation in the criminal acts at Hungry Hall.

They knew well how the wretched boys were tortured by want of food.

They saw and understood the reason of their lean and hungry visages.

But they were entirely ignorant of the cause of so many disappearances.

"Expelled from the school."

Such was the pretended fate of all those who made sudden exits from the Hall.

They never troubled to make inquiries.

They had enough to do to screw and make shift against a rainy day.

But now that they had left Hungry Hall behind them, they began to think that either he was a lunatic, or that he was under the influence of some deadly fear.

Mrs. Carver was roused out of her sleep of a night by the loud outcries of her husband, who would ask her most incomprehensible questions, and glance round him in terror as if fearful of every shadow.

Even in the daytime a knock at the door would startle him, and if anyone glanced at him more intently than usual in the street, he would at once think that he was the object of some malevolent scrutiny.

This, of course, was sure to have its effect on his constitution.

And it did.

He grew thinner, as it were, day by day.

His rubicund visage began to assume a pale sallow hue.

His eyes were restless and bloodshot, and his hands tremulous.

This condition became worse after the receipt of a letter from the vicinity of his old school; and worse still, one day, when chancing to light upon an English newspaper, he saw the advertisement in regard to Hungry Hall, the account of his flight, and the return of the scholars to their homes.

Then there was the reward offered for the capture of Dr. Carver, *alias* Hepburn.

And then, too, the account of the horrors which had been discovered at the old academy told him that things were gradually but certainly closing round him.

Mrs. Carver, coming suddenly into his room, found him sitting by the fire clutching the paper in his hands, and gazing staringly into the flames.

He was so lost in thought that he did not even observe her entrance.

She stole up to him and placed her hand upon his shoulder.

But she had no time for speech.

Leaping up, he clutched her by the throat, and shook her angrily.

"No, no!" he screamed; "you shall not take me! No, no! I did not do it. There are others worse than I am. Away, and leave me in peace."

"Hush, hush, my husband!" cried Mrs. Carver, in great alarm. "You will raise suspicions of something wrong if you call out thus madly. Why do you make such strange statements? You are not guilty of any crime."

Then he dropped down into his chair

and sobbed, saying convulsively, in a low and agonised voice—

"No, no, wife, I am not guilty. I am not guilty!"

But this calmness was only for a time.

He was thoroughly stricken with the fear of arrest.

He had always (strange anomaly!) been kind to his wife and family.

But now he grew irritable and morose.

They saw, of course, this change with great anxiety.

Not guessing at the real cause, they at last set it down to illness produced by a sudden change in their mode of life.

But speculation soon became vain.

One night, returning from some journey—the destination and purport of which he did not tell them—he went shivering and wet through to bed.

The next morning he was in a raging fever.

Now was the time that they began to learn more and more in regard to his secrets.

But even now all his explanations were given in a style so disconnected, that it was very difficult to understand of what he accused himself.

Wild indeed were his ravings.

Now some boy would follow him with angry eyes and outstretched arms.

Now another would stand by his bed and mock his agony.

Now another would sit upon his chest and jabber at him.

Now the phantom of some murdered man would call upon him for atonement for the past.

Thus much they could tell from his wild words.

And little by little light seemed to dawn upon the mind of Mrs. Carver.

She knew how the boys used to be so often disappearing.

But she said nothing to her daughters of all this.

Whatever crimes her husband had been guilty of should be sacred from them.

At last the reaction came, and the fever leaving the brain, the body was exhausted unto death.

His mind became perfectly clear.

But his physical powers were gone for ever.

It was useless to try and disguise from himself the fact that his days were numbered.

Others saw it plainly.

Of what use would it be for him to fight against the truth?

Then began a battle with his own heart.

What was it best to do?

To die and leave all unsaid?

Or to try and make a late atonement?

It was a long time before he decided.

But at length, when the Destroyer was advancing with giant strides, he made up his mind, and sent for a magistrate and a notary.

To these he made a long and detailed confession of all that he had done.

Before them were laid bare the secrets of those dismal days at Hungry Hall, and the awful mystery, too, which overshadowed the home of the Pendarvens.

Of course, as a matter of form, he was placed under arrest.

In other words, two gendarmes guarded his bedroom door.

But he was unable to move.

Death had him fast, and remorse and terror at the memory of his misdeeds hastened on the inevitable event.

At length, on the very evening that news of his confession reached England, he breathed his last.

No one knew the feelings of that dark spirit ere it winged its flight to other worlds.

But whatever they were, no one shared them.

He died in silence, save for a few murmured words to his family.

A more cowardly and dastardly assassin never passed through the gates of Death.

And yet he died as he did in his own bed, from which many a less guilty man would have been dragged brutally.

The confession was not sent straight to the authorities at the English headquarters.

It was forwarded to Rupert Pendarven, care of Dr. Walton at Blakesley Hall Academy.

This was the only address of the Pendarven family which the ex-schoolmaster knew."

"The atonement I wish to make," he said, "is for the sake of this Rupert Clifford—or Pendarven, as he has a right to be called—for he is the heir to the property, which the murder of his father gave into the hands of Hubert. It will be doing this lad far more good to give him my confession than to send it to the police."

These were the last words spoken by Dr. Carver, *alias* Hepburn, to the French notary and magistrate.

They decided to follow his advice.

A complete and careful copy was made of the confession of the dying man, and this, signed and sealed, was taken care of at the *conciergerie*.

Of course, Dr. Carver, who thought to make amends for his hideous crimes by this late confession, could not know that Rupert had quitted the school, and was now once more with the gipsies in the wild woods.

CHAPTER LII.

IN WHICH THE DARKNESS CLOSES ROUND HUBERT PENDARVEN.

WHEN Hugh Blacklock went dashing by his enemies on that tempestuous night, pale and wounded, he made straight for the castle.

His mind was full of deadly hate against everybody.

He was in both mental and bodily torture.

His wounds were deep and painful.

And now it seemed as if his last "comrade" had deserted him.

Bitter indeed was his anger against Hubert Pendarven for deserting him in the hour of danger.

Yet what was he to do?

If he betrayed him, he would be, as it were, signing his own death-warrant.

However, as to one thing he was determined.

Hubert Pendarven should pay dearly for his desertion.

He rode on at a mad pace all the way until morning dawned.

Then finding that he had not approached near enough to Pendarven Castle, he resolved to remain in hiding during the day, and continue the journey as soon as darkness fell.

He made a hasty purchase of some food and spirits as he dashed through a village at daylight, and then urging his tired steed forward once more, he made his way into a dense wood not far distant from the castle.

Here he remained all day.

He expected by doing this that he would not be disturbed.

He reckoned that the officers of the law in pursuing him would make their way first to Pendarven Castle, and would scarcely think of searching for him in these dense plantations.

It was very dark when he at length deemed it prudent to show himself at the gate of Pendarven Castle.

He was not liked by the rest of the

servants, but they knew that he was the confidant of their master; and consequently, in spite of the strange inquiries which had been made after him that day, he was at once admitted.

He found Hubert in his study.

He was evidently under the influence of excitement, and had been drinking freely.

He noticed, as Hugh entered, the dark scowl on his features, and knew at once that the interview was not to be a pleasant one.

"So you escaped?" he said, putting a chair for the ex-gamekeeper, and pouring out some spirits for him.

"Escaped? Not as you think," said Blacklock, after he had swallowed the fiery liquid. "I was nearly killed, then arrested and flung into the round-house. I made my escape from there, but I know I am pursued, and before to-morrow night you must make arrangements by which I can leave England at once. It is not safe for me to remain in the country another twenty-four hours.'

"Then what about me?" said Hubert. "If it is not safe for you, it is not safe for me."

"Oh! as for you, you must shift for yourself," said Hugh Blacklock. "You have thought only of your own interests, so just give me a cheque for two thousand pounds and let me be off ere it is too late."

Hubert, who was glad to get rid of him at such a price, said—

"That is not extravagant. If at any time you want more, and I have it, you can ask me. I too am going abroad. Why not go together?"

"Why not?" said Blacklock; "I can't think why you stick to the old place when there is a halter almost round your neck."

And though there was a large fire in the room, and it was very warm, he shuddered.

"I cling to the place for the sake of Ralph," said Hubert, "but to-morrow I shall go."

To-morrow!

We are all dreaming of to-morrow, knowing little what it may bring.

"Where are you going?"

"Right off to Spain."

"I'm with you then," said Blacklock. "I don't think I'd stay another hour in England if I could help it. Ugh! how cold it is. I've caught cold sleeping in that cursed wood!"

"I feel raging hot," said Hubert, as he drank off another half tumbler of spirits; "but what are you going to do with yourself to-night?"

"Stop here, up in my old room," he said. "I couldn't trust myself up at the cottage alone, and I feel cramped too all over."

"Very well," said Hubert Pendarven. "Very well, you can remain here if you like; you'll be better in the morning perhaps, after a good bed and a drop of strong grog to warm you."

"You're right, and when shall we leave the place?"

"To-morrow."

"At daylight I hope."

"No, not at least for me. I shall not leave till evening, as I expect some one here whom I must see."

"Perhaps you'll have some visitors you don't expect, and don't want," said Blacklock, "if you wait too long. Oh! what pain I am in."

"You'd better get to your room at once," said Hubert, and he rang the bell for the servant.

In a few minutes Blacklock had been taken to his room, where he had a warm supper, and a stiff glass of grog.

The last thing he looked at that night was the cheque for two thousand pounds, which Hubert had given him.

It was two in the morning when the master of Pendarven was aroused from his slumber by a loud knocking at his door.

Ever ready to take alarm at the slightest thing, he sprang up, crying—

"Who is there? What is the matter?"

"It's only me, sir," said Hurst the butler.

He had long since noticed the strange ways of his master, and was used to his sudden starts and exclamations.

"What is it then?"

"I'd like to come in and speak to you, sir, if you don't mind," said the man, "as it's something particular."

"Very well," and in a moment the butler was admitted.

He had a white, scared face, and his master felt a greater alarm than he cared to own.

"Why, you look as if you had seen a ghost," he said, with a forced laugh; "what is it?"

"It's Blacklock, sir. You see he sleeps next to me, and he keeps jumping up and screeching out and saying such funny things, that I thought it would be best if you came and had a look at him."

"I will," said Hubert; and with a ghastly fear at his heart he hurried on his clothes, and telling Hurst to wait for him, took the butler's lamp and went up alone to the bedroom of the ex-gamekeeper.

As he went in he could hear the ravings of the man plainly.

Indeed, every now and then his voice was raised so loudly that it echoed through the house.

"Help here! I never killed him! 'Twas Hubert! Ah! away, away! I will confess all. Only spare me! I cannot die, with all these sins upon my head. I will tell everything if you will but listen to me and promise me freedom. Ah, there they are again! Away, horrible vision. Away!"

Hubert closed the door.

"Ah!" he said, "this is worse than I feared. This wretched fool has caught a fever, and if his tongue is allowed to wag much longer he will be my destruction."

"Blacklock," he said, suddenly, as he went to the bedside.

The effect was electrical.

The wounded man, who was suffering terrible tortures, and who was, moreover, in a raging fever, sprang up with a yell.

"Ah!" he cried, "there he is again! The demon who lured me to destruction. Avaunt, fiend! I have confessed—I have confessed! It is you who did the murder."

Great beads of perspiration stood on the brow of Hubert Pendarven.

Without the aid and companionship of this man, who had been with him in all his desperate deeds, he felt indeed alone.

He was in the face of a danger now which was all the greater, because it was unforeseen.

"This must be stopped at all hazards," he said; "the blood I have shed runs in such rivers, that another little streamlet will not much matter. If he lives, my existence is not worth one moment's purchase."

"Drink, drink!" shouted the fever-stricken man. "I parch—I parch!"

A smile passed over the lips of Hubert Pendarven.

"Now is my time," he muttered; "he shall feel no pain or thirst again."

With these words on his lips he quitted the room, and passed quickly down to the bedchamber, where he had left Hurst.

"He is in a raging fever, Hurst, I see that," he said; "give me my medicine chest. I must give him one of my composing draughts. He is raving about some crime he has committed, and if his words were heard by others it would bring disgrace on the whole household."

"Yes, sir," said Hurst.

This he thought was all that it was necessary to say.

He had his own ideas about matters.

But he did not consider it prudent to give tongue to them unless he had certain proof.

He gave his master the medicine chest, and then waited while he poured out twenty drops from a small bottle, which he had often seen him use.

"That will make him sleep till morning," said Hubert, as he mixed the dark-looking liquid in half-a-pint of water. "He won't disturb anyone until long after I am up. Don't mention his ravings to anyone."

"No, sir."

"You needn't stop up, Hurst," added Hubert Pendarven, as he began to ascend the stairs, followed by the butler. "I'll guarantee you against any further disturbance."

On reaching the next landing they separated, Hurst going into his own room, and his master into that of Blacklock.

The latter had fallen back exhausted, when Hubert had quitted the bed-chamber.

But when he saw someone again entering the apartment, he sprang up and yelled once more for drink.

"Here you are, my friend," said Hubert; "drink this."

He handed to him the deadly draught, and Hugh Blacklock drank it eagerly.

Then he relapsed upon his bed with a deep-drawn sigh.

"Ah!" he said, "it will all be better soon. The police will be here directly, and then, when I've unburdened my mind to them, I shall be easy."

Hubert smiled.

"I don't think," he murmured to himself, "that you will ever be troubled on that score."

And he sat down by the remnants of the fire to watch the effect of his "medicine."

It was not long in seizing hold of the patient, and after several attempts to speak, he at last became perfectly still.

Hubert went over to him presently, and spoke to him.

"Are you awake, Blacklock?" he said.

No answer came.

He bent over and listened.

No sound was to be heard.

He got the lamp and held it close to the eyes of the gamekeeper.

They were already glassy.

"Ha!" muttered the master of Pendarven, "it does its business well. He is well-nigh sped. When morning dawns there will be in the world one enemy less for me."

He slowly and noiselessly left the room, and as he passed the butler's door, he knocked at it softly.

"Hurst," he said.

"Yes, sir."

"Don't disturb yourself, Hurst," said Hubert. "I only came to tell you that he is sleeping quietly now. Don't say anything about him to the other servants. I will see to him in the morning. His words may make a wrong impression if they are heard by the other servants. Good night."

"Good night, sir."

And so they parted.

Hurst turned over to his sleep without the slightest suspicion of the awful thing which had happened in the adjoining chamber, Hubert to snatch if possible a few more hours' rest before the terrible day which awaited him.

He had no fear, no remorse in reference to what he had done.

He knew that he could arrange to hoodwink Hurst until night-time.

" ' NO, NO, I DID NOT DO IT ! THERE ARE OTHERS WORSE THAN I AM !' CRIED CARVER."

Then he would have a few hours' start. and he cared not what might happen.

But still, though he felt only pleasure at the death of Hugh Blacklock, he could not rest as he had wished.

The phantoms of his evil days were ever around him, and warned him of swiftly-pursuing vengeance.

He felt that darkness, in fact, was closing around him.

CHAPTER LIII.

THE END.

THE next morning passed quietly.

Hubert Pendarven had succeeded as he had intended in keeping Hurst and the others out of Hugh Blacklock's room.

He took him in a light breakfast, and afterwards some wine.

And yet all the time he was lying stiff and stark.

" I don't think he'll be much trouble now," he said to Hurst, after his last visit. " He seems quiet and easy, and there'll be no need of a doctor, I'm glad to say."

And so as Hurst, in common with the other servants, had no affection for Hugh Blacklock, he made no remark, and, indeed, troubled himself no more about the matter.

So the day sped.

Eagerly Hubert Pendarven looked forward to the night.

At length, just before sunset—about an hour before—he passed into the grand old dining-room, which was situated just above the lawn terrace, not far from the entrance hall.

He was used now, ever since the death of his wife, to dine alone, except upon those occasions when special guests were invited ; but on this occasion he felt a most terrible loneliness over him.

He was just discussing a second course, and planning an immediate departure now that the person he had expected had not arrived, when he was suddenly astounded by seeing the door open, and several persons enter unannounced.

Their coming was so noiseless, that he felt dread overcome him as he saw them.

But it was only a moment before he recognised the leaders.

Reuben, Rupert, Owet and Merrifield, and Carter Smith.

The others were strangers.

" What is the meaning of this intrusion ? " he said, rising, and trying to speak haughtily.

" It means," said Reuben, who was pale and ill, but nevertheless, firm and resolute——" it means, Hubert Pendarven, that your game is up. This is Rupert, son of Richard Pendarven, the brother you murdered. Ay, glare not at me. I say again," repeated Rupert, " the brother you murdered ! Denial is useless now. Here, in my hand, I hold the confession of Hepburn, *alias* Dr. Carver, who was one of the gang who came with you to this place on that awful night many, many years ago. Here is the confession of another, and here another, three out of the four who saw you strike your brother down in cold blood.

" Here, too, is the marriage certificate of your brother Richard and Mona Lehman, which, through a man named Fred Frost (since dead) we found at Melton Church.

" The game is up, Hubert Pendarven ; the bright day is over, the darkness has come. What have you to say ? "

"What have I to say?" cried Hubert, with pale lips. "Simply this. If Rupert has proved his legitimate right to this place, let him have it and welcome. But I deny that my brother died by my hand. He fell in our struggle, and struck his head. But I am innocent of taking his life.

"You lie!" cried Reuben. "We heard from his dying lips the story of his wrong."

"And what do you propose doing?" asked Hubert, who was standing close by the open French window.

But no answer was given to this question.

At this moment there was a rush of horses' feet, and then loud voices, as the riders drew rein at the front entrance.

In another instant Hurst, the butler, rushed into the room.

"Four constables are at the door, and demand to see you, Mr. Hubert!" he cried. "The servants can scarcely keep them back."

"Let not the servants trouble themselves," said Hubert Pendarven, with wonderful calmness. "Let the men enter."

He listened intently, while all present waited with anxious suspense.

But they were unprepared for what instantly followed.

Just as the footsteps of the newcomers were heard coming up the stairs, Hubert made a sudden dash through the open French window, and leaped from the terrace to the lawn below.

It was a daring leap, and Reuben and the others ran forward, expecting to see him lying helpless, at any rate, on the ground.

But, apparently unhurt, he was, when they saw him, running like a deer towards the front entrance, where stood the horses of the constables.

Reaching these, he seized one, leaped on its back, and hitting the others right and left to disperse them, he galloped off at a headlong pace towards the lodge gates.

The steed he bestrode was a splendid one; but knowing what a desperate chase it might be, he dragged off a low bough as he flew along to act as a whip.

Reaching the lodge he saw Mrs. Jobson, the wife of the lodge-keeper; he reined in a moment.

"Someone's very ill up at the castle," he said; "I've rushed off without my hat. Lend me one of Jobson's."

The woman, wondering greatly at his pale and wild appearance, did as she was directed, and away he went at a break-neck pace along the highway.

But he was not long unpursued.

The constables lost no time in mounting their horses, at last three of them did, and were soon following in splendid style.

The sun was now setting in gold and purple splendour.

But the dusk would soon be here, and then they might run the risk of losing sight of their quarry; and so they pressed forward at an unmerciful speed.

The road at this point went straight on for miles without any cross thoroughfares.

And so as they sped on they could see the fugitive long ahead.

The horses were pretty much of a strength and quality, and so, although they urged their steeds to the utmost speed, they knew that "Dick," the horse which Hubert Pendarven rode, was quite capable, with the start he had, of giving them the slip if he was ridden properly.

On, on they went in the deepening twilight, over Brampton Bridge, through Pentath village, by the side of Lord Sibley's park.

Just at this point, a hare leaping suddenly out of the hedge startled his horse, which shying, threw him and fled, dragging the reins from his hands and nearly throwing him on his face.

He looked round him in desperation.

There was no use in attempting to catch the horse, which was careering away like a mad thing far ahead.

He knew, however, that at the side of Lord Sibley's estate was a large and dense wood.

Here he could find thick coppices and dark tangled cells, where he could defy detection.

There, he thought, he could conceal himself, and perhaps, after all, have revenge on those who had driven him from his home a hunted fugitive.

Of course, while he was thinking, he was not losing time.

He ran along the road at the top of his speed, and arriving presently at a small opening, he forced his way through, and began his scramble through the dense foliage.

But his pursuers had by this time gained upon him greatly, and in a few minutes after his entrance into the thicket, they dismounted and were forcing their way after him.

One of them unslung a short carbine he wore in cavalry fashion, and aiming at the flying murderer as he fled, fired.

The shot took effect, and with a gasping cry Hubert Pendarven fell forward.

In another instant, however, he had regained his feet, and was plunging on again.

But the short delay was disastrous to him.

By the time he had reached a small open space, his foes were upon him.

"Halt! or we fire," said one of the constables, as they all presented their weapons.

He turned and faced them, with a double-barrelled pistol in each hand.

"If I die, so do some of you," he said; "I hold four lives in my weapons here."

"We must risk that," said the leader calmly; "it is our duty to take you alive or dead."

The reply was a bullet aimed with such precision, that it passed through the constable's cap.

The next instant there were four reports, and the smoke clearing away disclosed Hubert Pendarven on the ground.

"Seize him! we have him now alive," said the head constable.

But he was wrong.

Ere they could reach him, and wrench his weapons from his hand, he had placed one of them to his mouth, and in another instant he was dead.

The base assassin had gone to his account.

* * * *

We have little more to tell.

Hubert Pendarven was buried in an obscure corner of the churchyard, away from all the rest of the family.

Ralph was well provided for, and under the circumstances, decided to change his name and live abroad.

This he did so completely, that none of his relatives ever saw him again, though they received many letters from him, in not one of which he failed to express contrition for the part he had played at school.

The fear of death alone brought Sir Charles Alreston to his senses; on his supposed dying bed he forgave Reginald and Gladys, who both came to him at once on his summons.

He did not die, however, but lived to see his son married again, and to be present also at the wedding of Rupert and Gladys, which took place three years after the death of Hubert Pendarven.

Leigh Glindon was present also with his bride, the veritable Susie Brandford, whom he had once escorted home by such roundabout ways, after her adventure with Mr. Meekly.

Reuben and Miriam were there too, and the dusky sons and daughters of Bohemia also gathered in Alreston Park, and hurrahed loudly as the carriages containing the bride and bridegroom went gaily along the drive.

On the morning of the next day, Dr. Walton received wedding cards.

They were contained in a huge envelope, in which were the title deeds, giving the freehold of Blakesley Hall Academy, its grounds and the beautiful farm of Holme Dale adjoining, to him and his heirs for ever.

All were made happy at the school that day, for enclosed also was a large cheque to be spent on a gigantic treat for Rupert's old schoolfellows.

And so, with sunshine over all, we drop the curtain upon our story.

Happy in the love of Gladys, of Reuben, and of Miriam, in the respect of all his friends, in the possession too of worldly riches, Rupert Pendarven never in his most blissful moments forgot the days when he was known at Blakesley Hall as the Gipsy Schoolboy; and where he had passed through so many and perilous adventures.

" WITH A GASPING CRY HUBERT FELL FORWARD,"